Billy the Kid's
Last Ride

Billy the Kid's Last Ride

A Novel

JOHN A. ARAGON

SUNSTONE
PRESS

SANTA FE

Sunstone books may be purchased for educational, business, or sales promotional use.
For information please write: Special Markets Department, Sunstone Press,
P.O. Box 2321, Santa Fe, New Mexico 87504-2321.

Cover design ▸ Jeff Fielder
Book design ▸ Vicki Ahl
Body typeface ▸ Minion Pro
Printed on acid free paper

Library of Congress Cataloging-in-Publication Data

Aragon, John A., 1952-
  Billy the Kid's last ride / by John A. Aragon.
    pages cm
  ISBN 978-0-86534-847-9 (pbk.)
  1. Journalists--Fiction. 2. Billy, the Kid--Fiction. 3. New Mexico--Fiction.
I. Title.
  PS3601.R343B55 2011
  813'.6--dc23
                                2011045567

WWW.SUNSTONEPRESS.COM
SUNSTONE PRESS / POST OFFICE BOX 2321 / SANTA FE, NM 87504-2321 /USA
(505) 988-4418 / ORDERS ONLY (800) 243-5644 / FAX (505) 988-1025

To Sheila, who listened and even encouraged my
bewildering ruminations.

PART ONE
PRETTY WILLIAM

1

¿QUIEN ES?

A few obituaries were written and Garrett tried to cash in. And for a while three wooden crosses stood over the outlaws' graves. Sometimes señoritas they had known left flowers and said prayers.

There were starlit nights when drunken Texas cowboys and local caballeros laughed, yipped at the moon like coyotes, and used the crosses for target practice. They acted as if they were shooting at Charlie, Tom, and Billy themselves. But this they would never have dared while the outlaws lived.

"¡Cobardes! Cowards!" The Kid would have laughed.

The New Mexicans who lived in the abandoned fort all drifted away and the old adobe buildings crumbled to dust.

In 1912 the United States government paid men to dig up the soldiers' graves. They took whatever they found there to the National Cemetery at Santa Fe. Some people said they accidentally took Billy there too. The Kid would have had a good laugh at that.

Then the Pecos flooded its banks, and when the waters receded nothing was left, until the straw-grass returned in the spring. But the outlaws' old amigos could never forget them, and they drank raw mescal and sang ballads, called corridos, in the New Mexican cantinas.

■■■

"We take you to the graves, Señor Percy. We ride in the motor car, no?" Rosario hopped with excitement when she said, "motor car."

Percival Baron Chesterfield looked across his writing desk, through quarter-inch thick bifocals, at Rosario's divine form illuminated by lamplight in the doorway, and framed by the black New Mexico night.

"But why you want to go there? Señor Percy, there no is nothing there."

Rosario frowned at that thought—realizing that if he knew the barrenness of the place, Señor Percy might not go to the graves—and she would not ride in the motorcar.

Percy looked down at his typewriter and piles of books and papers, and back up at Rosario. "Because...well, because...I'm not sure."

Now the girl was smiling again. She stood there, wearing a low-cut, white cotton smock and a red cotton dress, with a deeper crimson wool sash tied tightly about her waist that emphasized her lithe, womanly figure. She wore a silver necklace and cross. Her sleek, impossibly thick hair, blacker than the night, flowed over her shoulders and blouse, and some of the curls seemed suspended, resting on her breasts.

Percy had first seen Rosario Salazár three days before, when he arrived in Lincoln and took a room in one wing of the Salazár family's sprawling adobe. From that first moment, Percy thought Rosario was the most beautiful creature he had ever known. Her physical beauty was greatly augmented by her constant enthusiasm and insatiable curiosity about the world beyond Lincoln County, New Mexico. Rosario seemed to take every chance and excuse to come to Percy's room, offering coffee, tamales, chocolate, and endless questions.

Percy could not answer Rosario's question. He had no idea why he wanted to see the graves. Everything about his life seemed hopelessly complicated as never before.

Percy was thirty-eight years old, but he had always felt mature beyond his years and he considered himself a confirmed bachelor. Until now, he would never for a moment have considered the possibility of a romantic liaison with a girl like Rosario, uneducated and twenty years younger than he. In fact, the only person with whom Percy had ever considered romance had been Miss Juliana Pritchard—and nothing had come of that.

Juliana was niece to Mr. Magruder, Percy's boss, chief editor and majority shareholder of the New York Daily Herald. At thirty years of age, Juliana was classified by most people as a spinster. In her youth, she had attended Chapin, then Vassar. She wanted to work at the newspaper as a reporter or copy editor. But such jobs were not available to a woman—not with so many equally well-educated family men competing for positions that opened so rarely.

So Mr. Magruder hired Juliana to assist him with chores around the offices. Three days a week she worked about the lobby, near Percy's desk, filing, answering correspondence, and performing such other tasks as Mr. Magruder might require. Occasionally, Miss Pritchard and Percy found time to talk, and her good sense and cheerful company moved Percy.

Once, years ago, as Percy and Miss Pritchard laughed together, as they often had, he had almost asked her to share ice cream with him at the corner soda shop. In that moment, Percy thought he saw an invitation in Miss Pritchard's eyes. But then he thought that such a suggestion would be reckless. After all, Miss Pritchard was Mr. Magruder's niece. Why would she want to go with Percy for ice cream? It was a stupid idea, and Percy was not a reckless man. So he had repressed his feelings and the words were never spoken. In the years that followed, he had sometimes recalled that moment, and wondered.

But for the most part, Percy was content with the routines and rhythms of his life. He awoke each morning at his apartment in Yorkville, near 98th Street and Lexington Avenue. Each weekday morning he ate the same breakfast of eggs and boiled potatoes, then rode the train to 23rd Street. In good weather, he would walk to the Herald's offices in West Manhattan. In poor weather, he took a cab. He returned home at exactly the same hour every evening. He read several newspapers every day, and walked in Central Park before bed every night. He purchased groceries every Saturday morning at ten o'clock.

For sexual release, Percy had, for years, visited a prostitute in one of the better Hell's Kitchen tenements on the first and third Saturday of each month at precisely three o'clock in the afternoon. "Mrs. Madigan" was more than ten years older than Percy, and quick and businesslike, so Percy always made the three-thirty train back. He felt that Mrs. Madigan was a sensible and steady choice for this purpose. Yes, Percy had been content with his life and work. But now, looking at Rosario, he felt hopelessly confused.

It had been a month, though it seemed only a day, since Miss Pritchard had brought the message that Mr. Magruder wanted to speak with Percy. In Magruder's office that day, Percy's satisfactory and orderly life had begun to turn upside down.

Percy had been appalled right from the moment when Mr. Magruder informed him that he—Percy—was on his way to New Mexico to write a series

of articles about Pat Garrett for the fifteenth anniversary of Garrett's murder.

"Who's Pat Garrett?"

"My God, man, Garrett was the lawman who killed Billy the Kid."

"Bill the who?"

"Billy the Kid. Worst western outlaw that ever lived. Cold-blooded killer. He loved to kill and he was proud of it. He bragged that he killed twenty-one men, not counting Mexicans or Indians, before he was twenty-one years old. Why, he even threatened to kill Governor Lew Wallace. Just think. If he had done that, Ben Hur might never have been written. Thank God for men like Pat Garrett."

"But, Sir. Who cares about a sheriff who killed some obscure outlaw? This news must be at least forty years old. My asthma's been bothering me, Mr. Magruder. By the time I get inoculations and a passport, change my money, and get to Mexico, it will be 1923. Then it will have been sixteen years since Garrett died. Who cares about a sixteen-year anniversary? For that matter who cares about a fifteen-year anniversary?

"Damn it, Chesterfield! It's New Mexico, not Mexico. New Mexico is a state. Has been for ten years. You don't need inoculations."

"But, Sir. My weight problem. My back hurts all the time. My doctor says it's caused by my stomach pulling it the wrong way. Travel exhausts me. And my article on the Teapot Dome scandal is almost done."

"Percy. You're an idiot. There are always scandals. People are crazy about this cowboys-and-Indians, sheriff-and-outlaw stuff. Don't you ever go to the moving picture shows? And the books by that writer fella with the funny name, Zane Grey? They're selling like hotcakes. If we're gonna compete with the big boys, our paper has to give the people what they want."

"Please, Sir. Why do I have to go to New Mexico? We've got the best libraries in the world. I can take the train, do the research right here in New York City, and have your articles done in a week."

"Listen to me, Mr. Chesterfield. We are journalists. We rigorously investigate the facts we report. We're not writing a goddamn dime novel here. I want you to check the records in Santa Fe and talk to the old-timers who knew Garrett. I want you to come up with a new angle on what made Garrett so great. People love old-fashioned heroes. And that stinking war in Europe turned all

our doughboys into atheists and perverts! Here are your train tickets and some background materials. You leave on Wednesday."

So Percy had done as he'd been told. He'd packed his bag and caught the Trans-Continental for Santa Fe, where he'd dutifully done his research, making extensive notes. But everything about the place had disturbed him. The hills were covered with juniper bushes and rabbit sage, which the locals called chamisa. The spores caused Percy's nose to run and his eyes to water constantly. Sometimes he felt he could hardly breathe. The 7,300-foot altitude compounded his problem. The massive adobe building called The Palace of the Governors, and the Romanesque cathedral, on the plaza of the ancient city, were pleasant to look at, and there were some buildings constructed of fired brick that had been brought from the East by rail. But the rest of the town was made of mud huts that looked like they were melting. The streets were unpaved and there were no trains to get around the town. The whole town wasn't big enough for a train to go anywhere. Percy had to walk, sweating, everywhere. The dirt wasn't just in the streets. There was dust in the hotel, and even in his suitcase.

Percy's nerves were badly on edge in the town, which seemed full of ragged Pueblo Indians, dirty cowboys, and crazy Mexican bandidos. Then there were the bohemian artists: they just painted, drank, gambled and howled all night in the back alleys. No one—not even the staid Hispanics who kept their daughters in at night—paid any attention to the strange ladies Percy had noticed in their midst—the ones that didn't quite fit in. Girls from back east looking too much like small, lean men, wearing short hair, suits or dungarees, and boots. They sat on the benches in the plaza brazenly kissing their more feminine companions, and strolled down the portáles, holding hands. Percy now understood why the stodgy matrons back in New York always whispered, "She went Santa Fe" upon learning that one of their female social contacts now preferred women.

The food was all made of strange little legumes, called pinto beans, corn, and pork, and covered in red sauce that tasted like fire and caused Percy's bowels to run. He survived mostly on coffee.

But Percy had even worse problems. He could not complete his assignment in Santa Fe, where he could find no one who had known Pat

Garrett. He learned that Garrett had never even lived in Santa Fe.

Percy was terrified, but he managed to choke down his fear and send a telegram to Mr. Magruder. Magruder's reply was terse (although it did include a reminder to Percy of the cost telegrams). Magruder told Percy he'd arranged through the local newspaper, The Santa Fe Daily New Mexican, for him to have the use of a 1921-model Hupmobile so he could travel to a place called the Pecos country, where Garrett had actually lived.

Percy felt that the Hupmobile was the first good thing that had happened on the whole trip. It was a beautiful machine. Four cylinders. State of the art. Forest green, with gold pin stripes along the doors and fenders.

And so, despite the barking dogs that pursued him, Percy felt great pride and hope when he set out for the Pecos country in the Hupmobile. Wearing goggles provided by the Daily New Mexican and a silk scarf he had purchased in a curio shop on the plaza, he dodged pigs and chickens and motored past wagons and burros, heading south along a dirt road called the Old Pecos Trail, for the town of Lincoln.

But the period of elation was short-lived. Outside of town, the empty road seemed endless. Percy grew lonely, and when the wind blew dust stung his face and clogged his runny nose, and he felt he would choke to death. The finest dust somehow penetrated his goggles, swirled around, mixed with his constantly flowing tears, and formed mud streaks around his eyes. After eight hours, as Percy approached the town of Capitán, a tumbleweed leapt into the Hupmobile's open cab and struck Percy with such force that the missile disintegrated around his head. He had to stop, and he spent half an hour picking thistles out of his temple, cheek, and left ear.

At Lincoln, two brown youths astride bare-backed horses, some farm hands, a couple of cowboys, old ladies, a few dogs, and an assortment of poorly clothed children, gathered around the car as Percy stepped onto the viga-supported portál of the Salazár family home. A hawker brought a tray of beer, and even the old ladies drank, chewed tobacco or smoked cigars as the little crowd contemplated the Hupmobile.

Señor Pacifico Salazár stepped out, thumbing his suspenders, and accepted Percy's letter of introduction. As Señor Salazár read the letter, the women and children of his household peered out from the doorway and whispered questions about the man on the porch with the red eyes, muddy face, bloody ear, and strange, green vehicle.

That was the first time Percy saw Rosario. She had a slight overbite and prominent front teeth, and her full lips pulled up in the most dazzling smile Percy had ever seen. She had been smiling at Percy ever since. What she smiled about Percy didn't know—but he knew he liked it.

Now, three days later, as Rosario stood in the doorway of Percy's room asking about the motorcar, Percy was filled with confusion. The feelings that Rosario engendered in him were such as he had never known. He felt they could be described only as "wild," and that they threatened to destroy the very foundation of everything he had believed about himself and his ordered world.

"I just don't know why I must see the graves, Rosario."

She placed her hands behind her and leaned back against the doorframe. She pursed her lips thoughtfully, and looked down at her bare feet.

"What are you thinking, Rosario?"

She looked up, smiled, and glided across the room and around the table. She leaned back against the desk, almost sitting, and her knee touched Percy's knee. She leaned forward, glanced around the room in conspiratorial fashion, and locked eyes with Percy.

Percy waited several moments, then asked, "What?"

"Señor Percy," she said, seductively. "Mañana…"

"Yes?"

"When we go to the graves…"

"Yes?"

"You tell me many things of New York, no?"

Percy laughed. He thought it was the first time he had laughed since he had been ordered on this perplexing mission. "Of course, Rosario."

Rosario seemed to leap from her place and dance in an instant out the door. "I wake you early!"

Percy heard the girl running at full speed down the porch to the Salazár family's sleeping quarters.

When Percy finished laughing, he turned back to his writing and the research materials on his desk. Rosario had charmed him so. He felt much

better—not so nervous. He was beginning to feel like his old self: a newspaper man. He had been suffering from an ever-increasing feeling of dread that the conflicting sources he had so far uncovered would prevent him from writing the articles Mr. Magruder wanted. But Percy now felt a bit of confidence that his articles would be acceptable if he could just report the truth.

He looked at the two obituaries Mr. Magruder had provided, which announced the death, at age twenty-one, of the desperado the newspapers called Billy the Kid. The first, from the Santa Fe Weekly Democrat of July 21, 1881, read in part:

No sooner had the floor caught the descending form, which had a pistol in one hand and knife in the other, than there was a strong odor of brimstone in the air, and a dark figure with the wings of a dragon, claws like a tiger, eyes like balls of fire, and horns like a bison, hovered over the corpse for a moment, and with a fiendish laugh said, "Ha! Ha! This is my meat!" and then sailed off through the window. He did not leave his card, but he is a gentleman well known by reputation, and thereby hangs a 'tail.'

The other had appeared in the Grant County Herald on July 28, 1881. It read in part, "He was a low-down vulgar cut-throat with probably not one redeeming quality."

Magruder had also given Percy a book written by Pat Garrett himself and published in 1882, with the amazing title, The Authentic Life of Billy the Kid, the Noted Desperado of the Southwest, Whose Deeds of Daring and Blood Have Made His Name a Terror in New Mexico, Arizona and Northern Mexico, by Pat F. Garrett, Sheriff of Lincoln County, N. Mex. By Whom He Was Finally Hunted Down and Captured by Killing Him.

Percy had kept busy in the three days since his arrival in Lincoln. He'd located and spoken to several aged, native New Mexican men who claimed to have known both Pat Garrett and the kid who had called himself William Bonney. They had seemed mostly interested in talking about Bonney.

Now Percy began typing his hand-written notes of those interviews. A man named Miguel Otero had told him, "To all those who knew his mother, his

courtesy and benevolence of spirit were no mystery."

Don Martín Chávez had said, "Billy the Kid was a perfect gentleman and a man with a noble heart. In all his career, he never killed a native citizen of New Mexico, which was one of the reasons we were all so fond of him. He had plenty of courage. He was a brave man and did not know what fear meant. They had to sneak up on him in the dead of night to murder him."

Added Jose Garcia y Trujillo, "Su vista penetrava al corazon de toda la gente. His look pierced all our hearts."

Percy flipped through the pages to the back of Garrett's book. Garrett said that William Bonney's last words, spoken at midnight on July 14, 1881, were "¿Quien es?" Percy knew that the words meant, literally, "Who is?" or "Who is he?" Percy had already begun to learn how to pronounce the Spanish words and he liked their soft sound. He mouthed the words in a bare whisper: "¿Key-en es?"

His lamp-flame flickered and died. Percy sat in the dark room, thinking of the young outlaw, dead those forty years. "¿Quien es?" he wondered, "¿Quien es?"

2

EXILES, MAY 1881

The symbols had been left there by anonymous sojourners in futile defense against fated passage to oblivion.

The Kid's black stallion, Bala, still looked fresh and Ledoux's new pinto looked okay too, but the other horses were lathered and blowing hard when the five riders pulled up before the mouth of the canyon.

"Por aquí. This way." Montoya said.

Jesse Evans pulled a bandana from the breast pocket of his frockcoat, pushed back his Stetson, and wiped sweat and sand from his forehead and blond eyebrows. He looked at the towering sandstone cliffs that rose on either side of the entrada and he looked back across the immense, saguaro-, yucca-, cholla-, mesquite- and sage-covered plain the riders had just traversed. It was dusk and the darkening shapes of the sages and cacti melted and faded together into a soft, gray-blue blanket that stretched and curved away to the purple embers of twilight smoldering on the distant horizon.

Evans looked back at the opening which cleft the flat-topped row of cliffs running out of sight, north and south, and up at the piñon, juniper and cedar that grew atop the mesas. He gazed above and beyond at successive levels and mounts which rose into ponderosa and Douglas-fir forests, still alight and glowing in the sinking sunlight, toward the great, high Mogollon rim that runs along the southern Arizona-New Mexico line.

"Yer loco," Evans said, peering into the deepening shadows of the canyon. "If them blue-boys follow us in there, we'll be trapped."

"No," Montoya said. "Hay un ojo de agua dulce, zacate bueno, y una salida que sube para las alturas, y hay sitios donde un hombre puede defenderse contra muchos. There is a sweet-water spring, good grass and a way out to the heights and there are places where one man can defend against many."

"He's right," Croft said, "When I was scoutin' fer them blue-coats we chased Victorio here. There's good cover in there. We couldn't ride in without gettin' a lotta men shot. We had ta ride north and come up the next cañon. We left a squad here ta pen 'em in. But by the time we come back over the top, the Apaches was gone. There's a trail up and out the far side. And there is a good spring in there."

Evans studied their back trail for sign of pursuit. "You see anything, Billy?"

They all knew the Kid had the best eyes. Billy pushed back his Mexican sombrero and scanned the plain. "They're not comin'. Why would they? Them soldados got Killian's cattle back. They can't drive 'em an' chase us. An' they don't care. It's not their job. They're restin' up somewheres, prob'ly drinkin' by now. You boys go on. I'll watch here awhile."

Evans, Croft, Ledoux and Montoya rode up to the spring at the head of the canyon. The waters seeped out into a surrounding bosket of oak brush, carrizo, cattails, grass, cedar, juniper, some small Doug fir and blackjack ponderosa, then sank below the sandy arroyo floor.

The outlaws hobbled their horses, built a fire, and sat against the cliff wall in the arced shelter of a low, hollowed cavern. The domed ceiling of the ancient grotto was blackened by smoke of fires precedent and numerous beyond reckoning. Their fire illuminated and the exiles contemplated ancient glyphs, cut through the soot. The symbols gamboled and cavorted across the black stone cielo and they had been left there by anonymous sojourners who, in their time, had fraudulently usurped the role of lesser gods and cast their creations of tiny myths over the artificial firmament in futile defense against fated passage to oblivion.

A huge, fallen ponderosa lay before the cave, between the outlaws' fire and the spring below where the horses rested and browsed.

The Kid sat at the mouth of the canyon and waited until it was good and dark and he was satisfied no enemies followed. But movement in the conifers atop the cliffs alarmed him. Leading Bala, he walked up the draw and kept in the moon shadows against the canyon wall. After a while, he saw the light of his amigos' fire, and as he got closer he could hear Evans and Ledoux arguing.

"God damn you, Ledoux. If you'd a' scouted Killian's spread like you was told and like you say you done, you'd a' known them troopers was around.

You almost got us all killed. And where'd you git that pinto with no brand? There's somethin' yer not tellin' us. And I don't like ridin' with no liar."

"Settle down, Jesse. I looked the place over an' talked to a couple a' campesinos, but I got my own business, too."

"Not when yer ridin' with an' s'posed to be lookin' out for us, you don't. I don't know if I should whip yer mangy hide 'er just shoot you down right here."

"Ten cuidado. Be careful," Ledoux said in a low, menacing tone.

The Kid was close now and he saw a dozen Gila Apaches moving down from the narrow cleft and twisting trail, which ascended the angle where the cliffs met and the canyon ended. He crouched in shadow behind a slabstone, broken from the canyon wall, directly across the draw from his amigos' fire. The wash was narrow here, so Billy leaned his Winchester against the sand-lith and drew his revolvers as the Gileños filtered into cover around the spring.

"No! ¡Tu tengas cuidado, eh!" Montoya said to Ledoux, and Montoya put his hand on his pistol as a warrior aimed his rifle at the unsuspecting fugitives.

Billy shot the Apache in the back of his thigh and the Apache fired too, but his aim was ruined and his bullet only sliced across Croft's ribcage. The warrior's leg gave way and he collapsed without a sound. The outlaws dove for cover behind the ponderosa, Bala leapt away and Billy ducked as bullets splattered against the face of his stone shield and the cliff behind him. A chieftain shouted and the Apaches stopped firing. They crouched and glanced about, knowing their backs were exposed to the Kid. There was a long silence.

"They shot me Billy! Kill 'em!" Croft yelled.

The Kid called to Montoya. "Ask 'em what they want, Patricio. Tell 'em we don't want no trouble and we ain't got no extra horses or nothin' else to give 'em."

Patricio and the Amarind headman spoke in a mix of Apache and Spanish. The chieftain laughed bitterly. Then Patricio answered the Kid.

"He says they want the pinto. They say it's theirs. And they want Ledoux. They say he killed their kinsman and forced his woman. But she's alive. He says you might shoot some of them, but you won't get them all. He says the mountain gods make a joke. Maybe we all die together tonight but no matter: Ledoux must pay with blood. Sangre por sangre."

The Kid stood on the high bank of the arroyo across from his compadres. Ledoux crouched behind the ponderosa, out of the Apaches' line of sight and fire, but the Kid could see his bowler and the top of his forehead.

"Open up on 'em, Billy!" Ledoux called, "You got 'em cold."

The Kid rose up, shot Ledoux through the head and ducked back under a handful of bullets loosed in response by the Apaches.

There was another strained silence, then Montoya and Evans pushed Ledoux's body over their log cover and Ledoux lay bloody, twisted, and limp before his accusers.

"Tell 'em the gods' joke don't work tonight. We men got a choice an' no reason to die just so them mountain gods can laugh. Tell 'em to take the pinto and go."

"He says you shot his man."

"Tell 'em I could a' killed 'im, easy. I can kill a lot of 'em right now. They shot Croft. We're even. Sangre por sangre."

"He says this place is holy. If we're here at dawn, we all die."

The Apaches backed up the draw, two supporting their wounded brother, another leading the pinto, and they slipped up the twisting, water polished stone trail out of the canyon to the forested plateaus above.

The outlaws rode at a brisk canter down the arroyo, out of the canyon, cut north over the desert, and fled into the night.

Near dawn, the desperados found another ravine, and passage up to the high timber. The next day they topped the rim and descended through cool forests of huge and majestic ponderosa pine and fir to Silver City, New Mexico Territory. Evans and the Kid were known there so they waited in a walnut grove while Montoya and Croft entered the town at night and found a drunken doctor to sew Croft up and girdle his broken ribs.

They rode south and skirted La Mesilla where the Kid had been sentenced to hang only two months earlier. He had been tried by a jury there, and condemned for killing Sheriff William Brady in broad daylight on the main street of Lincoln town. He had killed his guards and escaped. He was hunted in Arizona, New Mexico, and West Texas. He had told friends that he only hoped to live long enough to kill Sheriff Pat Garrett, for Tom and

Charlie, and to kill the governor, Wallace, for his lies.

The outlaws rode on, rustled some steers and sold them to a butcher on the Mexican side of El Paso Del Norte. They ate, drank and slept in a bordello there. Then they rode for the Pecos country, where they figured they still had some friends.

They rode across a great flat waste of low mesquite, jimson, Russian thistle, milkweed, rabbit sage and cactus, toward cobalt blue mountain ranges shimmering on the eastern horizon. The riders spread out of each other's dust and spoke not at all. They dug for water in the lowest parts of the arroyos they crossed.

As he rode, the Kid had plenty of time to think about how he had killed Ledoux on the judgment of an instant. He felt no remorse: Ledoux had betrayed his own compañeros. The Kid felt only pride for his excellent shots, which had stopped the Apaches, visited instant justice and retribution on Ledoux, and saved the tiny band of desperate amigos to ride another day.

He rode on and thought about how he had come to this point, hunted and condemned—how he had come to this strange place and time of his imminent ending. A place so far from that of his birth in New York City, just twenty-one years past.

3

ARIZONA TERRITORY

I Frank P. Cahill, being convinced that I am about to die, do make the following as my final statement.

Percy could not sleep, no matter how he willed it. He had missed two appointments with Mrs. Madigan, and he had that feeling which he could only describe as "frisky." And he felt an obsessive need to understand the bandit and killer, William Bonney. And so, Mrs. Madigan's immense and opulent bare white breasts, Rosario, Miss Pritchard, and William Bonney boiled by turns to the surface of Percy's consciousness as he tossed under heavy, loom-woven wool blankets that were so scratchy as to penetrate the yellow pajamas—monogrammed on the breast pocket in royal blue with his initials, PBC.

He often found his path to sleep by reading favorite passages from Homer. But now his beloved leather-bound copies of the Iliad and the Odyssey lay abandoned on his nightstand, as even his stalwarts, Ajax, Diomedes, and Achileus had, this night, utterly failed to defeat wakefulness.

Percy's most acute problem was that the little adobe room in which he reclined was freezing cold. It was late November, and he was informed that this year's weather was exceptionally mild; so mild that Rosario went about barefoot in the evenings. But only a few hours after sunset, the temperature plummeted; now, as Percy occasionally poked his head out from under his blankets, he could actually see the steam of his breath.

A cast-iron wood stove stood in one corner of the room and Percy resolved to make a fire. He arose, slipped his brogues over his argyle-covered feet, and headed out to the woodpile.

He shivered in the mist that rose from the Rio Bonito just below as he piled a prodigious load of fagots onto his left arm, swayed, and barely regained equilibrium by adding the support of his right arm. He further secured the load by placing his chin on top. As he staggered back toward the porch, he felt

a tickle, as if a feather touched his cheek. He felt it again. He craned his head back and looked at the bundle of wood in his arms.

He saw the beady eyes, obscenely bloated abdomen, and mass of angular legs of Latrodectus hesperus, the black widow, as she crouched there, her chelicerae extended, ready to bite his corpulent lower lip. In the instant before he screamed and hurled his bundle of wood toward the sky, he saw little cotton-like egg sacks on the wood and a score of her tiny offspring scurrying about. Percy's short legs were fat and thick, but he still almost fell as he staggered backward, slapping at his face and neck, and one of the falling logs struck his head and caused lights to erupt behind his eyes as he careened into the corner pillar of the portál. He glanced back at the woodpile, and thought he saw swarming movement throughout, revealed in the moonlight, as he fled back into his bedroom door.

He darted about the room, lighting and placing candles, one in each corner and three on his desk. I'll see them before they can get me, he thought. He tucked his pajama bottoms into his argyles, against the eventuality that the little beasts might attempt an assault by running up his legs.

Percy now knew he would not sleep this night. He angrily yanked a blanket off his bed, inspected it carefully, wrapped it around his body, pulled the top over his head like a hood, and sat there, huddled over his desk like some ancient, angry monk on vigil.

There was nothing to do but get back to work, and he began flipping in most irritated fashion through his piles of notes. But writing always calmed Percy. As he began studying his notes from his research at the state archives in Santa Fe, he was inspired by the feeling of detective work, as though he were hunting Billy the Kid just as Garrett had done.

He remembered the brilliant deductions he had made when, turning a page in the state library, he had discovered several exemplars of the Kid's handwriting. There was a bill of sale for a horse, a signature on a receipt for a bottle of whiskey, and a letter written to the Governor of New Mexico and author of Ben Hur, Lew Wallace.

Percy had been greatly surprised by the Kid's handwriting. Researching a savage killer, he had expected to see a crude and brutish script. But the boy's writing was even and precise. The cursive letters flowed across the pages, each exactly the same height and slanted consistently at a ten degree angle to the right. The lines were perfectly straight, though the pages were unruled. The signature, "William Bonney," displayed graceful spirals on the first line of the "W" and rising end of the "y."

Percy knew that the boy's name was not "William Bonney." He had felt a sort of perverse hometown pride when he read, in source after source, that William Bonney had been born in New York City in 1859. He was probably Henry McCarty, the son of one Catherine McCarty who had come to New York from Ireland fleeing the great potato famine. The greater weight of authority held that they lived in the Irish Fourth Ward of Manhattan. Nothing was known about the Kid's father, though there were rumors he had been killed in the Civil War.

These facts, together with the handwriting and Percy's knowledge of New York history, allowed him to deduce, as a detective would, many things about the infamous New Mexico outlaw.

First, the boy's mother loved him. Yes, this deduction seemed obvious. All mothers love their boys. But this mother loved hers enough to see to his education. In the late 1850s and early 1860s, the Fourth Ward had been infested with ruffians and scores of gangs, including the Whyos, the Plug Uglies, and the River Pirates. The dives that flourished around the Bowery were favorite resorts of pick pockets, sneaks, panel thieves, badger game experts, lush workers, and knock-out artists.

The handwriting showed that Catherine had protected her son from these influences, and that he was an intelligent and a disciplined student who had learned his lessons well and completed at least a primary education.

Percy also deduced that the boy had probably spoken with at least a slight Irish accent.

But there was a riddle which, Percy felt, was essential to understanding the essence of the boy's nature: a person's name is usually an accident of birth, but William Bonney had chosen his own name. What did it mean?

Percy knew that Catherine and her sons, Henry and Joe, would have spent nights in Irish public houses in New York, where people drank thick, dark beer and sang songs of Irish heroes who fought, with sword and shield, against tyranny and impossible odds. The heroes usually died in great, final

battles, but their names were remembered. "William Bonney" would have been understood, to the Irish, as meaning, "Pretty William." Percy searched his memory for the melodies. Was there a song of Pretty William?

He continued reviewing his notes. It seemed that Catherine and her boys had drifted west, seeking a new life. They were perhaps in Indiana, perhaps in Wichita. By 1873, they were in Santa Fe. Catherine was consumptive. She might have moved west to seek a new life for her boys, away from the hopeless streets of New York. And Percy knew that, in those days, it was believed that the dry, high desert air of New Mexico could cure tuberculosis.

At Santa Fe, Catherine married her companion, William Antrim, and the lost little family traveled south and west to the boomtown, Silver City, at the base of the Burro Mountains, near the New Mexico-Arizona border.

Percy's research showed that Catherine had died there when Henry was fifteen years old. The boy learned to deal cards from his older brother, Joe, who, at age eighteen, worked in a saloon and casino.

The boy stood in the doorway of the miner's little cabin. The room smelled of blood, urine and sickness.

"Take care of my boys" his mother, Catherine, said.

"Now no more of that," Mrs. Trusdale replied.

"Take care of my boys, promise me." And there was bloody spittle on Catherine's lips.

"You know I will, Catherine."

After Mrs. Trusdale left, Henry and Joe sat on the bed, held Catherine's hands, and wept bitterly as she died.

"Stop looking at the whores, Henry!" Joe reached out and gently ruffled the boy's hair. The boy laughed at his brother. Then he dealt, like lightning, ten cards. Some from the bottom, some from the top, as the boy chose. He had learned to shuffle so after the usual cut, the cards he wanted were on top, and he had a good sense for what cards ended up on the bottom. He could deal either way.

Joe smiled. He had always known that his little brother was smarter. Joe was pleased that he had shown the boy a way, maybe, to survive.

"That's good, Henry. Now just remember one thing. Always sit where you can see everything. If any of them seem like they're even thinkin' you're cheatin', pull your gun. Cover 'em all. Take the gold, an' get out, an' don't go back."

The orphan boy was arrested for stealing a keg of butter from the back of a rancher's wagon. Then arrested again, for holding some laundry that another boy, "Sombrero Jack," had stolen from "Celestials sans cue." The boy was captured, but he escaped from the Silver City jail by climbing up the chimney.

Percy's research showed that at 15 years, the boy had crossed the western mountains, Apache country, to Arizona Territory. Wanted for escape in New Mexico Territory, Henry had changed his name to "Henry Antrim."

Henry worked as a cowhand there, at a ranch owned by a man named Hooker. But he was let go by a hard foreman—Bill Whelan—who disdained the small boy's ability to do his job working the calves at the fall roundup, or rodeo del campo.

Henry was good on horseback, rounding up the calves and driving them down from the high country to the rodeo camp. He was good with a rope, and he had a close connection and mutual understanding with his horse. He was gentle on the bit and with his spurs. His mount quickly came to understand that by responding alertly, it would avoid harsher treatment. Many men were heavy handed, and never learned to win their mounts by gentle treatment.

The boy thought his fine skill with la riata, his lariat, and his excellent horsemanship, would be appreciated and entitle him to the job of roping the calves and dragging them to the fire, where they would be castrated and branded. But there were many skillful ropers and fine horsemen and the green newcomer had a lot to learn before he could secure the plum job at the branding.

"You want me to do what?"

"Look, boy. Yer lucky we don' run ye off, green as ye are. Now I'm gonna explain this t'ye just once. When the roper drags the calf to the fire, Mackie an'

Acuña 'll take his tail an' his head, bring 'im down, an' hold his legs. Ye grab the ball sack, cut the end at about two inches up, reach in, pull the stones out, an' roll the sack up the strings. Ye gotta cut the strings as far up from the cojones as ye can. Don' use no knife, the blades're too sharp. The calf 'll bleed to death. Ye bite the ball-strings, high-up as ye can."

"Bite'em?"

"That's right. Crush an' rip the ball strings. Pluck the nuts off. A ragged cut an' the steer lives. A clean cut an' the steer bleeds ta death. Once ye pluck the nuts, just walk ta the fire, take the iron an' lay on the brand."

John Mackie, the Scottish-American army deserter, liked the boy and saw his confusion. "Mr. Whelan, sir. Forgive me sir. Which of us ever plucked the stones without seein' it done first? Let me do the pluckin'. The boy can hold the legs."

Whelan looked darkly at the two. "Do as ye please. Git et done right."

The first bull-calf was black and white. He was about 200 pounds, and he kicked and fought hard as they bulldogged him to the ground. Henry only weighed about 120, but held the bull's legs and Mackie ripped out the animal's testicles and branded him. They did it again and again. By three o'clock Henry was exhausted, and a two hundred pound calf got loose and kicked him in the chest before clipping Acuña's jaw with his hooves.

"¡Chíngate, cabrón! Fuck you ass," Acuña protested.

Whelan watched and frowned.

"You pluck 'em now," Mackie decided.

The next bull-calf was big, too. The roper, Joe Buck, roped him well, and dragged him, kicking, to the fire. Acuña twisted his head down, and Mackie jerked his tail and kicked out his legs. Henry cut the scrotum, pulled out the testicles, and severed the epididymides with his teeth. His mouth filled with blood and it was on his chin and neckerchief. The next time, the boy decided to do it the easy way. He cut the seed strings with his knife. He branded the animal and it skipped away.

"Don' do that." Mackie warned, as he glanced over at Whelan, who sat his appaloosa and watched everything.

As they continued, the boy bit some and occasionally used his knife.

But when the first calf he had cut fell and died on the edge of the herd, Whelan rode up and ordered him off the place.

By 1877 Henry resided at the Hog Ranch—a loosely connected warren of saloons and bordellos that served Fort Grant, Arizona Territory.

The accounts Percy read told of soldiers and miners deceived and fleeced by a young boy's unlikely skill at cards. The sources said that Henry and John Mackie, who had also been fired from Hooker's ranch, enjoyed great sport stealing horses from officers and enlisted cavalrymen busy enjoying the pleasures of the Hog Ranch. The two thieves were so successful that the commanding general at Fort Grant had declared the Hog Ranch off limits to all personnel.

By the age of 17, Henry was beginning to take an interest in good clothing. He had outplayed a gambler so badly that the man had to give up his suit, shoes, and bowler. The man's friends were angry, but the boy showed he was ready and the men gave the victim a frockcoat to cover his nakedness, and they walked reticently out of the little shack where the game had been played.

Henry walked proudly down the street in his new, ill fitting, store-bought gambler's shoes, plaid suit and bowler. Then he saw cavalry horses tied outside George Aikin's saloon. He moved through shadows to the fine prizes only to find that all four horses had long leads tied to their bridles. Four officers, all in blue, brass, and braid, stood stiffly erect at the bar inside, holding the ends of the leads, evidently supposing the precaution would prevent the theft of their horses. Henry laughed at their unwarranted confidence.

He moved cautiously to the window, looked in, and signaled to his lover, who went by the name of "Bonnie Bueno" [Pretty Good]. She winked back, and approached the officers. She caressed their ears, shoulders, and necks, laughed and joked, and took pains to bend forward at every opportunity, revealing her ample cleavage. Henry cut the leads, tied them to hitching posts and led the horses away.

He rode with his spoils toward Tombstone. The Arizona nights were warm, and on the third night he slept easily.

He awoke to the softest sound, the nicker of a horse. He opened his eyes in the chill and soft light of dawn. He saw high-topped rawhide moccasins

circled and crossed with cut-leather thongs. He saw billowy cotton breaches above the moccasins, a colored wool breech-cloth. A belt with hammered conchos of Mexican silver, a calico shirt, bandoleros, a turquoise necklace, and arms cradling a Sharp's rifle in the most casual attitude. He could see the man grinning. Dazzling white teeth. The man's dark face was mostly obscured in the shadow of the sun, which rose behind him, casting a halo around his long, blue-black hair.

Officers and troopers from Fort Grant sat their horses behind the Apache tracker. Henry started and reached for his six-gun but the click of a single action Colt's behind his ear, held by the Master Sergeant O'Connor, proved that resistance was futile.

At Fort Grant the civilian blacksmith, Frank Cahill, welded chains onto the boy's thick wrists. But the moment the steel cage door slammed shut and the jailers walked out, Henry worked his small hands out of the manacles. He had been doing well at poker and horse theft, and he kept money buried in a lock-box. The skeleton key in his pocket was small and he used it to work the lock on the cell door. The jailer was drunk, and Henry disappeared.

Three days later, Cahill was drinking and gambling at the Hog Ranch. "Ya know, boy, I'm from Ireland. Galway. And it shames me to see our kind stupid as you are. What makes ya think ya can walk out of the gaol, and just sit here playin' cards after stealin' horses?"

"I dont think it. I'm just doing it." Henry grinned as he hauled in another pot.

"Yeah. An' maybe the rest of ya are stupid as this dumb potato eater. Does one of ya notice that he wins every time he deals?"

The players looked at each other, but no one said anything.

Henry's face clouded. Cahill's charge was serious enough to get a man shot. Henry had won a lot and he decided to avoid confrontation with the entire table.

"You know, Frankie, you're right. You are. I just came here to get my things. I'm leaving tonight for California."

The boy smiled casually, gathered his money, stood up, and walked to the bar, where he whispered with Bonnie while keeping an eye on Cahill and the others—losers all. Cahill's luck didn't change, and soon he stood at the bar, drinking, next to Henry and Bonnie.

Cahill tossed back a shot and looked at the Kid. Henry wanted no trouble, but he was not going to look away.

"Yer a stinkin' pimp," Cahill said.

Henry took this as a slur against his lover, although, in truth, if there is virtue in chastity, her virtue could hardly have been defended. The boy felt the insult must have stung the girl, and his anger flared. "You're a son of a bitch."

The blacksmith grabbed Henry's lapels, head-butted him, and hurled him down to the floor. Henry was on his feet in an instant, but Cahill came forward like a bulldog, shoulders lowered, and drove the boy back through the open door. Henry landed on his back. The blacksmith, on his knees, straddled Henry's torso, cocking back his elbows and throwing down mighty blows. Henry slipped some, and blocked some, but some landed square and bounced his head off the boardwalk. He managed to pull his .41 from his waistband, and jam it into Cahill's side. Cahill's eyes grew wide and he grabbed at the gun, but there was a sharp pop and his body buckled, slumped, and doubled into fetal position as Henry pushed him off and sprang to his feet.

The boy waved his gun from side to side, covering the excited crowd as he backed and stumbled down onto the road. He saw Bonnie standing, dismayed, among the witnesses.

A fine bay named Cashaw, a racer of some repute, was tied there. Henry loosed and mounted her, and galloped into the night, crouched low like a jockey and looking back, gun in hand, lest any should venture a shot.

Percy could well understand why the boy rode away. He was already wanted for stealing horses. Now, Cahill was killed. The New Mexico border was only one hard day's ride away, and who could tell what a jury might do?

Percy found that the Cahill killing was well documented in cavalry dispatches, a coroner's jury indictment and in memoirs of witnesses. And there was Cahill's own statement signed on his deathbed the following day, in which he omitted to tell how he had beaten the boy:

My name is Frank P. Cahill. I was born in the county and town of Galway,

Ireland; yesterday, Aug. 17th 1877, I had some trouble with Henry Antrim, otherwise known as Kid, during which he shot me. I had called him a pimp, and he called me a son of a bitch; we then took hold of each other; I did not hit him. I think I saw him go for his pistol, and tried to get a hold of it, but could not, and he shot me in the belly. I have a sister named Margaret Flanagen living in East Cambridge, Mass., and another named Kate Conden, living in San Francisco.

4

WILLIAM BONNEY

Now the kid called himself "William Bonney," or "Pretty William," the name of an outlaw hero and prolific lover as told in Irish song and legend.

As the outlaws rode for Fort Sumner, in May 1881, Jesse Evans was thinking too, weighing the dangers against the benefits of again riding with the Kid. They had ridden together for a short time, four years earlier, then they ended up on opposite sides in the Lincoln County War. Now they rode together again, but Jesse saw bad trouble on the horizon. On the one hand, the Kid's gun was very useful—the shot that had killed Ledoux had been a damned good one.

Texas Rangers wanted Jesse for breaking out of the Huntsville prison, where he had begun a twenty-year sentence for killing Ranger George Bingham in a running gunfight, and the Pecos and Fort Sumner were damn close to Texas. Jesse's crimes in New Mexico Territory had not been forgotten, but many would be hard to prove and the powerful men he had once served had sanctioned others. Still, if Texas Rangers caught up with Jesse in New Mexico, he would want to have the Kid with him.

But on the other hand, the Kid was wanted for killing lawmen in New Mexico Territory, and it was more likely that Sheriff Pat Garrett, cattle detectives, U.S. Marshals or cavalry would first corner the Kid. Then the Kid would need Jesse's gun, and Jesse wanted nothing to do with that.

He decided it would probably be best to separate from the Kid. Problem was, the Kid was cocky and hotheaded and he expected everyone to be as loyal to their amigos as he was. Ledoux was a good example. Leaving the Kid now might be dangerous. Jesse had to figure a way to do it in a time and place where it would not involve a confrontation.

Jesse rode on and thought of how he had first met the Kid. Looking back, he knew it had been an unlucky day.

Jesse had ridden into the tiny collection of adobe huts, and ruined walls of the old fort at Apache Tejoe, with Frank Baker, Jim Croft, and three other rustlers. Four, if you counted the body of Emilio Machado, which hung across his saddle. The men trailed thirty Spanish cattle they had taken near La Mesilla. It had looked like they got away clean, until a bullet ripped through Emilio's upper leg and through his hamstring before coming out his knee. Jesse and his boys all remained mounted, unlimbered their rifles, and fired hot volleys at Mariano Barela's posse as they rode forward through the mesquite brush.

"Stupid Mexes!" the rustlers jeered as the posse-men, equipped with only six guns, were driven back.

Jesse's rustlers kept control of the spooky herd and tried to tie off Emilio's wound even as they moved on, but they failed to stop the blood, and Emilio finally fell off his mount and died.

Ike Clanton, Bill Brocius, and Johnny Ringo stood in the shade at Apache Tejoe with their herd of thirty-four steers and heifers, rustled in Arizona, grazing nearby.

"Bad luck?" Ike asked as he regarded Emilio's corpse, with its blood soaked pants and a boot that hung off it, dripping blood.

Jesse glanced at Emilio and back at the Arizona outlaws. He tried to buck up, and faked a grin. "You know, Ike, another day, another bullet." He nodded, "Bill, Johnny."

Johnny Ringo chuckled and spat some tobacco.

"How many you bring?" Ike asked.

"Thirty. You?"

"Thirty-four. We trade and you pay gold for four."

"Suits me," Jesse said, "three dollars on foot?"

"Good enough. Who the hell's that?"

"Just a buncha Mexes," Jesse said.

Johnny Ringo frowned, "No, that one's a gringo."

Jesse dismounted, and walked with the Arizona rustlers over to the little group of card players, sitting on blankets in the shade of a cottonwood.

The Anglo boy had just won a hand, and he collected a pot consisting

of some coins, a pair of gloves, and a straw sombrero that he immediately put on his head.

The boy looked up at Jesse, Ike, Bill, and Ringo. Ike and Bill wore goat-hide chaps and sombreros, and sported waxed, pointed mustachios and chin-whiskers in the popular style called "The Imperial." Johnny Ringo and Jesse Evans were clean-shaven, and they wore Stetson hats with gracefully curved brims. Instead of chaps, Evans and Ringo wore knee-high, heavy leather gators over their boots. Jesse wore a wool frock coat and Ringo wore a Mexican bolero jacket cut short at the waist with fancy lacework on the cuffs and broad lapels.

The four outlaws looked at the boy and exchanged amused glances. He was wearing the same light cotton plaid gambler's suit that he had worn for the whole two weeks since he had killed Frank Cahill. His pants were filthy and torn. One foot sported a shoe and a sock. The other had been bare since he lost a shoe in the fight with Cahill. The boy's ragged, store-bought suit was about two sizes too big for him, and when he placed the plain, loosly woven Mexican sombrero on his head, his appearance was withal so strange that all four rustlers were forced to hold back from laughing out loud.

"You playin' strip poker with these Mexes, boy?" Jesse asked.

Henry rose to his feet, clearly exposing the Colt's .41 that was stuck in the waist of his trousers. His cheeks flushed red, and his blue eyes flashed anger.

When Ringo saw the gun and the look, he recoiled a bit and rested his palm on the handle of his six-gun.

"What if I am?" the boy answered.

Jesse chuckled. "It's all right with me, amigo. It's a free country, ain't it? I'm Jesse, these here are Ike, Curly Bill, an' Johnny Ringo." Jesse flashed his winning smile.

Henry relaxed a bit and, aware of his absurd appearance, grinned back.

"Well, that's right! Hell yes! It is a free country. And if you want to play a hand, I'll bet these coins and gloves against your boots."

Everybody laughed.

Jesse considered the kid's ragged figure. "How old're you boy?"

"Seventeen."

Jesse concealed his surprise. The boy looked no older than fifteen, and would have been small even for that age. "You got a horse?"

"I had one. A fast one. She wasn't mine, but I had to leave between two suns and I had no horse nor time, I had to leave presto change-o. But once I got here I sent her back."

Jesse, Ringo, Curly Bill and Ike exchanged incredulous glances.

"Lemme see if I git this, boy. You say you stole a horse an' then gave'r back?" Said Jesse.

"That's right, she belonged to a friend of mine."

"What's your name, boy?

"My friends call me 'Kid.'"

"That's not what I asked."

Henry hesitated. "Henry Antrim" was now wanted for murder. Henry rolled his eyes up to the sky for a moment and Jesse knew that what came next would be a lie.

Now the Kid called himself "William Bonney," or "Pretty William," the name of an outlaw hero and prolific lover as told in Irish song and legend.

"William Bonney, eh?" Jesse responded, glancing at Ike and Ringo.

"Sure."

"Sure. You know how to trail cattle, boy?" Jesse asked. He glanced back over his shoulder at Machado's body, hanging across his saddle. "'Cause I know where you can git some boots, and another horse, no luck about it, and we need another hand."

Ringo and the Clantons drove the New Mexico cattle west toward Tombstone, and Evans and his people drove the Arizona cattle east.

Jesse's bunch rode from Apache Tejoe toward Mesilla. At the base of the Burro Mountains they broke up. Jesse sent Frank Baker and the others on with the herd and he waited with William on a ridge overlooking a mining camp. At midnight, they rode down, cut the hobbles, and drove off five horses that grazed near the miners' tents. Someone shouted and the miners came out shooting. Jesse and the Kid returned fire and Jesse had to ride back, curse the boy, and order him to break off the fight and move on.

They took the main road and met a stagecoach headed for Lordsburg. Jesse and William sat their horses in the middle of the road and Jesse ordered the driver to stop and throw down his weapon. He obeyed.

"Now, throw down the strong-box, Floyd."

"There ain't no money nor gold nor silver in it Jesse, I swear."

"Throw it down. You got a key?"

"I swear I don't, Jesse."

Jesse dismounted, shot the lock off, kicked the box open, and cursed when he saw that Floyd told the truth.

"Goddamnit, Floyd. Yer gonna pay for this."

"Now hold on a minute, Jesse! I got no say who sends what in the box."

"Yeah, but you're gonna pay."

Jesse looked at William and William looked puzzled and hesitant. Jesse laughed, stepped over to his saddle wallet and took out a bottle of rye whiskey. He tossed it up to Floyd and winked at William. "Drink it."

"Drink it all?"

"No. Leave two shots for me an' Billy here."

Floyd had a hard time drinking the bottle down and Jesse and William both laughed. Jesse decided he liked the boy. He enjoyed schooling the boy in his lawless ways. But when Jesse offered the last whiskey-shot to William and William declined, Jesse asked with some displeasure, "My whiskey ain't good enough for you, Kid?"

"I don't drink whiskey. I've tried it. I don't like strong spirits. It makes me feel slow."

Jesse and William moved on with their stolen horses and stopped at the little station called San Ysidro. The station-master, Gomez, fed and watered the horses. William spoke in Spanish with Gomez, and, inside, with Gomez' wife and children.

"Bring us food and whatever you got to drink," Jesse ordered.

"Señor Jesse, I am contento to help with your horses. But if you want more, you must show that you can pay."

"Pay? Sure Gomez. I'm gonna pay you. You know me. Just chalk it up for now. We got business in Mesilla."

"Sí, señor Jesse, I know you well. You no pay me nunca."

"I ain't askin' again, Gomez. Get it out here, pronto."

Gomez nodded to his wife, and she brought beans and pork simmering

in red chile, and some corn tortillas. William looked ruefully at the woman and her children and rolled a cigarette. Jesse shoveled food into his mouth so fast that he was barely able to ask, "You ain't eatin', Kid?"

"I ain't hungry."

"How'd you learn to talk Mex so good?"

William looked angry—he looked like he might be about to draw. Why should the Kid care that we're makin' some Mexes feed us? Jesse wondered. Then the boy seemed to calm as he answered the question. "When we come here, the gringos didn't think so much'a me ma. She lived with Antrim, and the people talked among themselves but they made sure we heard. The matrons said we were bastards. The Spanish people we met in church never said nothin'. They brought us food even when they had nothin'. We went to their weddin's and burials. It ain't hard to talk Spanish. It's real simple."

"So, are you?"

"What?"

"A bastard." Jesse grinned.

William looked at Jesse for several moments, and Jesse saw death in William's eyes. Jesse considered whether he should draw right there, but the boy looked ready and Jesse decided his best chance was to charm his way out.

"Don't get me wrong, Kid. I didn't mean it like that," and Jesse smiled his most sincere-looking smile.

"No, I didn't think you did. I killed a man at Fort Grant for callin' me somethin' hurtful to a woman. You can call me what you want. But me ma was no bitch."

"I didn't mean it like that."

William stood up, tossed some coins on the table to pay for Jesse's meal, and walked out. After that, Jesse always knew to be careful of the Kid. And now, as he rode and remembered all that had happened, he thought that he was still alive only because he had learned that lesson.

Jesse finished eating. He arose, sneered at Gomez and his family, picked up and pocketed the coins William had left, and walked out the door.

They drove their stolen horses through Mesilla, and when they rode out William had picked up a beautiful bay, pacing mare.

"How the hell'd you do that? I didn't even see you."

William laughed. "Presto change-o!"

Jesse watched the boy, trying to look composed as he wolfed down a plate of beans at John Kinney's rancho at Rincón, five miles west of Mesilla. Jesse could see that the Kid was hungry even though he didn't want to admit it, and that he was happy to have a horse and boots, even if one stunk of Emilio's blood.

"You must be bloody bolloxed ta bring a stranger here," Kinney complained to Evans as he regarded William's unlikely and ragged appearance.

"Come here, John," said Jesse, and drew Kinney, the ruddy-faced, Boston-born, ex-cavalry sergeant aside.

"John. Listen. I know who this boy is. He's the one that shot and killed that army blacksmith at Fort Grant. He's wanted here in New Mexico, too. He can't say nothin' 'cause he's as likely to hang as we are. And I'll tell you what. We gave 'im some shells for that .41 he carries. He practices all the time. He can shoot like the very devil, with both hands."

"Well, Jesse, he looks loco to me. But, hell, how many misfits do we got already? If he don't work out, bury 'im in the desert. Nobody'll miss a tramp like that. Anyway, we need men. Dolan and Riley got another army contract for beef. I want you to send Segovia to Seven Rivers with the cattle yer already drivin'. Morton and the Seven Rivers boys have already got a hundred. Dolan needs about eight hundred more to meet his contract. I want you to ride south with ten men. Frank'll ride north with ten. Herd every damn steer you find, and cut east. Meet in our camp in the Guadalupes in three weeks. Riley'll be there. Join up with the Seven Rivers boys an' take the herds to Fort Stanton. I got a few loco cowboys an' vaqueros. I'll meet you there, too."

As Jesse recalled, his troubles with the Kid had begun at the camp in the Guadalupe Mountains. Everyone was there: Kinney and his men, Frank Baker and his detachment, and Jesse and his bunch.

They had ridden hard and had close to five hundred head rustled from everywhere a hundred and fifty miles around. The Evans-Kinney gang, 'The Boys,' numbered sometimes as many as thirty, and twenty or more were

present on the night John Riley of The House met them at their camp in the Guadalupes.

The trouble started when Riley read a newspaper article from the Mesilla Independent. At first it was fun. Some damn editor named "Fountain" had written an article exposing "the chain," the association of rustlers that drove and exchanged rustled cattle through West Texas, New Mexico and Arizona. With false bills of sale, brands didn't matter. Cattle from one territory could be sold in another. The loose affiliation of outlaws just traded them and moved them from east to west and west to east.

In his article, Fountain named The Boys and called upon decent citizens to rise up and deliver "hempen justice." Everyone laughed and Jesse, John Kinney and Frank Baker dictated a letter in response:

RESOLVED: That we shall take the first opportunity of getting even with the Independent "Clan" and regret that an unwillingness to experience the sensation of "pulling hemp" has operated as an obstruction to the carrying into execution heretofore our intentions in this regard.

RESOLVED: That the public is our oyster, and that having the power, we claim the right to appropriate any property we may take a fancy to, and that we should exercise the right regardless of consequences.

Then the trouble with the Kid started. Riley read another article, which said that a group of The Boys had eaten and drunk at a station run by eighty-one-year-old Chaffrie Martinetti. This was true. It was Frank Baker's squad. When Martinetti demanded payment, Baker told him to "chalk it up." This was the standard practice of all The Boys. But Martinetti rapped his knuckles on the table.

"¡Paga me!"

Frank came out of his chair and backhanded the old man, hurling him into a table, and onto the floor. Frank pulled his six-gun, spun around, and shot Benito Cruz, Martinetti's son-in-law, as he raised a rifle. Frank, enraged, gave Martinetti a few good kicks as he left.

Now Riley read the newspaper report saying that both Cruz and Martinetti had died. Riley presented this fact as positive news that would re-enforce many other acts of intimidation The Boys relied upon to ensure that no one would oppose them, or testify against them in any court of law. The mood in the camp was festive, and Frank Baker received the news with pride.

"Why'd you kill that old man?" the Kid asked.

Things got quiet. Jesse still remembered how the Kid had looked when he said that. The Kid was sitting on his saddle behind the central fire.

In the weeks since Jesse had met the Kid, he had come to learn that the boy was nothing like the buffoon he had at first appeared. He didn't drink, and he didn't pay women, though they seemed to like him. He had used his money to buy a frock coat, three good bib-shirts, and denim pants suitable for range or town. The Kid wore fine Mexican, hand-tooled boots. He had invested in equipment, and now wore two double-action .41 Colt's Thunderers, carried a brand-new .44-40 Winchester, and had a saddle and leather saddle-wallets as good as any in the outfit. He spent his time in cantinas, saloons, and at the campfires, joking and gambling. And he always seemed to win. He spent freely on ammunition, and he practiced his draw and aim at every opportunity. The Kid was fast. He used more ammunition then anyone the outlaws had ever seen.

Now the Kid looked calmly at Frank Baker, staring out from under the brim of his new, tightly woven, Mexican sugarloaf sombrero, and awaited the answer to his question.

Everyone watched in silence.

"What?" Baker asked.

"I said, why'd you kill that old man?"

The Kid sat, leather cuffed wrists resting on his knees and there was no hint of insolence in his voice or physical attitude. But Baker and everyone else took the question as a challenge. Frank Baker was Jesse Evans's best friend, and he looked at Jesse, who rose to his feet and stepped over by Frank in an unmistakable gesture of support.

"You don't tell me who to kill, boy. Unless you want me to start thinkin' who's next," said Baker.

The Kid seemed totally unperturbed by the bellicose response.

"I ain't tellin' you nothin'. Why would I? I'm just sayin', why?"

Baker understood violence and simple physical power. He understood

little else. So now, when the Kid spoke so calmly, with total confidence but without any hint of belligerence, Baker didn't know what to think, do, or say. He looked around the watching faces. He hadn't even thought about why he'd killed the man, but he did now. He realized that he didn't know why he had beaten Martinetti. He thought for moment, then laughed it off. He looked around, raised a bottle to the crowd and declared with great hilarity, "'Cause he interrupted my supper!"

The Boys all shouted their approval at the cold-blooded assertion. Jesse relaxed and sat back down, and the gang went back to laughing and drinking.

But Jesse kept glancing back across the fire at the boy who sat at the edge of the darkness, the boy who almost always joked and laughed, but now just sat there in calmest reflection, and Jesse understood that the boy sat in the place which demanded judgment of himself only and where strength and most deadly genius were already conceived.

5

ROSARIO AND MATÉO

Just a coyote in the forest.

A woman's voice, laughing or crying out—Percy couldn't tell—tore his attention from his writing. He stared at the door, cocked his head, and listened intently. He heard it again. The high pitched tones of the woman's voice outside sounded at first alarmed, then happy. Percy clutched his blanket over his head and around his neck even as he arose, cautiously approached the window and, barely parting the curtains, peered out across the Salazárs' garden to the edge of the forested banks of the little Rio Bonito. He discerned, in shadow at the far edge of the garden, Rosario's form leaning back against an oak tree. Matéo Romero, the handsome, strapping young man Percy had already seen around Lincoln in days previous, leaned over Rosario, one hand on a branch above, the other about her waist.

Percy's eyes grew wide and he was transfixed as he watched Matéo kissing Rosario. Rosario laughed and turned her head aside, allowing Matéo to kiss her neck and cheeks. But each time he tried to turn her head toward him, to take her lips, she pushed him back, allowing only the briefest kisses on her mouth. As he became more persistent, she protested in a high keening tone: "Matéo! No!" Matéo then relented and returned to kissing her face and neck only, and Rosario's laughter returned.

Percy knew he had no claim on Rosario. He was surprised at the lightning bolt of fear, jealousy, disappointment and excitement that shot through his belly as he watched Matéo kissing Rosario—as he watched Rosario, cautiously and playfully approaching that aspect of her nature which she must, ultimately, find irresistible and to which she must some day yield.

Percy's heart and loins heated at this vision and knowledge of the girl's desire, however innocent and tentative. Yet he also felt a sudden shame at his voyeurism and lechery and he released the curtain allowing it to fall

back, foreclosing his view through the window.

Percy considered himself a man of the world—a newspaper man from the tough streets of New York. He considered that, although he had never himself engaged in such frivolity, he could still understand that he had just witnessed nothing more than some quaint country courtship ritual. Rosario was in no danger, he decided, and he turned back toward his desk. But before he could take two steps, he heard Rosario cry out again, and this time there was no playfulness in her voice. Percy leapt back and jerked the curtain aside. He saw Matéo, his hand at Rosario's back, forcefully pulling her hips against his. With his other hand, Matéo grasped the back of Rosario's neck, forcing her face forward, and he seemed to be drinking deeply from her mouth, muffling her protests. He released her neck and clutched at her breasts, and Percy again clearly heard a cry, almost a cougar's growl, of alarm.

Percy stepped to the door, pulled it open, glanced at frame and threshold to assure himself no black widows lurked there, then stepped out onto the porch—allowing the spring-hinged screen door to slam closed behind him. The noise had the desired effect.

Matéo recoiled. He seemed shocked to see Percy's robed and hooded form standing on the porch. Rosario, hammering the back of her fist on Matéo's chest, managed to break away. Percy looked past her and locked eyes with Matéo as Rosario leapt up onto the porch, stepped behind Percy and gratefully grasped his arm at the biceps as she looked over his shoulder at Matéo.

For a moment, Percy saw indecision in Matéo's eyes. The look quickly turned to anger and resolve, and Percy saw the muscles of Matéo's huge chest and quadriceps rippling beneath his clothing as he crouched, then began to charge forward. Suddenly there was the sound of another door slamming, and Matéo slid to a halt and retreated into the shadows of the bosque. Percy turned and looked down the porch at Señor Salazár as he walked toward them, frowning, shotgun in hand.

Since his arrival in New Mexico, Percy had been studying and rapidly learning Spanish, and he had no trouble following the conversation which followed.

"Rosario! ¿Que haces aquí a esta hora? What are you doing here at this hour?

Rosario looked over Percy's shoulder at her father, then lowered her eyes. "Nada, Papi, vió la luz en el cuarto del Señor Percy, y solamente vino a ver si necessitatba un poco de chocolate o algo. Nothing, Daddy. I saw Señor Percy's light and I came to see if he needed some chocolate or something."

Rosario, still grasping Percy's arm, turned her head and glanced up at him, clearly imploring him not to disclose her tryst with Matéo, then she hung her head, and looked back down at the porch.

Percy's eyes widened with fear as Señor Salazár's eyes scanned his daughter. She was still panting and clutching at Percy's arm, her hair disheveled, a deep blush across her cheeks. Señor Salazár's eyes narrowed as he looked at Percy, then gazed through the open door at Percy's rumpled bed. Percy glanced toward the bosque, where he saw Matéo's figure melt away and disappear in shadows—and Percy realized he had been very badly framed.

"This is the truth, Señor Chesterfield? She has been here with you all this time?"

Percy discerned an element of menace in the father's voice.

Even as Señor Pacifico Salazár asked this last question, Rosario released Percy's arm and stepped away from him. Percy understood that Rosario moved away from him to make their situation look less compromising, but in so doing she had made him a fair target for the double-barreled shotgun which Señor Salazar held, pointed down at the porch just in front of Percy's feet.

Percy knew he had to think and speak quickly, but everything had suddenly become so complicated. Should he lie to his host, who had treated him fairly and kindly? Or should he attempt to defend himself by telling the truth and betraying Rosario's secret? And what if Señor Salazár had heard the sounds Rosario made with Matéo? Percy realized he probably had—that was what had awakened him.

If so, Percy thought; and if I say it was me, he'll likely shoot me right now. But Percy realized, and with great sadness, that he could never betray Rosario. And he figured he was probably guilty, after all, as he recalled the lusty thoughts he had been having about her. Percy faced the fact that in his heart, he had reached a decision—if he ever got the chance to have Rosario in his bed he would take it, Señor Salazár be damned. And what, Percy thought, on a spiritual level, is the difference between a sin chosen and a sin executed? Percy

realized that he loved Rosario. Exuberant, irrepressible, devastatingly beautiful Rosario. Rosario. Percy decided he could do worse than to die in an attempt to protect her. Looking at the blue-barreled shotgun, Percy considered that, probably, it would be painless to take the blast at this range. A flash of light, then darkness. That would be all.

All these thoughts ran through Percy's mind in a few seconds. Percy clenched his blanket about his chest with both hands, looked with sadness on Rosario one last time, blinked back a tear and confessed:

"Yes, Don Pacifico, she was with me."

"What were those sounds I heard!?!" Señor Salazár angrily demanded.

"¡Nada Pápi!" Rosario broke in. "¡Un coyote en el bosque, nada mas! Nothing, Daddy! Just a coyote in the forest."

"¿Donde está Áyax? Where is Ajax?" Señor Salazár replied as he scanned the porch and garden.

Percy fully understood the point of Pacifico Salazár's question. Áyax was the Salazárs' immense canine, longhaired, brown, mangy, half hound and half wolf. Percy resented the way Áyax constantly sniffed and lifted his leg over the Hupmobile's tires. But Áyax clearly had ferocious potential so Percy had never attempted to interfere with the animal's territorial prerogative where it came to the Hupmobile. Now, Percy realized, appreciating the irony, that his fate depended on Áyax's presence or absence. Because Áyax would never suffer a coyote to remain for long, yipping about the Salazár's garden. If Áyax was anywhere about, Señor Salazar would know Rosario lied. He would know that the sounds which had awakened him were no coyote but rather sounds of Rosario's passion. And, Percy knew, he would then surely pay with his life; both for supposedly making love to Rosario, and for their insulting attempt to lie about the coyote.

Pacifico, Rosario and Percy all looked urgently around the garden discovering no sign of Áyax. Pacifico, clearly unconvinced, looked darkly at Percy and, shaking his head in disbelief, wheeled on his heel and started back toward the main house.

"¡Vaya pa'dentro, niña! Get inside, girl!" Pacifico ordered as he walked away.

Rosario hesitated only long enough to look with undisguised gratitude into Percy's eyes for a moment, and to briefly caress his cheek. Then she quickly followed her father into the main house. The door slammed behind them.

Percy stood shaking and trying to breathe as he watched the Salazárs' lights go out. Although it was bitterly cold, he realized that there were beads of sweat on his forehead. Long moments passed and Percy finally gathered himself, stepped back to his own door, looked down to make sure no black widows lurked on the threshold or his blanket, then reentered his room. He closed the door, staggered back to his desk and collapsed into his chair. He took a deep breath and exhaled slowly. He sat there for several minutes, blinking—amazed at all that had happened in such a short time, and at the fact that he still lived and breathed.

He thought with pride how he had protected Rosario. He still felt a glowing sensation on his cheek where she had gratefully touched him. He thought of how she looked at him with affection as she turned away, and his stomach glowed as if a thousand spring butterflies fluttered within.

And Percy began to calculate. Surely, he thought, Rosario would not forgive Matéo and she would see him—Percy—as her champion and deliverer. He dared to hope that Rosario would recognize that he was superior to Matéo by far. And then, a profound realization washed over him.

Percy realized that his life had been lonely. He now knew that he wanted to marry Rosario. He began to think what it could be like to possess her, to take her with him back to New York, to live in bliss with her there.

After a time, he calmed and turned back to his work. As he happily reviewed his notes and again began to write, Rosario still haunted his soul. He felt he now understood, as never before, the power of woman. Now, he felt he could well understand how it was a woman who had finally caused William Bonney to break with Jesse Evans and The Boys.

6

SEVEN RIVERS

**She was no whore, but she lived in Seven Rivers
and chose that place because it was free.**

The Banditti broke up and drove their strings of rustled cattle down from the Guadalupes into the Pecos River Valley, to the Beckwith ranch near Seven Rivers.

Seven Rivers was founded in 1867 when one Dick Reed built a trading post on the site, which was a good stopover for Texas cowboys pushing herds up the Rio Pecos. Reed first called the place Dogtown for its abundance of prairie dogs. But the name was later changed to Seven Rivers, a reference to the seven springs that flowed from there down to the Pecos.

L.G. Murphy, Jimmy Dolan and John Riley, the principals of The House in Lincoln, kept a herd near Seven Rivers. It was known as "the miracle herd" because it never grew any smaller, no matter how many army and Mescalero Apache reservation beef contracts The House filled.

Seven Rivers lay at the base of a vast public range dominated by John Chisum, The Cattle King of New Mexico. Chisum ran 100,000 head of cattle from Seven Rivers, two hundred miles north along the Rio Pecos all the way to the Bosque Grande.

Seven Rivers was a haven for gamblers, rustlers, drovers and itinerants of every stripe. There were so many shootings in the town that all the saloons' doors were easily detachable at the hinges so as to provide handy stretchers for the dead and wounded.

Folks who lived in Seven Rivers admitted that no one could live there who did not steal from John Chisum. But it went both ways. At fall roundup, Chisum's cowhands swarmed over the range and drove every yearling they encountered into Chisum's branding camps, regardless of the brands on the mothers the calves followed.

Now Seven Rivers rustlers and others gathered at Beckwith's, assembling a herd of a thousand to fill The House's latest government contract. When The Boys rode in with their contribution they found a festive atmosphere. Men, women, and children had gathered at Beckwith's to support the confluence of the droves of rustled cattle, and to socialize at this event, which would support the community through the upcoming winter.

Buck Morton was foreman of The House's drovers. He received incoming cattle, paid the rustlers who brought them, and hired many to stay on for branding and the drive north to Fort Stanton, near Lincoln. This year, Morton hired Jesse Evans, William Bonney, Frank Baker and many of The Boys to stay on, as Jesse was an expert at altering brands and only he could be counted on to keep control of the lawless men who rode for the Banditti.

The lush lines of huge, shady trees that lined the seven streams pleased William. He did his share of work during the days, and spent his nights gambling in Seven Rivers. When he had off-time, William practiced his shooting. Children and young women, drawn by his fire, always gathered to watch, encouraging William to show off. He would ride back and forth, hanging from his saddle, shooting targets from under his horse's neck like a Comanche. He would drop a bandana from his horse, then ride back at full gallop and snatch it off the ground. The little crowds shouted and clapped at these antics. William delighted in their pleasure.

The Banditti didn't think too much of William's displays. Those who watched the excited young females in the crowd generally looked like they had just eaten lemons.

"I'd like ta see'im do that ridin' toward my shotgun," Frank Baker was once heard to remark.

It was on The Boys' fifth day at Seven Rivers that the Belle of the Pecos observed one of William's little shows. She was Evangelina Duprée, from New Orleans by way of Galveston. Her beauty was legendary and people referred to her as The Belle of Pecos, or—if they were addressing her directly—just Belle.

The first time William saw her face, he was hanging off his galloping mare and looking under her neck, so that Belle appeared upside down. She had come to help out at the roundup, for pay, and she wore dungarees and a plaid wool shirt rolled up to the elbows. But her full lips, her blue eyes, and the

even features of her face, framed by shimmering brown locks and the straight lines and sumptuous curves of her frame beneath her baggy clothing, were nonetheless magnificent; and William almost fell off his horse. But he held on, regained control of the animal, turned back, rode up, and tossed her the stinking bandana he had just secured with the chivalry of some knight of old presenting his lady with a veil of finest gossamer or oriental silk.

Belle was twenty-seven years old, and she lived as she pleased. She was no whore, but she lived in Seven Rivers and chose that place because it was free. She had given herself to more than a few men, but disdained them all, as they invariably thought that one night of pleasure entitled them to own her. But she would be owned by no yahoo-buffoon, whatever his sexual prowess.

Having caught the dusty bandana, Belle almost fell over laughing at the boy's exaggerated air of gallantry. Thinking she was impressed, he rode on down the little line of his admirers, glancing back at Belle, puffed with pride at what he regarded as his impressive exploits.

At the noon meal that day, Belle watched William by the tables laden with beef, corn, squash, and chile under the shade trees near the streams. And he watched her. Flashing his buck-toothed grin, he ladled a dollop of chile con carne onto a tortilla, walked over, and offered it.

"Did you try this? Señora Romero made it. It'll blow smoke outta your ears! I'm Billy."

Belle laughed. "I know, Billy. I'm Belle. And I've tasted Señora Romero's chile con carne before. You are not going to get me to taste it again."

William laughed. "Too bad," he said. "I was hoping it might heat you up some."

"Well, it did leave me rather warm," she replied, and smiled, looked away and back again, finally leveling her gaze on the boy's eyes. She did not blush. Billy thought for a second, then tossed the burrito into a pack of scavenging curs, causing a brief snapping scuffle which neither Billy nor Belle noticed.

"Can I ask you a personal question?" Billy asked.

"Aren't you a little young to be askin' personal questions of a Miss right off, like that?"

Billy grinned. "I'm eighteen," he lied.

The boy looked so young that Belle was at once surprised and skeptical; but she was amused that such a young fellow would be so bold. She decided to call his bluff, and continued to meet his gaze without opprobrium.

"Go right on straight ahead and ask then," she said, smiling.

"Do you like rock candy? 'Cause I got some in my saddle wallet down by the rio."

"Well, let's go, then."

They walked away from the gathering and passed into the deepest shades of the bosque, where Billy had left his saddle and kit by a spring-fed brook. Once they were out of sight of the gathering, Billy dared to take her hand and Belle, older and wiser as she was, accepted the boy's advance with amusement.

"Look here," he said as he pulled two paper bags from his satchel. He withdrew a large sugar crystal from the first bag and extended his hand. When she tried to take it, he tossed it into the air and caught it in his mouth.

"Presto change-o!" He laughed and offered another.

She seized his wrist, and took the candy. She sucked the sweet rock and smiled as Billy sat by the brook, pulled off his boots, and dangled his feet in the soothing water. He stretched out his hand. She took it, joined him, unlaced her high shoes, rolled up her pants, and dabbled her feet in the flow.

William opened the second bag and produced a pint of whiskey, which he held out to Belle.

Belle could barely conceal her amusement. "You go right ahead."

William took a sip and coughed a little.

"You don't drink much do you?"

"Not much."

She took the bottle and swallowed about a fourth of it. As she lowered it from her lips, William removed his sombrero, held it before them like a screen against watchers who were not there, and kissed her. She shrugged and allowed the advance. She liked the worldly boy. His face was pretty and smooth, like a girl's. They kissed for a long time, but Belle broke it off with a deep, throaty laugh at the brashness of this young fellow who obviously believed he would seduce her, right there, with a piece of candy and a shot of whiskey. The very thought made her laugh harder and harder until she fell

back onto the ground, clutching her abdomen.

William blushed, confused, and he lowered his sombrero. When he did, he saw Buck Morton, the drover foreman, striding forward, his face red and twitching with anger.

"Git away from that girl! Git yer grubbin' Irish paws off her!"

William sprang to his feet. Belle took in the scene, reclining on her elbows, and hung her head back, laughing harder still. William and Morton squared off, each with a hand suspended over his six-gun.

"You little bastard! I been courtin' that girl day an' night for three months now. Get ready to answer!"

Belle laughed harder yet, but she managed to roll onto her side, push herself onto her knees then rise to her feet. She stepped between the two rivals, facing Buck Morton.

"Courtin' me? Courtin' me, you say, Buck Morton? Is that what you call it?" Belle walked over to Morton, took his wrist and pulled him after her back toward the camp. "Courtin' me? Well, Buck Morton, if you ever wanna 'court' me again, you better shut the hell up and leave that sweet boy alone."

William frowned when she said "sweet boy," and Morton glared back over his shoulder as Belle drew him off toward the round-up.

William was hot at Morton's interruption, and Belle's casual attitude and abandonment. He decided to let it go and ride into Seven Rivers for a card game. He saddled his horse at the corrales. As he was checking his cinch, he saw Morton, Frank Baker, and Jesse Evans coming his way. They were all heavily armed, as always, and their faces looked grim. Morton was in the lead. William gently pulled his reins, turning his mount so that she stood as a shield between them. He placed his Winchester over the hind-bow of the saddle as if he were about to tie it on, pointing it conveniently in the general direction of Morton, Baker and Evans. The three stopped about ten feet away, at the edge of the corral.

"Jesse." William nodded.

"Kid."

"You dirty little saddle bum!" Morton broke in.

Baker spat and grinned.

"You get outta this camp," Morton said. "Get out now. Don't never come back to Seven Rivers or I'll have you like a coyote hide on my fence."

"Is that what you say too, Jesse?"

"It don't matter what Jesse says," Morton said. "I'm foreman here. I just said it. Get out." Now, William was even hotter than before, but he tried not to show it. He was thinking he could take Morton and Baker. And he wanted to. But with Jesse on their side, the odds seemed a little too long. How far was Jesse prepared to go?

"That's fine with me. I was just leavin' anyway. Give me a minute to round up my bay." William glanced over his shoulder at the filly he had pilfered in Mesilla, and back at Jesse.

"Sorry Kid. You ain't takin' the bay," Jesse said.

"I paid for her outta my share. She don't belong to The Boys."

"No. She don' belong to The Boys. She don' belong to you neither. She belongs to Mesilla sheriff, Barela. That's his daughter's horse. Barela's posses are slow an' poor-armed. There's a reason for that. John Kinney keeps Barela happy, an' Barela ain't cheap. An' right now, Barela ain't happy at all. He done told Kinney, git the horse back or he's breakin' out the Winchesters. Sorry Kid."

William walked his saddle-horse toward the corral gate, keeping her more or less between him and the others. Rather than mount up, he walked her well past the gate, and from a distance he called back, "I'll see you on down a straight lane, Buck!"

Then he swung onto his saddle and gave the mare his spurs until he was out of rifle range.

Percy's research suggested that William Bonney rode alone northward, into the Pecos River country. For a few months, he enjoyed gambling and dancing and sparking the girls in the eastern New Mexican towns: Lincoln, Fort Sumner, Puerto de Luna, Anton Chico and Las Vegas.

Good as he was at cards, odds are odds and the Kid supplemented his income by the trade he had learned from Evans and Kinney.

From the time he had first come to New Mexico, the common Irish boy and his family had been consigned to the lower classes, and Billy had always associated with the poor, Hispanic people of the territory. He was smart, open and quick, and he spoke good Spanish.

In the Pecos country, the Kid stole cattle and horses from wealthy Anglo ranchers, especially the Texan cattlemen who were driving huge herds up the Goodnight Trail from southwest Texas into New Mexico and Colorado.

It had been only thirty-five years since the United States had attacked Mexico, fought into Mexico City, and extracted the treaty of Guadalupe Hidalgo, in which Mexico ceded New Mexico to the powerful northern gringos. Residents of New Mexico didn't care. They had as little connection with Mexico City as they did with Washington.

The treaty guaranteed that New Mexicans would keep their property and receive equal treatment under North American laws. But once General Kearney rode into Santa Fe and hoisted the North American flag, all power went to the Anglos. The change of government and laws had been mostly peaceful, but the Norte Americanos immediately began acting like conquerors. They took over all government positions and imposed an entirely English-speaking court system.

A "Court of Land Claims" was set up to convert Mexican land titles to North American ones, but the average Spanish-speaking New Mexican people had no understanding of this procedure and the court was used fraudulently by Anglos to take title to native New Mexican lands. Some of the oppressed New Mexican people fought back by outlawry against the invaders, especially against Texans who had repeatedly tried to invade New Mexico before the Mexican War, and then again during the Civil War.

The resistance of the poor and dispossessed seemed to the Kid like the resistance his Irish ancestors had faced to class oppression, battled, and commemorated in legend and song. Of course, the Kid was no economic theorist. He just fit in naturally with the common Spanish families whose earthy and Catholic culture was so like his own, and he instinctively joined in little, defiant forays with those who had nothing. They used their power of stealth and knowledge precedent of the land and people to take means of livelihood from the newcomers who claimed all and possessed more than they could possibly use or protect.

The Kid partnered on these small raids with native New Mexicans like Patricio Montoya. Patricio and Billy became loyal friends.

He rode back south and took a job as a cowhand with John Chisum.

After a couple of months of wrangling, just three weeks before his eighteenth birthday, William Bonney took his pay and rode west for some cards, drink and girls, to Lincoln town—a powder keg with a lit fuse.

7

SEÑOR PERCY'S CHALLENGE

This place has always been very dangerous.

Percy kept studying his notes and typing. It was very late, and he leaned back in his chair and rubbed his eyes. Then he thought he heard something. He sat up straight and listened carefully. He heard it again: the soft sound of footsteps creeping down the portál.

There was a gentle knock at his door, the door opened, and Percy's heart leapt into his throat as Rosario stepped into the room and closed the door behind her. Now the girl wore a long cotton gown, which descended to her ankles, a heavy, woven wool shawl around her shoulders, and buffalo-hide moccasins.

"Señor Percy, despensamé, excuse me," she said, and she stepped forth bearing a vessel of oil for Percy's lamp. "I saw that your lamp was dark." She removed the glass, added oil then re-lit it.

Percy realized that his mouth was open and he closed it as he tried hard to look only into her eyes. He had seen at a glance how the bright lamplight pierced her thin gown below her shawl, revealing the devastating contours of her hips and legs. The effort of looking only into Rosario's eyes caused him to smile and, as always, she smiled back.

She hesitated, then suddenly rushed around the desk to Percy's side, bent over him and embraced him for long moments. He felt her shaking with emotion. Then she drew back, her face only inches from his, and smiled the warmest smile Percy had ever seen.

"Señor Percy, I come to give you mi gracias—my thanks—for protect me. You are gentilehombre, a gentleman."

Percy's heart soared at this statement as he began to believe that his hopes to win the girl would be swiftly realized. He swelled with pride and felt a rush of heat in his cheeks.

"Rosario. Darling girl. De nada. It's nothing."

Rosario straightened, stepped back and pulled a carved pine chair up beside Percy's. She sat next to him, leaned forward and took his hand.

"Señor Percy, you are from Nuevo York, but your ways and ours can no be so different. You comprende. You understand. My father, he kill you if he think you and I were...juntos...together. You are very brave man."

Percy felt waves of joy rush through his heart. He calculated his next move. At first he thought to embrace her, crush her lips to his and take her. But Percy's cautious nature held him back and he next considered dropping to his knee, kissing her hand and begging that she marry him. Again he found himself incapable of action and before he could decide, he saw tears well up in Rosario's eyes.

"Rosario. What's wrong?"

"Señor Percy. Yo tengo miedo. I have fear." And her voice cracked.

"Please Rosario, you must not fear love. And you must not fear Matéo. I swear to protect you from him, with all my strength." As Percy said this he felt great pride at the eloquent words that had somehow escaped his mouth, words such as he had never before thought himself capable. But at the same time, he felt a fool. How would he protect Rosario from the Herculenian Matéo? Percy knew that in any physical contest with the tall, lean, powerful young man, he would stand no chance. But before he could speak further, a look of astonishment came over Rosario's face. She straightened, released his hand and said, "Señor Percy. You no understand me. I no fear Matéo."

In an instant her hand disappeared beneath her shawl, then darted forward and suddenly she was holding a gleaming, razor-sharp blade, three inches long, against Percy's throat.

"I no have fear of love and no have fear of Matéo, Señor Percy. I have fear that I kill Matéo if he again try to mount me as the stallion mount the mare. This is why I thank you. Because if you did not come to me before, I would have killed him. Then Matéo's family hang me or shoot me. If my father try to stop them, they shoot him too. Matéo have big family. I give thanks to you because you save my life, and Matéo's. And my father."

Rosario withdrew the blade from Percy's neck and returned it to its hidden place beneath her shawl between her breasts. Percy took a deep breath

and exhaled slowly. His thoughts swirled in confusion. What Rosario said next caused his hopes to plummet and filled him with alarm and jealously.

"I come for your consejo—your counsel—Señor Percy. You are a gentleman from Nuevo York. Muy civilizado. How do I teach Matéo to be a gentleman like you? To treat me with respect, so that I can love him, and in time, give myself to him? "

Percy's heart plunged into despair at these words, but he considered himself to be a problem-solver, and he decided to stall for time.

"Let me think a minute." Percy stood up, stepped over to his night stand (he staggered a little, feeling drunk with shock), and he took up and charged his briar pipe. He lit it and puffed several times until the tobacco burned brightly and the smell of sweet brandied smoke filled the room. Percy returned to his chair, sat down, and looked at Rosario who sat stiffly erect and wide-eyed, awaiting his counsel.

Percy puffed and thought how to answer the girl's question. He understood she was in danger. And he was not willing to give up his hope of having her for his own. He knew he had no experience in matters of the heart, but he thought nonetheless that there must be a way to protect Rosario from Matéo, show her that she could not love Matéo, and prove to her that he himself was her soul mate.

Rosario sat in rapt attention and waited as Percy smoked. A plan and trap (which he thought devilishly clever) formed in Percy's mind.

I am a writer, Percy thought. I will beat him with my weapons: words.

"Rosario," he said at last, "you must talk to Matéo in broad daylight, in town with people around so he cannot act so as to give you offense. You must explain to him that before he can touch you, he must talk to you. Explain to him that he must win you with gentle words, with poetry."

"Poetry, Senor Percy? ¿Con rimas? With rhymes?

"Yes. Poetry. The kind that by writing it, will soften and civilize Matéo's heart. By writing poetry, he will have to look inside himself to find the tender part of his own nature. Once he does this, he will be changed."

"But Señor Percy, I no understand. How do I show him what you mean?"

This was just the opening Percy had angled for. Now he could tell

Rosario, covertly, exactly how he felt, and he could demonstrate his superiority by offering a love poem that Matéo could never match.

"Let me show you."

Percy took up his pen and began to write, pretending to compose a poem, which actually consisted of the first and last verses of "First Love" by John Clare. Percy glanced at Rosario's look of admiration as he pretended to create the ditty, taking pains to pause often, as if in thought, with a most loving expression on his face. He changed the title of the poem, and finally nodded with satisfaction. Then he lifted the paper, held it before him, raised his chin to what he expected would present a noble profile and he began to read. He spoke the words gravely, in his deepest voice, and he glanced at the girl's eyes as she listened enraptured and quivered with emotion:

> Rosario
>
> I ne'er was struck before that hour
> With love so sudden and so sweet
> Her face it seemed like a sweet flower
> And stole my heart away complete.
>
> I never saw so sweet a face
> As that I stood before
> My heart has left its dwelling place
> And can return no more.

"Oh! Señor Percy! ¡Sí! Tomorrow, Matéo will come to ask me to ride with him as he always does. But I will tell him no. I tell him he must learn to win me with gentleness and sweet words before I will be with him again."

Percy was content with this answer, confident that the young Matéo could not match his own intellect and education. Percy even felt a twinge of guilt at his own satisfaction at the thought that Rosario would surely be disappointed if Matéo should even attempt to write a poem.

And now, Percy made his final move—which he fully expected would bring the matter to a quick and satisfactory conclusion. He signed his name

at the bottom of the paper, then said, "I have an idea, Rosario. Why don't you show this poem to Matéo to help him write his own?"

"Oh, gracias, Señor Percy! The girl took the poem with a look of awe, folded it, carefully opened her shawl and pushed the paper down into her cleavage next to her dagger.

Percy felt a pleasant trill of malice as he thought: If the brute can even read, he will know that writing to be a shot across his bow and a challenge to fight in my battlefield—the realm of letters.

"You are so kind to me, Señor Percy," and Rosario leaned forward, wrapped her arms around Percy's shoulders and planted a long kiss on his cheek. Percy felt a sweet rush of warmth in his loins. But before she finished, the door flew open, and she and Percy both bolted to their feet and stood blushing, facing Rosario's grandmother, Doña Flora, who stood in the doorway, hands on hips, glaring at them.

"Vaya a su propia cama, niña," the woman said. "Get to your own bed, girl."

Rosario had told Percy that Doña Flora was her maternal grandmother, practically her mother, as Rosario's mother had died giving birth to her. Rosario's many younger siblings in the house were children of Señor Pacifico Salazár's second marriage.

Rosario obviously did not fear Doña Flora as she feared her father, for she dared to smile and give Percy a quick parting kiss on his forehead before she lowered her eyes and rushed past Doña Flora and out the door.

Percy was left standing red-faced before Doña Flora's withering gaze. He knew that she clearly saw the lust and perfidy in his heart.

Doña Flora shook her head. "Ten cuidado, Señor Percy. Usted juega con fuerzas aquí que usted no puede entender. Y este sitio siempre ha sido muy peligroso. Yo tengo sesenta años y yo se lo que el amor puede hacer a nostotros. Yo rezo a Dios que usted viva bastante tiempo para encontrar lo que busca aquí y regrese vivo a su hogar. Be careful Señor Percy. You play with forces here you cannot understand. And this place has always been very dangerous. I am sixty years old and I know what love can do to us. I pray that you will live long enough to find what you seek here and return safely to your home."

With that, Doña Flora turned and pulled the door softly shut behind

her. Percy sat back in his chair. He felt he had understood most of Doña Flora's Spanish words and he repeated them silently to himself: You play with forces here you cannot understand. This place has always been very dangerous.

And Percy was certain that Doña Flora spoke the truth. He feared he had made very bad mistakes in lying to Señor Salazár and baiting Matéo—both within the span of a few hours. Now as he turned back to his reading and writing, he thought how little William Bonney understood of the powerful forces at play when he rode into Lincoln in November, 1877.

8

LINCOLN TOWN

A festering nest of jet-black, deadly scorpions swarmed all about the base of the Yucca.

In late May, 1881, the Kid rode with Jesse, Patricio, and Croft, condemned and exiled. Posses, army detachments and bounty hunters patrolled the southern highway to the Pecos and Texas, so the outlaws rode cross-country on hidden game and Indian trails, which they knew well. They crossed the Jornada del Muerto, the Dead Man's Journey, and the immense, scorching, absolutely white gypsum sand dunes beyond, where nothing grew. The Kid saw a single yucca plant on the white sand waste and he rode toward it thinking he might find sign of water there but as he approached the lone living thing, Bala suddenly whinnied and skipped aside. A festering nest of jet-black, deadly scorpions swarmed all about the base of the yucca and the Kid passed and continued across the bleak white desert dunes, which stretched out of sight into blinding, reflecting waves of light and heat. The Kid rode on in contemplation of his life and considered how, by chance, three years earlier he had ridden into Lincoln town at the precise time that set him on course toward choices foreordained by his nature and the nature of his people and bearing undeviate toward his now manifest destination, life and all dreams of life entirely forfeit and the doors of his fate then closed irrevocably and forever behind him.

Percy's research revealed that William Bonney rode from Chisum's into the town of Lincoln in November 1877, a few weeks before his eighteenth birthday.

Lincoln was a one-street town with a couple of stores, some cantinas, a hotel, stockyards and a smattering of houses. It was home to just forty-five families, but it was the mercantile center of the whole county. The county itself covered an area of 27,000 square miles, and people living in villas and ranchos, big and small, for a hundred miles all around did their business in Lincoln town.

The sheriff, William Brady, had come to New Mexico with the California column, which helped drive invading Texan confederates from New Mexico during the Civil War. Brady had mustered out of the army after the war and settled on a ranch near Lincoln. He was elected sheriff in 1869 and again in 1877, and in that role he supported the rights of the "gringos"—the foreigners—against the native New Mexicans.

L.G. Murphy and his young associate, Jimmy Dolan, owned the main store in Lincoln, called "The House." They sold farm and ranch supplies, many types of imported spirits and brokered local produce. Murphy and Dolan enjoyed a near monopoly in Lincoln. They received government contracts to supply the Mescalero Apache reservation to the south with beef, mutton and other supplies. Murphy and Dolan charged exorbitant rates for goods to Hispanic and Anglo shepherds and farmers. They gave credit to the unsophisticated at usurious rates. Then they obtained court judgments against, and foreclosed ownership to, lands of those who owed them.

Murphy and Dolan made financial contributions and paid fees to powerful politicians and lawyers in the territorial capital, Santa Fe, and they supported election campaigns of the judges of the district court in La Mesilla, 200 miles away. The most powerful member of the power brokers who made up the Santa Fe Ring—even more powerful than the governor—was U.S. Attorney John Catron. John Catron lent money to The House and held interests in The House's cattle contracts with the army. Catron used quiet title suits to fraudulently acquire six million acres of lands from native New Mexicans, making him the owner of the largest area of privately owned land in the United States and its territories.

The Kid rode into Lincoln from the North. About halfway though the little town, the houses were set back so that the road widened into a placeta, or open, common area. A little courthouse and a church stood on one side and a torreón—an old, round, stone, two-story tower—stood on the other.

The torreón had been used by the village's earliest settlers for defense

against raiding Indians. The Hispanic settlers took shelter there against Apache, Comanche, Kiowa, and, sometimes, Navajo raiders. Their women and children huddled on the bottom floor under a five-foot ceiling. The men on the floor above them fired muzzle-loaders through narrow loopholes at any raider who dared approach. But the stern war parties usually stayed back and looted the village of its stock, produce and goods as the defenders watched, despondently, from the torreón.

Now the torreón had not been used for many years and as the Kid rode by, marveling at the medieval-looking structure, three "soiled doves" sat at its base, smoking. The whores wore black, billowy, ankle length skirts and their shawls were pulled up, modestly, over their heads so that only their faces and the parts of their hair over their foreheads were visible.

A young woman stood up and walked into the placeta to the place where the young rider must pass her.

"Hola, caballero. ¿Que buscas? Soy Gabriella. Hello, gentleman, what do you seek? I am Gabriella." The girl's face was delicate and beautiful, her smile, welcoming.

William had rarely paid for a woman but he had been lonely on Chisum's range and he warmed to the girl's friendly greeting and the graceful lines and curves of her frame which defied concealment despite her modest dress. William pulled up, regarded the pretty girl and returned her smile.

"¿Pués, no tráes otro frajo? Mas que eso, no se que busco. Do you have another smoke? Beyond that I don't know what I seek."

Gabriella pulled her shawl back so that it hung around her shoulders exposing her beautiful hair and she did not draw it around her so the clean curves of her breasts invited the boy.

"Qualquiera cósa que quieres, jóven. Whatever you want, young man." And she stood on the dirt plaza, rolled a cigarette, and handed it up with a smile.

"¿Quanto cóbras? How much do you charge?"

"Tres dolares. Three dollars."

The price was more than twice the common market but Gabriella anticipated negotiation. Most vaqueros would respond with an offer of one dollar and the deal would be struck somewhere in between. She shifted her

weight and placed her hand on her hip, further revealing her pretty figure.

William had a generous nature and he already liked the girl.

"Get on up here." He pulled his boot from his stirrup so that she could place her foot and mount and he caught her arm, pulled her up behind him, and they rode down the forested bank of the Rio Bonito. An hour later they returned and they kissed many times before William helped Gabriella to dismount.

It was dark now and William rode on down the paseo and stopped before a brightly lighted house with many horses tied in front, from which loud, drunken laughter emanated. The place seemed to be a public house but William tied his horse, put on his frock coat, and knocked on the door.

A sturdy, very handsome dark-skinned man with slicked-back black hair pulled the door open and looked William up and down.

"¿Si?"

"Soy Guillermo, tengo sed y busco un juego. I'm William. I'm thirsty and seek a game."

"Soy Juan Patrón. Páse. I'm Juan Patrón. Come in."

William entered a smoke-filled room. He was surprised how many people were in the little house. Men and women sat on chairs and bancos, long wooden benches, lining the walls. Children scurried about. By the fireplace, a guitar-player and a violinist played. Juan introduced William to James H. Dolan.

Jimmy Dolan had been a drummer boy for the union army. He had mustered out of the service at Fort Stanton with the rank of corporal. Major L.G. Murphy had mustered out at the same time and Murphy had opened the business called "The House." Jimmy was Murphy's right-hand man. Murphy drank more whiskey than anyone anybody in Lincoln had ever seen. When Jimmy Dolan would refuse to join him, Murphy used to say, "Have another, Jimmy. The definition of an Irish homosexual is a man who prefers women to drink."

But Jimmy was young, he had grown up poor and he was ambitious as hell. He did not give himself over to whiskey as Murphy did. Now Murphy lay drunk and useless in The House and Jimmy took responsibility for running the business. William knew Dolan was the man The Boys and the Seven Rivers

men dealt with when they rounded up huge herds, rustled from Chisum and a lot of others, and delivered them to Fort Stanton to honor The House's contracts. Jimmy was now the de facto leader of The House and the main economic power in Lincoln. And he looked it. Jimmy wore a store-bought suit, and buffed leather shoes from Chicago. He wore a plush, wool overcoat and fedora.

Jimmy was about ten years older than William, but they were the same size and Jimmy looked into William's eyes.

"William Bonney, eh?"

"My friends call me Kid."

"Well, 'Kid' it is then. God knows, we've got enough 'Billys' around here. It's good to meet you, Kid. Us Irish 've got to stick together in front of all these Mexicans in this God-forsaken country."

William grinned and shook Jimmy's hand. He thought he might work for Jimmy. He looked to the back of the room where the only other Anglos in the place, Charlie Bowdre, Dick Brewer, Jesse Evans and Buck Morton sat at a little table playing cards. Cards was what William had come for. Before entering the game William stood for a few minutes and listened as the musicians played and sang a passionate corrido—a ballad—about a great hero.

> Don Hernando was a mighty man,
> His horse Goliath was the best in all the land.
> He rode from Las Vegas to the Llano Estacado
> Where he killed buffalo with his lance only.
> The Comanche dared not oppose him
> When he made love to their princess, Tzotín.
> Her heart broke when he rode away.
> She feared she would not see him after that day.
> But when the tornado came to take her village,
> Don Hernando appeared on the bank of the Pecos.
> Goliath leapt the Pecos, Hernando roped the tornado.
> He conquered the wind and dragged it far to the north.
> But God struck him with lightning, punishing his pride.
> Tzotzín followed and held him as he died.

The Comanche warriors refused to bury him.
His body was left to lie on the plain.
But his seed grew in Tzotzín's womb.
His decendents were the greatest warriors
the Comanches had ever known.

William walked over to the card game. Jesse and Morton saw him at the same time.

"Shit." Jesse said.

Morton glared. But Bowdre welcomed him, in his soft Southern accent.

"Howdy boy. You play poker?" Bowdre's wife Manuela stood by him, resting her hand on Charlie's shoulder.

"Well, I've played some. But you might have to remind me of some of the laws, though." William looked at Jesse wondering if Jesse would expose him as a sharp.

Jesse pocketed his money, knowing that now he could not win. He looked at the table, shook his head at the boy's fraud, but said only, "Well, boys, I'm kinda tired. It was a hell of a long drive from Seven Rivers."

Jesse stood up, and gave Juan some money for the tequila and food he had enjoyed.

"Well, that's good, Jesse," Brewer said. "Just don' be ridin' for the Rio Feliz, now."

Brewer was John Tunstall's foreman. He and Bowdre had recently tracked and arrested Jesse and Frank Baker for stealing Tunstall's stock on the Rio Feliz. Brewer had delivered Evans and Baker to County Sheriff William Brady, in Lincoln. But Brady was Dolan's man, and Jesse "escaped" within days. Brewer and Bowdre knew they could do nothing about it. So they now sat playing poker with Jesse. But Jesse knew that if Brewer and Bowdre caught him again, this time they would simply hang him on the range.

Jesse had decided not to challenge Brewer again. "Don' worry about it, Dick," he said. "I got a pocket full a' silver from this last drive. I'm just gonna get some sleep." And Jesse walked out.

William was sorry to see Jesse go. He had hoped to make Jesse pay for the bay mare he had confiscated.

William joined the game and acted like he couldn't deal. On his deals, he shuffled awkwardly and this allowed him to see many cards and arrange the best cards below the center of the deck. Then, when Dick, Buck, or Charlie cut the deck, William knew aces and face cards were on top. William dealt his cards from the top, and everyone else's from the bottom. William was most interested in taking Morton's money, and he cleaned Morton out. Morton glared at William and left the game. Now William played with only Dick and Charlie. He decided they were pretty good fellows and he was already way ahead on Morton's money so he played more or less fair and enjoyed the company.

It was after midnight when the game broke up. William, Dick, and Charlie walked out the door together. As they unhitched their horses, they heard the clicks of shotguns being cocked. William turned and looked at a tall, powerfully built man with a walrus mustache, standing with a shotgun leveled at his chest. Three other men stood behind Sheriff Brady and their shotguns were leveled at William, too.

"Lift up your hands, boy," Brady said. "We're takin' your irons."

William raised his hands and Deputy George Hindeman stepped up and took his guns and the rifle from under the offside stirrup of his saddle.

William looked at the sheriff's star on the lapel of Brady's coat. He now knew this was Brady and he knew Brady worked for Dolan and protected The Boys.

"I see you are a lawman. But I ain't broken no laws within this county."

"What is it, Sheriff?" Brewer demanded, "The boy ain't done nothin!"

"You an' Charlie ride on, Dick. This is county business."

Brewer and Bowdre already liked the boy. But he immediately lost their support when he said, "I know you to be Sheriff Brady. I ride for Dolan and The Boys."

When Brewer and Charlie heard that, they mounted up and rode off.

"You don' ride for Dolan an' you don't ride for The Boys no more. You think you can lie to me, boy?"

William looked past Brady, and saw Morton standing and grinning in the dark behind him.

"What do you say I done?"

"I say you done stole the horse of Sheriff Barela in Mesilla. There's a warrant for your arrest."

"Show me the paper, then."

"The warrant is on its way. I ain't gonna let you ride out before it gets here. You ain't got no protection from The Boys no more, and Dolan says you don' ride for him."

Hindeman, standing behind William, swung the butt of his shotgun like a bat, and lights exploded behind William's eyes.

Brady marched in the lead. Two deputies followed, dragging William. He came to, got his feet under him, and walked between them as they approached the town's calabozo, its jailhouse.

As they walked toward it, William considered the small adobe building. The little square structure looked like it would be easy to escape from. But when they opened the door and pushed him through, he saw a trap door in the floor. A deputy pulled the trap up and Brady ordered William to climb down. He descended a ladder into a log-lined pit. Someone threw an armful of hay down for him to make a bed, then the trap door slammed down, and William heard a chain slide through the door handles and the click of a lock.

It was pitch dark in the dungeon. William's eyes slowly adjusted, but before he could see much, a voice said, "Welcome to this here calabozo. It's good to have some company."

William could barely discern a huddled figure in the corner.

"I'm Billy Wilson," the voice said. "What'd you do ta land in this here God-forsaken hole?"

"I didn't do nothin' that I know of," William lied, rubbing the lump on the back of his skull. "I'm Kid. What'd you do?"

"I killed Robert Casey. He owed me wages for riding his range on the Rio Feliz. He got hot when I told him to pay up or throw down. It was a fair fight, but the jury didn't see it my way. They say I done it for Dolan. But if I done it for Dolan I wouldn't be here. I had no protection.

"Dolan came here yesterday. He said he ain't gonna give orders for me to be broke out. He done said he's usin' me to show the whole county, nobody better kill nobody, 'less he says so.

"They held me at Fort Stanton. I broke out but they shot me up pretty

good an' drug me back. They brought me here two days ago. They're gonna hang me in three days."

"Can you walk or run?"

"I think so."

"Then, it's your luck I'm here," William said. William bent, dug down into his sock and brought out his skeleton key. He walked over to Wilson and felt his wrists, looking for a keyhole. But the manacles were welded on. Wilson's hands were big and William knew Wilson could never extract them from the cuffs. Then William felt his way up Wilson's chains to where they were attached to the wall. They were bolted into the wall.

"Shit." William said.

"It's okay, Kid. Just keep me company. To tell the truth, I'd just as soon die as keep sittin' here in this shit-hole."

9

JOHN CHISUM

For an Englishman, you got darn little understandin' of what a street fightin' Irishman like Jimmy Dolan is willin' to do.

"It's war," John Simpson Chisum said.

Chisum, Alexander McSween, John Henry Tunstall and Tunstall's foreman, Dick Brewer sat at a table in Tunstall's store across and just down the street from The House.

Tunstall, twenty-four-year-old scion of a wealthy London family, was new to Lincoln. He had invested a great deal of his family's money to open a mercantile business, two ranches, and the first bank in Lincoln County. Tunstall had been induced to invest there by Alexander McSween, who claimed to be a lawyer, although he had never graduated from the law school he had attended back in Missouri.

McSween and Brewer had acted as proxies to file claims on range land for Tunstall under the Desert Lands Act. Tunstall's store threatened to break The House's mercantile monopoly and Chisum was The House's main competition for government beef contracts.

John Henry Tunstall was pleased with the progress he had made on his family's behalf. He was only interested in pursuing his businesses and now, Chisum's declaration of war at once confused and alarmed him greatly.

"Mr. Chisum, sir, we live in civil society. What can you mean by this talk of war?"

"What happened, John?" Brewer asked Chisum.

"You better wake up, Mr. Tunstall. Why do you think we ain't gettin' no contracts for beef? It's because The House is usin' Seven Rivers men and The Boys to sell our cattle to the government for only five dollars a head," Chisum replied. "We pay and they sell 'em for less than it costs us to raise 'em, brand 'em, and drive 'em. And if you think Jimmy Dolan is gonna let you run a store

right across the street from The House, then you understand nothin' about this here Territory.

"Two weeks ago, my foreman, Jim Highsaw, tracked missin' cattle to Beckwith's place at Seven Rivers. He dug up a pit and found about a thousand Jinglebob ears. A Seven River's man tried to stop Highsaw, they drew, and Highsaw killed 'im.'"

"Please, sir, what is a 'Jinglebob' ear and why would men kill for it?"

Chisum just stared dumb-founded at Tunstall's ignorance.

"John Henry," Brewer explained, "Mr. Chisum invented and registered an ear-cut to prevent rustling. You make two slices on the ear an' the middle part hangs down. They call it a dew-lop. People can often change a brand, but they can't change a dew-lop. So The Boys and the Seven Rivers men are cuttin' off the ears and selling the beef. A thousand ears means five hundred rustled cattle."

"I see," Tunstall said, amazed, and he raised a handkerchief to cover his frowning lips.

"That ain't all," Chisum continued. "We rode down to Beckwith's to arrest the culprits. But them adobe walls are four foot thick and after three days of shootin' we had to pull out. My drovers don' git paid enough ta charge an' die.

"Then, some of my men met Dolan an' the Seven Rivers bunch drivin' cattle ta Fort Stanton. Custom here says any man who shares a range can check brands on another man's herd. But Dolan's bunch started shootin' when my men tried to ride up. If that ain't proof I don' know what is."

"Please let me say, respectfully, Sir, these facts alone do not constitute proof in the law," lawyer McSween advised.

"I ain't talkin' about proof in a law-court, McSween. I'm talkin' about grounds ta fight."

John Tunstall replied, "Mr. Chisum, sir. You have been my best customer since I opened my store. And your kind counsel in the ways of this place, which is foreign to me, has proven you a true friend. I therefore hope that you will consider in the spirit of friendship, my view that your actions, and those of your agents, in the assaults you describe on the Beckwith holdings were precipitous and ill-advised. Surely, these are matters that should be brought to

the attention of the sheriff and settled in the courts. And what does your talk of war have to do with me? We English know from long experience that war is bad for business."

"What does it have to do with you? They take what they want from anybody that don't fight back. They're organized. You gonna let 'em take your cattle? You gonna let 'em take your store? If you stand alone, they will. Now I'm in a fight. If we fight alone, one at a time, they'll take us one at a time. We gotta stand together and make a plan to stop their rustlin'."

"Are you suggesting that we approach Sheriff Brady together? If so, I will be most happy to assist you in this endeavor. Mr. McSween shall represent us in drawing up the complaints."

Chisum shook with frustration at Tunstall's lack of understanding. "Goddamnit! For an Englishman, you got damn little understandin' of what a street-fightin' Irishman like Jimmy Dolan is willin' to do. Hell, I'm from Texas and I understand Dolan better than you do. McSween. Brewer. Are you two gonna explain this to Mr. Tunstall before he gets killed?"

Tunstall stiffened and his face grew pale on hearing Chisum's claim that the situation involved some danger to his personal safety. He looked wide-eyed at Brewer and McSween, the only men he trusted more than Chisum.

Brewer spoke first. "Look, John Henry, you gotta understand who these people are. Sheriff Brady was in the union army with Murphy and Dolan. He owes 'em money. And he's a tough Irishman. His deputies are all tough hombres, too. Murphy and Dolan still got plenty of contacts with the army at Fort Stanton. And they're in with the politicians in Santa Fe. Remember when Jesse Evans and Frank Baker stole our stock and we caught 'em and took 'em to Brady? How the hell do you think they escaped so fast? Mr. Chisum's sayin' we can't count on the law. Dolan owns the law."

"I don't entirely agree, Dick," McSween responded. "There are plenty of people in this county who want justice, and they vote. If we can expose Dolan and Brady there may be a political solution."

"You expose Dolan and Brady, you're dead," Chisum responded. "This war ain't about stoppin' 'em. This war is about showin' they gotta leave us alone. They can steal from anybody else they want. We gotta put gun hands on our ranges till they all know they die where nobody knows about it, if they

screw with us. That's the only court that matters. If they attack one of us the other's gotta come quick."

All were silent. They looked at Tunstall. He straightened his necktie, cleared his throat and spoke with hesitation. "I think I understand, Mr. Chisum. You are saying that by alliance, and by preparing to meet force with force in the field, the consequences of full-scale war may be avoided. This is a concept long recognized on the continent and in Britain. I am quite willing to invest in security forces necessary to protect my holdings. But where do I find these 'gun hands' you speak of?"

Alexander McSween responded, "John Henry, I agree with your decision. But I recommend that we keep legal and political options open as well. Toward that end, I wish to advise you that there is a young man who formerly served Mr. Dolan and he is being held in Sheriff Brady's jail right now. The word in town, spread by Dolan's own men, is that this young fellow is a respected fighter. And he would know a great deal about Jimmy Dolan's operations and use of the Seven Rivers men and The Boys. He is now at odds with them."

"I see," Tunstall replied. "You are saying he could be doubly useful, as a soldier and as a source of information in legal or political battles. Very good, Alexander. We must secure his services."

10

THE HOUSE

Why are we here?

The moon was full. All windows were covered so the outside of The House was dark. The Masonic officer called "The Tyler" guarded the front door with a drawn scimitar. Inside, on the second floor, the Ancient Free and Accepted Masons met in a place representing the Unfinished Sanctum Santorum or Holy of Holies of King Solomon's Temple.

Lawrence Murphy, owner of the The House, was drunk and his young partner, Jimmy Dolan, was very embarrassed as drunkenness was conduct unbecoming a Free Mason in Lodge Assembled. But Murphy was the Worshipful Master of Lincoln Lodge.

Dolan was exceptionally concerned because this night U.S. Attorney John Catron, Territorial Governor Samuel Axtel, Mesilla District Court Judge Warren Bristol and District Attorney William Rynerson, official visitors from the Grand Lodge at Santa Fe, were in attendance.

Murphy received the passwords from the east and west, assuring that all present were Free Masons, sworn to secrecy, then he rapped his gavel on the little stand before him three times.

"Brothers, I now open the Lodge of Masons. See that The Tyler is at his post and seal the door."

"Why are we here, Murphy?" Catron demanded. "It better be about your late mortgage payments, and I'm tellin' all the brethren right now, I've given our brothers, Mr. Murphy and Mr. Dolan all consideration due to fellow Masons, but I will foreclose their interests if I don't get answers tonight."

Murphy sat in the Worshipful Master's throne at the head of the hall and he seemed to be falling asleep. Jimmy Dolan knew his mentor was dying of cancer and drink and he trembled in the knowledge that all his ambitions

hung on this meeting and that he must now stand on his own before the most powerful men in the Territory.

Dolan spoke. "We've worked for years to build this place and we were doin' good till that Englishman, Tunstall, come here and used his family's money, and the money McSween stole from us, to undersell us and break us, no matter how much he loses. His bank is givin' out loans, cuttin' off the interest we used to make on sales.

"John Chisum is interferin' with our cattle operations. His drovers round up our yearlings and him an' Tunstall cut their beef prices and they got the next army beef contract."

"What concern of that is mine?" Catron responded.

Catron looked around at Axtel, Bristol and Rynerson and they seemed to agree, but then Murphy stood up.

"You call yourselves Free Masons? You claim brotherhood? You assemble here to support one Mason against another? You forget that we deal straight, and that the wall's strength endures only when all the blocks are in place."

Murphy's eyes flashed that old Irish fire and Jimmy Dolan was inspired in the vision of his dying Irish brother standing up in this strange land against the powerful Santa Fe Ring.

"He's right, John," Governor Axtel said to Catron. "You can wait a little longer for your money can't you?"

"Maybe so, but then what?"

"I say we give those upstarts a taste of what it means to fight us."

"What's your plan?"

"William," Axtel said to District Attorney Rynerson, "why don't you just indict Chisum and that two-bit shyster McSween? Fight bail. Judge, you'll know what to do when they appear in your court. That'll stop 'em long enough for Jimmy an' Lawrence to git caught up on their payments to Mr. Catron."

"Yeah, but that doesn't solve things. With the competition from Tunstall this business is goin' down in the long run. There's no reason to indict Tunstall," Catron replied.

"No, John," Judge Bristol responded, "but I see how we can deal with Tunstall. He's tied in enough with McSween that I say they're partners. If Jimmy will just send me some writs of attachment, I'll sign 'em. Sheriff Brady can seize all Tunstall's assets. Before the matter can be heard, a mob—maybe The Boys or Seven Rivers folks—might just break in and clean out that store. I don't care how wealthy Tunstall's family is. They ain't gonna want to keep supplyin' the whole county for free forever. If they do, we'll do it again. In the meantime, Jimmy, you make sure that Kinney, Evans and The Boys make Tunstall's herd their first choice."

All the members of the Free Lodge Assembled sat back and grinned, contemplating the great majesty of their powers combined.

11

WILSON'S FATE

What did it matter if the Kid shed a tear?

In two days, William had made little progress filing the link on Billy Wilson's chain with his belt buckle.

"You smell that?" Wilson asked.

William had been trying to remain cheerful, telling jokes and singing songs. He thought he had sung his favorite, "Silver Threads Among the Gold," about a hundred times, but now he stopped filing and sat down against the wall next to Wilson.

"Yeah, I smell it."

"My flesh is rottin' where they shot me. There ain't no cure for that, even if I could get out of here. And there ain't no way you are gonna git through that link before tomorrow. Even if you did, there ain't no time to dig outta here."

"I'm sorry," William said.

"It's okay, amigo. I'd rather die of a quick neck snap than of stinkin' rot."

The two sat for a while in silence. They heard the rattle of the chain being withdrawn from the trap door above. The trap opened and the dim light that flowed into the dungeon burned their eyes. Brady's men lowered the ladder and Brady called down, "Get on up here, Bonney. John Tunstall's done posted enough bail for you to buy Sheriff Barela five horses, better than the one you stole."

"Who's John Tunstall?"

"Are you gonna sit there yappin' or are you gonna climb up here? 'Cause I'm a busy man and I'm about to close this trap back down."

William looked ruefully at Wilson.

"Go on, Kid. I only got one more night to wait. You been kind to me and I won't never forget it. Leastwise, not before tomorrow."

Wilson grinned and William smiled back at the brave joke.

"Well, all right then, amigo."

"Well, all right then."

They shook hands.

"Will you come to my hangin'?"

"I'll be there."

"Hasta la vista. Until we see each other again."

"Hasta la vista."

That night, William again drank and gambled with Brewer and Bowdre. William usually didn't drink much, but Wilson would be hanged in the morning and this night was an exception. Brewer and William staggered into the Wortley Hotel about three a.m. and it seemed to William that he had only slept for a moment when Brewer said, "Get up, boy. It's Billy Wilson's time. He was good company to play cards with and whatever he done, he needs a few friends to help 'im over."

William and Dick walked out, crossed a little garden and passed through the gate on the white-picket fence to where Charlie and Manuela Bowdre, and Tom O'Folliard stood waiting. They could see the hanging platform, made of green, freshly cut wood, standing next to The House a short distance away. Jimmy Dolan stood on the balcony of The House, surrounded by gunmen, and looking down at the scaffold and the people gathering about.

William walked down the street with his new amigos. The Kid's face was grim and sour. William didn't like hangings—even when they involved people he didn't know. William had seen three hangings, on two occasions. In Fort Grant he had witnessed the hanging of two San Carlos Apache brothers. He had watched, horrified, as the sheriff, Ryan, fit a black hood over the first brother's face. Ryan started to pull a mask over the second brother, Nah Diaz. Nah had been totally calm, but now he turned his head toward the sheriff, craned his neck forward, opened his eyes, wide, like a bug, and said, "Boo!"

Ryan and half his stern, heavily armed, walrus-mustached deputies jumped back. Nah laughed and the crowd laughed, too. Ryan, humiliated, stepped back up and yanked the mask down over Nah's sparkling white grin. That's what Billy liked most about all the Indians he had known. All of them, Apaches, Navajos, Pueblos, had a hell of a sense of humor. The Kid felt real

bad when the trap slammed down on Nah and his hermano.

In Socorro, New Mexico Territory, Billy had seen an ex-slave, John Henry Anderson, hanged. From everything Billy had heard, Anderson was probably innocent. From everything Billy had heard, it was usually Indians, blacks and Mexicans that got hanged. But Anderson didn't complain. He just called out calmly and graciously in his profoundly deep voice," I want you all to know, I have been kindly treated by Sheriff Russell and his assistants."

Now the Kid was going to have to see it all again.

William Bonney walked with his new friends up to the edge of the crowd surrounding the gallows. A chain of bluecoats circled the scaffold, arms ready, as Wilson, bandaged and chained, was led, limping, up the stairs.

"We're with you, Bill!" Brewer yelled.

"Yea heariee!" the others yelled.

Bill looked down and saw his friends.

"Thank you boys, and adiós!"

"You got anything to say?" Sheriff William Brady asked in an impatient, disapproving and unimpressed tone.

"Just this!" Bill laughed, and he sang a profane song and tried to dance a jig, bent and wounded as he was. The crowd cheered. Bill told the minister to go to hell; then he told the sheriff, "Let 'er go, Willy, I'll die game!"

Brady sprung the trap and Bill Wilson dropped, jerked, then dangled for ten minutes. The little crowd was mostly gone and the Kid wanted to go too, but his new friends, Tom, Charlie and Dick remained forlornly, as soldiers put Bill in his coffin at the foot of the stairs.

"He's breathin'!" a woman cried.

The blue coats carried Bill back up the stairs and Brady hanged him again.

"What 'er you cryin' about?" Brewer demanded of the Kid. Brewer's drovers looked at the boy.

William wiped a tear from his eye with one finger. "Shut up," he said.

Brewer looked insulted and challenged, and Tom and Charlie and the other drovers were shocked and embarrassed. They looked anxiously at the Kid and Brewer. All saw danger in the boy's look. Brewer shrugged. "Let's go."

What did it matter if the Kid shed a tear? Bonney had known Wilson in the calabozo, and the others had all known him too.

William and his new pals drank and gambled together for two more days. William ran out of money about three a.m., the second night.

"Loan me two dollars, Charlie," William said. "I've got a damn good hand."

Charlie had already folded. He pushed the boy two dollars, but the Kid's hand wasn't good enough and Buck Morton took the pot.

"Looks like you're out of luck and money," Brewer said, and stood up. He swayed on his feet. "Vamonos. Let's go."

William, Tom and Charlie followed Dick out, down the street to their horses. They all had difficulty walking, but they were fine in their saddles.

"Where we goin'?" William asked.

"Tunstalls."

It was a sixty-mile ride. After the first five miles in the cool, bracing air, William said, "You boys 're makin' me sober. It's a damn waste of money!"

William laughed and they all laughed with him, and they always would, until the day of their deaths.

Percy was extremely tired. He pushed away from his writing desk, leaned his head back and rubbed his eyes. He had worked all night. Dawn was about to break over the high escarpments on either side of the valley of the Rio Bonito. A rooster crowed, and a pale light filled the blue mist over the rio.

He looked around the room, assuring himself that no spiders had entered. He got up, stepped over to the door, opened it, and peered carefully outside; no spiders in sight. He looked across the garden at the privy that stood in dawn light on the high bank above the thick underbrush lining the Bonito. A few chickens scratched there and the Salazárs' formidable dog, Áyax, half wolf and half hound, lying on the porch, raised his head and returned Percy's gaze.

He decided it was safe. Pulling his blanket tightly around himself, he crossed the yard to the privy. He opened the door, hung his blanket over it and entered.

Percy usually read a newspaper as his bowels moved, but now he sat in the privy and continued reviewing his notes and findings concerning the strange case of William Bonney.

He regarded the process of evacuating one's bowels as the most distasteful act human beings must endure, even when, as back in New York, he enjoyed indoor plumbing, and he was glad to be finished. He arose, cleaned himself with pages from an old newspaper that lay on the seat beside him, and opened the privy door. He stepped out—and froze.

He stared straight into the eyes of a huge longhorn steer that had wandered into the yard and stood facing him, complacently masticating greens from the Salazárs' winter garden. The prodigious span of the beast's horns extended several feet on either side of his head, to the edge of Percy's peripheral vision. Percy glimpsed the deadly black point of one horn, which seemed to be aiming at him, as he jumped back into the privy.

He yanked hard, slamming the privy door against the frame. Now he felt an overwhelming urge to evacuate again, but as he turned around he saw an immense specimen of Latrodectus hesperus crouched malevolently on the edge of the seat he had just vacated.

Percy recoiled, hitting the door with his upper back. The door flew open. He wheeled and looked again at the longhorn. The monster's powerful neck was now extended down and his head and horns tossed back and forth as he ripped vegetation from the earth.

Percy slammed the door closed again, held it in place and pressed up against it as he looked back over his shoulder at the black widow on the bench behind him. He still held his thick sheaf of notes in one hand, and he folded them in half and determined to use this weapon to kill the spider. He turned and slowly raised the paper bludgeon over his head while still holding the privy door tightly closed against the longhorn. His hand trembled.

He heard a door slam, and looked back through the moon-shaped cut in the outhouse door to see Rosario walking toward the longhorn. She held a bag of chicken feed in one hand and tossed feed about the yard with the other. The chickens converged on her vector.

"¡Vayate! You go!" Rosario sternly ordered the bovine. The longhorn took a step back, but he was loath to abandon his rich pasture and he pawed the earth and started forward toward Rosario.

Áyax seemed to come from nowhere, viciously snapping his fangs and leaping at the longhorn's face. The chickens scattered, flapping their wings ineffectually.

"¡Vayate!" Rosario commanded again as the steer tossed his horns back and forth, holding Áyax at bay even as he backed up, turned, and scampered off.

Percy's left hand, which held the door strap, trembled uncontrollably and caused the door to bump rhythmically against its frame.

Rosario straightened, then craned her elegant and slender neck forward, peering at the outhouse door. "¿Señor Percy?"

Percy threw the door open and stumbled toward Rosario, glancing back at the black widow. He regained his equilibrium and checked his flight as he reached her, and she placed one hand on his chest and grasped his upper arm with the other.

"Señor Percy. ¿Que pasa? What's happening?"

He put a hand on her shoulder for support and bent his head forward, gasping for breath.

"Señor Percy. ¿Estás bien? Are you well?"

"Rosario," he panted. He drew her toward him, and rested his head on her shoulder. "There are spiders, and that bull tried to kill me!"

Rosario smiled and leaned back so she could look into Percy's eyes. Then she drew him nearer, tightly embracing him.

"Esta bien ahora. Estoy aquí. It's all right now. I'm here." And Rosario's rich voice as she said that was the softest, sweetest, and most reassuring Percy had ever heard.

She took Percy's right arm with her right hand, curled her left arm around his waist, and led him back toward the house.

Áyax growled. Rosario and Percy looked over and saw the longhorn standing at the edge of the garden, wavering between fear of Áyax and the desire to feed. Percy recoiled and Rosario stepped over, interposing her body between Percy and the steer as she led him back to his room.

"¡Matalo! Kill him!" Rosario commanded Áyax, and the dog bristled and charged forth, growling and barking in most savage fury, and drove the steer, tail twitching, down the road.

Rosario led Percy into his room, and he sat on the edge of his bed.

"Rosario. Thank you. I couldn't sleep. There were spiders everywhere."

Rosario looked around the room. "Quedate aquí. You stay here."

She stepped out the door and returned with a bound-straw broom. She raised it to the ceiling and swept a cobweb from between the vigas directly above the spot where Percy had sat, reading and writing all night. The cobweb disappeared and yet another a black widow dropped onto Percy's chair. Rosario smashed it with the broom, and swept it off the chair and out the door.

Percy's eyes rolled up to the ceiling where the spider must have lurked, directly above his head, all night. He fainted and collapsed on his bed.

Rosario looked with compassion and great affection on the unconscious man, and tenderly covered him with a thick wool blanket, which had been woven by a Navajo woman in the desert, and the woman had woven the blanket with great care, creating symbols carefully calculated to honor and in no way offend the gods of the mesas.

12

JOHN TUNSTALL

Turn loose now, you sons of bitches! I'll give you a game!

The Kid was with John Tunstall the day Dolan sent a gang of hired guns down the street to tell Tunstall to close his store and get out of town. William stepped out onto the portál before the thugs got to the door. Jesse Evans was foremost among the men Dolan had sent.

The Kid wore two Thunderers and he challenged the whole bunch to draw.

"Turn loose now you sons of bitches! I'll give you a game!"

By then, William had been working for John Tunstall for a month. The Englishman was only twenty-four years old, but he acted like a father to William—encouraged the boy and seemed to enjoy his company. Tunstall had given the Kid a horse, a saddle, a Winchester and a new pistol. William had been very proud to receive these gifts. He'd thanked John and said it was the first time in his life he had ever had anything given to him.

John Tunstall said he would show William and all his hands—which included William's new amigos Bowdre, O'Folliard, and the foreman, Brewer—how to become successful and respected. Tunstall claimed that success would come surely and only by dealing honorably in all business affairs and all social relationships in sparsely populated Lincoln County, a place which, Tunstall claimed, offered tremendous opportunity, and where they would all make their fortunes.

Life for William finally seemed good and promising. He was happy living with Tunstall and his new amigos. Everyone seemed to like him, and he thought it must be kind of like having a family.

John Tunstall's actions as well as his words inspired confidence in the hands who accepted him as their patrón. Tunstall was developing a promising ranch and he had opened a bank in Lincoln town. He had also built and opened

a store in direct competition with The House, which had dominated the town for years. Tunstall was easily able to undercut The House's prices, which had been set when The House had enjoyed a monopoly prior to Tunstall's arrival. Then farmers and ranchers had to sell their goods at deflated prices and were paid in credit rather than cash for The House's goods, which were sold at inflated prices. Thanks to his lower prices, business flowed away from The House to Tunstall's new store, and Tunstall saw this as proof of his philosophy that financial success would come naturally and inevitably from honesty and fair dealing.

Tunstall's principles may have been solid, but Tunstall's associate, Alexander McSween, who claimed to be a lawyer, although he had never qualified, did not follow the same code of ethics. McSween had met Tunstall in Santa Fe and had convinced him to come to Lincoln to seek his fortune.

L. G. Murphy and Emil Frtiz had originally owned The House. When Fritz died of cancer his family hired McSween to collect Fritz's life insurance policy. Although Murphy and Dolan claimed Fritz owed the money to The House, when McSween collected $8,000 from the insurance company, he refused to pay it over to Dolan. He claimed that most of it was owed as attorney's fees. Dolan sued McSween and McSween was ordered to pay, but he did not, and he had no assets that could easily be seized. Even title to his house—an adobe building right on the main street of Lincoln—was held in a relative's name.

When McSween associated with Tunstall, Dolan assumed they must be partners, and he figured that they were using The House's money to build Tunstall's store and capitalize Tunstall's bank. In fact, the money was all Tunstall's, sent by his family from England.

Now Dolan's men threatened McSween and Tunstall, and the Kid was prepared to do whatever was necessary to defend Tunstall and his new amigos.

Rumors that the Kid was a pistolero and wanted for murder, brought by Evans and others, had circulated through Lincoln town and now, when the Kid stood on the portál and demanded action of Dolan's thugs, everyone looked to Jesse Evans. The Kid stared at Evans, too, and Evans, wisely, backed down from William Bonney. Slowly, the whole bunch backed off.

Dolan watched, seething, from the portál of The House, just down the street.

But Dolan didn't need to rely only on his gun hands. He still had Judge Bristol at the District Court in Mesilla and the rest of the Santa Fe Ring behind him. Dolan figured if he could drive Tunstall out of business by legal action, he could then easily take revenge on McSween, and he saw how to use the dispute over Fritz's life insurance benefits as a way to eliminate the competition from Tunstall. Dolan decided to start by shutting down Tunstall's ranch. Without notice to Tunstall, Dolan obtained a Writ of Attachment from Judge Bristol directing Sheriff Brady to attach Tunstall's cattle and seize all Tunstall's horses. That would leave Tunstall with a ranch with no horses—and no way for his men to get to Lincoln to defend McSween or the store. Dolan had a good laugh at those thoughts when his lawyer delivered the writ.

Dolan sent word to Sheriff Brady that he would need a lot of men to execute the writ. Tunstall had many horses and, besides the standoff with the Kid, there had been many other bellicose encounters between Dolan's men and Tunstall's. Dolan's men outnumbered Tunstall's by far, but they were mere hirelings, mercenaries. Dolan knew that Tunstall's men were loyal and bonded like brothers to each other, to their English patrón, and to the ideals he espoused.

John Tunstall did not understand the deadly realities of life in the bought-law New Mexico Territory. However, his men were aware of them, and for a time, the commitment and determination of the few would check the cynicism and avarice of the many and the powerful. Until February 18, 1878, Bonney, Bowdre, O'Folliard, and Brewer would successfully protect the aristocratic, naïve English idealist from the mortal danger to which he seemed oblivious.

13

THE LINCOLN COUNTY WAR

This road is short enough.

Jimmy Dolan sat in Sheriff Brady's office, leaning back on the hind legs of his chair, resting his boots on Will Brady's desk. Nobody else would have dared such a thing, but Dolan had supported Brady's bid for the shrievalty with money, guns, and the influence he had bought in Santa Fe.

"It's your duty, Will, to serve this writ, soon as ya can."

"I know my duty, Jimmy, and I've always executed your writs and auctioned the lands and houses of those that've owed ya. But this is no light thing you're askin'. I evicted Bowdre and Brewer off their ranchitos based on your writs. Your titles were good, theirs weren't. But you sold 'em the bad titles and they had no lawyers. It was all legal accordin' to the courts, but they're mad as hell and they're likely ta fight. All them Tunstall's are likely ta fight."

"They might want to…but that English lily won't let 'em. And they'll do what he says, if ya take enough men."

"That's what I'm sayin' t'ya, Jimmy. We need ta prepare, careful, ta execute this writ. I'll need a lotta men and time ta get 'em together and ready. It's a sixty-mile ride. And right now I've got business ta handle at my own place. I ain't been home in three days."

Dolan laughed and shook his head. This was just what he had hoped for. Bowdre and Frank Freeman had beaten Brady to within an inch of his life a year before. Bystanders had saved him. Then, Brady and a posse killed Freeman at Bowdre's ranch. Yes, Bowdre would fight, and Dolan was pleased to see Brady's hesitation.

"I understand you've got other business," Jimmy said soothingly, "I'm not askin' ya to do it yourself, Will. As high shire-reeve you've got posse comitatus just like in the old country. I've got thirty men ready right now and I want it done now. They're bleedin' me ev'ry day, Will."

Brady hesitated. He knew what could happen. "Can they read and understand the writ?"

"They understand, Will. Get the horses and bring 'em back here. It's that simple."

Jimmy Dolan and William Brady stood in the street before Dolan's mounted mob, and Dolan handed the writ up to Buck Morton. Jimmy Dolan had paid him well and appointed him posse foreman. Thirty others from Seven Rivers and The Boys sat behind Morton. Just outside of town, Jesse Evans and Frank Baker waited to join the posse, once they were out of Brady's sight.

"Raise your right hands," Brady said. "Do you swear to execute this writ?"

The posse rode to Tunstall's ranch on the Rio Feliz. There they met Bill McCloskey, who brought a message from Tunstall. Tunstall had heard about the writ and he was driving his remuda of sixteen horses into Lincoln to submit to Brady and have the matter decided in the courts. Bonney, Dick Brewer, and Charlie Bowdre rode drag at the rear of the remuda, about a half-mile behind Tunstall and John Middleton. The Kid glanced back over his shoulder and saw Dolan's posse as it topped the hill and charged.

The posse-men began firing, and bullets kicked up the ground, causing the Kid's horse to buck and skitter. He reined her in and followed Brewer and Bowdre across a ravine and up a steep hill, and took cover behind big boulders. The Kid levered a round into the firing chamber of his Winchester and took aim. But the posse did not follow them, but instead cut south after Tunstall and Middleton, who were concealed from the Kid's view in a bosket at the head of the strung-out horse herd.

Middleton and Tunstall heard the shooting behind them and as the posse came forward through the piñon and juniper stands, Middleton knew what it meant. "Come on, John! Follow me!" Middleton shouted at Tunstall, "For God's sake, come on!" He spurred his mount and raced to join his amigos, Dick, Billy and Charlie.

"What, John?" Tunstall stammered.

Tunstall started to follow Middleton, but hesitated, stopped, and turned back to face the posse. He thought he could talk to them, give up the horses, and fight in the courts. Middleton was right. Tunstall was wrong.

The posse-men had nothing to say. Buck Morton rode up and shot Tunstall in the chest. Then Frank Baker dismounted, put the barrel of his six-gun against the base of Tunstall's skull and pulled the trigger. Others pumped bullets into Tunstall's screaming horse.

The Kid watched from the hill top above and saw Morton and Baker gallop into the woods after Tunstall. He saw Middleton break from the forest headed towards him, and as Middleton rode up, the Kid heard the shots that killed Tunstall. He cursed under his breath and watched as a few posse members came out of the woods and looked up at his position. But Dolan's men weren't about to charge uphill over open ground at forted men with good rifles. They withdrew back into the cover of the trees. The Kid could hear them, distantly, laughing as they drank from flasks, and they laid Tunstall next to his horse, tucked his overcoat under his head like a pillow, put his hat on the dead mare's head, and placed a blanket over man and horse as if they were bedded together in a grotesque burlesque.

The posse rode back to Lincoln with the horses, including one that belonged to William. They left Tunstall's copy of the writ stuffed under the tail of his dead mare, a fine thoroughbred that Tunstall had greatly favored, and man and beloved horse lay on blood-soaked New Mexican ground, staring blankly into one another's empty eyes.

William Bonney reckoned Sheriff Brady owed him a life and a horse.

Once the killing started, it picked up fast. McSween had no pull in Mesilla but he got John Wilson, justice of the peace in Lincoln, to issue constable's warrants to arrest Dolan and known members of Brady's posse. There was a warrant for Sheriff Brady, too.

Wilson deputized Dick Brewer, William Bonney, Charlie Bowdre, Tom O'Folliard, and ten others. They called themselves "Regulators." They swore an oath, which they called the "Iron Clad," to avenge Tunstall and any others of their number who should fall, and never to betray each other by word or deed.

McSween summoned Lincoln Constable Atanacio Martinez and demanded that he arrest County Sheriff Brady. Martinez figured he'd probably get killed, but he was bound by honor to do his duty, and he agreed to confront Brady. The Regulators hesitated, doubting the wisdom and feasibility of

McSween's order—all except William. He was angry at the loss of his horse and furious about Tunstall's murder. "I don't give a damn. I'm with you, 'Nacio," he said.

Tom O'Folliard was about William's age and they were fast friends. "I'm with you, Billy," he said.

Brady had been seen entering The House. Atanacio, William, and Tom walked down the street, stepped up to the doors and threw them open. They faced Brady and a ring of pointed guns. Brady's men disarmed them. They treated Constable Martinez with restraint but they beat O'Folliard and the Kid and threw all three of them into the calabozo. Brady released them a few days later, but he kept the rifle Tunstall had given the Kid.

Now, William figured, Brady owed him a life, a horse, and a rifle.

The Regulators decided to hunt and take only those of Dolan's who left Lincoln alone or in small groups. Spanish friends pointed out the trail of four posse members.

Jesse Evans, Frank Baker, Manuel Segovia, and Buck Morton sat resting their horses in shade under the only tree in sight on a grass plain thirty miles south of Roswell when the Regulators topped a ridge a half mile away. The four immediately mounted up and galloped away from the approaching Regulators.

The Boys pulled out their rifles and wildly fired back at their pursuers, who were at the edge of rifle range, and the Regulators answered every shot with fire that proved equally ineffective as they raced forward undeterred.

With Brewer and the others on his tail, William led the pack after Baker and Morton when Evans and Segovia split off. Now it was twelve men chasing two, and The Boys' horses began to fail after five miles. As the Regulators gained ground, Baker and Morton pulled up and took cover in a low bog, amidst cattails and high grasses that offered only the illusion of cover. But now they could aim well and the Regulators backed off out of range and encircled their prey. They dismounted and crawled forward on their bellies through the grama grass, maintaining steady fire, keeping Baker and Morton down. The Boys managed to return fire, defiantly and at great risk. As their ammunition ran low and the Regulators' circle tightened, they saw in parley their only hope. Baker tore a white sleeve from the arm of his long johns, tied it

to his rifle barrel, and waved the flag of surrender as high in the air as he could reach without exposing his torso or his head to his enemies' guns.

"Brewer! Let's talk! I got no dispute with you!"

"We got every dispute. You killed John Tunstall. Now you run outta' trail."

"I didn't kill 'im. But you're forcin' this fight."

"I am."

William was on the opposite side of the circle from Dick Brewer, and keen to finish the fight. Brewer's tough words inspired him, and he was crawling forward for the kill when Brewer said, "Give up your arms."

"And let you kill us?"

"We'll take you in for trial." The minute he said it, Brewer knew it was a mistake. Where would they take Morton and Baker? To Brady? That was where The Boys had gone for safety after killing Tunstall. But Brewer believed that what he was doing was right, and there had to be a way to make it right. "We got legal warrants for your arrest. We'll take you in for trial. I give my word."

"Show me the papers."

"I'm comin'. If you shoot, you're gonna die here and now."

"We won't shoot. Let's do this legal an' civilized. I'll take my chances with a jury."

Brewer stood up, raised a hand for his men to hold fire, and walked forward, warrants in one hand and his rifle in the other. Baker stood up too, rifle lowered and pointing at the ground. He gave his rifle and pistols to Brewer, and read the warrants. Buck Morton did the same.

"I'm sorry you surrendered," Brewer said. "That's not how I wanted it."

The Regulators rode north with their prisoners and spent the night at John Chisum's South Spring Ranch. The next day they rode through Roswell, which was little more than a post office, where Baker and Morton deposited letters with the postmaster, Ash Upson. Morton wrote to his uncle, a lawyer back in Tennessee:

I have no fear of dying but if I do not reach Lincoln alive I ask that you arrange for a full investigation.

Baker wrote to his sweetheart in Seven Rivers. His hand trembled as he gave Ash Upson his letter, and Ash noted the Regulators' grim faces. "Is there anything else I can do for you?" Ash asked.

Bill McCloskey spoke up. "Don't worry, Ash," he said. "Some of these boys've talked about makin' their own law. But they don't mean it. If any man wants to harm these men on the road they'll have to kill me first. They'll get safe to Lincoln."

William raised an eyebrow and steamed at McCloskey's declaration. McCloskey had carried John Tunstall's last message to Jimmy Dolan, telling Dolan that Tunstall was headed to Lincoln to submit to Brady's writ. McCloskey had formerly ridden for Dolan and the Seven Rivers men. He was a friend of Morton's, and he had only recently joined Tunstall. And William knew, now more surely than ever, that McCloskey was still Dolan's man. He had joined Tunstall as a spy, informed Dolan of Tunstall's route to Lincoln, and now he was trying to protect Tunstall's killers.

The party rode on. Charlie Bowdre was thirty years old, the oldest man present. But Brewer was the leader. Charlie, Brewer and William rode abreast, ahead of the others, and Charlie argued with Dick Brewer.

"You can't be serious, Dick, takin' these assholes to Brady. Remember when Jesse and Frank stole our horses and stock and we tracked them down and turned them over to Brady? How long did it take for them to 'escape'? Brady is Dolan's man and these two are too. How Goddamn stupid are we to keep handin' the cubs back over to the wildcat? I say we give 'em what they earned with no more talk. If we ain't got the balls to fight back, this country's never gonna change an' we deserve what they give us next. Dolan's done took our ranches. Next he's gonna give us what he gave Tunstall. Goddamn it, Dick. We rode hard after these turds. Now we gotta finish it."

"You think they won't kill you in a minute, like they killed John, if you let 'em go?" William added. "This is a groundhog case. They killed our amigo. If we just let 'em go then we don't deserve nothin' he ever gave us."

"I said we're takin' em in for trial."

Brewer kept thinking about the things Charlie and William said. He knew they were right in their own way. But he had given his word, and that was another kind of right. They rode on, and when they came to a side trail to

Lincoln through Agua Negra, Brewer led the party off the main road.

Frank Baker was a cold killer, and he knew exactly what he would do if he had any of the Regulators under his power. He had only surrendered because he was about to die and surrender was his only slim chance. He had figured they would kill him pretty quick, and when they didn't, and rode for a day and a half for Lincoln, his hopes had begun to rise, as did his contempt for Brewer.

That stupid bastard is really gonna give me over to Brady, he thought.

But as Brewer headed the party off toward Agua Negra, Frank's fear returned and turned his face white.

"Hey, Dick! Where we goin'? I say we take the short road. I'm tired a' ridin!"

"This road is short enough. An' we won't meet none a' your friends this way."

Frank clenched his teeth and sneered, and William looked back at him. Frank met his gaze for a moment, and looked away.

Brewer led the party a ways forward, and then off the trail up to a big oak tree with a good hanging branch. He wheeled his horse and Charlie and William did, too. He nodded at John Middleton. "Get 'em off their horses and tie their hands."

Morton and Baker sat side by side on their horses, not a yard apart.

"Now hold on a minute, Dick, you said we was gonna be tried. You done give your word," Buck Morton said.

"This is your trial right here. Did you kill John Tunstall?"

"Hell no!" Morton shouted, hoping to muster some credibility by the loud and emphatic denial.

"How 'bout you Frank?" Brewer asked, casually and ironically. Frank Baker looked around at the cold faces surrounding him. He held no hope, but managed to answer in an equally casual tone, "Nope."

"Well all right, then. Let's hear some witnesses. I'm first. I seen you two ridin' hard at Tunstall just before I heard the shots that killed 'im."

"I seen you, too," Charlie Bowdre said. "You see anything Kid?"

Morton and Baker looked at William.

By custom, three witnesses justified a death sentence. Baker knew the Kid would condemn him, but he expected to see malice and hatred in the Kid's eyes. He saw none of that. No hatred, no compassion or pity. No sign of satisfaction or triumph. The Kid simply spoke the truth.

"Yeah. I seen 'em," he said.

A long silence followed.

Baker knew there was no profit in argument. But Buck Morton figured he might as well make one more bitter accusation.

"None 'a you seen nothin'!" he said. "I know, 'cause I seen the tails a' your horses when you run for cover." He looked around the circle of Regulators and was surprised to see some faces clouded with doubt. He saw Brewer's and Charlie's faces colored with shame.

William laughed. "Well, that's real good, Buck. 'Cause if you seen the tails of our horses, then I guess you're sayin' you were right there when Tunstall got shot."

Everyone knew the trial was over but McCloskey still played for a new trial. He nosed his horse up between Baker's and Morton's. "Now look, Dick. This is no right trial. You know it. Now, let's just keep ridin'. Take 'em to Lincoln like you done promised."

Baker and Morton both felt one last ray of hope. They could see that Brewer and Bowdre were still stunned by Morton's accusation of cowardice. The other Regulators also seemed to waiver. But when they looked at the Kid, they saw perfect assurance. He grinned with cynical knowledge of McCloskey.

"You think I don't see your hole card, McCloskey? 'Cause I got a rope right here for you, too. You ride for Dolan. I always knew it. You killed Tunstall as sure as these two poor bastards did. They were just a little more honest in the way they done it." William made no move for his six-gun.

He didn't have to. McCloskey immediately backed down.

"Well, now hold on Kid. I ride with you. I say what I think. But that's all I can do."

Morton's horse stood on McCloskey's right. He knew McCloskey would no longer defend him, and he took his last chance. He snatched McCloskey's six-gun from its holster. McCloskey tried to grab it but Morton shot him through his side. Morton spun the gun toward Brewer, Bowdre and Bonney, but Bonney had already drawn and his bullet blew through Morton's neck and

spine. Baker spurred his mount and pulled a pocket pistol he had concealed in the breast pocket of his frock coat, and the Regulators were all firing now. Morton and Baker and their horses were riddled with bullets before they hit the ground.

In the silence that followed, a few shepherds crept cautiously forward through the brush. They looked wide-eyed at the carnage and made signs of the cross.

"Traigan espadas?" Brewer asked them. "Do you have shovels?"

"Sí, Señor."

Brewer tossed a couple of silver dollars on the ground before them.

"Don't it seem kinda strange, Billy?" Tom O'Folliard asked as the Regulators rode for Lincoln. "We rode for two days with them boys and now they're dead. Dead. We killed 'em. It seems real strange to me."

William frowned and seemed to be staring, blankly, at the road. "Yeah, Tom. It is strange. That's how it is. But they deserved it. I never intended to let them birds reach Lincoln alive."

Jimmy Dolan had been shocked when he learned that the Regulators had warrants and had even had the gall to try to arrest Sheriff Brady. He sent heavily armed riders to Santa Fe with a letter to John Catron. Catron flexed his political muscle and on March 9, 1878, the same day Morton and Baker were gunned down at Agua Negra, Territorial Governor Samuel B. Axtell, escorted by U. S. Cavalry, rode into Lincoln.

Axtell met with Dolan, and issued a proclamation:

John B. Wilson's appointment as Justice of the Peace is null and void and all his purportedly official acts, including issuance of arrest warrants, are void ab initio.

Thus, with a stroke of his pen, Governor Axtell turned the Regulators into outlaws and murderers, wanted for killing Baker and Morton. Axtell then borrowed $1,800 from Jimmy Dolan, signed a promissory note and left town.

The Regulators' leader, Dick Brewer, didn't care what Axtell said, and the Regulators remained defiant. They rode back to Lincoln for instructions from McSween. They were settling their horses in an adobe corral when Sheriff Brady and three deputies came riding down the street.

The Regulators fired, all at once, over the adobe wall. Brady and one deputy, George Hindeman, pitched off their horses. Two others reached shelter across the street. Brady pushed himself up with his arms and said, "Oh Lord," then collapsed and died.

Eighteen-year-old William Bonney, seeking justice, ran out into the street to take Brady's rifle and his blooded Arabian stallion.

Deputy Billy Matthews fired from a window, grazing Bonney's hip. The Kid retreated, but he was seen and recognized by many witnesses.

Percy's reseach revealed that Sheriff Brady's assassination polarized the county even more than had Tunstall's—if that were possible.

A "posse" led by Jimmy Dolan raided Tunstall's ranch and stole all the cattle on the place. The Kid and Charlie Bowdre exchanged shots with Buckshot Roberts near San Patricio but no one was wounded. Then the Regulators caught up with Roberts at Blazer's Mill. Roberts killed Dick Brewer and wounded several other Regulators, but the Kid put a bullet in Roberts' gut and he died the next day.

Seven Rivers men ambushed the Regulators at Charles Fritz's Ranch, killing Ab Saunders and the Regulators' new leader, Frank McNabb. Then the Seven Rivers men rode to Lincoln, where they were repulsed by the Regulators, leaving several dead.

The Regulators attacked Dolan's cattle camp at Black River where the Kid killed Manuel Segovia, another member of the posse that had killed Tunstall. The Boys riding under John Kinney ambushed the Regulators near San Patricio and raided the village, terrorizing its inhabitants.

A posse of Seven Rivers men ambushed some Regulators near Roswell but fell back in a running gunfight. They gathered reinforcements and for a time laid siege on the Chisum South Spring Ranch.

Dolan had obtained a warrant for McSween's arrest. The Regulators protected him, fearing he would be killed if captured. But McSween finally got tired of running and returned to Lincoln with the Regulators and allies from Picacho, all told about forty men, for a showdown.

14

EL CHIVATO

"Now," he said, and we all followed him out.

Percy awoke after only an hour. He peered out from under his blankets and saw no black widows anywhere. He got up and dressed. He lifted a container of gasoline, walked out and around the house to the dirt road in front, and filled the Humpmobile's gas tank in the delicate morning light.

He saw Rosario standing down the road talking to Matéo Romero. The handsome young man sat bareback astride a white, magnificently muscled quarter horse. Percy could not hear the young peoples' conversation but he saw Matéo gesture, clearly inviting Rosario to climb up behind him for a morning ride. Percy saw Rosario shake her head and point back, directing Matéo's gaze toward Percy and the Hupmobile. She handed Matéo Percy's poem and Matéo read it, looked at Percy with great malice, then turned his horse and rode off.

"¿Que, por favor, puedemos ir, ahóra? Can we please go now?"

Percy turned and looked at Rosario's grandmother, Doña Flora, standing, frowning, behind him. Percy understood that Doña Flora would accompany him and Rosario to Fort Sumner and the graves. Doña Flora knew where the unmarked graves lay, and it was also imperative that Doña Flora accompany Percy and Rosario as they drove out of Lincoln in order to prevent the inappropriate speculation and gossip which would surely arise if Percy and Rosario should ride alone together through the town, not to return until nightfall.

Doña Flora was only sixty years old. She stood straight and her figure was still lean beneath her long wool dress and wool shawl which she clutched tightly over her prodigious bosom against the cold November morning air. Time had been kind to Doña Flora. Her dark and noble Spanish face exhibited wrinkles only at the corners of her eyes and Percy thought they looked like tiger stripes when she smiled. She was still a great beauty and Percy could see where Rosario got her looks.

Percy took Doña Flora by the elbow, guided her to the Hupmobile, opened the door and helped her up. Rosario joined them carrying a basket containing burritos—corn tortillas wrapped around beans and chile marinaded pork—and apples. Áyax jumped into the car too.

Percy took the wheel and Rosario bounced with undisguised excitement as he fired up the engine and drove the car through the town. Residents watched, and Percy filled with pride at the two great beauties sitting beside him.

They headed south down the valley of the Rio Bonito. After twelve miles the road turned along the Rio Hondo and Rosario suddenly pointed to a low adobe with grass growing on top of an earthen roof supported by stout vigas and latillas. The dwelling was barely visible among the cottonwoods.

"Look Señor Percy! This is the house of my grandmother's cousin, Yginio. Yginio Salazár. Señor Percy, Don Yginio knew Señor Pat Garrett. Do you want to stop?"

As they cut off the road toward the house, Percy saw Don Yginio, tall, lean as a rail, splitting wood near the back. As Yginio walked toward him, Percy gazed at his exceedingly dark visage, fissured by wrinkles like the face of a bare granite mountain, and his well-trimmed white beard, thick as a brush.

Don Yginio embraced Rosario and Doña Flora. Rosario introduced Percy and he shook Percy's hand with a grip like iron.

"Que pasan pa' dentro. Come inside."

The ladies sat on two simple chairs before Don Yginio's woodstove and Yginio and Percy sat on upright pieces of unsplit firewood. Don Yginio poured strong coffee and the Salazars spoke for a bit about their family—weddings, births, and burials.

Then Rosario said, "Tio, Uncle. Señor Percy has come from La Ciudad de Nuevo York to learn important matters of our people."

Not at all taken in by the girl's enthusiasm, Don Yginio turned his attention to Percy and looked him over critically. Percy thought he detected a look of mistrust in the old man's eyes and he decided that he had best speak quickly and carefully.

"Don Yginio. Thank you for having me in your home. I have been sent here to report about the sheriff, Pat Garrett, and his enemy, the outlaw Billy the Kid. Rosario tells me that you knew Mr. Garrett."

Yginio frowned. "Yes, Mr. Chesterfield," he said in heavily accented English. "I knew Garrett. But I knew the Kid better. I rode with him in the war. We never called him 'Billy the Kid.' This is only what his enemies called him—the powerful gringos who stole our land, and used The House to steal our goods and livestock to keep us down."

With that rebuke, Don Yginio looked away from Percy, staring into the fire. Percy understood that he had started badly, and he feared that he was about to lose his witness. "Don Yginio," he said. "Forgive me. Por favor. I know little of this place. I am only trying to understand. Please be so kind as to teach me. How should I refer to William Bonney?"

Percy looked at Doña Flora for support, and Doña Flora gave Yginio a nod indicating her approval of Señor Percy.

"Most of his amigos called him 'Kid' or 'Billy,'" Don Yigenio said at last. "But all the Spanish people called him 'El Chivato.' This was a term of great affection. It means 'kid,' like a beautiful young goat. In his last years he began to get whiskers on his upper lip and chin and when he rode the range, to raid the gringos' cattle and horses, he could not shave. So when he would return to the settlements and plazuelas, he seemed to have a fine, blonde, down beard of the sort the gringos call 'goatee.'"

Percy imagined Billy with his blond hair riding into the plazuelas among the darker New Mexicans. "I would be grateful if you could explain to me how an Anglo boy like El Chivato could gain the affection of the native New Mexican people," he said.

"To us, El Chivato was no Anglo," Don Yginio replied. "A man's color does not matter. El Chivato was a young man. But he was muy macho, very brave, like one of us. And he could smell the truth."

Percy was perplexed by this enigmatic answer.

"The truth? What is the truth?"

Don Yginio gave Percy a fierce look, then looked back into the fire for a long time. Percy dared not speak. He watched and waited. And at last Don Yginio relented.

"When Tunstall came here, he gave us hope that we could sell our goods and livestock for fair prices. El Chivato was no fool. He knew that Tunstall and McSween got him out of jail because they wanted to use him. But El Chivato was a man of honor. He gave his word. El Chivato had always been in trouble. Tunstall and McSween gave him his first chance to go straight.

"But the Dolans murdered Tunstall, and dashed all our hopes. We decided to fight back. We tried to defend McSween. We called ourselves 'Regulators,' an honorable name. But we knew that the sheriff, the governor and the Santa Fe Ring would never allow justice. We were young men, and our true mission was revenge—pitiless war on those who had harmed us. And El Chivato was a vengeful young man. He only understood that a loyal friend must kill any man who kills his friends. This is the pagan code. The killing went back and forth. It was war, which God seems to have decreed to be the state of all mankind.

"When the war started, El Chivato was just one soldier among many. He was always ready. He kept his gear together, he rode well, and he responded immediately to any order. We all loved him. He was always laughing—but in a quiet, not boisterous, way. He would dance and laugh, gamble and laugh, ride and laugh, and kill and laugh."

Don Yginio's voice warmed and his face grew more animated as he talked about his old comrade in arms.

"He was always in the forefront of every action. The fight at Blazer's Mill is a good example. We were there hunting members of the posse that killed Tunstall. Buckshot Roberts was a tough old scout and he had led Dolan's posse to Tunstall. He did not know we were at Blazer's when he rode in. He tied his mule to a tree on the other side of the river, and walked up to the mill. Brewer and many others wanted to just shoot him down. But Frank Coe convinced us to stay inside and wait so that he could talk to Roberts and accept his surrender. Coe walked out and met Roberts and they walked to the porch at the back of the mill.

"Coe told Roberts we were all inside. He told Roberts he would die if he did not surrender. They talked for half an hour but Roberts just repeated, 'No.' 'No.' 'No.' "Finally we got tired of waiting. All ten of us walked out and around the corner to demand Roberts' surrender. Charlie Bowdre was in the lead."

Filled with growing passion, Don Yginio rose to his feet and began to wave his arms to demonstrate what happened next.

"Charlie said, 'Surrender your arms.' Roberts said, 'Not much, Mary Ann,' and he pointed his Winchester and fired from the hip. Charlie drew and fired too, but Roberts' bullet hit Charlie in his stomach, ruining his aim and knocking him to the ground. But the bullet ricocheted off Charlie's cartridge belt, and it ripped off George Coe's trigger finger. I saw the bloody finger flipping up through the air as Roberts fired at El Chivato. El Chivato had already drawn, but Roberts' bullet zipped along his forearm and his revolver flew from his hand. Roberts' next shot hit John Middleton in the chest, throwing him back and down. Roberts kept levering and firing all around with great speed. We all scattered for cover. All except El Chivato. He charged Roberts as Roberts backed up, still firing, and stepped through the back door of the mill. El Chivato grabbed Roberts' rifle barrel. Roberts stuck it in El Chivato's belly and pulled the trigger, but he was out of bullets. El Chivato yanked the weapon away. Roberts slammed and latched the door, but El Chivato drew his second revolver and, firing with his left hand, shot through the door. His bullet tore through Roberts' belly, but we did not know that at the time.

"Charlie thought he had hit Buckshot. He lay, doubled over in pain behind a wood pile, next to Dick Brewer. We had wounded men now, and Charlie said, 'Let's go, Dick. I dusted him. He's sure to die.' But Brewer was very angry and said, 'I'm not gonna let him live even one extra minute.' We all fired at the door.

"Inside, Roberts pulled an officer's pattern Springfield off the Blazers' mantle, and he cracked the door open and watched the smoke from our guns. That is how he knew where we were. When Brewer rose up for a shot, Roberts fired. His bullet tore the top off Brewer's skull and splattered us all with blood. We rode out and we were very sad and discouraged that just one man killed our leader and wounded so many of us. But El Chivato had gained stature in all our eyes for his quick thinking and fearless acts.

"We fought many battles after that. El Chivato was always in the forefront." Don Yginio sat down. "Only an hour before the Regulators were finally destroyed, El Chivato became our leader."

"Tell us," Rosario said, nodding, leaning forward.

"We were trapped in McSween's house in Lincoln," Don Yginio continued. "We had been fighting for five days. Dolan's men, the Seven Rivers men and The Boys under Jesse Evans and John Kinney opposed us.

"On our side were the Regulators and twenty men from Picacho riding with Don Martin Chávez. It was a stalemate until the last day, when Dolan used his political connections to bring the United States Army under Colonel Dudley. A troop of buffalo soldiers rode in with a mountain howitzer and a Gatling gun. They needed only to point these powerful weapons at the houses occupied by the McSweens, forcing our allies to flee into the countryside.

"At last only ten of us remained with McSween in his house. The troopers then backed off and the Dolans, the Seven Rivers men and The Boys surrounded the house. There was constant gunfire and the Dolans managed to soak a window sill with coal oil and set it afire. The fire burned slowly from one room to another, yet we kept shooting. Finally, night fell and we were crowded into the last room. The Dolans waited on the other side of the adobe wall that surrounded the house, about twenty feet away. They knew we must come out, and they held their rifles ready.

"McSween hung his head and covered his face with his hands. All gave up hope—all except El Chivato. He took control. He said we must have courage and we must go out shooting. He leaned against the door frame chuckling and smoking a cigarette.

"At last he finished his cigarette and tossed it aside. 'Now,' he said, and we all followed him out. At first we thought it a miracle. No shots greeted us. The Dolans were sitting behind the wall. They did not expect us to come out so soon. But then one man looked over the wall, then another. I was behind El Chivato, who held both his six guns ready. I saw him raise his guns. He fired at the wall, throwing dust into the air, and the Dolans ducked down. We ran for the gate on our right. The Dolans all rose up. They were behind the walls, on our left and straight ahead. We all fired at them, and they fired back. The explosions were constant. The flashes of the guns added to the illumination from the burning house that lit the garden, bright as day. The constant roar of the guns was terrifying. I followed El Chivato. Looking past him, I saw John Kinney rise up, aiming right at him. El Chivato fired, Kinney twisted to duck back but El Chivato's bullet carried away Kinney's mustache. Next to Kinney,

Jim Beckwith aimed his rifle at El Chivato, but Tom O'Folliard, at my side, fired his rifle and blood blossomed around Beckwith's eye and rose like a halo around the back of his head.

"At that moment a bullet hit me in the shoulder and I fell to my knees. I tried to keep shooting and another bullet hit me in the back. As I fell forward onto my face I saw Tom and El Chivato pass through the gate. For a moment I saw them returning fire from buffalo soldiers in the street. I stretched my hand out to them, but they ran left toward the Rio Bonito and passed behind the wall, beyond my vision. Even as darkness took me I could hear the shouts, screams and moans of McSween and the rest of our men as they were all gunned down in the garden. Blood fell down like rain all around me.

"I awoke a little later. I dared not show that I was still alive. I opened one eye. The Dolans were all around. They ordered McSween's servant, George Washington, El Negro, to play his fiddle. They were all dancing and drinking. I heard sounds coming from Tunstall's store and I knew they were looting it. Then I heard John Kinney's voice right next to me –'I'm gonna finish this one off.'

"I heard the cock of a gun. I said a silent prayer for God to receive my soul. But God denied my prayer. He decided I must live, for Jesse Evans's voice answered, 'The greaser's dead, John. Why waste a bullet?' In that moment I knew Jesse saw that I was alive, but he wanted to give me a chance.

"I awoke at dawn. The Dolans were gone, except for a few who lay in drunken slumber on portáles lining the street. I crawled away. I do not know how I endured the pain. It seemed I crawled, slowly, for hours along the Rio. I reached the house of Doña Flora's father, and they concealed me at great peril to their lives.

"The Regulators who did not die that day all left the Territory. The war was over. The rich and powerful had prevailed again.

"But all the people were happy that El Chivato had escaped. We learned that Charlie Bowdre had met El Chivato and Tom in the forest with fresh horses. For two years after that, those three amigos rode free through the Pecos country. They lived mostly at Fort Sumner on the edge of the Llano Estacado, which had no law but the word of its dueño, Don Pedro Maxwell. El Chivato liked Don Pedro and Don Pedro liked him, even after he heard the rumors that

El Chivato had made love to Don Pedro's sister, Paulita. What could Don Pedro do? El Chivato had a gay, open spirit. He was a graceful dancer and Paulita adored him.

"In time I reunited with El Chivato at Fort Sumner. And that was when I met Pat Garrett. He had been a buffalo hunter on the llano, but he left that sad and declining trade and married Apolonaria Gutierrez. Pat and El Chivato were friends. They drank together. El Chivato never drank much. Garrett always did. They both loved to gamble. Sometimes they would kneel on blankets in the plaza and throw dice. Garrett was the tallest man most of us had ever seen and El Chivato was undersized, so we called the pair 'Juan Largo and Little Casino.' El Chivato used to laugh at Garrett: 'You're one long-legged son of a bitch!' And Garrett would laugh back, teasing the boy about his buckteeth. 'What's a man to do, Kid?' he'd say. 'I've got to reach over because I can't eat pumpkins through a picket fence like you can.'

"El Chivato, Tom and Charlie were wanted everywhere except at Fort Sumner. They could not start ranches so they gambled and made their living by raiding the rich gringos' cattle and horses. These men knew all the little settlements on the Pecos, they attended the fandangos and our people adored them, especially El Chivato, because they defied the powerful."

Percy continued to sit spellbound and silent as Don Yginio stepped across the room and took up his guitar. As he tuned it, he said, "Not a day has passed that I did not think of El Chivato, since the sad time I learned of his death. El Chivato always told us to fight."

And Don Yginio played and sang:

> Oh timid Mexicans don't be afraid.
> Listen to the sound of the bullets,
> The bullets of those gringos say:
> chee chee cha ree
> If you don't kill me, I shall kill thee

15

A TALE OF BEN HUR, A TALE OF THE CHRIST, A TALE OF BETRAYAL

I don't care to open negotiations with a fight, but if you'll come at me three at a time I'll whip the whole damned bunch of you!

Leaving Don Yiginio's home, Percy continued driving down the dirt two-track road toward the Pecos River.

"Do you want me to show you how to drive the car?" Percy asked Rosario.

"Oh! Sí, Señor Percy."

Rosario was a quick study, and she was ambidextrous, so Percy was amazed at the co-ordination she displayed as she enthusiastically worked the clutch, the brake, the gearshift and the steering wheel. Before long, Percy was perfectly confident that Rosario could guide the car up the empty road. He pulled notes from a folder and quickly lost himself in his studies of Garrett, the Kid and New Mexico Governor Lew Wallace.

Percy's research had shown that, by 1878, most Americans thought the "wild west" was pretty much settled. Railroads and telegraph lines spanned the country. Except for a few Chiricahua Apache bands that hid out, mostly in Mexico, every American aboriginal tribe had been rubbed out, or nearly so—even the powerful Sioux and Cheyenne—and their survivors consigned to reservations.

Electric lights, telephones, phonographs and vaccines against disease were in development. In the east, people were playing tennis, and baseball and football leagues had formed and adopted uniform rules. People liked to read dime novels about outlaws, battles with "wild" Indians, and gunfighters, whom they regarded merely as a part of the past.

In Arizona Territory, New Mexico Territory and east and south Texas, many cowboys, outlaws and lawmen, including William Bonney, Jesse Evans,

and Pat Garrett enjoyed the novels too. But they didn't know it was over.

Americans were shocked and fascinated by news reports of bandits, shootouts, brash lawlessness and the "Lincoln County War" in a strange place called "New Mexico." In the wake of the battle in Lincoln and the killing of McSween and so many of his supporters, President Rutherford B. Hayes himself was concerned enough to send a treasury agent, Frank Angel, to investigate and report back. On Angel's recommendation, the president decided to replace Territorial Governor Samuel Axtell with General Lew Wallace.

Lew Wallace had been the youngest Union general in the Civil War. He was one of the judges who had presided at the trial that had condemned the killers of Abraham Lincoln. Wallace was dispatched to Santa Fe with orders to investigate the situation, end the Lincoln County War, and impose order on the territory.

Wallace entered the Palace of the Governors in Santa Fe, where Spanish, Mexican, and American governors had resided in succession since 1610. In truth, Wallace was more interested in finishing his novel, Ben Hur: A Tale of the Christ, than he was in governing, but he became angry when he learned that troops from Fort Stanton had assisted the Murphy-Dolan faction in the battle where McSween and so many of his faction had been killed. He was also concerned by reports that his predecessor, Governor Axtell, had borrowed $1,800 from Jimmy Dolan.

Wallace had heard from people who were bitter about how Colonel Dudley helped the Dolans kill McSween, and he was aware that the English government was protesting Tunstall's murder.

Congress had passed the Posse Comitatus Act, on June 18, 1878, forbidding federal forces from intervening in civil disturbances between citizens of the states and territories, and Governor Wallace devised a two-part plan to end the Lincoln County War. He would extend amnesty to all who had fought in the war, except Colonel Dudley, and people such as eighteen-year-old William Bonney who were already under indictment for murder. He would remove and perhaps court martial Dudley for violation of the Posse Comitatus Act. That, he thought, should satisfy everyone.

But, without consulting Wallace and despite the Posse Comitatus Act, President Hayes issued a proclamation concerning Lincoln County, New

Mexico Territory. The president declared he would use the military to enforce the laws of the United States, and he commanded all insurgents to disperse and retire peacefully to their respective abodes before noon on the thirteenth day of October, 1878.

When Wallace issued his proclamation extending amnesty and issuing a general pardon for "...offenses committed in said county of Lincoln in connection with the aforesaid disorders between the first day of February 1878 and the date of this proclamation," he was criticized by neutral citizens who had felt protected by the president's order. They claimed Wallace was inviting outlaws and warring factions back to Lincoln.

Wallace's efforts to have Dudley removed were rejected by General Sheridan, Commander of the Department of Missouri, by his superior, General Sherman, and by the secretary of the Department of War.

To the Kid, these developments seemed nothing new. The law supported both sides. The district court had issued writs against McSween and Tunstall; the justice of the peace had issued warrants for the Murphy-Dolans. Now, the Dolan faction used the army and state prosecutors to keep after the Regulators, as per the president's order, despite the governor's proclamation.

The Kid decided to make his own peace. He wrote a note to Dolan's chieftain, Jesse Evans, saying that he and his boys wanted to take advantage of the governor's amnesty and come in.

The Kid, Jose Salazár, Tom O'Folliard and Charlie Bowdre rode into Lincoln after sundown. They stood behind a low adobe wall. Dolan, Evans, Edgar Waltz, Billy Matthews and Bill Campbell stood across the street.

"Bonney's impossible to treat with!" Jesse Evans yelled. "I say we kill 'im an' get it over with for good, here and now!"

William called back. "I don't care to open negotiations with a fight, but if you'll come at me three at a time I'll whip the whole damned bunch of you!"

Waltz played the diplomat and convinced everyone to sit down and talk. The two groups moved forward warily, holding rifles and shotguns, shook hands in the middle of the street, and moved into a cantina to negotiate and write down the terms of their peace. One of the provisions of the agreement stated that no member of either faction would testify against any other in court. No member of either faction was to shoot any member of the other, without

first giving notice that he had withdrawn from the agreement. Then they all went drinking together.

The Dolans adhered to the agreement for about two hours. On the way to get some canned oysters, the drunken Bonney-Dolan crowd ran into Houston Chapman, the lawyer for McSween's widow Susan.

Chapman had come to Lincoln to fight Dolan in the courts. He had been conducting town meetings, trying to drum up political support for Susan McSween against Dolan and The House. Dolan's man, Billy Campbell, pulled his gun, aimed at Chapman's feet and ordered him to dance. Chapman refused and spoke defiantly. Dolan drew and fired at Chapman's feet; the shot shocked Campbell. He flinched and shot Chapman in the chest. His gun was so close it set Chapman's coat and vest afire, and the badly burned, smoking corpse still lay in the street the next morning.

Billy and his crew took their first chance to excuse themselves and ride out. The faithless peace was over.

Governor Wallace traveled to Lincoln to personally investigate the killing of Chapman. Having finished Ben Hur, Wallace wanted badly to justify his policies to President Hayes, and to complete his mission to end the Lincoln County War for good.

William Bonney wrote a letter to Governor Wallace:

I have heard that you will give one thousand ($) for my body, which as I understand it, means alive as a witness. I know it is as a witness against those that murdered Mr. Chapman. If it was so I could appear at court, I could give the desired information, but I have indictments against me for things that happened in the late Lincoln County War and am afraid to give myself up because my enemies will kill me. The day Mr. Chapman was murdered I was in Lincoln at the request of good citizens to meet Mr. J.J. Dolan, to meet as a friend so as to be able to lay aside our arms and go to work. I was present when Mr. Chapman was murdered and know who did it, and if it were not for those indictments I would have made it clear before now. If it is in your power to annul those indictments, I hope you will do so as to give me a chance to explain. Please send me an answer telling me what you can do. You can send answer by bearer. I have no wish to fight any more, indeed I have not raised an

arm since your proclamation. As to my character, I refer to any of the citizens, for the majority of them are my friends and have been helping me all they could. I am called Kid Antrim, but Antrim is my stepfather's name. Waiting for an answer, I remain, Your obedient servant, W. H. Bonney.

Wallace responded:

Come to the house of old Squire Wilson (not the lawyer) at nine (9) o'clock next Monday night alone. I don't mean his office, but his residence. Follow along the foot of the mountains south of the town, come in on that side and knock at the east door. I have authority to exempt you from prosecution if you will testify to what you say you know. The object of the meeting at Squire Wilson's is to arrange the matter in a way to make your life safe. To do that the utmost secrecy is to be used. So come alone. Don't tell anybody—not a living soul—where you are going or the object. If you could trust Jesse Evans, you can trust me. Lew Wallace.

Governor Wallace sat at Squire Wilson's table. At nine o'clock William Bonney stepped through the door, his Winchester in his right hand, a Colt's Thunderer in his left.

Billy agreed to turn himself in and testify against Major Dudley and Dolan. Wallace gave his word he would pardon the Kid. Tom O'Folliard would surrender, testify and be pardoned as well.

William Bonney cautioned the governor to be sure of the men who would accept his surrender, as the Dolan faction would take any opportunity to kill the Kid. William said, "I am not afraid to die like a man, fighting, but I would not like to die like a dog, unarmed."

William and Tom were held on a loose house-arrest at the Ellis house in Lincoln and at Juan Patrón's house. They entertained visitors, played cards, whispered at the windows with señoritas and enjoyed nightly serenades by their Spanish-speaking friends.

Billy testified against Dolan and Dudley, but they were both acquitted. Then William waited for the governor's pardon, but he had been betrayed: he never heard from Wallace again. The district attorney, Rynerson, a Dolan-

Catron man, was preparing to try and hang the boy. One morning, at dawn, William slipped his hands out of his cuffs, walked over to Juan Patrón's trastero, opened it and removed his pistols and rifle. He told his guards he was leaving. They said nothing. The Kid nodded, and the guards handed over the key to Tom's handcuffs. The two of them, well armed, walked down the street, mounted up and rode out. Governor Wallace issued a proclamation offering a $500 reward for the Kid, dead or alive.

For the next two years, Billy and his amigos lived by their wits, rustling cattle and dancing, gambling, and courting the girls in the little plazuelas up and down the Pecos. They bedeviled posses, cavalry columns, and Seven Rivers vigilantes. When they were challenged or pursued, they fought.

In Bob Hargrove's saloon at Fort Sumner, Texan Joe Grant, drunk and belligerent and probably thinking of reward money, was on the edge of picking a fight with William all afternoon. At one point, William admired and examined Grant's pearl-handled pistol. When he turned to leave, Grant drew, aimed at the Kid's back and pulled his trigger. The hammer clicked down on the empty chamber that William had rotated into place against this very eventuality. The Kid drew as he whirled about, and put two bullets, one on top of the other, into Grant's chin and brainpan. He twirled his pistols, slipped them neatly back into their holsters, and laughed.

"Joe, I've been there too often for you."

16

TOM

Well, Tomás, there's only one fair way I know to settle this question.

In summer moonlight, Tom O'Folliard and William Bonney rode a hidden game-trail through shadows of the cottonwood bosque along the Pecos River until they drew near a shallow ford. The trail forked there, and the boys sat their horses at the crossroad.

"Bueno, Tomás, mi amigo. Aquí estamos otrá vez. Okay, Tom, my friend, here we are again."

Tom spoke Spanish even better than William did, and the friends often conversed in that language.

Tom had lived in Coahuila, Mexico, for the first seven years of his life. His parents died there, so Tom was an orphan, like William, and they were the same age. Like William, Tom had been a rustler. When he first came to New Mexico, from Uvalde, Texas, Tom made his living rustling Jimmy Dolan's rustled cattle. When Dolan's men figured him out, and intended to hang him, he naturally joined the McSween faction at the start of the Lincoln County War. But Tom and the Kid were also quite different.

People called Tom "Bigfoot Tom" or "Big Tom O'Folliard" because he was six feet, four inches tall. He towered over the diminutive Kid. But he wasn't really big, just tall: he was lanky as a rail.

Tom had been a very poor shot until he met William, who taught him how to shoot pretty well. Tom idolized William, first because of his reputation and marksmanship, then because of the courage he had displayed the night he led Tom out of the burning McSween house in the face of so many blazing guns. Once they'd cleared the killing floor and the Rio Bonito and reached safety, Tom, shaking with adrenaline, had passionately embraced William and declared, "¡Tu eres el mas macho, mi amigo! You are the most manly, my friend!"

But now, Tom's interests and William's conflicted.

"Sí, aquí estamos otra vez, hermano. ¿Para donde vamos? Yes, here we are again, brother," Tom said. "Which way do we go?"

The trail to the right would take the boys to Fort Sumner, where William sought love; the trail to the left, over the hills to a hidden valley and the little settlement called Escondido, where Tom's amor would be found. But they could not split up. Posses, cavalry, and bounty hunters were always a concern. It was the boys' custom for one to keep watch through the night, for law, while the other enjoyed the blissful pleasures of love.

William laughed, as he always did at the initiation of this, the friends' custom and ritual.

"Well, Tomás, there's only one fair way I know to settle this question."

Tom pulled one leg from his stirrup, crossed it over his saddle and sat waiting as William rummaged through the pocket of his frock coat for a deck of cards.

"What's that, mi amigo?" Tom asked as he always did.

"We cut."

Tom was always amazed at how expertly William could shuffle a deck of cards in his hands, even as he sat in his saddle. William extended his hand and the deck, offering Tom the cut.

Tom looked at the deck, hesitated and frowned. "Ayee, mi amigo. Can I ask you a question?"

"¿Como no? Of course."

"Why is it that when we cut cards, you win nine out of ten times? I ain't no numbers man, but I figure we should more less each win about half the time. You wouldn't cheat a friend out of a night with a pretty girl, no? Maybe we just ought'a flip a silver dollar."

William grinned; but he winced, too, with guilt. "No, Tom. We don't have to flip no silver dollar. I got a feeling you're gonna win tonight. Go ahead and cut, hermano."

Tom looked at William with some mistrust, but then reached out and lifted the top half of the deck. He turned it over and displayed the four of clubs. "Shit!"

"Damn, Tom. You don't make it easy, do you? I better shuffle again."

Tom started to object, then shrugged and remained silent, forlornly slumped in his saddle, one foreleg across the pommel. William reshuffled again and again, sitting his horse and grinning at Tom. When he finally cut, he drew the two of hearts, the lowest card in the deck.

"Vamonos para Escondido!" William laughed.

Tom laughed too.

William held the horses as the boys watched the Ortega house from concealment in a ponderosa stand at the edge of a freshly plowed field. When all the lights went out, Tom moved stealthily to Santina's window and knocked gently. William watched as she slipped out the window, embraced Tom and followed him, holding his hand, into the woods. William withdrew into the brush, selected a point from which he could watch the road, hobbled the horses, and sat smoking, Winchester at his side.

There was only a vague suggestion of light in the eastern sky when Tom returned.

"Goddamn it, Tomás! You been gone all night. I'm tired as hell."

"Sorry Billy, we fell asleep."

"Well, muchas gracias, amigo. I like to sleep too." Billy laughed wryly and shook his head. "Shit."

The boys guided their horses down a steep incline to the road and cut east, spurring their mounts to a trot.

"Billy, how'd you do that?"

"What?"

"With the cards."

William chuckled. "I'll tell you, amigo. It takes practice. If you ever get where you can settle down and sit still, I'll teach you."

"Billy?"

"What?"

"I aim to marry that girl."

"Shit."

"I got more bad news for you, amigo."

"What?"

"From now on, we're flipping silver dollars."

"I can do that too."

"No, Billy. We're flipping my silver dollars."

The boys rode, laughing, into the dawn and toward the crossroads.

Finally Pat Garrett, the hunter, was elected sheriff of Lincoln County. The governor, the Dolans, all the powerful ranchers, and the Santa Fe Ring supported him. His charge was to stop William and his amigos. And Percy's research showed that besides Garrett, the U.S. Cavalry, and the Seven Rivers posses, other forces were gathering against the Kid, Tom, and Charlie.

17

CHARLIE SIRINGO

I figure your life is worth a ci-gar.

Curious children trotted around the tall Texas cowboy, and businessmen, fine ladies, and common workmen and women all noticed him as he made his way from the train station through busy streets to the Pinkerton Detective Agency's Chicago offices.

Charles Angelo Siringo still wore his broad Stetson, chaparejos, and high-heeled boots. His Colt's .45 was holstered on his left hip in reverse-draw position. His Winchester was slung, barrel down, over his back.

He left his untanned, spotted, cowhide bag in the lobby and passed through the carved doors of William Pinkerton's office.

"Hello, Charlie, good to see you."

"I came as soon as I got your telegram, Mr. Pinkerton."

Pinkerton gestured and Siringo took a Windsor-backed seat before the black walnut desk.

"I've got your report on the Smith brothers' case here. It says you hired on as a cowhand at the Smith ranch, made love to the boys' sister and learned their whereabouts. You notified the authorities and the boys were arrested in Price, Utah."

"Yes, Sir. I've got the second report right here." Charlie removed a folded sheaf of papers from his vest pocket and pushed it across the desk toward Pinkerton. "My time sheets are there, too. I figured they'd get here faster on the train with me than by post. I hope you can endorse a draft for me right away, Sir. It's a lot of time. I spent two weeks in the calabozo with them Smith brothers."

"It's no problem, Charlie." Pinkerton looked at the papers before him. "Why don't you just tell me?"

"Yessir. Would you have any tobacco, sir?"

"Surely, Charlie. Please forgive my lack of hospitality."

Pinkerton took a cigar from his desk drawer and passed it. Charlie struck a match on his boot heel and puffed forcefully on the cigar. He savored the hot smoke, loosed a series of rings, and grinned as he continued.

"Well, sir, after I made love to that pretty, dark-eyed girl, she showed me a letter from her brothers, written and mailed in Price, Utah, after the hold-up, showing that they were in hiding in that neighborhood. In the letter they stated that they were soon to leave for a certain town in Arizona. I also saw photos of the Smith brothers and secured their descriptions. Then my heart grew cold for that pretty maiden and I 'hiked' back to join Sheriff Shores. He at once wired his brother-in-law, Roe Allison, who was his under-sheriff, to search for the Smiths around Price, Utah, as their letter had been mailed there.

"We then started for Denver, where we boarded a Denver & Rio Grande train for the line of Colorado and Utah to take up the trail. After retiring in the sleeper, Shores received a telegram from Roe Allison at Green River, saying that they had captured the Smith brothers and their accomplice, Rhodes, and would meet our train at Montrose with the prisoners. After dark the next evening our train arrived in Montrose ahead of the eastbound train carrying the prisoners. I consulted with Shores, and we decided the best plan was for him to put his handcuffs and leg-irons on me and pretend that I was a desperate character whom he had captured up the Gunnison River that day.

"When the train pulled into the depot, I was taken aboard and placed in a seat near the other prisoners. I acted sullen all the way to Gunnison, where we arrived around ten o'clock in the morning. The whole town of Gunnison turned out to see us desperate prisoners. We were marched with our leg-irons on through the streets to the Court House and jail, a distance of half a mile. The snow was over a foot deep and the sidewalks were lined with people, so that we had to walk in the street single-file. I brought up the rear and gave the spectators some hard, contemptuous glances. Sheriff Shores told me afterwards that several people said I was the toughest looking criminal in the bunch.

"All four of us were shoved into a steel cage just large enough for us to lie down. We were given a few greasy quilts and blankets and our meals were put into the cage. There were no other prisoners in the jail, and it was my wish

that we be kept in close confinement for a day or two, as confessions can be secured much easier in that way.

"Our cell was spattered with human blood, where a short time before a man had cut his own throat from ear to ear, in the presence of an officer who was unlocking the cell to take the fellow into court. After cutting his throat he laid the knife carefully on a shelf, shook his fist at the officer, and fell over, dead. Shores told us this story when we asked about the blood. We also learned that this cell had been the home of the man-eater, Alfred G. Packer, who had killed and eaten the choice parts of five men. He had been taken to the penitentiary for life a few years previous.

"My three bedfellows were a dirty lot, alive with vermin, as they had been in hiding on an island in Green River for several weeks. And one of the Smiths had a bullet wound through the head, which gave out an odor that put the finishing touch to the already foul air in the cell. He had received the wound in a fight among themselves; at least, that was their story.

"After a few days of solitary confinement I secured a full confession of how the train was held up, and they told me how they had remained in hiding on an island in Green River up to the time of their arrest.

"After two weeks in jail I was taken out, supposedly by an officer from Wyoming who was taking me back there to be executed for murder. I had confided in my companions, telling them of breaking out of jail in Wyoming after being sentenced to hang. The boys really shed tears when I shook hands with them prior to being handcuffed to the officer.

"I didn't have to appear as a witness against these men, as they confessed to the train hold-up after they were convinced that Shores had a 'cinch' case against them. They gave up the gold and bank notes and were each sentenced to a term of seven years in the Colorado penitentiary."

Pinkerton and Charlie both laughed.

"Well, Charlie. You sure can spin a yarn. Good work. How are your wife and daughter?"

"Just fine, sir," Charlie lied. His nineteen-year-old wife was dying of consumption.

"The reason I ask, Charlie, is because I've got a new assignment for you. It's going to be very dangerous and I want you to think carefully before accepting it. There are aspects of the assignment, however, which you may enjoy. It will require you to return to Texas. I do not want you to accept this assignment if you feel it might be too dangerous."

Siringo was angered at Pinkerton's suggestion that any assignment might be beyond his abilities, but he concealed his displeasure and casually blew smoke rings over Pinkerton's desk.

"What is it?"

"We've been retained by Mr. Charles Goodnight, President of the Texas Panhandle Cattlemen's Association. It appears they are having severe problems with rustlers. In particular, one William Bonney, the one they call 'Billy the Kid.' The cattlemen want it stopped. As you probably know, the Kid is already under indictment for killing lawmen, so it doesn't really matter how you stop him. I see you brought your Winchester. It is in good repair?"

"I'll take the train to Wichita and ride on down into Texas."

Charlie rode the remnants of the Chisolm trail into the Texas panhandle.

Damn fool hoe-men, he thought as he observed the barbed wire and tilled earth encroachments on the once sacred cattle trail. He had driven, and seen driven, thousands of cattle up that trail.

When a pack of dogs charged out, barking, from a nearby farmhouse, Charlie slipped the knot that held his Winchester across the hind-tree of his saddle, raised the weapon and shot the leader of the pack. The animal leapt, twisting and yelping in the air, then dropped and lay still. The others sniffed the corpse and sidled off.

Damn fool hoe-men, he thought.

At Tascosa, Charlie met with the leaders of the Panhandle Cattlemen's Association, Mr. Goodnight, Mr. Morris and Mr. Moore of the LX brand.

"Charlie," Goodnight said, "we want you to pick a few fightin' cowboys and ride ta New Mexico Territory. That little band 'a rustlers from down on Rio Bonito 'r sellin' our cattle to Coughlin in Tularosa. He sells 'em to the army on the Mescalero reservation."

"Well," Charlie replied, "you didn't mind much when the Kid was sellin' you horses outta New Mexico Territory."

"You got a problem, Charlie?" Goodnight asked. "Because when Mr. Pinkerton said we could count on you, and you bein' from here an' all, we were pleased. But we need to know, 'cause they say you were once friendly with the Kid."

"No, Mr. Goodnight, Sir. I got no problem. The Kid is good-natured. Yeah, I like 'im. I gave 'im a Havanna ci-gar and a meerschaum ci-gar holder one time. Right here in Tascosa. He gave me a book. A buncha nonsense about what a tough gunfighter he is. He signed it for me. But I've got no problem, Sir. Business is business. The Kid's a kid. He don't understand the country's changin'. He won't live long enough to ever know it. I'll take Big Foot Wallace, Jim East, Lee Hall and Cal Polk."

"That's the spirit, Charlie," Moore said. "I'm givin' you this expense money. Five hundred dollars. You'll take just one horse apiece. Corn is scarce this year. If ya need more horses ya can buy 'em in New Mexico. We already sent Frank Stewart ahead with some other tough hombres. You try to catch up to 'em. Try to find that sheriff, Garrett. He's huntin' the Kid too."

"The problem is, Charlie," Morris said, "they don't steal enough to make much of a difference. But it's the Kid's name. Every paper you look in, it's 'the Kid this' and 'the Kid that.' Now, as long as the Kid stays alive, laughin' at all of us, every other damn kid's gonna think he kin do the same thaing. After awhile, it does matter. We're businessmen. It's gotten expensive enough to where it's cheaper to pay Mr. Pinkerton an' you."

It was dark and snowing hard when Charlie Siringo and his heavily armed crew rode into the little village of Anton Chico, New Mexico Territory. Stewart and his men were there and they were expecting Garrett and his posse. Wallace and the others billeted with Stewart in a low-roofed, dirt-floor adobe while Charlie Siringo rode north to Las Vegas, leading two mules, to purchase grub, corn for the horses, and extra ammunition.

He entered the hall of Vicente Silva on the Las Vegas plaza. The hammered-tin ceilings were high and the room was well lit. He had a few drinks of powerful aguardiente, then sat against the wall, feeling a warm glow and admiring the beautiful young women who danced with the clientele to guitars and violins. After awhile, he chose a girl and took her upstairs. When he returned, Charlie stepped up to a black jack table and placed a bet.

Charlie played a few hands and held his own. Then the dealer clapped his hands, held them up, open, to show he held no cards or money, and stepped aside. William Bonney took the dealer's place. The Kid still had snow on his sombrero and he pushed it back to hang behind him.

The Kid shuffled the cards and grinned at Charlie.

"Hello Charlie, I hear you're lookin' for me." The Kid grinned bigger. "Here I am!" He laughed.

All the black jack players stood and backed away from the table, leaving Charlie alone to meet his fate.

The Kid nodded to Vicente Silva, who stood off to the side, leaning on his bar, watching the confrontation. Silva walked over, bringing the Kid two bottles of aguardiente. Silva sneered at Charlie, walked back to his place, and looked on with grim amusement.

The Kid reached out and filled Charlie's glass to the brim. "Drink up," he said.

Charlie took a sip.

"Drink it all," the Kid said, and there was no hint of laughter in his voice.

Charlie drained the glass and the Kid filled it again.

"Now drink that."

Charlie drank it all and coughed. "Now look, Billy, you been rustlin' cattle in Texas and my people are tired of it."

Billy was pleased to see that Charlie would show some backbone.

"Rustlin' cattle? Rustlin' cattle?"

The Kid laughed so hard he looked like he was about to fall over, and Charlie looked for a chance—but he could see the Kid was keeping an eye on his gun hand the whole time. The Kid finally calmed down and said, smiling, "If you're lookin' for rustlers you should go on down the Pecos and shoot John Chisum. Then ride back to Texas and arrest Mr. Goodnight. Now they're cattle kings. But everybody knows them two branded untended Texas range cattle while the owners were fightin' or dead in the war."

The Kid was still grinning and sighing from his laughter as he said, "Now place your bet."

Charlie put two dollars on the table.

"More," said the Kid.

Charlie laid down twenty dollars.

"That will do," the Kid laughed, and dealt the cards. Before he turned over his hole card, he said, "You know, Charlie, you should probably set your hog-leg on the table, so we can relax."

Charlie's head was spinning and he stared at the Kid. Why would the Kid invite me to draw my pistol? he asked himself.

Both the Kid's hands were visible, holding the deck, but his grin looked as challenging and deadly as the snarl of a keen hound-dog below a treed mountain lion. Charlie wondered if the Kid had men behind him, ready to shoot him down.

The Kid leveled his gaze, looked into Charlie's eyes and chuckled.

"Put it on the table."

"I'm gonna do it real slow, Kid."

Charlie took his Colt's below the handle, raised it slowly and carefully, and placed it on the table before him.

Billy took the weapon and placed it to his own right, well out of Charlie's reach.

"Looks like you lose," Billy laughed. He turned his hole card over and took Charlie's bet. He filled Charlie's glass again.

"Now drink that," he said. "Now place your bet. Fifty would be good if you expect to get your money back." The Kid was laughing again.

Charlie tried hard to focus as they played, hand after hand, but Billy made him drink until he was sick. The place had quieted down and night had yielded to the gray light that shone through the front windows when Charlie said, "I got no more money, Billy."

"I believe you, Charlie," Billy laughed.

Charlie was so drunk he feared he would vomit on the table. He wasn't sure he could make it to the door even if Billy didn't shoot him, trying.

"Good morning!" Billy laughed harder. "Now Charlie, you gave me a ci-gar once. My mother told me that a good man never forgets a kindness. I don't know what they're payin' you but I figure your life is worth a ci-gar. Now we're even. I don't want to see you on the road. ¿Comprende?"

"Sí, comprendo," Charlie said.

The Kid walked out.

"We're leaving at dawn. How many of you are comin' with me?" Garrett asked.

Charlie Siringo had arrived at Anton Chico the night before, without supplies or money, and he sat in the corner by the fire in the little bare adobe room.

"You can take East, Hall and Polk," Siringo said. "I'm takin' Wallace an' ridin' down to White Oaks to look for LX Brand cattle."

Rosario drove on, blissfully absorbed, but the road was so bad that the Hupmobile could only make about twenty-five miles an hour. After two hours, Percy asked her to stop. He stepped down and walked over to relieve himself behind a scraggly juniper tree. He drew his penis from his trousers and unloaded a strong urine stream onto some moss-covered rocks. The gurgling sound of Percy's piss hitting the ground seemed to grow louder, then split into two distinct sounds: one of falling water, the other the chilling, dry, rasping death-warning of a diamondback's rattle.

The perfectly camouflaged, coiled, gray-brown snake had been sunning herself there in the mild November morning until the piss stream ran down along the ground and disturbed her. Percy, looking down at his penis in his hand, saw the reptile's head rise up and cock back, three feet away, ready to strike. A white stripe graced her jaw-line, mimicking a macabre grin. Percy felt a sickening weakness in his bowels. He had no idea the snake couldn't strike from that distance. He cried out, pinched off his piss-stream with his hand and flexed his quadriceps so that he flew backward and hit the ground on his backside. A fountain of urine arced into the air and fell, soiling Percy's trousers. He rolled over and scurried away on all fours, looking back as the serpent slithered off and disappeared in the prairie-grass. He scrambled to his feet and back toward the Hupmobile, stuffing his penis into his pants as Doña Flora and Rosario laughed uncontrollably.

Rosario suddenly cut the wheels hard and floored the accelerator, pushing the Hupmobile onto a railroad track and across a bridge over the Pecos. The wheels bounced violently over the rail-ties.

Percy dropped his papers and recoiled, and his face turned even whiter then it had already been, as he looked down at the foamy rushing water below and at the oncoming train ahead.

"Faster, Rosario!"

They barely made the far bank. Rosario jerked the car off the tracks and sped down the embankment as the train rushed by. She and Doña Flora seemed unconcerned but Percy, shaking from head to foot, shouted, "Stop, Rosario! Let me drive."

"We are here now, Señor Percy! Only one mile more!"

She accelerated back, south now, down a slight incline, then braked, and Percy looked up a gentle rise toward the unmistakable, crumbling, ruined adobe walls of once-powerful Fort Sumner.

Rosario and Áyax lept from the car, and Rosario ran, laughing, up the hill. Percy followed, holding Doña Flora's arm. They were only halfway to the ruins when Doña Flora stopped.

"Este es el campo santo. This is the graveyard."

"Where?"

"Aquí. Here." And Doña Flora extended her arm and moved her hand in an arc that seemed to encompass the whole horizon and half the world.

"But where is the Kid buried?"

"Aquí está la tumba. Here is the grave." Doña Flora pointed down at her feet.

"Are you sure?"

"Sí. Yo recuerdo muy bién. Yo estába aquí ese mañana cuando le enteráran. I remember well. I was here that morning when they buried him."

Percy stood for a moment and looked around at the empty place. He looked up at the old ruins, back at Doña Flora, and down again at the bare earth between them. Percy stood in silence, then heard the slight stirring of a gentle breeze and the distant laughter of Rosario, who was cavorting with Áyax, picking flowers, and chasing rabbits on the plain above.

This place was once filled with life, Percy thought. People lived here. They made love, bore children, dined, danced, sang songs, gambled, battled their enemies, and wept as they buried their dead. For a moment, he thought he could almost see people carrying the Kid's coffin down from the ruins.

Ghosts, he thought.

Then real movement caught his attention. He turned to see a rider followed by two men on a mule-drawn spring-wagon coming across the plain.

The men stopped fifty yards away and Percy walked over to meet them. The rider was Anglo, older than Doña Flora, and the men on the wagon looked Mexican.

"Abájalo aquí. Put it down here," said the Anglo, as he swung down from his horse and turned to meet Percy.

"Howdy. I'm Charlie, Charlie Siringo."

"Percival Chesterfield. New York Daily Herald."

They shook hands.

"New York City? What brings you way out here, Mr. Chesterfield?"

"You're Charlie Siringo?"

"Yessir. That's what they call me."

Percival removed a notepad and a pen from the inner breast pocket of his tweed jacket. The Hispanic men wrestled a massive granite tombstone toward the back of the wagon and Percy asked, "Mr. Siringo, did you really know Pat Garrett and William Bonney?"

Siringo frowned and glanced briefly at Percy as he rolled a cigarette. "Yeah. I knew 'em both. That's why I'm here. You a writer?"

"I'm a reporter."

"I used to write some. But you seem to be huntin' pretty old news out here."

Now Percy frowned. "That is very true, Mr. Siringo. I guess it's not news at all. I'm not sure exactly what it is. I read your books. You once hunted William Bonney. What was he like?"

Siringo's eyes betrayed sadness. Maybe shame. "Well. That was a long time ago. About the best I can tell you is that the Kid was a boy who used to laugh a lot. Garrett was a man. He used to drink a lot."

Percy jotted notes on his pad. "Mr. Siringo, now that I've come to this

place where the Kid spent so much time, I'm wondering why he came back here. He lived here more than anywhere. Didn't he know they would look for him here?"

"I expect he did."

"Then why did he come back?"

"Well, son, I got a pretty good idea. But when you figure 'propriety' and 'gossip' and all, I guess it ain't for me to say. There is only one person who has a right to say, if she will."

"Who?"

"Paulina Maxwell. Now her name is Paulina Jaramillo and she lives just a few miles up the road in the new town of Fort Sumner. If you want to know, drive up there and ask her. I got no right to say more."

"Pat Garrett caught up with Billy the Kid before you did."

Siringo looked up for quite a while at the old fort. Then he said, "Well. That ain't exactly true. I caught up with the Kid before Garrett did."

"What happened?"

"We played cards," Siringo said mildly. "Then Billy decided to let me live on. I guess I owe him for that. It's been a long time comin', but we took up a collection in Santa Fe. The Kid's buried right around here somewhere."

The workers used ropes to lower the tombstone onto the ground. Percy looked at the carved inscription. It bore the names of Charlie Bowdre, Tom O'Folliard and William Bonney. At the top it said: "PALS."

Percy, Doña Flora, Rosario and Áyax pulled up before a brick and mortar, pitch-roofed house in the new town of Fort Sumner. Percy thought the structure rather modest considering the great wealth Paulina Maxwell's family had once enjoyed. Paulina stood on the porch, watching and waiting, as if she had expected the visitors.

Percy and Rosario stepped down from the Hupmobile.

Doña Flora remained in the cab, and Paulina and Doña Flora greeted each other from a distance.

"Flora," said Paulina.

"Paulina," Flora replied.

Percy noted that the greetings were rather cold and neither of the women prefaced the greetings with "Señora" or "Doña" which would have been more respectful.

Áyax slept on the porch and Paulina, Percy, and Rosario sipped coffee at Paulina's table.

"Billy was a good boy but he was hounded by men who wanted to kill him because they feared him."

Percy didn't know how to ask his most burning question, so he attempted to approach it obliquely.

"Mrs. Jaramillo," he said, "I have heard that William Bonney was what they call a 'ladies' man.'"

"Billy the Kid, I may tell you, fascinated many women. In every placeta in the Pecos, some little señorita was proud to be known as his querida. He was always smiling and good natured and very polite and danced remarkably well, and all the little Mexican beauties made eyes at him from behind their fans and used all their coquetries to capture him and were very vain of his attentions."

"But Mrs. Jaramillo. Please forgive me. Were you Billy's amor?"

Paulina's eyes seemed to look far away, perhaps into the past, and she smiled and focused her gaze back on Señor Percy. "I? No, Mr. Chesterfield," she said enigmatically. "I know who she was though. But she was not I."

"¿Porque estás tan triste, Señor Percy? Why are you so sad?" Rosario asked, as Percy frowned and sullenly guided the Hupmobile south toward Lincoln.

"Because, Rosario, Mr. Siringo made me think Paulina and Billy were lovers. But she denied it. Now I have no idea why he returned to Fort Sumner when he could have fled the New Mexico Territory and lived."

"She's a lying bitch," Doña Flora said.

Percy was shocked. He had no idea Doña Flora spoke English and he would never have expected such a bitter and profane exclamation from the reserved matriarch.

"She denied her amor for fear of her brother, then for fear of her jealous husband. Now, Jaramillo is dead and she still denies Bee-lee because she is vain

and fickle and she fears the gossip of the idle. She will carry her lies to her grave."

Rosario looked with great amusement at Doña Flora and Percy, then tilted her head back, raised her chin and smiled ecstatically as her beautiful hair streamed behind her in the New Mexico wind.

18

HUNTED AND CONDEMNED

The sun set, casting a blood red onto the snow and clouded winter sky until the blood was lost in darkness.

Now, as Billy rode for Fort Sumner, in May 1881, with Jesse, Croft and Patricio, he remembered and missed his best pals, Charlie Bowdre and Tom O'Folliard. He remembered what Charlie had told him about his meeting with Pat Garrett and the sad truth of Garrett's words.

Bowdre had met Garrett in December of 1880, on the snow-covered road between the low pine-brush dotted foothills and the grass and sage plain that descended to the Pecos valley. Soft snowflakes drifted down and the men shivered in their saddles.

"You got men followin', Patty?"

"No, Charlie. I sent word I'd come alone, and you should well know I'm a man of my word. I've come in good faith under my guarantee. But it's cold and it's been a long ride. Now what'd ya want?"

"I want to come in, Patty. I want to live in peace with my wife. Manuela's a good, beautiful woman."

"Charlie, I'm gettin' real tired a' this. It's gettin' old. I've told you and the governor's said it as well. You can come in. But you've got to quit O'Folliard and Bonney. They're dead. Sure as if they're already in the ground. There's nothin' more you can do for 'em."

"They're like brothers to me, Patty. You know some a' the shit we been through together. I won't ride with 'em no more. But if they come to my place, there's no way I can swear I won't give 'em a roof or somethin' to eat."

Garrett's eyes were stern, sad, and grim.

"I'm real sorry to hear that, Charlie. But I guess I understand. And it's too bad. You know what I'm gonna do though, and I'm tellin' you, honest. I'm

gonna keep comin'. I'm gonna sleep on your trail. Rain or snow, I don't care. And I'm gonna have to kill you."

Bowdre scanned the horizon, looked back at Garrett and nodded several times.

"Yeah, I guess I see that, Patty."

"Here." Garrett leaned forward on his saddle and handed Charlie a Mexican-silver flask: good whiskey against the cold.

"Damn! That's good, Patty!"

"Yes it is, Charlie. It's sweet. Like life."

"Thank you, Patty…and…goodbye…hasta la vista."

"Hasta la vista."

"What'd'e say, Charlie?" Billy asked.

"It's no good, Billy. I can't go back."

"That's bullshit! But don't worry about it, amigo."

Billy was cleaning his Thunderers. He raised one, spun the clean chamber and flipped it back under the barrel. He laughed. "I guess we need another new sheriff!"

O'Folliard and Billy both laughed.

"I'm not worried," Charlie said. "I was just…wishin'…things could be different."

Now the little band of rustlers was down to four: Billy, Tom, Charlie, and Dave Rudebaugh. True to his word, Garrett and his men doggedly stalked the outlaws through sleet and snow and they slept on the outlaws' trail. Garrett finally outguessed his prey, and on the night of December 19, 1880, he stood tall and implacable on the portál of the old Indian hospital at Fort Sumner. Charlie Bowdre's wife Manuela was inside, bound and gagged, and Garrett's posse was ready and aiming all around him as the outlaws rode in through deep, moonlit snow.

Pat Garrett waited until he was sure he recognized the men, then he gave the signal and the lawmen opened fire.

Billy, Tom, Charlie and Dave drew and fired shot after shot. The posse men ducked under cover; the outlaws cut away on their mounts and high-tailed it out, still firing back, keeping the posse-men down. But Tom O'Folliard reined up after only a quarter-mile, and walked his horse back to the fort.

"Drop yer guns!" Garrett shouted.

"I can't," Tom said. "You've killed me."

Lawmen walked up and caught him as he sagged and dropped from his saddle. They carried him into the old adobe room where they were encamped and laid him on the floor. Then they played poker and waited for Tom O'Folliard to die.

Tom moaned and kicked. "God damn you, Garrett!"

"I wouldn't talk like that, Tom, you're about to meet God Himself." Garrett threw down his hand and it was straight, and his men groaned.

"Go to hell, you long-legged son of a bitch."

"Shut up and take yer medicine, boy," Barney Mason said.

Tom managed one last quip: "Oh, yeah. It's the best medicine I've ever taken." Then he was gone.

Next morning, Garrett paid Jesus Silva to build a coffin and dig Tom's grave.

Bonney, Bowdre and Rudebaugh rode through the night. Dave knew his horse was hit, but he gave her his espulinas and without mercy, and the mare served on until she dropped into the snow at dawn after twenty-five miles. Billy and Dave doubled up and the men rode on. Two days later they ate at Wayne Brazil's ranch, warmed up a little, picked up fresh horses and rode out.

They got to the abandoned rock house at Stinking Springs as the sun set, casting a blood-red onto the snow and clouded winter sky until the blood was lost in darkness. That's how William always remembered his last night with Charlie Bowdre.

Garrett and his men shivered in the snow and they were waiting at dawn when Charlie stepped through the door, carrying a bag of oats for the horses. Bullets ripped into his stomach and chest, and he reeled back inside.

"They killed you, Charlie!" William said. "You can still get revenge. Go back out there and take a few of 'em!"

Charlie, dazed and in shock, staggered back out and wobbled toward Garrett. Pat stepped up and caught him as he fell.

"I wish…I wish…" and Charlie Bowdre spoke no more.

The posse shot Charlie's horse and it fell, blocking the stone doorway. William had brought his horse inside the rock house for the night and he wanted to ride, shooting, through the door and take his chances, but now he knew she would not approach the blood scent of Charlie's dead gelding. After a few hours, Bonney and Rudebaugh grew hungry. They could smell bacon being cooked by Garrett's posse. Garrett promised Bonney and Rudebaugh they would not be lynched, and they surrendered.

Lawmen and prisoners rode to Fort Sumner. They laid Charlie's body on the plank portál. Manuela wailed, then sprang like a tigress on Garrett and pummeled him until his men pulled her off. Dave and Billy were chained together, but Paulina Maxwell held and kissed Billy and they all ate dinner together on December 24, 1880.

Garrett led his men and their prisoners first to Anton Chico, then on to the jail in Las Vegas, where an angry mob gathered. Rudebaugh had killed jailer Lino Valdez the previous April, trying to break out a friend. Leaders of the mob demanded that he and Bonney be given up to hempen justice. But Garrett and his men faced them down, and got the prisoners onto the train to Santa Fe.

At Santa Fe, Billy was held alone, chained to the floor, for three months. He wrote letters to Governor Wallace at the Palace of the Governors on the plaza, three blocks away. "I have done everything I promised," he wrote. "You have done nothing you promised." But Wallace was touring the east coast, signing copies of Ben Hur, and he either did not receive or ignored the Kid's letters. Wallace was no longer interested in New Mexico. He was expecting an appointment as ambassador to Turkey.

Garrett took the Kid down the Rio Grande Valley to La Mesilla. A lawyer was quickly appointed and Billy was tried for the murder of Sheriff William Brady. The trial lasted two days. Jimmy Dolan and others testified that they had seen the Kid run out and take Brady's rifle and horse as Brady lay dying in the street.

William Bonney testified in his own defense. He admitted he had been with the Regulators the day they killed William Brady and Deputy

George Hindman. But he claimed he had not shot at Sheriff Brady. He made the unlikely and transparent claim that he only shot at deputy Billy Mathews. William claimed he had a special grudge against Mathews.

On cross-examination William could not explain how he could have missed Mathews at short range with plenty of time to aim. He could not explain how Mathews escaped unwounded while Sheriff Brady was hit by more balls than there were Regulators.

It didn't matter, anyway. The judge instructed the jury that the Kid was guilty of murder if he had participated and acted in concert with others.

William was quiet and hopeless, yet defiant. A reporter from the Santa Fe New Mexican wrote, "He has no friends here."

The Kid read the article and thought, "All my friends are dead."

On April 13, 1881, Judge Bristol ordered William Bonney to stand and asked if he had anything to say. William reflected on the irony of the fact that, of all the killers in the Lincoln County War, he would be the only one to hang. "At least two hundred men have been killed in Lincoln County in the past three years, but I did not kill all of them."

Judge Bristol ordered that William Bonney be confined at Lincoln "... until May 13, and on that day between the hours of nine and three the said William Bonney, alias Kid, alias William Antrim, be hanged by the neck until his body be dead." Judge Bristol looked down from his high bench at the upstart, William Bonney, and repeated triumphantly: "Dead, dead, dead."

William laughed. "You can go to hell, hell, hell."

Two days later, a reporter interviewed the Kid, who said, "Advise persons never to engage in killing."

Deputy Marshal Robert Olinger thought himself a gunfighter and a tough hombre. He had killed two men by ambush. And he was a huge man, nearly as tall as Garrett and much heavier. Many of Olinger's friends called him "Big Indian." But Garrett called Bob "my killer deputy."

Olinger was among the party that brought Billy from La Mesilla to Lincoln for execution. He had a mean streak. He despised the Kid, jealous of the boy's reputation as a real gun fighter, and Bob stayed on at Lincoln to help

guard Billy and to see him hang. He relished the thought of hanging the Kid and he enjoyed taunting the boy.

Murphy was dead of natural causes, a rare thing in New Mexico, and Jimmy Dolan now owned and operated Tunstall's store. The county had bought The House and put it to use as a courthouse and jail.

The county had not yet installed barred cells, so Garrett held William in a room on the second floor and his shackles were attached by a padlock to a six-foot chain tether. The door to William's room was kept open and Garrett, Olinger or J.W. Bell sat in the hallway outside the doorway and watched William constantly. Several other prisoners were allowed to roam freely through the hall, and through a big room next to William's. Others sat, chained to steel bolts on the floor, in a room across the hall, and they watched Billy through the open door. Sometimes Garrett or J.W. Bell played cards with William at a little table in his room. William had escaped from jails in Silver City, Fort Grant, Lincoln, Fort Stanton and Albuquerque, and he knew he would hang if he didn't do it again.

Bob Olinger returned with William from the privy. William, in leg irons, hobbled to his chair at his little table. Olinger stepped back and leaned his shotgun against the wall. "This is your chance, boy. I ain't holdin' no shotgun now. Would you rather sit still and hang, or die tryin' to live?"

The prisoners all about looked up alertly and watched with anticipation.

Billy knew that Bob, who fancied himself a gunfighter, would love a reputation as the man who killed the Kid, trying to escape. Billy grinned, thinking of the lurid and false tales Bob would tell. Still…it was tempting.

"I'd rather live the rest of today, Bobby," said Billy, coolly concealing his temptation. He knew Olinger hated to be called "Bobby."

Now Bob really wanted to hurt the boy. "Well, if you're too much of a coward to even try, then I'll just watch you hang."

"Oh, I don't know, Bobby. You know what they say. There's many a slip 'twixt the cup and the lip!" Billy laughed.

Bob reached down and took up his shotgun. "The cup's gettin' pretty damn close to the lip. But have it your way, chickenshit."

"I will," Billy said. "Thank you, Bobby." The Kid smiled innocently.

Olinger fumed. The Kid was winning the conversation, but Olinger held an ace in the hole.

"You know, we're not gonna drop you off a trap. Garrett's goin' tomorrow to order special lumber for a new kinda hangin' machine."

All the prisoners were staring. Wary, Billy tried to hide his concern, but his curiosity was too much. "Whad'ya mean, Bobby?"

"They got a new way a' hangin'. Garrett read about it in that there magazine, Scientific American."

Billy wanted to stay cool. He wanted to maintain his feigned air of confident indifference, but he could not. "How can there be a new way a hangin'?"

Olinger nodded, smiled, and took his time, savoring the boy's anxiety, before he answered, "Just think about it. It's real simple. If we don't drop you, how else can we do it?"

Billy looked at his wrists and hands, chained and resting on the little table before him. He knotted his brow and frowned. "There's only one way to hang. Same for everybody."

"Well, I guess you're no scientist, then, boy." Olinger let a few seconds pass, and smirked at William's dumbfounded and urgent look of curiosity. "What we're gonna do is tie the rope to a real heavy weight. We're gonna spring a lever and drop the weight. Now, I've been thinkin' and talkin' a lot with Garrett about this. It's pretty damn interestin'. 'Cause you see, if we leave too much slack in the rope it'll jerk your head right off. But if we don't leave enough slack it'll just pull you up and you'll twist and kick for a long time. A real long time. But if we do it just right…we'll jerk you to Jesus!" Olinger laughed hard. "Jerk you to Jesus!"

Olinger laughed so hard he had to wipe a tear from his eye. He composed himself with a deep, almost musical sigh. "We know what can go wrong 'cause they already tried it a couple a times in Arizona Territory. They ain't got it right yet. I guess you could say we're gonna do a sorta scientific experiment with your neck! So I'd just like to know. Do you want us to use a lotta slack or none at all? How much slack? Just tell us, and we'll measure it out any way you say."

Now Olinger wasn't laughing. He looked calmly at the Kid and said,

coldly, "It's the least we can do." He glanced around at the other prisoners, who were all staring in expressionless horror. "Maybe you shoulda tried ta take me, chickenshit." Olinger cocked his shotgun and pointed it at William's throat, as he knelt and clicked the padlock shut on William's shackles, chaining him to the floor.

William stared at his chained wrists on the table before him. If they ripped his head off, he thought, his body would collapse on the platform and his head would probably fall out of the noose and land on his body. It might roll some. Blood would pour out of his neck-stump. There would be a lot of it.

How much slack? he wondered.

"Ahh Bee-lee, it makes me so sad to see you in this trouble. I would do anything I could to help you."

"I know you would, Juan." The Kid smiled sweetly. There was a tear in his eye. "Maybe there's one last favor you can do me. Remember those two chicas we spent time with that time at Seven Rivers?"

Juan thought. They had never spent time with two girls at Seven Rivers. "What?"

"You remember. Those two we held and caressed down by the Pecos."

Juan remembered when the two of them had practiced shooting by the Pecos, and he understood what William was talking about. William's "girls" were Colt's Thunderers.

"Oh, yes!" Juan said, lustfully. "Of course I remember! How could I ever forget?"

"I'd just like to see either one of them two girls one more time before it's too late. But the only time I ever get out of here is to shit. I guess it wouldn't be too romantic to see a girl in the shitter!"

The boys both laughed at the Kid's vulgar joke.

"'Course Garrett would never allow such a thing, but he's leavin' town on Thursday to pick up the beams for my gallows. They're all cut and ready. Very considerate of him," the Kid chuckled.

Juan sat still and thought how to speak clearly, yet in code. "You know the fat one, Dolores? Sorrows? You know…the one that made so much noise when you banged her? She might be able to come see you Thursday. Or

Wednesday night. But if you saw her in the privy…she might grab your ass!"

The Kid understood Juan would find a way to fasten a gun under the rim of the seat in the outhouse.

"You promise me you'll ask her, Juan? It's my last chance."

"Don't worry amigo. Te doy mi palabra. I give my word."

Billy was hoping, hard, and he even prayed, that Juan would come through and leave a loaded gun in the privy. But he couldn't be sure, and he found his own chance before he got his evening turn in the privy that day.

Garrett had ridden to Blazer's Mill to pick up the lumber for Billy's gallows. Olinger took all the prisoners except Billy to eat supper at Wortley's Hotel, across the street and a few doors down.

Billy was alone with J.W. (James) Bell. The amiable ex-Texas Ranger was both overconfident and kind to Billy. After all, at Santa Fe, Garrett had ordered special leg and hand shackles, weighing fifteen pounds, made and welded onto the Kid.

Bell sat in Billy's cell and played cards with the boy. Billy was an excellent card player, but he acted as if his manacles hampered him. He casually tossed a card onto the edge of the table, where it teetered, then fell to the floor between him and Bell. When Bell bent forward and down to pick it up, Billy hit J.W. as hard as he could with both hands and heavy steel chains.

Bell fell, stunned and nearly unconscious. Billy dropped to his knees, stretched to the end of his chain, and hammered his fists and chains down hard again, bouncing Bell's head off the floor. He grabbed Bell's shirt at the collar and shoulders and dragged Bell's body forward until he could reach Bell's keys and gun.

He turned the key and the padlock that bound him to the floor snapped open. He hobbled in his leg shackles toward the armory door by the top of the stairs. Bell, coming to, struggled to his feet and staggered toward Billy.

Billy turned and covered Bell with cocked .44.

"Settle down, J.W."

Bell was even clearer now, and he stepped sideways past Bonney and rushed to the stairs.

"Hold up, J.W!" Billy ordered, and he shuffled after Bell.

Bell cut around the corner and leapt down the stairway. Billy liked Bell, but he couldn't let him go. Billy cleared the corner and fired a hasty shot that ricocheted down the wall after Bell. Bell took the stairs in three bounds and, as he reached the bottom landing, Billy aimed better and fired again at the middle of Bell's back.

The bullet that killed Bell and blackening globules of lung blood blasted from Bell's chest, and splattered the wall at the base of the stairwell. Bell hit the wall, cut left and ran a few more steps, as killed deer often do, out the back door and into the yard. There he collapsed and died in the arms of Godfrey Gauss, who had just walked out of his house behind the jail. Gauss lowered Bell to the ground and ran for the street.

Billy hit the armory door with his shoulder and all his weight. He selected a double-barreled shotgun, broke it open, loaded it and stuffed shells into his pocket. He shambled and hopped as fast as he could back to the window overlooking the street where he knew Bob Olinger must come.

Billy saw him, way up the street.

Olinger had been walking out of Wortley's with his prisoners when he heard the shots. He left them standing in the street and jogged toward the jail, Colt's .45 in hand. Gauss stepped through the gate at the corner of the courthouse. Bob stopped and Gauss excitedly told him that the Kid had killed James Bell. Olinger looked up at the window of Billy's cell. Gauss did too. There was the Kid, looking down double barrels.

In view of what he must now do, Billy decided not to say "Bobby."

"Hello, Bob."

Bob tried to swing his pistol up into action, and Gauss jumped back.

Olinger flew backward off his feet when the double load of shot slammed into his chest and shoulders. His back hit the ground, hard, his feet flew up and one boot flipped free through the air and landed, upright, in the street behind his sprawled body and from the red-hot shot, burnt shirt, and mass of blood that had been Olinger's chest, a wisp of steam rose into the cool, April evening New Mexico air, and it dispersed there as quickly as did the breath of God, which now, forever, departed the still clay that had been Garrett's "killer deputy," Robert A. Olinger.

Gauss was terrified. He turned to run.

"Hold up, Gauss!"

Gauss froze.

"I wouldn't hurt you!"

William looked at the few bold spectators who were already moving cautiously forward, staring at the body, looking up at Billy.

"But you can tell everybody," and William scanned the crowd, sternly, "I hold the courthouse and I hold this town! Now, go get me one of Judge Leonard's horses. He's my friend and he won't mind lendin' one. And get me an axe or somethin'. The sooner I get outta these chains the sooner I'll clear out."

William walked around and stepped out onto the balcony where he could watch the street. He tried not to show it, but he was shaking with stress, relief, adrenaline, remorse, exaltation and fear. Would Garrett ride in? Would some friends of Dolan try it? Billy wanted badly to get on a horse and get out of Lincoln.

Gauss threw a pickaxe up to William. The Kid only took time, and it took an excruciatingly nervous half-hour, to break one link of the chain that held his ankles, and the sun set as he cut strips from a blanket and tied the chains to his belt.

Gauss saddled and brought a skittish, hammerhead pony that belonged to Billy Burt.

"Take 'er 'round back."

William Bonney re-entered the courthouse and, trembling and manacled as he was, managed to strap on a holstered Colt's .44, two cartridge belts and spurs. He stuck another revolver in his belt, stuffed saddlebags with two more pistols and ammunition and slung them over his shoulder. He fixed a Winchester under the cartridge belts at his back. He checked the street from a window and then, shotgun raised, walked out the back door.

Gauss and a few men and women, whom Bonney recognized as friends, stood under the stars watching him, and looking at Bell, bloody on the ground.

"I'm sorry I had to kill but I couldn't help it," William said ruefully. "Tell Bill Burt I'll send his horse back in a day or so."

William tried to mount the pony, but his rattling chains caused the animal to skip back and he fell to the ground. He sprang to his feet, covering the crowd with his shotgun, then managed to swing up onto the saddle. William

walked the animal calmly around the building, chains and shotgun across his pommel. He didn't have time, and didn't recognize everyone who stood there, so he glared a menacing warning at the lot, looked down at Olinger, and said, "You won't round me up again, Bob."

The Kid felt unbounded elation boiling up in his heart. He wanted to burst, hightail it, fly and sprint away, shouting with joy. But William had always possessed an ability to remain clear, calculating, and effective in hot action, even when his lethal acts were motivated by anger, passion or desperation. He didn't want to encourage pursuit by looking scared. So he affected a cool, calm air, tossed the shotgun onto the ground and nudged his pony to an easy, deliberate trot with a gentle touch of his rowels. People watching at the edge of town heard William laughing quietly as he cut across the Rio Bonito and rode to freedom.

True to William Bonney's promise, Bill Burt's horse walked back into Lincoln five days later and words of the boy's honor were spoken and whispered in Spanish, even by those who opposed him, throughout the county. But William's Irish and Anglo enemies on the ranges and in the halls of power in Santa Fe and Washington had no such impractical regard or admiration for his dash, and they invoked, swore and affirmed English curses, oaths of vengeance and pledges of merciless retribution.

William rode east onto John Chisum's range. It was there that he stole Bala from one of Chisum's cow camps. The Kid was amazed and greatly pleased at the power and strength of the half-broke, elemental stallion of nearly sixteen hands, and he was glad to have taken Bala from Chisum's people because, though he had claimed to support McSween and the Regulators, Chisum had never pitched in when the fight got hot.

Near Fort Sumner, William met his old friend and former Tunstall-McSween fighter, Patricio Montoya. Patricio was wanted, too, and they rode together. They rustled and sold cattle; then rode north to one of William's old hideouts, a cave near Los Portáles. Jesse Evans, Jim Croft and Maríano Ledoux sought shelter there too. Evans had escaped from Huntsville prison in Texas, where he had been serving a twenty-year term for killing Ranger George Bingham in a running fight and general shootout. Ledoux and Croft were both wanted for robbery and murder. All three had ridden with William and The Boys, and then opposed William and Patricio in the Lincoln County War. Now all five were alike exiled and hunted, and once more allied themselves and rode together.

They tried for California, though none knew the way across the southern Arizona deserts. But they were turned back when Ledoux's negligence and treachery prevented them from raising a stake by theft and sale of Killian's cattle. Posses, volunteers, cavalry and lawmen along the Arizona-New Mexico line hunted them.

Now, in May, 1881, the riders ascended a grass, yucca and cholla cactus-covered plain, and passed between the Sierra Blanca and Guadalupe mountains into the Pecos Valley, headed for Fort Sumner. They were well known and wanted on the roads and towns of the Texas panhandle, and they knew not the way across the Llano Estacado. So they were barred from the west and east.

William rode on and thought he might escape to the north. One of his friends, Romulo Ortega, had tried. But a family at a ranch where Ortega had stopped to rest had reported his presence near Pueblo, Colorado. Ortega was taken on the road by cavalry and jailed in Pueblo.

Billy heard what happened next from cowhands who were there.

One cold night, only an old, drunk sergeant was guarding Romulo, when a vigilance committee walked in and took the soldier's weapons and keys. They opened Romulo's cell.

"Be a man and step out here. Don't make us go in there'n take you."

Romulo stepped out. As they prepared to tie his hands, one vigilante took pity on the prisoner. "Ye can bring yer coat if'n ye wanna."

"I won't need it."

They took him a little way down and across the street. They stood Romulo in the back of a wagon and threw the rope over a branch of an oak tree. But the branch was too thin, so when they lashed the wagon team the branch bent till Romulo was standing in the street. He hopped and twisted, trying to breathe, but the noose's thirteen knots gave no slack, and Romulo heard the jeers and laughter of the crowd as urine blackened his trousers and he passed

into darkness and the branch bent even more, so that in the morning he was found half-dangling, half-kneeling, soiled and dead in the street.

Billy the Kid was better known, by far, than Romulo Ortega. The whole country, from the president right down to the governor, marshals, sheriffs, powerful cattlemen and ordinary citizens from the east coast to the west knew of his impossible escape, and awaited news of his run and how it would end. People in England knew too, and they hoped their murdered countryman's lone champion would, somehow, prevail.

So Bonney didn't figure he could run north, east or west. Sometimes, around the fire at night, the outlaws talked about Mexico. But they had no clear plan. They were just riding to Fort Sumner to see their friends.

William Bonney wanted most of all to see his lover, Paulina Maxwell. When he had escaped after being confined for months in Santa Fe, La Mesilla, and Lincoln, he had visited several of his sweethearts in the little settlements and plazuelas in the Pecos country. These kind Spanish girls had without exception generously and compassionately shared their magical favors with him. But the voluptuous, passionate, eighteen-year-old Paulina, princess of the great Maxwell ranch at Fort Sumner, was William's favorite.

Now, after three weeks in the saddle, the outlaws approached Fort Sumner and William Bonney was overwhelmed by his desire to embrace Paulina, to see the dark depth of her eyes, to breathe the light of her smile, to smell her earth, and drink her rain.

It had been a long day, and Percy was exhausted when he drove back with Doña Flora and Rosario from Fort Sumner into Lincoln. But the trip to the graves had clarified many things in his mind, and he retired to his room and set to work revising his manuscript.

In Percy's view, "Pretty William" was no cold-blooded killer. He was a thief, a gambler and a rustler and more escape artist than killer. He had stymied military men and posses, government agents, bounty hunters, vigilantes and lawmen, for years. He had escaped from jails in Silver City, Fort Grant, Lincoln, Albuquerque and Fort Stanton. Yes, the boy had killed men. He killed for revenge against those who killed his friends. And he killed men who intended to kill him.

The native New Mexican people adored the Kid because he had brilliantly defied the very same incomprehensible powers that oppressed them: the president, the governor, the American law, and those who used it for their own profit. And he seemed to laugh and dance with Spanish beauties all the while. Percy considered a statement made by Miguel Otero, who had once been the governor of the New Mexico Territory: "William Bonney had his share of good qualities and was very pleasant. He had the reputation of being considerate of the old, the young and the poor; he was loyal to his friends and above all, loved his mother devotedly."

An hour after sunset, as Percy put the final touches on his manuscript, Rosario appeared in the doorway and he found her still more alluring than ever before, which until then he would not have deemed possible. She had rouged her cheeks and lips, and pulled her hair back tightly over her head into a high roll held in place by a sparkling silver comb. The intricately laced rebato of her low-cut, Mexican linen blouse stretched below her cleavage, revealing the stunning curves of her breasts, and crossed beneath the crowns of her shoulders. Her tight, long sleeves ended in ruffled lace that circled wrists adorned with silver bracelets.

Percy knew not what alchemy she had employed in lengthening and thickening her eyelashes. Her woven red, wool dress, with alternating striations of triangles and stripes, tightly cinched around her delicate waist, hung straight down from the angular curve that emerged when she shifted the axis of her hips to rest her weight on one leg.

"Vamonos para el baile, Señor Percy. Let's go to the dance."

"A dance?"

"Sí, este es la noche del baile. Yes, tonight is the dance."

Percy felt confused, and looked back longingly and with great hesitation at his books, his notes, and his manuscript as Rosario took him by the arm and led him out and down the street to the old Montaño store.

Inside the softly curved adobe structure, the men and women of Lincoln drank, smoked, gossiped, and danced, and children dashed about. In one corner three guitarists, a fiddler, a harmonica player and a man with a huge pueblo-drum played rancheras and ballads.

Rosario guided Percy to a seat against the wall, where many tipsy men of Lincoln regarded him as something of a celebrity for his ownership of the Hupmobile and offered him one shot after another of powerful aguardiente. Though he wasn't much of a drinker, Percy felt bound by courtesy to accept the hospitality. He was already flying high when Rosario pulled him from his chair to dance with her.

"I don't know how to do this."

"I show you! Like this!"

As Rosario pulled and pushed him about the floor, Percy discovered the skipping rhythm of the ranchera, eventually managing to keep up and move his short, thick legs and bulky torso in perfect time with Rosario's graceful movements. The dance flowed over and through him. Percy gave himself up to it as he and Rosario moved up and down the floor and around and around and the musicians played piece after piece.

Even as he fell more deeply in love with Rosario, Percy thought that he was understanding the essence of the Kid.

The Kid knew this very thing, heard this very music and was taken by these same dances and Spanish beauties, Percy thought, and he felt communion.

Suddenly, a hand on Percy's arm restrained him. He stopped dancing and turned to face the young Adonis, Matéo Romero.

"I dance with her now, por favor."

Percy released Rosario, and stepped back. Matéo took her hand and attempted to slip his arm around her waist. Rosario recoiled and pushed Matéo back, hard.

"¡Desgraciado! ¡Estoy bailando con el Señor Percy! Disgraceful one! I am dancing with Señor Percy!"

Matéo reached out, grabbed Rosario's arm and pulled her back toward him. Percy, with the courage of aguardiente, put his hand on Matéo's arm. Like lightning, Matéo slammed his fist into Percy's nose between his eyes, snapping the bridge of his glasses and sending him to the floor.

Several of Lincoln's leading men rushed forward to defend their distinguished guest and the honor of their town. But, before they could intervene, Rosario sprang like a tigress into Matéo's face, striking, scratching, kicking and driving him out the door.

Everyone rushed out after them. Percy slowly struggled to his feet and stumbled after, dazed and half-blind. Percy saw Rosario hurling insults at Matéo, who sat his horse in the middle of the road fifty yards away.

Stoked by aguardiente and adrenaline, Percy staggered across the road and mounted his Hupmobile. He fired it up, floored the accelerator, and charged right at Matéo. The crowd shouted and cheered and Percy thought he saw Matéo draw a blurry object, perhaps a pistol, as he plunged irrevocably on to meet his destiny, and Matéo's.

He closed his eyes and gripped the wheel with white knuckles. Long moments passed. Opening his eyes, he saw a pig in the road, slammed the brake pedal and pulled the wheel to his right, causing the Hupmobile's rear wheels to spin around in a cloud of dust. He caught a blurry glimpse of Matéo riding up into the hills, and drove the car slowly back to the cheering crowd. When he stepped down from the car, Rosario was foremost among those who rushed up.

"¡Tu eres mi heroe!" she said, as Percy fainted and fell backward onto the dusty road. "You are my hero!"

They carried Percy to his room. He was dimly aware of Rosario pouring more aguardiente down his throat, and tenderly tucking his blankets beneath his chin. He descended into darkness and dreamed, falsely, that he had captured the Kid.

As Percy slept and dreamed of the Kid, Matéo Romero slipped through the forest and climbed the Salazárs' adobe wall outside Rosario's room. He tossed pebbles at Rosario's window until she opened it. He began to play his guitar and he recited an old Spanish poem by Adolfo Becquer:

> The shadowy swallows will once again return
> and their nests on your balcony hang.
> Their wings will again brush your windows
> as they playfully call;
> But those who paused in their flight
> your beauty and my joy to behold,
> the very ones that learned your name and mine,
> those...will never return!

The jungle-like honeysuckle will once again
up the walls of your garden climb;
and once more at twilight, lovelier than ever,
its flowers will bloom;
But those crystallized masses of liquid,
those dewdrops we saw tremble
and fall, like teardrops at the close of the day...
those...will never return!

Once again upon your ears,
the ardent words of love will fall;
your heart from its profound sleep
perhaps will awaken;
But mute, enraptured and on bended knee,
as only God before his altar is adored,
as I have loved you...do not deceive yourself,
in that manner you will never again be loved!

PART TWO
EL CORRIDO DE BILLY THE KID
[BILLY THE KID'S BALLAD OR RUN]

19

HELEN

When love is forgotten, where does it go?

When Placido and Francisco Trujillo and two other caballeros drove their remuda of twenty excellent, blooded Arabian horses through the gates before Robert McCulloch's headquarters on the Pecos, Robert thought it could be true that the Trujillos bred the finest horses in all of Mexico.

Robert and his black foreman, Esau Gates, stepped down from the portál before the sprawling adobe ranch house where they had been sitting with their wives, Helen and Esther. They stepped forward to welcome the Trujillos and receive delivery of the caballada.

Robert liked the horses but he didn't really like the Mexicans. He didn't like the fancy lace work on their vests or the rows of small silver conchos connected by little silver chains they wore down the lace-adorned outside legs of their tight-fitting pantalones.

Placido and Francisco wore flat, round-brimmed, brown cordobeses with low cylindrical crowns banded by wide, silk ribbons. Those were common enough and they didn't bother Robert, but the Trujillos' men wore lace-decorated, high-crowned sombreros with prodigious brims that, Robert thought, were absurdly large.

Robert didn't like the way the Mexicans rode, either. They sat too erect in the saddle, and they pushed with their legs in opposition to the rise and fall of their horses' backs. They reminded Robert of the aristocratic Union and Confederate cavalrymen he had known and despised when he and his brother, Angus, had marched through Georgia with an Irish New York regiment in 1865, sixteen years before.

Robert and all his cowboys also supported their weight with their legs as they rode, but they moved with their horses and sat more relaxed on their saddles. It was said the cattlemen rode with four or five joints of their backbones below the cantle.

Robert's wife, Helen, was just nineteen years old and she was excited and fascinated by the visitors, whose arrival brought change to the daily routine of the isolated ranch. Helen was delighted when she was introduced to the Trujillo brothers. Francisco complimented her beauty, then swept his hat from his head across his torso and bowed deeply. Helen was thrilled when Placido exclaimed that it was a great honor to meet her and he took her hand, raised it to his lips, bowed slightly and pierced her blue eyes with his gray ones.

Helen's father had been killed by Chiricahua, and the McCullochs had looked after Helen and her mother ever since. Helen had not known her mother was dying when she and Angus arranged Helen and Robert's marriage and the union of their ranches. Helen was only sixteen at the time. Robert was forty years old and he had lost two wives in childbirth. The infants had died too.

Helen had felt she was ready to be a woman and she embarked enthusiastically on the adventure of marriage. She was confident she could give Robert the sons he longed for. Helen's experience of intimate relations with her husband and her assumption of her wifely duties over the big household made her feel proud and grown up.

Helen loved the rare occasions when she and Robert attended weddings, fandangos, even wakes and funerals, in the little town of San Pasqual, twenty miles away. But social occasions were all too rare and Helen was now excited to receive the different, interesting and gallant Mexican visitors into her home.

The mood at supper was festive. Afterward, when Robert, Helen, Gates and Esther, their English partners, Albert and Sarah Rowe, and the Trujillo brothers moved to the hide-covered bancos around the fire in the great hearth, the New Mexican servants, Rosa and Maria, watched and listened as they ate at Helen's big, intricately carved walnut table.

Esau Gates had fought for a colored regiment in the Civil War and he had saved Robert's life in a hand-to-hand mêlée, bayonet against saber, when the infantry lines had been broken and mixed by a desperate rebel cavalry charge near Savannah. No one in the New Mexico Territory had ever heard of a Negro foreman but all potential hands were warned, they would work for Gates, or move on. Esau was diplomatic in his requests to the cowboys. He always said: "Mr. Robert wants us to…" He handled the cowboys as wisely as he handled his horses. The cowhands who had seen Gates's courage in scrapes with outlaws or Indians were all thereafter heartened by his presence and protection on the lonely, dangerous range.

Gates and Esther lived in one wing of Robert's big adobe, and Robert and Helen were glad to have them there. Helen was aware that many people despised her colored friends and she was relieved and pleased when the Trujillos accepted without question the Gates's presence at her little celebration.

The Trujillos had brought fine tequila. Robert broke his rule against strong drink and allowed Helen to partake. The Rowes drank heavily and the Trujillos did too.

Francisco, called "Paco," laughed and tried to tell many jokes which did not translate well into his imperfect English. But Paco's attempts in the telling were very humorous in themselves and everyone laughed heartily. Placido played the guitar and sang ballads. Placido played a dramatic flamenco and Paco danced, stamping his heels and gesturing gracefully with his arms and hands overhead and all about.

Helen felt a warm glow from the tequila and she laughed uncontrollably when Paco pulled Rosa from her chair and danced, spinning her around the room, as Placido played a spirited ranchera.

Placido played a sweet melody and recited, in his impossibly deep voice, a poem about a love, lost and forgotten.

> Los suspiros son aire y van al aire.
> Las lágrimas son agua y van al mar.
> Dime, mujer: cuando el amor se olvida,
> ¿sabes tú adónde va?
>
> A sigh is air and returns to the air.
> A tear is water and seeks out the sea.
> But, tell me, woman, do you know?
> When love is forgotten, where does it go?

Helen spoke some Spanish, and she understood more. She grasped the meaning of the mournful and powerful ballad that Placido sang next. The song told of a married Spanish lady, Isabella, noble and beautiful, who burned with desire for the handsome and gallant caballero, Don Juan. Isabella took Don Juan to her bed and she glutted and slaked her lust there. After, Don Juan grew cold and showed little regard for the lady he had so eagerly and fully taken in carnal love. Isabella confided the insult to her brother, Hernando. Hernando killed Don Juan with a sword.

In their bed, that night, Robert raised Helen's gown, spread her legs, moved over her and satisfied himself, as he always did, in a brief act, his beard smelling of tobacco and of his dinner. Robert snored and Helen lay awake, glowing and recalling the pleasures of the wonderful evening.

Helen could not stop thinking of Placido and the song of the beautiful, lustful, daring Spanish lady. Helen had never imagined that a married lady could act like that. She had never considered that a woman would want to. But Placido and the song told, so matter of factly as if it were a matter of course, the astounding idea that a married woman could burn with such uncontrollable desire for a man.

The Rowes were from England. They had traveled in many countries and known many people. They did not seem to question, at all, the plausibility of the tale of the beautiful lady's desperate and reckless acts. The Rowes also seemed to accept, without question and with approval, the motive of Hernando who killed Don Juan, not because Don Juan had taken and enjoyed Isabella, but because Don Juan had not shown sufficient respect and gratitude for the lady's favors, so completely bestowed. The Rowes had clapped and shouted as the song reached its climax and Don Juan felt the cold steel of Hernando's sword in his belly, then died.

When Helen, as a young bride, had come to Robert's bed, the experience was, at first, painful. But Helen was eager for the adventure and, in time, she found it pleasurable. Two years passed and Helen did not conceive. One night, in a thoughtless, offhand joke, Robert compared Helen to a steer. After that, Helen felt hurt and anxious and she no longer enjoyed their attempts to conceive a child. Still, Helen had never considered the possibility of intimacy with any man but her husband.

There were many men on the ranch and some of the young cowboys were very beautiful. None had stimulated interest in Helen, such as that told in the song of the Spanish lady, Isabella, for Don Juan. The cowboys always acted so shy when they spoke to Helen. They held their hats before them and looked at the ground or at their boots. They could usually only stammer a "Yes, Ma'am," or "No, Ma'am," or "Thank you, Ma'am," when they spoke.

One night, when Helen sat in a window taking air at a fandango, she heard several of the young cowboys talking on the porch outside. They bragged, laughed and told explicitly of things they had done with a young Mexican girl in the town, and with whores. They derided and expressed contempt for the women they had used. But they expressed no shame, and even great pride, at their own exploits which they described in vivid detail. Helen had been surprised and shocked to learn the drovers' hidden thoughts and attitudes.

After Helen heard how the young men talked to each other about women, she began to notice how many of the cowboys, especially Jenkins, watched her, covertly and askance, from a distance. She noticed how they ran their eyes down over her blond hair, full bosom, delicate waist and over her flat belly and the broad, mature curve of her hips. Their eyes traveled from her hips down the length of her legs, almost as if they could see through her dress. Helen now understood the meaning of those looks and she resented them.

Now, Helen lay awake thinking of the wonderful and rare evening she had just enjoyed. She was fascinated and could not stop thinking of Isabella. She thought of how different Paco and Placido were from the men she knew. She thought of how the Mexican brothers had so confidently and gallantly complimented her beauty. She thought of Placido's deep voice and of his beautiful gray eyes with which he had, so openly, taken hers. In a dizzy, terrifying moment, Helen dared to think of taking Placido in the act of love. She immediately repressed the thought. Placido would not act like that. No one could think of it. Then she slept and she dreamed of the wanton Spanish lady. And she dreamed of Placido.

Riders had been dispatched when the Trujillos arrived and the next day neighbors came to the ranch. Food was spread on tables on the portál. Some of the visitors drank whiskey and the Trujillos' horses were tested in races of varying distances. The Mexican horses won most and placed highly in all. All

the Mexican horses showed superior qualities of agility and intelligence.

Helen and Robert presided, sitting together on a raised banco. Helen and Placido exchanged many glances. Helen blushed crimson when she looked over at Placido, standing in a group of men exchanging wagers, and she saw Placido gazing back at her, spellbound. Placido's smile sparkled and he nodded. Helen quickly looked away. She glanced at Robert. He did not notice Helen's discomfort.

The folk danced to guitars and violins in the big house, all alight, that night. Helen spoke briefly to Placido under the vigas on the broad portál. Placido told Helen she was the most beautiful woman he had ever seen. Robert was an experienced man, he had traveled great distances and had known two wives. Robert had also told Helen she was the most beautiful of all the women he had known. So now, when Placido said it, Helen knew Placido wanted to have her as Robert had. Placido brushed Helen's lips with his. Helen thrilled and immediately retreated back inside the ranch house.

The next day, Robert and Placido concluded the sale of the caballada and Robert, Gates and one hand set out with half the remuda on the two-day ride to Angus McCulloch's headquarters.

That night Helen stripped, washed with water from a painted tile basin in her candle-lit room and she brushed her hair. But on this night, unlike all others, her curtains were open. Placido leaned against a wagon just outside the light and watched her. Helen watched Placido, too, and she raised her nightgown and held it, covering her breasts and hips, as Placido walked forward with a slight swagger and stepped through the window. He held and kissed her gently at first, then more ardently and he gently took her gown from before her and guided her to her bed. As Placido crushed and bruised Helen's lips, breathed her breath, caressed her breasts and the soft curves of her belly, hips and thighs, he swore that he loved her, and always would, mute, enraptured and on bended knee as only God before His altar is adored, and Placido made long, slow love to Helen again and again and Helen knew passion beyond all dreaming and imagining.

Next morning, Helen felt like a stranger in her home. She had thought she could secretly take Placido. No one would ever know. But now she knew her life could never again be as it had been.

That night Placido came again as Helen knew he would and she was ready. He brought pantalones and chaps so Helen could ride like a man, not sidesaddle as Robert had always required. Placido had his own horse and the lovers took two of the horses Placido had sold to Robert the day before so each horse could rest in turn as the fugitives rode the others. They walked the animals across the wide yard past barns and corrales and passed under the gatehead. Then they rode at a good clip into the night, south, for Mexico.

20

ULYSSES

Drink to the wisdom of White Wolf!

Ulysses O'Laerte had known for two weeks that Angus and Robert McCulloch would come to his little spread on the Black River near where the New Mexico Territory bordered Texas. Six of Charles Goodnight's hands had stopped on their way back down the Goodnight Trail, headed for Pope's Crossing and Texas.

Word was spreading up and down the Pecos. A Mexican had stolen Robert McCulloch's wife. The Mexican stole horses too. That's pretty much how the trail drivers told it. But Ulysses knew Robert McCulloch, he knew Helen, and he knew Placido Trujillo's reputation. When the drovers said it was Placido Trujillo, Ulysses knew what had happened.

Ulysses knew what would happen next, too. The McCullochs would go, like two bulls rampant, into Mexico after Helen and Placido. Ulysses knew the McCullochs would expect him and his people to back them up. And Ulysses had been thinking hard, how to stay clear of this big trouble.

Ulysses's alliance with the McCullochs against outlaws—and Chiricahua, Mescalero, Kiowa or Comanche—had been useful for both sides. The McCullochs had a lot of men. Ulysses and Diego, their two teen-aged sons and Diego's nephew Ignacio worked their little spread with just two vaqueros. Because the McCullochs commanded so many guns, they had never been outnumbered in fights against large war parties or big gangs of horse and cattle thieves.

On the other hand, Ulysses and Diego with their deep knowledge of the territory and its people—Indian, Northern European, Spanish and Mestizo—and their skills as trackers and scouts had been invaluable to the powerful ranchers. And Diego, Ignacio, and Ulysses's two vaqueros were experienced "full blooded" men, tough in battle.

Ulysses was probably the best scout still around. He was as good as the Apache scouts the army sometimes used against the Chiricahua, but he knew a lot more about the northern territories than the Apaches did. When he was barely more than a boy, Ulysses had ridden with Kit Carson. He had known Don Luciano Maxwell and many other famous explorers and mountain men: men like Ouray, St. Vrain, Robideaux and Zan Hicklen. Ulysses knew both slopes of the Rockies and the passes through them, all the way north to Sioux country. He knew the plains east of the Rockies, the northern New Mexico mountains and parts of Utah, and he had ridden most of the way to California. And, of course, Ulysses knew the Pecos, the Bosque Grande, the Guadalupes, Sierra Blanca, the Gila, the Apache Sitgraves and the wide intervening plains and deserts.

Ulysses still favored clothing such as he had worn in the old days—a fringed, beaded, deerskin Cheyenne war shirt dyed green from the chest up, leather leggings which covered the silver buttons on his moccasins, gartered just above the knees, with buffalo-hide soles in which, when necessary, he could walk without leaving sign of his passage. Ulysses carried his Bowie knife in a scabbard made from the stretched hide of a buffalo tail. The tail's black end-tuff hung to his knees. He wore a full beard but he kept his beard cut short ever since a Cheyenne brave had grabbed hold of it and almost cut his throat in a scrape on the east slope of the Rockies many years before. But Ulysses wore his scalp hair long, in nostalgic deference to the old custom once observed between mountain men and Indians, as a trophy and gift of honor to any warrior bold and lucky enough to take it. The hair on Ulysses's temples and in his beard was streaked with grey. His eyes were grey, too.

Ulysses wore, even in summer, a broad-brimmed, brown, plainsman's hat of crushed beaver felt. In its wide, beaded band he sported three eagle feathers given him by a Lakota chieftain, the father of his tall, comely wife, Morningstar.

Now, for defense against men, Ulysses carried a Colt's .44 and a Winchester, which used the same ammunition. But in a painted hide quiver, Ulysses still carried his long, muzzle-loading .50 caliber Hawkin for big game or an occasional long-range shot at human enemy.

In the waning days of the mountain men and explorers, Ulysses had

done some scouting out of Fort Sumner for the army, against the Jicarilla Apache, the Mescalero, and the Comanche, until they were forced onto reservations. He had lost standing with the army when he refused to participate with Kit Carson in what Ulysses considered to be the brutal and shameful subjugation of the Navajo. Ulysses had ridden with the New Mexico Volunteers, the Colorado Volunteers and army regulars out of Fort Union when they whipped Sibley's rebels at Glorieta, near Santa Fe. At the time, Ulysses was just thirty-six years old.

It was just after the war, in 1866, that Ulysses had first met the McCullochs. Ulysses, old Diego, and Ignacio, the sixteen-year-old son of Diego's sister, had left Fort Sumner and the Bosque Redondo and ridden down into Texas and out onto the immense, seemingly boundless, yellow grass-covered buffalo plain known as the "Llano Estacado" where the wild and powerful Comanche still ruled.

The little group led a mule laden with trade goods—mostly steel knives—which they hoped to parlay for Texas cattle, she-stock, to start their own herd. Trading with the fierce Comanche on their own ground was always dangerous. So the three comancheros fell in with a larger party led by Saturnino Archibeque and his partner Esquibél, caballeros known to be unpredictable and murderous pistoleros. Archibeque's party numbered five and they brought a two-wheeled carreta drawn by oxen, filled with goods that included a barrel of whiskey.

Ulysses knew Archibeque was as likely as the Comanche to murder him and his people and he never let Archibeque out of his sight. The comancheros rode in uneasy alliance across the llano. They passed the Yellow Cliffs and reached the deep, broad, verdant cañon known as Valle de las Lenguas or "Valley of the Tongues." The place was so named because tribes who spoke different languages met there with English- and Spanish-speaking traders.

But the comancheros found no Comanche encamped there, so they continued on to another cañon, the place called Valle de Las Lagrimas, "Valley of Tears." It was here that tribes met and traded or sold Mexican and North American captives. The place was named for the grief that was witnessed there.

Many Comanche clans were gathered at Las Lagrimas and Ulysses and

Diego traded 200 steel knives, some steel canteens and some wool blankets for Texas she-stock, thirty in all, and for a blue, longhorn bull. Ulysses's group moved out immediately after the deal was made, fearing they might meet Comanche bands who would not honor the trade and would take the hard-earned herd.

Archibeque's group took longer to trade their goods and they remained at Las Lagrimas as Ulysses's people drove their stock south and west to Las Lenguas. Archibeque had hidden his cask of whiskey some distance from Las Lagrimas. Fearing the Comanches would arise to war once they drank, Archibeque left a man with a fast horse to tell the Comanches where the whiskey cooper was hidden, but only after Archibeque was well on his way with his heard of 150 Texas and Spanish cattle.

After driving hard for three days, Ulysses arrived at Valle de Las Lenguas and camped at a spring on the cañon floor, among cottonwood, blackjack ponderosa, oak brush, juniper and pecan and on good grass.

Right after nightfall, Ulysses heard Archibeque's group descend into the cañon. Archibeque made camp less than a mile up the wash from Ulysses.

Four hours before dawn, Ulysses broke out of sleep and sat upright at the sound of a owl. The sound echoed off the cañon walls and this meant it was made by no peregrine. It was a signal of the Comanche. Even as he reached for his Hawkin, Ulysses heard gunfire, a mighty bellow, then silence, from the direction of Archibeque's camp.

Custom demanded that white ally against Indian in this land, so Ulysses and Diego left Ignacio armed and concealed and they rode at a brisk pace up the cañon toward Archibeque's camp. When Diego judged they were just out of hearing of those in the camp, he and Ulysses dismounted and walked their horses cautiously and quietly up the cañon floor. They walked together with their horses on either side as cover from ambush, holding the animals by the bozales attached to the headstalls at the horses' chins and they wrapped the hair ropes around their waists so the horses could not get away if they had to start shooting.

Diego and Ulysses stopped and stood, electrified, as they saw four riders, Comanches, emerge from dark shadows, walking their horses brazenly forward to meet them. The Comanches rode more or less abreast, but one was a

little ahead, leading the others. He was White Wolf, the biggest Comanche and perhaps the biggest man Ulysses had ever seen.

White Wolf was naked from the waist up but he wore bracelets of Mexican silver on his wrists and above his elbows. He wore a war bonnet of eagle feathers and dappled feathers of other birds of prey. White Wolf wore a thick, Mexican cotton breach cloth looped over a rawhide belt and leather thongs tied to the belt supported buffalo-hide dusters folded over his legs to protect them from rough brush, cactus and mesquite thorns. The open backs of the crude chaps were tied by rawhide thongs behind the war chief's knees, and the chaps were well-worn and greased and molded to his legs by sweat. A quiver with a bow and arrows and a thick war shield, made of buffalo hide stretched over oak branches bent and tied in a circle, hung on the giant's back.

White Wolf's face and his scarred and heavily muscled torso were painted for war. One side of his face was painted black, except for a white stripe which ran across his eyes, like a mask. The white paint on White Wolf's face covered an empty eye socket, sewn closed by some medicine man after the chieftan had lost the eye in battle.

White Wolf carried Archibeque's Sharps rifle across the front of his worn Mexican saddle; the butt of Archibeque's Colt's dragoon protruded from his belt and Ulysses recognized Archibeque's bloody, dark, Spanish-red scalp hanging from the thong looped over White Wolf's saddle horn.

The warrior who rode next to White Wolf wore a round, fur cap with a single, small antelope horn twisting forward over his forehead. Ulysses knew this was the chieftain known by his surviving victims in the northern New Mexico Territory as Cuerno Verde. He was so named after another Comanche who had worn a similar headdress and terrorized the New Mexican pueblos and Spanish towns many generations before.

Blue Hand rode next to Cuerno Verde. Blue Hand wore a skull cap of tanned buffalo leather, fringed with sea shells traded from the south, suspended by leather thongs and hanging over his ears and neck. All the warriors were dressed like White Wolf, painted for battle, and they displayed the weapons and scalps of Archibeque's people.

Diego was fifteen years older than Ulysses, and he spoke pretty good Comanche. He parleyed with White Wolf. Then he explained to Ulysses, "He says Archibeque's whiskey was bad. Archibeque cheated them. So they came to take the cattle back."

Ulysses thought he heard careful footsteps of warriors moving through the brush around them. "Tell 'im we don' care. Tell 'em ta come parley in our camp at dawn."

By riding forward so boldly, the Comanches had placed themselves in a position in which some would be killed or maimed if they started a gun fight, so White Wolf nodded, granting his assent.

Ulysses and Diego backed down the trail watching the warriors, Ulysses ready with his Hawkin, Diego with his double-barreled escopeta. As soon as they reached camp, Ulysses's group moved out, hazing their little herd up and out of the cañon and out onto the universe of yellow, grass-covered llano. Ulysses scanned their back trail with a spy glass and four hours after dawn he saw the Comanches coming.

Only six, Ulysses thought. They left the rest to handle Archibeque's herd. Ulysses was encouraged. He thought his plan might just work.

The three comancheros hobbled their horses and let the cattle graze free. Ulysses led a yearling away, down wind. He killed it, took the finest cuts and kicked dirt and grass over the carcass to hold the blood scent from the rest of the herd against changing wind.

Ignacio made a little fire out of buffalo chips and some small branches Ulysses had brought. A pot of coffee was set to boil and the comancheros sat on blankets, facing the approaching war party. Diego and Ignacio concealed their revolvers, cocked and ready on their laps beneath their serapes. Ulysses's Colt was not cocked. It was in his belt at the small of his back.

The Comanches stopped at about the edge of rifle range and studied the three herders. Diego waived them in. Fast Raven, a young brave about Ignacio's age, stood holding the warriors' horses. White Wolf, Cuerno Verde, Far Killer, Blue Hand, and a burly man called Bull Buffalo came forward and sat at the fire across from the three comancheros.

They shared the meat Ulysses offered. White Wolf skewered his and roasted it on a short, immaculately polished, razor-sharp Spanish dagger taken by White Wolf's storied ancestor from a valiant conquistadór who had died fighting and unknown to his people and he had lain bloody in his armor in the

sun on this strange landing and end point of his now forgotten odyssey and quest, the Llano Estacado.

Far Killer, Cuerno Verde and Bull Buffalo ate meat too. Blue Hand ate nothing. Blue Hand was the oldest man present, even older than Diego. Blue Hand was named for his youth vision which showed him that he could kill any enemy he faced with arrow or spear loosed from his hand painted blue with pigment from the rocks and sands of the holy places in the deserts where the Navajo ruled. The vision had proved true throughout Blue Hand's long life. But the Navajo had been destroyed and exiled from their abode by the soulless, voracious whites with their honorless and all-powerful weapons. So, the blue pigment was no longer traded on the Llano Estacado. Blue Hand had once held magic but now it was gone and the night before, as he loosed his bow and killed Esquibél, Blue Hand had seen his own death sign, also foretold in his vision, a white hawk flying from the east across the crescent moon. As Esquibél had fallen back, the hawk seemed to rise, almost out of the life blood spurting from Esquibél's neck impaled.

As the falcon arced upward, Blue Hand saw the moon's silver sliver in its path. Blue Hand tensed and summoned all his magic, if any he had ever commanded, and he shouted with all his strength. But he could not shout the bird back and it crossed the moon, then cut and sailed, gliding, up the dark cañon. Blue Hand stood watching in dismay.

Now, Blue Hand sat at the fire, across from Ignacio, in lethargic resignation.

Ulysses skewered his meat on a long, sharpened oak stake he had brought from La Canada de Las Lenguas.

White Wolf talked to Ulysses, making no effort to conceal his belligerence. Diego translated: "I know of you," he said. "I have heard. You show the soldiers the ways to the places of the Apache and to the secret places of my people. For war. The Mescalero call you 'Far Traveler.'"

"No. I am not the one you say."

"No? Then tell me your name."

"My name is Trader. I come from far to the east. My people keep the secret of how to make the finest whiskey. I bring whiskey here to trade with the army. And with the Comanche, too."

White Wolf could plainly see that Ulysses was no white immigrant from the east and he was astounded by the boldness of Ulysses's lie. And yet, the lie made no sense. Ulysses obviously had no supply of whiskey and the army forts were far away. The giant warrior was confused by the sheer unlikelihood that anyone in such dire circumstances could assert such an obvious falsehood. There were so many better lies the man could have told. So White Wolf was forced to doubt, and consider the possibility that Ulysses spoke the truth.

"You treat me as fool. I know 'Trader' is no true name among your people. You have a Christian name. Say it."

"My Christian name is John."

"Jahhen," White Wolf said, attempting to repeat the English name. "What does the name mean? Who does it tell of?"

"John is the most common among Christian names. It is so common that it means 'Nothing,' or 'Nobody.' And I have earned no war-name. I am only a trader."

White Wolf was becoming ever more confused by the strange conversation. But Cuerno Verde saw that all was a ruse and he gazed calmly and cynically with amusement and murderous intent at the desperate and futile verbal maneuvers of the doomed white man. Cuerno Verde assumed that the three comancheros had cocked pistols under their serapes and he was thinking how to take them without loss or injury to his people. He rejected the idea of riding out and attacking later, perhaps at night. The whites might fire on them at a distance as they left. The Comanches were not yet adept with their newly acquired firearms. But here, only a few feet from their enemies, their spears were as fast as guns. The whites had been foolish to let them come so close. All were here, now. It would be here and now.

Cuerno Verde sat at the end of the half circle of Comanches about the fire. Cuerno Verde sat opposite Diego. White Wolf was on the other end of the line near Ulysses. Ignacio sat between Diego and Ulysses.

Cuerno Verde affected a casual, calm posture, but he was ready. He was wondering how long it would take White Wolf to break out of his befuddlement into action.

Ignacio was pale and trying not to shake. The boy's eyes were big and his jaw muscles clenched and spasmed. The Comanches all had pistols in their

belts and rifles, and spears lay beside them. Far Killer held a heavy, knotted, burl war club across his lap and in his right hand.

Cuerno Verde knew that as soon as White Wolf concluded that Ulysses really was the enemy he suspected, he would send his razor-sharp dagger flipping through the air to impale Ulysses's throat. All the Comanches knew White Wolf could throw that renowned blade with incredible speed and accuracy. The vanquished conquistadór's dagger had once been very long and it appeared to have been naturally whittled down from many sharpenings but, in fact, White Wolf had intentionally honed it for perfect balance.

Cuerno Verde observed that both of Ulysses's hands were visible and he held only a wood meat skewer. White Wolf would follow the dagger with his spear before Ulysses could react. But White Wolf was not yet ready to kill. He was enjoying his meat and he was still seeking to learn the wily scout's name. He was diverted by the man's unlikely, nonsensical words.

Blue Hand was roused, slightly, from his melancholic contemplation of death imminent. He was intrigued by the philosophical question posed by Ulysses's paradoxical claim. Perhaps he was meant to learn some final truth at this point of his ending. He asked, and Diego translated: "How can a name name nobody? A name gives knowledge of man, woman, animal, of gods or of the places beneath the four winds."

White Wolf took the logic of Blue Hand's question as proof that Ulysses was a lying enemy of the Comanche people.

Ulysses sensed that White Wolf was near to deciding and he saw Cuerno Verde tense, covertly.

"I can prove the truth of my name," Ulysses said. "Look." Ulysses pulled his serape from over his thighs, very slowly, so his action would not startle and ignite the Comanches. The warriors all looked with great interest and they saw two bottles of fine rye whiskey there.

"This is the whiskey I will bring to trade with the soldiers and with your people, too."

When Cuerno Verde saw that Ulysses did not conceal a pistol, as he had believed, he began to question his conclusions. Ulysses could see that he had diverted the warriors' intent. He answered Blue Hand. "I am 'Nobody' because my whiskey is the best. All who drink forget me."

All the warriors, except Blue Hand, were now bemused by Ulysses's nonsense and they were excited and eager to drink, eager to know the spirits.

Ulysses raised a bottle, held it before him, shoulder high, arms extended, opened it and passed it to White Wolf with great ceremony. "Drink to the beauty of the Comanche women!"

"Hum." White Wolf nodded his assent and approval.

The bottle was passed around the fire, handled by all but the boy, Ignacio. Diego only pretended to drink. When Ulysses received the bottle he raised it to his lips and blew bubbles through the liquid, thereby appearing to have taken a deep drought.

"Ahh!" he said, and again raised the bottle with exaggerated dignity. "Drink to the strength and bravery of the Comanche warriors!"

The first bottle, then the second, circled many times. Ulysses toasted the Comanches' land, their gods, even their horses.

Blue Hand became somber and morose. His shoulders slumped and he seemed to shrink into himself as he watched his kinsmen become ever more relaxed and chatty. Blue Hand felt profound disappointment as he watched the drama of his death unfold. He had thought he would learn some final truth. But there was no truth. He would die, drunk, among fools, duped by "nobody" but a lying murderer.

Ulysses slumped as if besotted. He put a small morsel of beef on his stake and extended it over the fire. He took the bottle, pretended to drink, then said, "Drink to the wisdom of White Wolf!"

He offered the bottle to White Wolf and he swayed drunkenly; his arm was low and not fully extended. White Wolf leaned forward and reached for the bottle circling in Ulysses's unsteady hand.

Ulysses drove his hot stake into White Wolf's eye. He released the stake, snapped derringer from sleeve to hand and shot Bull Buffalo even as he uncoiled, pulled his Bowie and dove to finish White Wolf.

Diego, hand on shotgun by his thigh, took time to raise the barrel only an inch and he fired the escopeta through fire and coals. Ash and sparks erupted and spewed to air as shot ripped into Far Killer's shin and groin.

Ignacio pulled his revolver, awkwardly, and pointed, shaking, at Blue Hand. Blue Hand remained still, locked eyes with the boy and projected only

the first note of his death song before Ignacio fired.

Diego swung his escopeta toward Cuerno Verde and managed to deflect spear thrust with gun barrel and Cuerno Verde released spear, dived left head over heel, and came up running toward Fast Raven, who struggled to hold the Comanches' panicked, skittering horses. Diego didn't have time to fire at Cuerno Verde because Far Killer was coming over the fire, maimed and full of rage, swinging his club. Diego blasted Far Killer and Far Killer was blown aside, but he still brained Ignacio as he fell.

White Wolf let out a growling scream and fell back slashing blindly with his dagger as Ulysses closed with him. White Wolf's strength was so great that the dagger cut through Ulysses's serape and leather shirt and opened a long gash across Ulysses's sternum, pectoral muscle and ribs as Ulysses drove his Bowie knife down beneath White Wolf's clavicle into his lung and heart. Bull Buffalo came up in terrible pain and grabbed Ulysses's hair and throat but Ulysses ripped his blade free of White Wolf and slashed backhand across Bull Buffalo's neck.

Diego pulled his .44 to shoot at Cuerno Verde but Cuerno Verde, holding his Sharps' in one hand, pointed back and fired as he vaulted onto a horse. The shot rattled Diego. He fired and missed.

Ulysses pulled his revolver from his back belt and shot White Wolf, Bull Buffalo, and Far Killer as they lay writhing and shaking on the ground. Blue Hand lay still, eyes open, obviously dead.

Once he was sure the nearest enemies were no longer dangerous, Ulysses fired his colt at Cuerno Verde. Cuerno Verde was riding hard and away, ducked low over his horse, and Ulysses missed.

Ulysses stuck his Colt's in his belt and extended his hand toward Diego. Diego tossed Ulysses his Hawkin. Ulysses cocked it, primed the pan from his powder horn, raised the long rifle and aimed at Cuerno Verde and Fast Raven, galloping away. Ulysses took his time, sighted Cuerno Verde and squeezed the trigger. Fast Raven cut behind Cuerno Verde as the Hawkin exploded and the boy's shoulders and head snapped back and he pitched dead into the straw grass. Ulysses lowered his Hawkin and watched as Cuerno Verde raced away and cut into cover behind a swale in the prairie.

Ignacio was breathing. Diego wrapped the boy's head in cotton cloth.

He soaked the cloth with cool water. Ulysses gritted his teeth as Diego sewed his wound with a bone awl and twine made from maguey fiber. Ignacio was only half conscious when they got him on a horse, tied him to the saddle and drove their little herd toward New Mexico Territory and the safety of the Bosque Redondo.

Cuerno Verde slowed his horse to a trot and rode back toward the sanctuaries of his people. How can they take vengeance, Cuerno Verde wondered, after being told that "Nobody" had killed White Wolf? Cuerno Verde realized that he alone knew "Nobody" and he alone must avenge the great defender of the Comanche people, the great warrior, the great chieftain, White Wolf.

In 1866, Fort Sumner and the Bosque Redondo were still an army post and reservation for Navajo and Mescalero Apache. Several thousand were encamped there when Ulysses's party arrived and camped with their little herd in the shelter of the great oak and cottonwood bosque along the Pecos river.

The tribes had been nearly starving but Charles Goodnight had arrived the day before on his first drive up the trail which would bear his name. Angus and Robert McCulloch had also arrived with a smaller herd, their first, of Spanish cattle they had driven in from the Rio Grande Valley.

Goodnight sold 1000 cattle to the agents at the fort and there was feasting and song at the fires, all along the bosque, that night. Ulysses and Diego walked to the fort after dark. They drank there, among rowdy Irish, Scottish, German and Anglo bluecoats. When they left, they found two of Goodnight's men—"One-Armed Bill" Wilson and Bill Taylor—standing outside the tavern. Goodnight didn't allow his men to drink, but the drive had been hard and dangerous and the men were on their own time. They were thirsty.

The two cattlemen stood outside the saloon looking in. They were both rank rebels, defeated but not vanquished, and they knew a fight would result if they entered and mingled with the Union soldiers. Diego went back and got the Texans a bottle of rye. The men drained the bottle at Ulysses's fire.

Next morning, Ulysses, Diego and Ignacio sat on serapes, drinking coffee and cleaning their guns in the shade of an immense alamo. Two vaqueros

stood by, visiting. Ulysses's Colt's dragoon lay loaded and capped beside him and he was cleaning his Hawkin when the young lieutenant, Davis, rode up with one trooper and with Goodnight, Taylor and Wilson. The McCullochs, new to the country, had come along too, to see how the young lieutenant would handle the situation. The riders sat their horses in a line before the comancheros.

Wilson looked very embarrassed. He had told Goodnight that some of the comancheros' cattle bore the "Lazy F" brand: Goodnight's brand. Goodnight claimed them. He figured the unbranded yearlings with the she-stock were, by rights, his too. After introductions, Davis explained the situation.

"In Texas, no honorable man would do anythin' but return his neighbor's cattle. Even the unbranded ones," Goodnight said.

"This ain't Texas, Mr. Goodnight," Ulysses replied. "In New Mexico Territory, them that's got the sand ta risk it 've always traded with the Comanche."

"How can you trade for cattle showin' another man's brand? You know they're mine. We all can see it. The Comanche stole those cattle and you know that too."

"I've heard of you Mr. Goodnight, sir. I heard you was a ranger and scouted against the Comanche. But I guess you didn't git close enough to talk to 'em. I guess you kin still learn somethin' about Indians."

Ulysses poured a big powder charge down the barrel of his Hawkin. "Indians don't steal cattle, sir. They capture 'em. They figure what they can take from them that can't hold on to 'em, 'er theirs. The Comanche don't figure they're doin' nothin' wrong raidin' cattle and they don't figure them that fights 'em 'er doin' nothin' wrong, neither. The raidin' and the war that goes with it 'er honorable pursuits. Both ways. Good sport too."

Ulysses inserted a patch and fifty-caliber ball into the Hawkin's barrel and rammed them down. Goodnight looked at Davis, astounded that the lieutenant was allowing the scoundrel to load the big rifle before his very eyes. "Now, we traded goods, bought with hard money, fer them cattle. We damn near lost our hair. Five that rode with us lost theirs."

Ulysses looked at the McCullochs. He noticed that Robert wore a belt with a U.S. Army brass buckle. Angus had a U.S. Army issue canteen slung from his saddle. Ulysses had heard the men's thick Irish accents during the brief introductions and he now deduced that the McCullochs had fought for the north. He knew the vaqueros who stood by didn't like the Texans either. Ulysses cocked the Hawkin and primed the pan, then rested the big gun across his knee so he needed only to raise it to fire at Goodnight, Taylor or Wilson.

"Now, I rode with Carson at Valverde when we whipped you 'Texicans,'" he said, using the old name he knew the vaqueros would hate. "This here Hawkin can make a hole big enough fer the Texas wind to blow right through. I don't figure you Tex-i-can rebs would want to come back here makin' more trouble. And I don't figure them cattle 'er yer's no more."

Goodnight was fearless, not at all intimidated by the ragged plainsman's threat. But he believed strongly in law, so he submitted the matter to Davis. "I've had my say. Mr. O'Learte's had his. Now you say. What's your decision, Lieutenant?"

Davis had ridden in, thoughtlessly, with only one soldier. He had never thought the situation might turn so bad, so fast. Davis knew Ulysses and his reputation as a hard man.

Davis looked at the three comancheros all armed and ready. The vaqueros looked belligerent, too. Davis knew the Texans would act and people could die, fast, if he awarded the cattle to Goodnight. But Davis had to do his duty. "Well uh," he said, "the brands—"

"Now hold on a minute," Angus broke in. "O'Laerte's got a point. He's entitled to be paid for his labor and for his cost."

Everyone looked at Goodnight and waited for his reaction to Angus's suggested compromise. Goodnight removed his hat, pushed his fingers back through his hair, then examined the hat while he thought. "All right then. What do you figure you're entitled to?"

The faintest smile moved Ulysses's lips. Ulysses knew he had Goodnight.

"Eight cents a pound, on foot."

The night before, Wilson, drunk, had let it slip that Goodnight had sold his cattle to the army for eight cents a pound. And that was quantity. A small herd, like Ulysses', would therefore sell for more. Ulysses's offer was perfectly calculated to be very fair, but useless to Goodnight.

Goodnight thought for a minute, exasperated, then slapped his thigh with his hat. "Keep 'em," he said, and he cut his chunky blue and started away.

"Mr. Goodnight, sir!" Ulysses called.

Goodnight stopped and turned back. Ulysses walked up, carrying a hide-covered bundle. "Gifts, sir. Ta honor yer fairness." Ulysses slapped the hide back revealing White Wolf's feathered, painted shield and polished dagger of Toledo steel. The painted shield showed a white hawk flying toward the moon crescent.

"These trophies belonged to a brave man, White Wolf. He lived and died, true to his warrior's code."

"Well I'll be…" Goodnight considered, then took up and examined the gifts. "Never thought of the bandit like that. But, if you've stopped that killer, White Wolf, then I guess you've well earned those cattle. I thank you."

Goodnight and his men rode away. Angus and Robert stayed and spoke awhile with Ulysses.

"It's good ta meet a white man who knows what he's about in this wild country. The land is plentiful and fine, sure, but dangerous still. We'd best stick together if its ever ta be properly settled," Angus said.

"Well, now, my compañeros 'd tell you their people've been settled here 300 years. But ye'r right. It's dangerous still. I'm sure we'll meet again. I've got one question for you though."

"All right."

"If shootin'd started just now, were you gonna throw down on me 'er them rebs?"

Angus thought carefully. "I didn't know then and I don't know now."

"That's what I figured," Ulysses said with a wry smile and raised eyebrow. "That's why I mentioned it."

As Angus and Robert rode out, Angus thought and shook his head, amazed at the cleverness of the tough scout.

In the years that followed, the McCullochs settled to the north of Ulysses's little rancho and they claimed great ranches. Robert had his own land—then, through marriage, Helen's. Angus's lands and herds, farther north, just south of Chisum, were greater still.

Ulysses and the McCullochs had allied against many enemies. The McCullochs had always come to fight when Ulysses needed it. Ulysses had always done the same for them.

Now, fifteen years after their first meeting at Bosque Redondo, Angus and Robert sat with Ulysses and Diego at Ulysses's table in his big log cabin on the Black River. Forty cowboys were making camp around two supply wagons near the well behind the house. Gates sat on the front porch.

Smoked venison, elk and beef hung in the breezeway between the main cabin and the kitchen and the McCullochs ate rich steaks, which Ulysses had cut there. Ulysses's Sioux wife, Morningstar, renowned for her beauty, sat at the hearth behind the McCullochs, grinding corn with metate and mano, making tortillas and listening as the men sat in council.

"The Mexican army ain't gonna allow a bunch a' armed Gringos ta just ride in and start trouble," Ulysses said.

"That's where you come in," Angus replied. "You can scout ahead, keep us clear 'a trouble. We've got ta ride in fast, hit them hard, get the girl, and get out fast."

"I don't know Mexico all that good."

"Ya know it good enough. We've never allowed outlaws to get off stealin' women or horses. Ya can't be sayin' we should start now. I seem to remember hangin' a few on this very ground with no complaint from you. For God's sake, man, this is Robert's wife we're speakin' of."

Ulysses sat back, looked at the table and thought for a while. The action the McCullochs urged was the most dangerous they had ever undertaken together. Many people were sure to die. Ulysses needed the McCullochs' friendship, but this was too important, too big, to just go along without at least trying to reason with the proud, deeply offended Irishmen. Ulysses tried to think how to talk sense, diplomatically, with the brothers, bent on war. He decided it just had to be said, straight out.

Ulysses spoke to Robert. "You say Placido stole the girl. But we all know, there's no way he could'a forced 'er, quiet, off yer place with yer people all around. The girl took just two horses. She left you with all her land, all her cattle and all her horses. And why would you want her back after what she's done? I figure Placido got the short end of the deal, anyway you look at it."

Robert's face flushed almost as red as his hair and beard, with anger. "It was already all mine. Land, cattle, girl, horses."

"We're gonna rest here tonight and tomorrow, then we ride out," Angus

said, with finality. "Once we get to Mexico, we'll travel at night, hide out in the days. Now, how many men can ya bring?"

Morningstar set her work aside and glared at the McCullochs' backs. Ulysses regarded her, amazed as always that the Sioux beauty had remained with him, living here in this dry country so far from her people and their plush northern lands, which she longed for, still. *She's just about ta scalp 'em both right now*, Ulysses thought, amused.

Ulysses looked at Diego. Diego nodded, ever so slightly. Ulysses looked back at Angus.

"It'll be me, Diego, Ignacio, and both our vaqueros."

Angus sat back and considered Ulysses's offer. Ulysses was leaving his son and Diego's son, both nearly twenty years old, behind, protecting them from the dangerous fight ahead. Still, Angus was satisfied. Ulysses was entitled to leave someone back. And, Angus knew, Diego was totally loyal to Ulysses, but Ulysses could not endanger Diego's son while protecting his own. Old Diego was tough as nails and he could still ride and shoot. Angus figured Diego's experience and cool steadiness were worth more in a gunfight than some lad's limber joints.

"How 'er ya fixed for ammunition?"

Ulysses and Diego exchanged knowing glances.

"We've got a few rounds," Ulysses replied.

Angus understood this to mean that Ulysses's people had plenty of bullets. Ulysses wasn't the type of man to get killed for lack of shooting back.

21

THE EVANS–KINNEY GANG

Diego wagged his finger and said it would be bad luck.

Angus McCulloch had seen the Kid around Fort Sumner and he had even been introduced to him, once, in Lincoln, before the Lincoln County War. At that time, Angus didn't think much of the buck-toothed, pint-sized, New York Irish cowhand. But he figured, if the boy wanted to work hard, maybe he could build a spread someday. Angus doubted the boy would, although the boy's boss, the Englishman John Tunstall, swore he saw qualities and the making of an honorable man in the Kid.

Ulysses and Robert had seen the Kid a few times too. And back in 1877, they had a near scrape with a gang, including the Kid, who were riding under John Kinney and Jesse Evans.

It was Ulysses's custom to constantly scout his territory. He was always ready for Kiowa, Comanche, Apache, and Mexican and North American bandidos. Ulysses's vigilance was appreciated by the McCullochs and other ranchers to the north. Angus referred to Ulysses as the wolf who guarded the southern borders.

It was summer and Ulysses was riding with his son, Telemako O'Laerte, called 'Maco'. They knew how to move, always concealed, below the ridgelines and though the conifers on the west side of their range.

From a height they saw two gringo riders scouting part of their herd, then meeting up to talk. Another man rode in from the direction of the little group of cabins where Ulysses, all his men, and their families lived. Ulysses cursed quietly as one rider rode out to the west. Now, Ulysses and Mako could only trap two.

The O'Laertes, father and son, walked into the trespassers' camp after midnight. The men opened their eyes and looked into rifle barrels. Mako took

the men's guns and bound their hands and arms. Then Mako rode to get Diego and the other caballeros.

Ulysses questioned the captives. They were young, both about twenty years old. The tow-headed, ruddy-faced boy with a blond, peach-fuzzed jaw claimed his name was Boyd Dixon. The shorter, darker lad, maybe part Mexican, acted tough and said his name was "John Smith." Beyond that, the prisoners refused to answer Ulysses's questions.

"All right. We'll do it yer way," Ulysses said and said no more.

Mako, Diego and the others arrived at dawn. Ulysses had John Smith taken about fifty yards away where he could see but not hear what was to be said and done to Dixon. Dixon was put on his horse under a broad oak tree. A noose was properly placed around his neck and the rope was slung over a branch and secured.

"What 'er you doin', mister? I ain't done nothin' but ride onto this range. And whose to say its yer's?"

"I don't know what you done nor what you ain't done 'cause you won't talk to me. But I seen you scoutin' my herd."

"We're just passin' through. It's a free country ain't it?"

Ulysses sighed and shook his head as if very tired. "This is what's gonna happen. Listen close 'cause yer life may depend on it. I'm gonna ask you some clear, simple questions. Now, you see Diego standin' behind you there?"

Dixon looked over his shoulder at the small, lean, grey-bearded caballero. Diego's dark, wrinkled face was as leathery as his greasy, worn chaps and chaleco. Beneath the brim of his dusty sombrero Dixon saw Diego's near-black pupils and there was no mercy in them.

Ulysses continued. "If you refuse to answer any question, I'm gonna let go of this horse's bridle and Diego's gonna quirt the animal. Then we'll bring John Smith over here and give him a chance to save his own life. You want to think real careful 'fore you answer each question. You want to be dead accurate, 'cause we're gonna ask Mr. Smith the same questions, next. If he says anythin' different from what you say, we know yer lyin' and Diego's gonna quirt both yer horses. He's gonna do it straight away. No more talkin', no more waitin', no more lyin'. I got no more time fer this. And I pretty much already fig'red out what yer doin', anyway. The only way Mr. Smith can say exactly what you say is if you both tell the truth. You understand me, boy?"

"Yessir."

"Who 're you scoutin' for?"

"Jesse Evans and Jack Kinney."

"Where are they?"

"We're all s'posed to meet up, in two days, about one-day ride west of here."

"So yer tellin' me they won't be here fer at least three days?"

"I guess that's how it totes up. Yessir."

"How many gun hands they got ridin' with 'em?"

"They're each bringin' about fifteen men."

"How long you been ridin' with 'em?"

"I've rode with Jesse for about two months. I ain't met Mr. Kinney yet."

"There's been a lot 'a raidin' west of here. Some folks been killed."

This didn't sound like a question and Dixon couldn't deny it so he said nothing. They put John Smith on a horse next to Dixon. Once his head was in a noose he confirmed everything Dixon had said. Ulysses told a young vaquero, Miguel, to take the information, ride hard, and bring Robert McCulloch. Ulysses warned Miguel to be alert and wary of ambush. Miguel raced away.

"We told you what you wanted to know. We told the truth. Git us down from here, mister," Dixon pled.

Mako was only fifteen but he had seen these things before. He knew and dreaded what was to come. He looked at his father and winced as Ulysses answered, " I ain't gonna do that, young man."

"But you said we could save our lives by tellin' the truth."

"No. I said you might save your life. But this truth don' do that."

John Smith bent his head and stared at the ground.

"But we ain't done nothin!" Dixon protested.

"You tried to bring thirty armed men against my people."

"They're just comin' for cattle or horses."

"You boys are well armed. Rifles, six guns. Bandoleros with plenty of ammunition. You plan on shootin' steers and horses?"

"Now wait a minute, wait a minute. I'm beggin' you. Just hold us for a few days. When Jesse gits here we'll talk to 'im. He'll pay you a fine fer what

we done. We got money, lots of it. He'll pay enough to satisfy you."

Ulysses thought carefully before he answered. Mako felt hope that Dixon had found a way so they wouldn't have to hang the two boys.

"I think yer prob'ly wrong about what you think Mr. Evans might do for you. He's more likely to pay the fine with lead. But even if yer right, I can't sell you back over to Evans. If I did, I'd just have to fight you another day."

"Give us over to the law, then."

"You see any law around here? That's why you boys do yer raidin' in this country, 'cause there ain't no law nowhere near. And I got no men to spare to watch you. We gotta git ready to meet up with yer amigos that's comin'. Now, I've answered all yer questions because I think its fair fer you to know that the things you say have been heard and thought over. But nothin' you say changes the reasons why its got to be this way. You best git ready now."

"Do me a favor, mister?" Boyd's voice cracked and a tear ran down his cheek.

"What is it?"

"Write my grandmother a letter. Phoebe Dixon in Mesilla. Tell 'er I'm hung."

"If I'm still alive after I meet up with Mr. Evans and Mr. Kinney, I'll surely do that fer you, son. You got anything to say, Mr. Smith?"

Smith stared at the ground and shook his head, no. Ulysses released the men's bridles, stepped away and turned his back. Diego whipped both horses at once and Ulysses heard the taunt ropes squeak and scrape the oak bark.

Ulysses gave Smith's horse to Diego and he reserved Dixon's horse for Miguel as a reward in case he returned quickly, with help. Ulysses divided the dead boys' kits, tack, knives, money, watches, weapons and ammunition among his men. For himself, he kept a fine new .41 single-action bulldog revolver they found in Dixon's saddle wallet. The hanged men both sported new hand-tooled boots and Ulysses offered them to anyone they might fit, but Diego wagged his finger and said it would be bad luck. All the vaqueros agreed.

Dixon and Smith were still hanging there when John Kinney, Jesse Evans, William Bonney, Jim Croft and twenty-six other outlaws rode up four days later. A piece of hide was nailed to the hanging tree. There was writing painted in blood on it:

DEER MISTAR KINY YOU BERY EM AND COME ON AHED

Kinney's scouts reported that Ulysses's homestead was now guarded by at least ten well-armed men. Ulysses, Robert McCulloch and close to twenty more men were riding west up the adjacent valley so they could turn south and cut the outlaws off from escape back toward the Rio Grande. Kinney realized that this maneuver probably meant Angus McCulloch would be coming with more men from the Pecos in the east.

You spell like shit but you're a tricky bastard, O'Laerte, Kinney thought, as he discerned the nature of the dangerous trap.

The outlaws retreated, west, and beat the ranchers over the rugged Guadalupe Mountains. The two forces came in sight of each other and only a few long-range shots were tried as the gang of ladrones broke from the high country and ran out onto the desert plains of the immense Tularosa basin, headed for their home country around the Rio Grande and El Paso del Norte.

The outlaws were too many to fight in the open without Angus and his men. So the ranchers turned back for their own Pecos country.

At the time, the ranchers knew nothing of William Bonney. It was only later, during the Lincoln County War, that they heard that "Billy the Kid" had ridden with Evans's gang during the attempted raid on Ulysses's herd in '77.

Now, after the Lincoln County War, vengeful lawmen hunted Billy for the murders of a sheriff and two deputies. But Ulysses, Angus, Robert, and many other ranchers were determined to hang or shoot Billy for rustling cattle and horses all along the Pecos—and in Texas, too.

22

FORT SUMNER

Is that how I look when you have me?

Billy and Paulina Maxwell lay peacefully in trance after love, among oak brush, carrizo, and fragrant lilacs in the shade of the great cottonwood bosque by the Pecos River at Fort Sumner. Billy lay on his side; head on his saddle wallets and Paulina nestled back against him. Billy's arm lay over Paulina's side in the deep curve above her hip and his hand cupped the smooth arc of her belly as he slipped into sleep and began to snore softly.

The lovers lay just above a placid pool where the Pecos widened and slowed before a natural stone dam. Paulina looked through their leafy screen and watched a group of Mescalero Apache women and girls descend the opposite bank to bathe in the popular swimming hole.

Three naked and shriveled grandmothers took sun and washed clothes on the rocks at water's edge. A group of middle-aged matriarchs sat together in the pool near the bank in water to their breasts, and laughed and gossiped about births and love affairs among their clans and the buffooneries of their men-folk.

An ancient warrior, Melquiádes, sat atop the far bank above the women holding an antique fusil that was even older than he was. He kept watch there to warn away any who might intrude on the privacy of the mothers and daughters of his tribe.

The younger women and girls laughed and frolicked in the pool. Foremost among them were Tzoeh and Evangelina, daughters of the chieftain Don Tenorio. The beautiful sisters were the pride of their clan.

"Look, Billy!" Paulina poked Billy's ribs with her elbow.

Billy mumbled in his sleep and tried to hold on to this dreams. Paulina poked him harder, and Billy opened his eyes.

"Look Billy. That's Tzoeh."

Billy looked down at the dark beauty. She stood facing him, water to her thighs, laughing and splashing water back at the young girls who screeched, giggled, and cavorted around her.

Tzoeh was as beautiful as any woman Billy had ever seen. He ran his eyes down over her wet, jet black hair, black eyes, joyous, white-toothed smile, impossibly ripe breasts, flat belly and mature, wide hips to the dark delta of her sex at the gap between her curved and soft, yet lean and muscular thighs.

"Isn't she beautiful? Am I as pretty as she is? Is that how I look when you have me?"

"Huh." Billy chuckled cautiously. Paulina's playful teasing amused him but he sensed danger. Paulina was renowned for her stormy mood changes and powerful temper.

"Look how pretty she is, Billy. Would you like to do it with her?"

"No, Paulina, mi amor, solo quiero en ti," Billy lied, but Paulina's suggestion coupled with the stunning, miraculous vision of the Apache beauty caused Billy to stir against Paulina's soft bottom. Paulina pushed herself up on one arm, turned and slapped Billy's chest, playfully.

"You liar! ¡Cochino! Pig! Look at you! You want her!"

"No, mi amor," Billy insisted. "Solo pienso en ti. No, my love, I only think of you." He reached out and cupped Paulina's breast, but now Paulina's mood was changing to real anger. She slapped Billy's hand away and rose to her feet.

"¡Cabrón! Liar! I know how you are! I know what you did with Celsa the other night and what you do with that slut Carmela in Puerto de Luna!"

"¡No, mi amor!"

Paulina arose, stepped into her dress, pulled it up to her waist and pulled her blouse over her head.

"¡Chingate, mentiroso! Fuck you, liar!"

Paulina snatched up her suede-topped, buffalo-hide soled moccasins and stepped back as Billy rose to his feet, reached for her and implored her.

"¡No, Paulina! Mi amor. Te juro. ¡Tu eres mi amor! I swear to you: you are my love."

"You bastard!" She laughed and she broke out of the little thicket and rushed down the bank. The sudden movement drew the Apaches' attention.

Tzoeh looked up and saw Paulina laughing and dancing away from Billy as he stood naked in the brush, arms extended, imploring her, and Tzoeh laughed and blushed as she locked eyes with Billy and knew he regarded her magnificence. All the Apache women laughed at his discomfort and at their sudden discovery of the lovers' secret.

On the far bank, Melquiádes stood and frowned at Billy. Billy, embarrassed, raised his open palms before him in a gesture of peace and surrender and he quickly bent, gathered his gear and slipped off, upriver, and disappeared into the forest.

In 1881, Fort Sumner and the Bosque Redondo were no longer a reservation for Navajo and Mescalero Apache. The fort and surrounding lands had been purchased from the United States in 1871 by Kit Carson's old amigo, Don Luciano Maxwell, and his wife Doña Luz. Don Luciano had passed to the other side in 1875; now his son Pete handled the family's ranching business. Pete's sister Paulina was like a princess there. And the old fort was the hub of a thriving New Mexican community.

But the Fort was still a popular meeting place for Puebloans and for Apaches and Comanches, who were granted leave by reservation agents to travel out onto the Llano Estacado to engage in traditional buffalo hunts.

Billy sat on the portál before Beaver Smith's saloon, talking with some vaqueros, two Texas cowhands and the drunk one-legged Scot named Wallace. Wallace still wore the same blue Union army blouse and sergeant's chevrons he had worn since his honorable discharge in 1862. Wallace was telling the story of the battle of Glorieta Pass, of how a rebel ball in hot action had shattered his femur and how he bit leather and screamed as the surgeon sawed his leg off and seared the wound against infection with a red-hot iron.

Billy watched as several Mescalero Apache clans and some Comanches, paroled from their reservations to hunt, packed up their mules and horses and headed out across the wide plaza, which had once been the fort's parade ground, toward the llano.

Chieftains and young braves, armed with bows, spears and many types of feather-adorned fire-arms, both antiquated and new, rode ahead on spirited prancing painted Mustangs which could barely be held back. Their dogs loped eagerly beside them and their women followed, leading mules and packhorses bearing bundles of supplies. Tzoeh and Evanglina were among the train of women, talking and laughing. Tzoeh saw Billy and her eyes sparkled with humor, recalling Billy's embarrassment which she had witnessed only hours before, when he had stood naked and pleading as Paulina skipped away while all the women laughed. Billy tipped his sombrero and blushed in the knowledge that he was the object of the stunning beauty's amusement.

As the tribes moved out, Billy saw Pete Maxwell coming across the parade ground from the Maxwells' big, two-story house built over the old officers' quarters.

"Don Pedro!" Billy greeted his old friend.

"Guillermo, ven por aquí. William, come over here."

Pete drew Billy away from his companions. Pete did not know the cowboys and he was unsure of their allegiances or knowledge of the boy's identity.

"Billy," Pete said. "I never thought I'd see you alive again." The men embraced.

Billy laughed. "You should have known, amigo," he said. "I'm not the kind to just lie down like a dog and then walk up and let 'em hang me."

"You shouldn't be here, Billy. They're looking for you. They expect you to come here. They've already been here and they'll be back."

"You know I'm too quick for 'em, Pete. Damn, it's good to see you."

Pete looked skeptical. And what he said next cut Billy's heart. "Billy. You've got to think about what could happen. I heard you were with Paulina today. What if they had come at you then? People could get hurt. Killed. Don't you even care about her? I thought you would be dead, hanged, by now, and I'm happy to see you alive and free. But it's no good. You can't stay here."

Shamed and hurt as he was at Pete's gentle criticism and clear eviction, the Kid nonetheless affected a brave air of casual indifference.

"Don't worry about it, Pete. We're leavin' right now. I just wanted to stop and see my friends, but we're headed out. Hasta la vista, amigo. See you later, friend."

"Sí. El joven es muy macho. Yes, the young man is very brave." Pete

thought, on hearing the Kid's casual farewell.

"Hasta la vista," Pete replied and again embraced the doomed boy. But, as he did so, stern, unyielding knowledge of the Kid's fate descended over the two and both knew it was unlikely they would ever again see each other in this life.

Billy turned and walked toward the corrales.

"¡Guillermo Bonito! Pretty William!" Pete called.

Billy turned.

"Do you have any supplies?"

Billy shrugged.

"Take ten of my steers."

Billy was hurt even more. He feared Pete was offering because he assumed Billy and his compañeros would rustle the cattle anyway.

"Don Pedro," Billy chided, "you know I wouldn't steal from you."

"Sure, I do, Billy. I know that. But I want you to have them. Eat one. Sell the rest. At least have a few dollars in your pocket, hijo. I'll send Epimenio to the corrales with a bill of sale."

"Pues gracias, Don Pedro," Billy bowed his head subtly.

"De nada, y no hay de que, Billy. Vaya con Dios. It's nothing, nothing at all, Billy. Go with God."

Pete watched the Kid walk away and he thought: Yes, Billy, take the steers, sell them and go to Mexico. Perhaps I should have warned you more clearly. But a man must do what he must—for his family. And if you come back here again for my sister, I swear before God my witness, I will give you up to Garrett.

23

EL PRIMER CORRIDO DE BILLY THE KID

You ride always, like a tumbleweed blown before the whirlwinds of God.

Evans, Montoya, Bonney and Croft did sell Pete Maxwell's steers. They rode south into Texas, headed for Mexico. They still had some money and it was well after dark when they arrived at Juan De Dios Aragón's inn and cantina which stood among nine other adobe houses and jacales at the crossroads called Santa Cecilia, thirty miles above the Mexican border.

The desert plain all around was moonlit sage, cactus, ocotillo, jimson and mesquite, but there were a few cedars and junipers around a small spring that supported the lonely little settlement that served as a waystation for travelers passing from Terlingua to El Paso Del Norte.

The riders corralled their horses and Montoya, Bonney and Evans donned silver-buttoned frock-coats from their saddle bags, dusted off their sombreros, and walked up to Juan's place. But Croft, ribs aching, lay his bedroll under a juniper behind the corrales and dozed and moaned there while his amigos drank and danced in Juan de Dios' house, which Juan called the Inn of the Media Luna.

Juan de Dios was a Spaniard, part Basque, who had come to the country by way of New Orleans only forty years before. He was tall, over six feet three inches, and he was blond and blue-eyed. Juan had been headed for Nevada where sheepherding kin had settled. But he had met Prescilliana Tapia at Santa Cecilia, and transfixed by her great beauty, he had remained there as years slipped away. Fifteen of their seventeen children had died in childbirth or infancy and their two surviving sons had long since left Santa Cecilia to settle in New Mexico Territory, at Anton Chico, north of Lincoln.

Juan de Dios loved to play the guitar. He played flamencas gitanos and Spanish ballads but he soon learned many rancheras and even some Anglo and Irish songs and jigs. Juan was very gregarious and he had traveled far in his

youth, so it was strange that he had passed so much of his life, trapped in a sort of limbo, in the isolated little village.

Juan loved to gamble and, over the years, he gambled away or otherwise squandered Prescilliana's flocks and even her lands, which had once been considerable. Prescilliana grew to hate her tall, handsome, dissolute husband. Her tongue was sharp and unrelenting and Juan claimed Prescilliana was a remorseless torturer—because she was dark and, it was rumored, part Comanche.

When she was three years old, Comanches had stolen Prescilliana. In those times it was the custom of Spanish and native peoples to raid and steal each other's children in order to punish their traditional enemies in unending feuds. It took Prescilliana's brothers two years, roaming the llano, to find her and take her back. The searchers finally rode into a transient Comanche village of only a few wickiups and tipis. The mature warriors were absent, hunting, and the five Tapia brothers with their lances and escopetas easily dominated the women, boys and old men of the tiny encampment. The Comanches offered no resistance and disclosed that Prescilliana was among them. They gave her over to her brothers and claimed she had only been taken because she was the daughter of a Comanche warrior who had secretly known great passion with Prescilliana's mother, Josefina Tapia. The Tapia boys ignored the insulting claim and rode home, joyously, with their lost sister now restored to them. But the rumor of her genesis was whispered among her clan and her deeply dark skin and eyes and high cheekbones seemed to support the truth of the Comanches' claim.

After years of marriage to the charming, useless Juan de Dios, Prescilliana felt nothing, not even anger, when he claimed that the source of their problems was in her savage and cruel Comanche blood. Prescilliana declared, correctly, that Juan de Dios was a "tomador, jugador y mujeriego: a drinker, a gambler and a womanizer." She called him "Juan del Diablo" and she departed Santa Cecilia never to return. Juan heard his wife had joined their sons in the north, but many years had passed without word.

But Juan de Dios remained. He had reached an age at which women were no longer particularly interesting to him but he played his guitar, tended his children's graves, served food and drink and gave shelter to those who passed the lonely crossroads on the bleak and dangerous Texas desert. Juan de Dios loved to drink and discuss philosophy and the possible ultimate destinations of the bodies and souls of the journeyers who stopped on their way. And so, Juan de Dios was greatly pleased when his old friends, Billy, Jesse and Patricio entered the long front hall of his adobe house which was the cantina at La Posada de la Media Luna.

"Guillermo!"

Juan loved Billy most of all, but he gave hearty abrazos, embraces, to all three outlaws.

The outlaws rested, ate and drank. Word of their presence passed through the villita and many of Juan's neighbors came to celebrate the guests' arrival.

Jesse was wary and uncomfortable. He was wanted in Texas, and the formidable Texas rangers seemed to roam everywhere. But after a few drinks, he loosened up, and Billy was as gay and cheerful as he had always been.

Billy had a sweetheart in the place, Florencia. She rushed to Juan's and into Billy's arms when she heard he was there. Juan played his guitar and an ex-rebel, Gardey, of Cajun blood, who lived in Santa Cecilia with Beatríz Baca, played the fiddle. Everyone danced and Billy knew all the steps and pasos. Billy and Florita whirled about the floor. The children of the tiny pueblo played and ran about the room and young mothers watched and nursed their babes, modestly covering their breasts with fans, shawls and brightly colored serapes.

Billy told the congregation his favorite joke, a long story about a pig with a wooden leg. When a visitor asked about the pig, its owner extolled the animal's virtues. The pig had awakened a family and led them, through the smoke, out of a burning house. The pig swam into a river and saved a boy from drowning. The pig led a search party to a young girl lost in the desert.

"But I was just wonderin' about the swine's peg-leg," Billy continued. "The owner said, 'Pues hombre, you don't eat a pig like that all at once.'"

Gardey fiddled an Irish jig in Billy's honor and everyone watched and shouted encouragement as Billy danced, Irish style, in the center of the room, hands on hips, tapping his toes behind his heels and kicking his legs forward with remarkable poise, speed and balance. Patricio slipped away with "La Gorda," whose real name was Marta—a woman possessed of immense and opulent flesh and curves.

It was very late and most had gone when Juan told Billy that he had made up a song, a corrido, about Billy's deeds.

"El Corrido de Guillermo Bonito," Juan announced.

Billy sat and shyly smiled as Juan played and sang the spirited corrido, and the other listeners shouted their approval of the dramatic verses: "¡Eso!" "¡Así!" "¡Que viva!"

Juan's Spanish rhymes told of Guillermo, a mere boy with no family, who had stood up like a man against the oppression of the common people, both Anglo and Spanish, by unjust and powerful men who falsely claimed legal sanction for their evil deeds. Juan sang of the boy's loyalty to his friends, killed one by one, and how the boy never forgot their kindness and how, again and again, he honored his vows to avenge his fallen compadres. Juan's song told how the boy's enemies had trapped, chained and imprisoned him, many times, and plotted to hang him. But the boy was shrewd as the wolf, fast and dangerous as the cougar and no jail could hold him. In Juan's version of the story, Billy had retrieved the pistol from the privy, shot Bell and Olinger and rode away, free. Guillermo continued to defy the president, the governor of New Mexico Territory and their forces infinite and invincible. Guillermo rode and fought on against impossible odds.

The listeners cheered, Billy grinned and blushed and Juan suddenly stopped playing. He looked around at Billy and the little group of campesinos who watched him silently with expectant, questioning expressions.

Juan looked back down, pensively, at his guitar and he played a slow, offhand progression of melancholy notes. Then he looked back up at Billy and said, "It's not finished yet."

The layers of meaning in the simple statement were understood by all.

"Muy bien." Bonney said. "When you finish it, finish it good."

It was two hours before dawn. There was a dying fire in the horno. Jesse lay, sleeping on a banco, Juan with guitar, sat before the fire working out a sweet, sad melody. Billy and Florita sat across the room, in shadow, against the wall by the door. They leaned their chairs back on two legs and Billy rested his boots on the table before them. Florita nestled under Billy's arm, her head on his shoulder, and they kissed and whispered.

"Vamonos para tu cuarto. Let's go to your room," Billy suggested.

The girl had greeted Billy so warmly and they had danced and laughed all night. So Billy fully expected Flora would grant him her immeasurable favors. But the pretty girl with jet-black hair and big brown eyes did not consent.

"You broke my heart, Beelee. You hurt me so bad."

"¿Como? What did I do?" Billy whispered sweetly, thinking he would need only to deal with some petty jealously before taking her.

"I was pregnant when you rode away. I didn't know what to do. But, soon, I understood I could not hope in you. I went to see La Viejita who lives on the mesa. She gave me a potion. I let our baby go, never to be. I had to. Forgive me." Flora looked at the Kid's face. Tears ran down her cheeks and there were tears suspended, quivering in Billy's eyes.

"I know you had to. I don't know why, but I never got the choice to stay still."

Flora caressed Billy's cheek. "Mi Guillermo Bonito. You ride always, like a tumbleweed blown before the whirlwinds of God."

The door opened and Angus, Robert and Ulysses walked in. They did not see, and walked past, Billy and Flora in the shadows on their left.

"Juan de Dios!" Angus bellowed. "You old diablo. Good ta see ya, and it'll be better ta see yer whiskey!"

Juan looked up, shocked and speechless at the sudden crisis. Jesse stirred, lifted his hat from over his eyes and rose quickly to his feet as he and the ranchers recognized each other.

Before the ranchers could draw, they heard the clicks of Bonney's Colt's Thunderers being cocked behind them, and his command: "¡No se muevan! Don't move!"

The ranchers froze.

"Now, raise your hands up real slow and empty."

Flora jumped up and backed away from Billy. Evans drew his .45 and covered the intruders from the front; Bonney had them from the rear. Angus, Robert and Ulysses raised their hands, open, above their shoulders.

"You got 'em, Jesse?"

"I do."

"Turn around," Billy said.

The ranchers turned to face the Kid. Billy walked forward, a Thunderer in each hand. The Kid looked the ranchers over carefully. Ulysses's fringed, buckskin sleeve hung below his wrist, and the Kid saw a leather string around Ulysses's wrist and leather strings descending below the sleeve.

"Get their side arms."

Jesse stepped up behind the prisoners, pulled pistols from holsters and set them on the bar.

"You still got em, Jesse?"

"I do."

Billy stepped up close to Ulysses. The barrel of the Colt's in Billy's right hand was pointed, nearly touching the bridge of Ulysses's nose. Billy holstered his other pistol and, never taking his eyes off Ulysses's face, reached up and fished Ulysses's derringer from under his right sleeve.

Ulysses's eyes betrayed a brief flash of fear when the Kid deprived him of the trick he figured might be his last chance. The Kid saw it and grinned.

Patricio walked in the back door, grinning, ready to be ribbed by his amigos for his tryst with La Gorda. When he saw Billy and Jesse covering the ranchers, his smile evaporated and he pulled his Colt's .45 Peacemaker.

Billy walked back and sat in his chair against the wall. He put Ulysses's derringer on the table, pulled his second Thunderer, and pointed with the gun at the chairs before him.

"Sit down," he said, amiably.

The ranchers complied.

Ulysses was looking around and listening, trying to figure some chance. He heard the metallic jingle of spurs and scrape of a bar stool as Evans moved and sat at the rude bar-board behind and to his left. Ulysses knew his only chance was to talk his way out and he was thinking what to say. But Angus spoke first.

"Now don't do anything stupid, boy. I've heard you're no fool. We've got about forty men outside. You start shootin', you're dead, sure."

Montoya walked quickly forward, looked out the window by the door, pulled the shades closed and slammed the thick wooden bolt into place across the door and frame.

"There are many men at the corrales," he said.

The Kid raised his chin, slightly, and grinned, very amused, his biggest buck-toothed grin. One lip was slightly raised in a sort of sneer; the Kid's eyes seemed to be half closed and Ulysses knew that what he had heard was true: the Kid was a calm, true killer.

"Well I don't know how you old boys found us, but the luck is bad both ways. We found you too." The Kid barely held back an ironical laugh as he spoke.

"We're not lookin' fer you," Angus said. "We've our own business and we're just headin' south. Now give us back our guns and we'll be on our way."

The minute he said it, Angus knew how false and absurdly impossible his claim and suggestion sounded to the outlaws.

Ulysses kept thinking hard as Robert broke in. "A Mexican ladrón stole my wife." Robert choked as he said that. "It's him, and only him, we're after. We don't care about you; we want no trouble with you boys. My brother's tellin' you the truth. Let us walk out of here. We'll ride out and won't look back. We give you our word."

Patricio's alarmed glare softened a bit as he considered that there might be a way out of the hopeless situation. Patricio looked at Jesse, but Jesse's face was hard and skeptical. Patricio looked at Billy and saw no chance.

"You're not lookin' for us. You don't care about us. You give your word. You know how many words I've heard? From people like you? From the governor himself? Do you give your word you didn't pay hard cash to that panhandle cattlemen's association that set a reward and 'er payin' hired killers to find us?"

Ulysses would have denied it but Angus and Robert were the type of men who believed it was wrong to lie under any circumstances. So they said nothing.

"And you, Indian fighter," Billy said to Ulysses, "you give your word you won't turn around and take us with all your men the minute you walk out of here?"

Ulysses had no compunction about lying if it might work, but he knew the Kid knew better. Ulysses would immediately, if he got the chance, shoot or hang the Kid. He knew it and he knew the Kid knew it. Ulysses knew he would probably die immediately if he were to insult the reckless boy's intelligence and

pride with a transparent lie. The only way out was to tell the truth. So Ulysses said it.

"No. I don't give my word. I would though, if I thought you'd believe it. But you an' me both know the minute I get free I'll try to kill you, no matter what Angus and Robert say or do."

Angus and Robert looked at Ulysses, astounded at this uncharacteristic and apparently suicidal honesty.

But Billy was pleased. The old scout had admitted the clear truth of the situation. They were enemies, both about to die, but with a little honesty between them.

"Yeah. Looks like we got us a old-fashioned Mexican standoff here. Juan, pour us all a drink. We're all goin' under, together, tonight. I'm taking these men with me and I hope a lot of their boys, outside, before I'm through. Then you can finish your song."

Flora rushed out the back door. Juan de Dios poured stiff portions of aguardiente for all and his hand was shaking. "Billy, you wouldn't kill unarmed men."

"What do you say, O'Laerte? Angus? Robert? Would you hang me if you had me unarmed and hog-tied?" Billy asked.

Again, Angus and Robert were too honest to deny it. Besides, the question was rhetorical; all knew the answer.

Ulysses raised his glass, saluted the Kid and drained it. "Ahh! You gave us yer best stuff, Juan! he said, cheerfully and casually. "Pour another one."

Juan poured Ulysses another.

Then Ulysses made his try:

"No, boy," he said. "I wouldn't hang ya if I had ya tied. And ya know why? 'Cause I got better use fer you. Angus and Robert told the truth. We're goin' ta Mexico ta fight the Trujillo family. They've got a lot'a guns. We're lookin' at a hard fight. That's the truth and the truth is the way out of this. We don't have ta trust each other 'cause we kin all know we want the same thing. We all wanna live. We kin all help each other do that. You boys ride with us. If ya do, ya help us git what we want. We want Robert's wife and we wanna live a hell of a lot more than we wanna hang you jest ta save a few cows someday."

Ulysses looked at Montoya standing by the door. Then he turned and looked over his shoulder at Evans and the pointed barrel of Jesse's Remington.

"You boys help us and we kin help you. We'll speak for ya to git the gov'ner's amnesty. You git clear of the law and ya won't have to be runnin', stealin' our cattle, no more. You kin settle down an raise yer own cattle. Hell, we'll give ya a few seed stock. So why would we need ta hang you? Jesse. Yer wanted here in Texas. Jest stay out 'a Texas. Mr. Bonney. We can't help you. Yer condemned. Maybe the gov'ner could pardon ya but he won't. We all know that. You killed three lawmen, not countin' Morton, Baker, Hindeman and Roberts. But you help us, ya help yer friends and ya kin jest stay in Mexico—and we wish ya luck. You can't trust my word. You know it and I know it. But you can know that I'd rather face the Trujillos' guns with yer guns by me. You boys 'er known, proven fighters. You kin take the McCullochs' word an you kin take the knowledge that I want ta live and I know the best way ta do that is ta ride with you, not against you."

Evans and Montoya were convinced. Everybody looked at Bonney.

The Kid had been ready and committed to kill and die. He had presented a casual air but, inside, he was ready to explode. It wasn't easy for him to back off now, at Ulysses's words. The boy thought for a while. He had not told his amigos, but he had planned to leave them in the morning, when they they rode out for Mexico. He had intended to ride north and attempt to kill Garrett and Governor Wallace in a final act of revenge. Now every thing had suddenly changed with this chance meeting with Ulysses and the McCullochs.

Ulysses's argument made sense, no matter how William looked at it. And a sudden realization and sadness washed over his soul. He realized he was tired of fighting and killing. He was tired of the endless cycle of death and vengeance. But he had to survive this night before he could begin to figure how to find a new life of peace and freedom. William took a deep breath and exhaled in a long sigh. "Can you get the governor's amnesty for Croft too?"

"Jim Croft's here?"

"He's out there."

Ulysses smiled. "That's damn good news. Four pistoleros are better than three."

24

EL DESTINO

Hablamos de los que nacen, los que casan y los que mueran.
We speak of those who are born, of those who marry and those who die.

The war party camped on the Rio Grande in a cottonwood bosque where the acequia split from the rio and ran above the fields of the little pueblo of El Destino. They would wait for the supply wagons, sleep, then descend into Mexico.

There was some mescal in the town and some of Angus's men partook. Bonney and the outlaws also drank at their campfire, apart from the cattlemen. A little adobe church with graceful arched buttresses, a modest tower and a great green brass bell stood on a stony hill above the pueblo.

After midnight, the Kid climbed the cerro to the iglesia and passed through the arched, gray cedar-supported portál, and low walls, into the "campo santo," the graveyard, before the church's tall, carved wooden doors.

The moon was only a sliver and the Kid lay on the grave of an ancient conquistador before its carved, massive, marble headstone crowned by a reclining, cold, slumbering angel.

The Kid looked up and wondered at the broad cloud belt of stars, which divided the firmament in half. He thought of how small we are, how brief our lives. He thought of his mother, dead and perhaps among the stars. He thought of how he was doomed to die young. He hoped he would go down in a good fight. Maybe, if he fought and died well, he would be remembered in songs, like the Irish heroes in the ballads he had heard when he was a child, or like the caballeros whose deeds were told in corridos sung in the New Mexican cantinas. Then the Kid began to hope that he could avoid his fate. He thought maybe he could slip away into Mexico, where the northern lawmen could never find him. He could start over.

The dry, rasping cackle of an old woman split the silent night. The Kid instantly pulled a pistol and sprang into a coiled, squatting crouch against the headstone. His alarm brought a fit of laughter from three old crones who sat in shadow under the stone arch against the doors of the old church. The Kid pointed his revolver and scanned the campo santo before the headstone, then slowly, carefully, peered over the stone at the women in the doorway.

Damn, he thought, if you don't get more careful, there won't be no fight at all.

It occurred to him that maybe he hadn't seen them because the old women were shrouded in black with black rebozos over their heads. The women laughed harder as the Kid, big eyed, looked at them, over his gun.

"Calmate. Calm down."

"Ven aquí nino. Come here boy."

"No tengas miedo hijo. Don't be afraid, son."

The Kid rose, looked back around to assure himself there was no ambush, then holstered his .41. He walked toward the women, ascended three stone steps and stood over them. He shook his head, shrugged and smiled.

"¿Que haces aquí hijo? What are you doing here, son?"

"Nada, pensado, nada mas, abuela. Nothing, just thinking, grand-mother."

"Sientate. Sit."

The Kid sat cross-legged before the women. The woman on the left held the cloth of her rebozo across her face so that only black, wrinkle-framed eyes and protruding tufts of white hair were visible.

"Yo soy Angela, I am Angel," she said

"Yo soy Magdalena. I am Magdalene."

"Yo soy Luz. I am Light."

"Yo soy William, 'Guillermo,'" the Kid lied.

"No, tu no eres Guillermo. You are not William," Luz said with perfect assurance.

The women all laughed.

Luz's entire face was visible. She had a Roman nose like a beak, gray eyes, thin lips, rotten teeth and wrinkled, translucent skin, like parchment.

The Kid's buckteeth protruded as he grinned, puzzled.

"¿De qué piensas, hijo? What are you thinking about, son?" Magdalena

asked. "¿De la verdad? ¿Del futúro? The truth? The future?"

"Solamente de las estrellas. Only of the stars," the Kid lied again. "¿Y ustedes, abuelas, qué hacen aquí, a esta hora? And you, grandmothers, what are you doing here at this hour?"

"Hablamos de los que nacen, los que casan y los que mueran. We speak of those who are born, of those who marry and of those who die," Magdalena said.

The women all laughed again.

Magdalena pulled a bottle of mescal from beneath her robe. The Kid laughed too. They all laughed and joked as they shared the bottle. There were three worms at the bottom of the bottle and Luz placed them, one at a time, on the Kid's tongue. After he swallowed the worms, the Kid's head slowly drooped forward. When his chin met his chest, he collapsed onto his side. He sensed danger and tried to reach for a gun, but darkness descended over his eyes.

The stars wheeled overhead and the Kid's darkness was illuminated by dream. In his dream the Kid rose to his feet and walked through the arched doorway into the church. A few candles burned along the walls, lighting colored retablos of the Stations of the Cross, and the Kid saw Magdalena, Angela and Luz seated on the chancel floor before the altar. Many other old hags, all in black, surrounded them. Each of the women held secret bones and other mysterious objects in their claw-like hands, and secrets were breathed and whispered from their withered maws and all among them.

The Kid stood before the black coven and looked past them at the painted, carved wooden Cristo who hung, crucified, behind the altar. The Christ was already dead, his skin a blue-gray color. His face, in death, still conveyed a profound sadness. Blood flowed from many wounds and ran down his face, neck, arms, torso and legs.

"We like ya, boy," Angela said, in Irish accented English. Her voice sounded like the Kid's mother, Catherine. "You are ambidextrous and you have two destinies. We give knowledge of these things so that you may choose freely and wisely,"

"You go to Mexico to make war against the Trujillos," Magdalena said. "In Mexico you may fight only to defend and give mercy to the helpless and oppressed. If you choose this path you will find a new life. You will live, thereafter; in peace and you will die an old man in your bed, as the washed, colored clothes of your grandchildren dry and move in the wind outside your window. Your children and theirs will remember you. But no song of your warlike prowess will be sung beyond the third generation."

"But," Luz said, "if you choose war of blood and fire and revenge—your own, or the McCulloch's—then the Trujillos will be destroyed and you must also die before your twenty-second year. But songs and tales of your valor will be sung and told for as long as human men live and walk this earth."

"Decide," said Angela.

The Kid awoke, and he lay alone, on stone, before the church, in the cold, gray light before the sun rose. The Kid sat on the top step of the threshold before the church doors. He picked up his sugarloaf-crowned sombrero, slapped dust from the hat and put it on.

It was the Kid's custom to always study his surroundings for sign of ambush before he moved each morning, but somehow today he knew there was no danger. He walked over and pissed against the wall enclosing the graveyard. Then he returned to his seat on the steps. He rolled and lit a cigarette. As he smoked, he watched the dawn and considered spring wild flowers among the gravestones. Then he strolled, casually, through the campo santo, passed the gate and descended to the war camp.

25

SCALP HUNTERS

La muerte no es nada. Death is nothing.

The McCullochs' war party rode two nights and half a day into Mexico, across an immense, seemingly boundless sage and saguaro plain.

They stopped and rested at mid-day at a poor well and ruined corral on a lonely crossroads. The cowhands huddled about the supply wagons. The outlaws lay apart from them in a suggestion of shade against the corrales, pulled their sombreros over their eyes and tried to sleep.

Ulysses and Diego had gone ahead, but their man, Lalo, kept watch and he was first to alert the McCullochs that a party was coming along the road from the east. It was too late to run, even if the riders turned out to be Mexican army, so all made ready and waited by the wagons and under whatever cover could be found.

Angus watched the approaching riders through a spyglass and soon announced that they were civilians, only ten in number. The riders stopped at a distance and studied the McCullochs' party before they came on.

The Kid was new to Mexico—he had only been in a few border towns—and he watched with great interest to see those who approached. He soon decided that the riders were probably not Mexicans. Seven of them were Anglos, ragged and on skeleton-like horses, nearly ridden to death. Three riders were Indians, Pawnees, such as the Kid had never seen. The Pawnees' heads were shaven except for high scalp locks, which towered above the crests of their skulls. Feathers in the hair at the napes of their necks dangled down their spines. Two of the Pawnees were naked from the waist up. They displayed blue tattoos on their foreheads, chins, chests and arms. One Pawnee wore a blanket around his shoulders and torso. All wore breechcloths, leather leggings and knee-high buffalo-hide moccasins. The Pawnees had quivers with bows and arrows slung on their backs; two carried breach-loading Sharps rifles, one a Kentucky long rifle and each had a Colt's revolver in his waist-strap or slung from his saddle horn.

The Anglos were also heavily armed. All bore repeating rifles in scabbards on their saddles. Two had shotguns as well. All the white men carried two revolvers hung at their sides, thrust into their ragged pants or boots or slung over their backs, and all wore bandoleros strapped across their bodies, filled with bullets. Their shirtsleeves and fronts were splattered with blood. One of the men had no shirt and under his coat, bloody bandages could be seen. He lay forward on his mount and swayed, barely hanging on.

The riders, and each of them, carried rawhide ristras of jet-black Indian scalps caked with blood, which dangled from the horns and hind-bows of their saddles. One of the Pawnees held a braided leather lead attached to the bridle of a good gelding. The gelding was as exhausted as the other horses. Two Apache maidens, prisoners, rode the gelding. One of the women was the beauty, Tzoeh, the other her sister, Evanglina. The women's wrists were bound together before them and blood stained their rawhide bonds.

When the Kid saw the scalphunters and their captives, he sheathed his Winchester, strode forward, blood boiling, and joined Angus and Robert as they stepped up to meet the mercenaries. The Kid was figuring which of the interlopers to shoot first. There were nine scalp hunters; the Kid had twelve shots. The Pawnees looked most alert and one held his rifle across the front of his saddle. The white man in the lead held a double-barreled shotgun pointed at the ground by his right leg. The Kid would take these first.

"Who would'a thought?" the leader said. He grinned, showing black gaps between the few brown, rotten teeth he had left. "I've always been lucky, though, an' it's the devil's own luck to find white men an' plenty a guns in this damned waste. I'm Cain, Cain Jackson."

"I'm Angus McCulloch. This is my brother, Robert."

"Well now, we're glad ta see ye. We took on a tribe a' Apache five days east. Chiricahua. The gov'ner pays good gold fer their murderin' scalps an' we're not shy ta dance. Only problem was, they was followed up by a war party. Chiricahua and some Comanche, too. They been huntin' us the whole way ever since. We lost six white men an' two Pawnee. Our horses is rode down. But we laid down about ten of 'em yesterd'y an' if'n they're ready ta folla' ag'in I don'

figure they'll try us if'n we're with ye an' all yer guns. What do ye here 'bouts?

"You're a damn liar," the Kid said.

Angus and Robert stared at him, shocked.

The Kid stepped forward, his hands poised over his Thunderers.

The scalphunters all straightened and drew their rifles.

"Those women ain't Chiricahua. They're Mescalero. They weren't in Mexico neither. They were on the Llano Estacado. Huntin'. I seen 'em in Fort Sumner eight days ago."

The ranch hands looked back and forth at each other behind their rifles and wagons, and Montoya and Evans stepped up by the Kid.

"You say?" Cain grinned his rotten grin, leaned his torso behind his horse's head so it was between him and the Kid. He slowly raised his shotgun until it was leveled at the Kid's chest.

"The bitches ain't wimin. They're scalps on the hoof, boy."

"That's enough, Bonney," Angus said. "Stand back. I'll say who lies. Get your man back to the wagons, Montoya, before he takes a load a' buckshot."

The outlaws hesitated, looked at Angus and back at the scalphunters.

"Go along lads," Angus said, gently. "I heard you. I'll look into it and I'll decide what's to be done."

Montoya and Evans backed up. Evans pulled the Kid, glaring, with him. All watched the scalphunters, and the three watched still, after they took cover behind the wagons.

"Take it easy, Billy. If Angus says, we'll get 'em when they're not so ready," Jessie said.

"Ye got yerself a wild boy there, McCulloch," Cain said. "Ye best let 'im know, white men gotta stick together down here."

"Some do. And how do you answer the charge that you kill innocent people?"

"Apache. Innocent. I said they're Chiricahuas. Innocent? You tell me."

"You came west, five days?"

"We did."

"And have ya seen sign of Mexican army?"

"No, but they're about, an' if'n ye ride with us, its safe passage. The gov'ner asked us here. He wants Chiricahua scalps. He feasts us an' gives us

wimin, drink an' gold. But ye never said, what do ye here? Inny bus'niss but the gov'ner's is ferbid."

"My business is mine alone."

"Then yer dead if'n the army finds ye. Yer tracks say yer goin' south. I say we ride t'gether. Safe fer ye, safe fer us'n. An' I say too, it ain't Christian ta leave us'n ta the savages. Sell us some o' them fresh horses. Ye got more than ye need. We got gold, an' we got scalps ta trade."

Cain cast a greedy eye on the McCulloch's remuda of twenty-five sleek, spare horses.

"Christian?" Robert broke in, "What you've done, you've done. But those women you bring look Mescalero to me. Give 'em over if you expect to ride with us."

Cain grinned and looked about at his compañeros. The white men all looked amused. The Pawnee were impassive.

"Them she-dogs is our'n. Won by blood. Pawnee an' white. We sell their scalps whin we're done with 'em. It's a way sworn in blood. Nothin' kin change it. But we trade gold fer fresh horses."

"We have our own use for our horses." Angus replied. "Go your own way and be damned."

The scalphunters, guns ready and warily watching the war party, turned their mounts, cut a diagonal from the road west and took the camino to the south.

The Kid was furious and he felt sick. He had always fought to be free. Now he was bound, constrained to honor the McCullochs' hypocrisy, for the sake of his friends. The McCullochs would fight to free one woman, wrongly taken, while they left other innocents to face terror, rape, torture and pitiless death.

At sundown, the ranchers camped in an arroyo which Ulysses had described and designated as their rendezvous. The arroyo cut a southwest diagonal and intersected the camino a mile below the ranchers' camp.

Just after dark, Ulysses and Diego arrived from the south. The ranchers made no fires and Ulysses and Diego sat on their blankets, leaned on their saddles and ate jerky and parched corn with Angus and Robert. They

talked and planned. Evans and the Kid joined the council.

Angus told Ulysses of the scalphunters but Ulysses already knew. He and Diego had watched the killers make camp at the arroyo near where it crossed the camino. Ulysses informed Angus and Robert of the route he had chosen for the next day.

"That's fine," the Kid said, "you men go that'a way tomorrow, but without me. Soon as my horse is rested a little more, I'm goin' after them lyin' killers. When I'm done, I'm goin' on south. I won't be back."

"We said we'd help your people if ya helped us," Angus reminded the Kid.

Robert eyed the Kid, belligerently, but he knew the Kid was ready. Robert could do nothing to stop him.

"Then you better tell 'em you're not gonna help 'em," the Kid said. "Or maybe their guns are good enough for you to stand up to your word for what they can do themselves. You men are cowards. I told you the women are Mescalero. I seen 'em at Fort Sumner."

"It's not our business," Robert said.

"I've got a responsibility to get our people in and out and it's a hard fight we're lookin' at," Angus added. "We can't be fightin' everyone we meet down here."

"There's nine men, eight in good shape, and them Pawnees won't let you git close," Ulysses warned. "They prob'ly knew me 'n Diego was watchin', and they was too smart ta show it. And they don't know who we are. They prob'ly figured who we was scountin' fer, but couldn't see us good an' they gotta be thinkin' we could'a been Apaches, scoutin' fer them that's followin' 'em. Their horses 're played out so they had ta rein up. But they'll be watchin' close."

The Kid replied, "I'll ride up, friendly like. Once I'm in close with 'em, I've got twelve shots and my Winchester, too."

"They know yer no friend. You already gave that away," Ulysses said. "If we help you will you at least ride with us to parley with the Trujillos?"

Angus broke in. "It's me that says what we'll do and I've said it. You know it, damn well. What're ya thinkin' Ulysses, ta say otherwise?"

"I do know it," Ulysses said, "but I want you to just think about this. First, I believe what the Kid says about the Apaches bein' peaceful and the

raiders bein' lyin' killers. What the Kid says is right for its own sake. We never let murderers, rapers or stock thieves off in our own country, why should we do it down here? Those bastards need hangin' or, easier still, shootin'. Second, the killers work for the gov'ner. They want our horses, you said it yerself. If they git to the capitol they'll bring soldiers back after us even if its only for a cut of our horses. Them Pawnee 'll track us fast. Third, there's a war party, Apaches and Comanches, followin' 'em. We've got ta hit the Trujillos and head north fast. Mexicans 'll be gatherin' behind us. We can't git slowed up in a fight with a war party. But if we give 'em back the wimin we kin ride on through easy. They may even help us. Remember, it's the Mexicans that pay them scum fer Apache scalps. Four, I seen their camp. Their horses are rode out. I've got a way figured so we can take 'em. Then it's no trouble with the army, no trouble with the gov'ner, no trouble with the war party

"Last of all, you, Robert, Gates and me, Diego and Ignacio are experienced fighters. Miguel's reliable too. But them young trail drivers you brung 'll need fighters among 'em to give 'em the spine they're gonna need. With the Kid, Evans, Montoya and Croft, we got almost twice as many fighters. The Kid has real big huevos. He's ready now ta take nine alone. He's desperado, he don' care and ev'rybody says he's dead accurate with them six guns."

Angus and Robert stayed quiet and looked back and forth from Ulysses to Billy.

Ulysses looked into the Kid's eyes, "Yeah, we need ya. But you need us too. If you go alone you'll die tonight and you know it. Even if you take most of 'em with ya, the wimin 'll still die too. I know how to take 'em all. So, I ask ya again, and for the last time, if we help you git the wimin, will ya ride with us against the Trujillos?"

The scalphunters' horses were exhausted, some near dead. The killers pulled up and into a mesquite stand above the arroyo, near where it crossed the camino. There was decent grass there and a little water just below the sand of the arroyo bed. The horses rested.

One of the Pawnee had been first to see Ulysses and Diego watching, on their bellies, behind a broad-branched juniper, nearly a mile away from the others. By hand signals the whole party was alerted. Ulysses and Diego had not

seen that they were followed by a lean, tattooed Pawnee, High Wolf, on foot, as they rendezvoused with the McCullochs. The scalphunters, informed that the scouts were with the Norteños, felt safe enough to build a small fire to roast some rabbits the Pawnees had taken by bow and arrow.

Cain figured that if Apaches and Comanches still followed, their horses would be equally played out and, he figured, the Indian war party would not attack knowing the McCullochs' powerful force was nearby. So he allowed a small fire and pulled a whiskey bottle from his saddlebag. The white men drank, all except Clay, who lay, clutching his bloody belly, dying, at the base of a small, scrub paloverde.

The Pawnees did not relax. One watched the arroyo, another watched the road. The captive sisters, Tzoeh and Evangelina, sat, hands bound before them, on saddle blankets watching the mercenaries eat and drink. On each of the five nights since they had been taken, the women had been thrown at least a scrap of jerky. But now they were given nothing and they knew they were about to die.

Tzoeh was the elder and, although her hands, tied before her, were blue and numb, she planned to defend Evanglina. Tzoeh held a stone, the size of her fist, concealed in her lap in the folds of her calico skirt. Evangelina watched Cain. Cain leered at Evangelina and Tzoeh as he sharpened his scalp knife.

Clay was groaning, coughing and breathing hard. "I'm cold, amigos," he said, "real cold."

Cain, Grimes, Scully and the other whites ignored him. They felt cocky. They had done a lot of damage to the women's kinsmen in the last fight, and they had ridden hard. So the killers passed the bottle of rye all around and they laughed and licked rabbit grease from their fingers.

"I'm cold…damn cold," Clay moaned.

"Ye got a will?" Cain joked. "Er kin ye even write? Leave me yer hair. It's long, black 'n greasy 'nough. Them stupid Mex'es 'ill pay gold fer it too."

Cain and the others all laughed.

"Yer all son's a' whores." Clay said. "I kin still ride, jist git me ta' that doct'r in the capitol. He'll fix me up. We'll all ride t'gether ag'in like always."

"We're not wastin' yer horse no more," Cain said. "We need 'er an' we need the horse them Apache bitches 'er ridin'. And long 's yer makin' yer will, leave yer share 'o their cunnys ta us'n, too, 'cause we're gonna collect right now."

All the white men laughed. Cain rose and walked over, past the captives to where Clay lay. Clay gripped his bloody abdomen with both hands. He lowered one hand and pulled his .44 partly out of its holster but Cain squatted by him and easily took the gun.

"Ya filthy dog." Clay coughed the words and bloody spittle was on his lips. "Ya dirty, filthy cheatin' dog, ya break our blood oath. Er ya fools gonna ride with a man who breaks the pledge?" Clay said, as Cain took Clay's money, firearms, knife and ammunition from his belt, coat and saddlebags.

"No, Clay, we done swore we'd never let the savages git ye. Yer done fer, we kain't take ye an' we kain't leave ye fer the Apaches," Cain said.

"Gimme some water at least."

"Shut up an' die like a man," Skully said. "We're tired 'o list'nin' ta yer whinin'. Ye know we kain't leave ye ta the savages."

Clay tried to say more but his words were lost in a bubbling gurgle and cough as Cain held Clay's hair and cut his throat with his own scalp knife. Clay kicked a little as he bled out while Cain scalped him.

Cain stuck the steaming scalp in his belt and looked into Evangelina's eyes. Then he stood and walked over to her. The other whites rose, approached and stood over the captives. Cain grabbed Evangelina by her hair, pulled her to her feet and clutched at her breasts. Evanglina tried to push him away but Grimes stepped up behind her, wrapped his arms around her torso and arms and pulled her back against him. Tzoeh sprang up and swung her rock, in both fists, at Cain's face. Cain knocked the rock aside and out of the Mescalera's hands with his forearm. He drove his fist into Tzoeh's mouth and she flew backwards, onto the ground. The scalphunters were all about. One chopped branches off the trunk of a paloverde and others tied Evanglina against it, her hands pinioned over her head.

Tzoeh was staked out, spread eagled, on the ground between Evanglina and the fire. High Wolf stood just outside the firelight, watching the arroyo. He remained in his place, but he turned to watch how the Apache women would die. The other two Pawnee came up, lay a blanket beside Tzoeh, sat and prepared a pipe.

Cain grinned and leered as he straddled Tzoeh's hips, on his knees,

passed his big knife before Tzoeh's eyes, then sliced off the small silver conchos which buttoned her purple, velvet blouse. Cain pulled the shirt open and gently rubbed the blade over Tzoeh's nipples while staring into her eyes, looking for sign of fear. The Apache turned her face and looked into the eyes of the two Pawnees who sat calmly, watching and smoking. They began to sing a death song and Tzoeh felt strangely comforted. She knew that these people were like her own. She would show them and they would see, know, respect, remember and tell how a Mescalera could die without crying out and without showing fear.

Cain sliced the waist of Tzoeh's calico dress and he ripped it from her body. He sliced off the leather waist thong which held her soft, tanned doeskin breech cloth over her sex. He ripped the thong away and ran the flat of his knife over her belly and pubic hair. The whites were howling and exclaiming, "Hell yeah!" Tzoeh began to sing her death song as Cain rose, stepped to the fire and held the blade of his knife over red coals.

In the arroyo, Ulysses signaled Diego and Ignacio to stay back out of sight, in shadow, under the eroded overhanging sandstone bank. Ulysses, face blackened with ashes and mud and bearing sage stalks in his collar and hat brim, crawled forward on his belly. He took his sniper's position behind a good-sized sandstone boulder that had separated from the bank and lay on the floor of the arroyo. Ulysses peered out from its base. Ulysses could see High Wolf, the sentry, one hundred fifty yards away, silhouetted in the firelight as he looked back at the fire and listened to Tzoeh's passionate song. Ulysses slowly pushed his Hawkin forward and took aim. Evanglina's higher, mournful voice wailed out, joining Tzoeh's song. Cain pulled his blade from the fire, stood and turned toward Tzoeh.

The Pawnees suddenly sprang into action and all the scalphunters turned, ready, pulling rifles and pistols as Patricio Montoya came into sight riding down the camino toward the camp. Montoya led six fine bridled horses on a long, braided-leather lead.

The biggest Pawnee, Long Soldier, strode back to his place between the camp and the camino. His brother, Dream Walker, moved back beyond Tzoeh and the juniper. He bridled the Pawnees' horses, unhobbled them and stood, watching, prepared for flight.

Montoya stopped, fifty yards away.

"¡Hombres! Traigo caballos para cambiar por las mujeres. Men! I bring horses to trade for the women."

Cain stepped forward, Colt's .44 in one hand, Bowie in the other. Cain glanced back at his men, all ready, behind him.

"It's a trap, boys," Cain said, quietly. "But once we kill 'im we'll outrun the others, on their own horses. Grimes, git my horse ready. We'll take 'im an' them seven fresh ones. Git ready ta move out fast. I'm gonna bring 'im in close."

Cain called to Montoya, "Esta bien, pase por aquí. It's all right, come on in."

Montoya rode slowly forward, but at an oblique angle, showing the scalphunters the horses' sides and concealing the Kid—who was hanging on a leather lattice, cleverly woven by Ulysses, between the last two horses in the remuda. As Montoya drew near the fire and passed Long Soldier, he called out.

"Necistamos las mujeres para pasar, en paz al norte. We need the women to pass in peace to the north."

"Now why d' ye lie?" Cain laughed. "Ye folks 'er headed south."

Cain raised and aimed his .44 at Montoya's chest.

High Wolf was facing away from the camp now, studying the arroyo, and the back of his skull blew out toward the fire in a sheet of gore an instant before the roar of Ulysses's Hawkin sounded. Montoya dived from his saddle to his right as Cain fired and missed. The Kid ducked out from behind the horses, firing both his six guns. Cain took two slugs in his chest and flew backward. The Kid shot Scully between the eyes and Scully collapsed like a ragdoll by Tzoeh's head. The Kid hit two others in an instant and Montoya rolled, came up on his feet firing and his bullets hit them too, but the scalphunters were firing back shot after shot even as they went down. Montoya's horse, Relampago, now leapt between him and the fire and another horse reared, screaming, and collapsed. Two other horses whinnied and cried out as they took slug after slug. Other horses bolted all about the fire. A killer named Leach fired at Montoya and his bullet ripped through Relampago's flank. Leach turned and ran for his horse. The Kid fired, and hit him just below the nape of his neck. His head snapped back and he hurled forward to the ground.

Diego, Ignacio and Ulysses ran forward. Diego and Ignacio fired

their Winchesters at Grimes and Dream Walker, but wounded neither. Dream Walker fired back. Grimes tried to bridle his horse, unable to mount up and shoot back at the same time. Ulysses loaded his Hawkin even as he moved in.

The McCullochs and all their men, mounted, came up out of the arroyo two hundred yards away and thundered forward, whooping. As they drew within range, the cowboys began firing their six guns wildly at Grimes and Dream Walker.

Horses danced around the Kid and Montoya but Long Soldier, behind them, got a glimpse of Montoya and fired his Sharps. The ball tore through the back of Montoya's left shoulder, knocking him to the ground. Long Soldier charged and drove his body into the Kid's back as the Kid aimed at Dream Walker. They hit the ground together and both of the Kid's guns flew from his hands. The Kid twisted onto his back and he was able, with both his arms, to tie up Long Soldier's right arm as Long Soldier pulled his knife up to a striking position. The Kid held on tightly to the immense warrior over him, allowing no striking room. Montoya, his left arm hanging uselessly, staggered forward and dove into Long Soldier, knocking him off the Kid. They tumbled through the legs of the panicked, kicking horses and rolled over the fire. Long Soldier came up on top. Long Soldier would have driven his knife into Montoya's neck but he sensed the Kid was scrambling for a six-gun. Long Soldier chose not to spare a moment; he leapt off Montoya and sprinted toward Dream Walker who struggled to hold the Pawnees' rearing horses in the firestorm.

The Kid came up on his knees, revolver in hand, and tried to fire at Long Soldier, but the gun was empty. By the time the Kid located his other .41, the Pawnees were well away, riding low on their mounts and cutting behind intervening mesquite brush and paloverde. The Kid fired, to no effect.

Ignacio had outrun Ulysses and he slashed the bonds that held Evanglina to the paloverde. Evanglina rushed like lightning to Tzoeh. Cain's body lay sprawled between Tzoeh's legs, his head on her thigh. Evanglina grabbed Cain's knife and cut the thongs that held Tzoeh's wrists. Tzoeh sat up, took the knife, cut her ankle bonds and sprang to her feet. Evanglina took two revolvers from dying scalphunters. She handed one to Tzoeh and she handed Tzoeh her ripped, blue, calico dress. Tzoeh wrapped and knotted the cloth around her hips and she stuck the revolver in the waist. Then she sat down on Cain, straddling his torso. She showed him his knife. Cain gazed through glazed, dying, barely comprehending eyes at the fierce, beautiful woman he had been about to torture, rape and murder.

Even as the McCullochs rode up, shooting every scalphunter who still squirmed on the ground, Tzoeh got off Cain, sliced open his breeches and cut his genitalia from his pelvis. Cain's spinal cord had been severed by one of the Kid's bullets so he felt nothing, but Tzoeh, blood dripping down her forearms and smeared on her bare breasts, showed Cain the organs before she stuffed them into his mouth, which was bubbling blood. Then she sat on his chest and scalped him. Cain had already passed into eternal darkness when Tzoeh leaned forward pushing his knife down through his heart.

Ulysses came up and aimed his Hawkin past some of the cowboys who were racing onto the plain after Grimes and the two fleeing Pawnees. The Kid, reloaded, next to Ulysses, was aiming and firing his six guns ineffectively at the distant fugitives. Ulysses squeezed the trigger. A moment passed, then Grimes's horse went down, tumbling, kicking in the air and dust. Grimes staggered to his feet and stumbled after the Pawnees, who raced away, far beyond him. Ulysses, calmly, but with amazing skill and speed, recharged the muzzle-loader and aimed again. The Hawkin roared, and a moment later Grimes's remote figure collapsed.

Six of the McCullochs' young cowboys raced after the Pawnees, howling, sporting, firing. The Pawnees, knowing they were well out of range of the camp and the McCullochs' main party, stopped and wheeled their horses. Dream Walker aimed and fired his long rifle. Bucky Johnson, riding ahead of the others, was blown back, out of his saddle, dead when he hit the ground. The other cowboys, silenced, reined up around him. The Pawnees calmly and deliberately walked their horses away, looking back, menacingly, defying any to follow. No one did.

After Tzoeh took her revenge on Cain, she rose and moved next to Evanglina. The brave Mescalera sisters were exhausted, half starved, shaking with cold and adrenaline and, despite the strong Apache ways to which they had been born, weaned and raised, they were confused and disoriented. The women held their revolvers ready, studying their rescuers for sign of hostile intention. Ulysses held his hand out, palm down, and passed it quickly across

his chest in sign of peace. Ignacio gave Tzoeh a serape to cover her nakedness. Evanglina then moved quickly among the scalphunters and dead horses, gathering the scalps of her kin into saddle bags before she and Tzoeh mounted horses offered by Diego.

The cowboys roped the scalphunters' bodies and dragged them a short distance from the camino into a cleft in the arroyo, where they would not be seen for some time. The scalphunters lay there, dead on the ground. Diego checked and bandaged Montoya and declared that the wound was clean through, blood flow staunched. Montoya was good to ride.

The cowboys shot the wounded horses and two that were ruined by exhaustion. They hazed the rest before them as they quickly moved out, leading Bucky's horse with his body slung over the saddle.

"Don't ya figure ya ought'a go after 'em an' finish it?" Angus asked Ulysses as they led their people away.

"No. It'd take time, maybe days, to ride 'em down an' take 'em. And it'd be real dangerous. Besides, I killed the white man. I picked 'im 'cause I don't figure the Pawnee 'll ride, alone, inta the capitol. They'd have ta' pass too many Mexicans an' some 'er bound to fig're 'em fer hostiles. Without white sponsors, them Pawnee 're outlaw 'round here, now."

The party tied in with the supply wagons and caballada and headed south for only a few hours. The cattlemen gave Tzoeh some new jeans from Bucky's saddlebag, and Billy gave her a clean bib shirt. They made a cold camp, buried Bucky, and bedded down.

Evangelina and Tzoeh lay their blankets between the Kid and Montoya. The Kid tenderly covered Montoya with an extra blanket, gave him water and tried to get him to eat.

"You saved my life, amigo. You almost got yourself killed doin' it. He could'a killed you, easy," the Kid said softly. "Mil gracias, I won't never forget it. You have my word, mi amigo…siempre, aunque pasada de la tumba. Always, even beyond the grave."

"Callate, shut the hell up," Montoya whispered, "La muerte no es nada. Viene a todos. Death is nothing. It comes for all. It is only importante how we live. We always protected each other and we always avenged our amigos. We still do and always will. No hay que decirlo. There's no need to say it."

Montoya moaned all night. The young Apache women held each other and shook and wept in absolute silence. Near dawn, Tzoeh lay her head and hand on the Kid's shoulder and chest. They looked into each other's eyes, then slept, fitfully. After that, Billy and Tzoeh slept together at each camp.

Three days later, the war party camped at dawn on the arroyo Fe De Amor. It was still spring and water ran over the sands. The supply wagons had fallen far behind. There was good cover and the Norteños would wait there a day, a night, and the following day before moving on.

The cowboys enjoyed the waters all day and at dusk William and Tzoeh took their turn. William, refreshed by the waters, sat naked on his saddle blanket and Tzoeh, wrapped only in the poncho Ignacio had given her, nestled against his ribs.

William looked into Tzoeh's eyes. She was strong, Apache. But William saw a tear in her eye and he brushed it aside with one finger. "Digame," he said. "Tell me."

Tzoeh looked into William's eyes. She hesitated. Then she felt trust and she said, "Beh-leh. I am…good…I you have…I you love. My heart fly like high bird. But I…lloro, I cry. They kill people…my people."

"Sí, yo se. Yes, I know. They killed my people too." There was a tear in William's eye as well.

"I give mi to you, Behleh. I give mi to you. A woman give to man she love. I cry for mi people. A woman cry for people."

"I love you too, Tzoeh. We're in Mexico now. We keep goin'. You and me. All we gotta do is find a way to get free of those damn McCullochs before they cause too much trouble, and we can ride down deep into Mexico. Nobody knows me here. We can live here."

"The Mexican hate Apache. They kill Apache."

"Not all of 'em. Only here in the north. The Mexicans are mostly Indians too. We'll go deep down south, where they ain't never seen no Apache. Till we get there, I ain't gonna let nobody bother you."

"I cry for mi people Beh-leh."

"I cry for my people, too."

26

FORTALEZA TRUJILLO

I am a man of honor.

The McCullochs, their vaqueros, the outlaws and the Apache sisters returned to the camino where it ascended a high mesa. They passed through a gap in its vertical, black-lava crown. On top, they found a vast plain dotted with conifers and cedar and covered with sages, manzanita, brightly flowering high-altitude cholla cactus, and wild, yellow gramma grasses. The plain stretched into the distance and, beyond, blue and snowcapped mountains rose above the high desert. The Norteños knew that the Trujillos and other haciendas lived at the base of the remote mountain range.

■■■

Ulysses sat at dawn on a rock just below the black basalt rim of the mesa, overlooking El Valle del Rio Scamandario and the Pueblo of San Apolonio.

About a half mile to Ulysses's left, the road on which the McCullochs were riding toward the town descended the mesa in a series of sharp switchbacks, passed over a narrow bridge and upper acequia and entered the town. The camino ran through outlying streets lined with adobe dwellings, jacales, mangers and coyote fences of thin, upright piñon trunks enclosing horses, burros, sheep, goats, pigs and poultry. The road then entered el centro where fine plastered houses of adobe and stone, some two- and three-stories high, and some bright with tiled wainscots, surrounded a broad cobblestone plaza.

There was a fountain in the middle of the plaza and a narrow stone gutter carried its overflowing waters across the square, through the town and down to the lower acequia madre and fields beyond. At the far end of the plaza was a high cathedral of carved stone blocks with a bell tower on one side.

The road crossed the plaza at the end opposite the iglesia and nearest

Ulysses. It passed before a long building with a wide portál, which housed a store and cantina. Rows of wagons, carts and colorful cloth-covered booths stood before the church. Farmers and artisans were marketing their produce and goods to people who were gathering there. Ulysses saw that the road passed the plaza, descended through more poor adobes and jacales and passed over the acequia madre, which ran parallel to the rio. Beyond the ditch and its short bridge were long fields of corn, beans, alfalfa, chile, melons, and fruit trees. Small, lateral ditches ran from the acequia madre through the fields toward the river.

The camino passed through the fields and over a wide bridge of stone and wood, which spanned the Rio Scamandario. Past the bridge, the road split.

The smaller fork of the camino continued straight south and rose in a few gentle switchbacks to the high hill on which the Trujillos' hacienda stood. Behind and above the hacienda, the land rose precipitously and the high, heavily forested mountains towered above and beyond where piñon, cedar and juniper gave way to ponderosa pine, fir and on the distant, soft blue heights, white-trunked stands of aspen. The east fork of the camino cut left, followed the river and twisted out of sight around the base of the mountains.

An immense pasture, enclosed by the longest corral Ulysses had ever seen, extended from the far side of the hacienda to the east, and followed the camino almost out of sight. A hundred or more of the Trujillos' fine horses grazed there on good, rich, green grasses.

To the west of the hacienda, the Rio Scamandario flowed down out of a plain at the base of the mountains. The river was shrouded there in cottonwood groves which had not been cleared for fields. Beyond the alamo bosque Ulysses could see the Trujillos' cattle grazing.

Ulysses studied the hacienda for signs of vulnerability. Clearly, the great house had been built by the Trujillos' ancestors for defense against Indians.

The hacienda was built of stone and mortar. The exterior walls formed a rectangle and no windows faced outward. Inside, the walls were lined with dwellings that surrounded a huge, cobblestone courtyard.

In one corner of the courtyard, to the right of the main house, were stables, a smithy and what appeared to be a small dairy. There was a well there, too.

The dwellings which lined the front and side walls of the fortress were one story and the roofs were a few feet lower than the exterior wall, forming a defensive parapet all around. At the rear of the courtyard stood the Trujillos' two-story stone hall and sleeping quarters. Ulysses could not see the back of the Trujillos' main house but he could see that the pitched roof of huge ponderosa vigas, planks and latillas ended a few feet shy of the crenellated back wall and parapet.

Ulysses noted that all the roofs of the enclosure were planked, shingled of wood and supported by pine vigas, latillas, beams and corbels. The huge, open gates at the front of the courtyard were made of thick old mesquite planks. The stables, smithy and dairy were made entirely of wood and thatch, probably filled with hay, and they were adjacent to and, like tinder, directly below the massive pine vigas and eaves of the main house.

If we can fire it, Ulysses thought, the whole thing will burn real good.

Ulysses heard a sound behind him; he spun around and raised his Winchester. He saw five people standing there, looking at him, mouths agape. They were Indians, campesinos. The older man, wearing cotton pantalones, fiber sandals, a colorful serape and soft, straw sombrero, held a live lamb slung around his neck and over his shoulders, forelegs in his right hand, rear legs in his left. A younger man stood next to him, bent under a heavy load of woven cotton and wool goods, which he also bore on his back, gripping rope ties at his shoulders. A barefoot Indian woman in an embroidered blouse and bright red and white cotton dress, wearing a small round wool hat over long black braids, stood behind the men. She carried pottery vessels in a net on her back; two young boys, barefoot in cotton pants and shirts, stood at her side.

Ulysses was shocked. He had used all his skill, guided the war party and avoided being seen for nearly two weeks. How, he wondered, had he now allowed five peasants to just walk unseen right up on him? Where had they come from?

The Indians all stared. Their eyes ran over Ulysses's Winchester, the big Hawkin in its beaded quiver on his back, and at his two .44's, one holstered on his thigh, the other in his war belt. They stared at his bowie knife and his crossed bandoleros loaded with bullets. They stared with wonder at his fringed, beaded leggings, strange moccasins and the eagle feathers in his hat.

Ulysses would have shot armed men in order to guard against danger to his own people, to protect their safety and chances of success. But he knew he could not murder these innocents. Ulysses lowered his rifle and attempted a friendly grin, which looked to the Indians like a snarl.

"Muy buenos dias," Ulysses said, knowing even as he said it that his ruse and feigned, nonchalant benevolence was entirely transparent to the Mexicans.

The older man released the lamb's front legs, removed his hat, placed it over his breast and replied, "Muy buenos dias, Señor."

The man looked away, down at the path before him, and walked by. The others followed. None of the adults looked back at Ulysses as they passed, eyes lowered, humbly, but the two boys stared wide eyed at the strangely dressed, heavily armed scout as they followed their elders down the footpath leading to the camino and San Apolonio.

Ulysses put his hand on the top of the black lava-rim rock, pushed down and leapt to the mesa's summit. He watched the Indians walk away, then strode into the piñon stand where his horse was hidden. He rode down the path, away from the peasants and, when entirely out of sight, he cut north, urging his horse to a long lope. He had to tell the McCullochs that their presence was now known.

As he rode, Ulysses thought of the valley, the town and the Trujillos' stronghold. Ulysses thought of Robert McCulloch's temper, Angus's determination, of the young green cowboys and of the unpredictable outlaws. He thought of his responsibility to get Diego, Ignacio and their vaqueros safely home. He thought of his wife and son. And he tried to figure what to do next.

Ulysses, Angus and Robert all agreed. With the element of surprise gone, they should enter the pueblo, show their strength and then parley with the Trujillos. Robert wanted blood, but he finally agreed that if he could get Helen back without it, that would do for now. The McCullochs would get their people out safely. They would find a way to get revenge later.

At noon the church bell tolled a steady warning as the war party came over the crest of the mesa, descended the twisting bajada del camino, crossed the bridge over the high acequia and rode right into the plaza—their rifles, revolvers and bullet-loaded bandoleros shamelessly and menacingly displayed.

People stood and stared at the invading gringos. There were corrales along the road south of the plaza between the cantina and the fields. The fronts of the corrales were made of pine poles, and the sides of black, lava rock. Angus ordered that the horses be placed there, fed, watered and guarded. But the horses were left saddled. The supply wagons were stopped in front of the cantina and store, across from the church. Cowboys rested on the portál and inside. Gates was left in charge and he posted and instructed guards all around. Gates would order all to mount up and attack if shots came from the hacienda.

Angus, Robert, Ulysses, Montoya and the Kid headed on without delay, down the camino toward the Trujillos' stronghold. Ulysses's people, Diego, Ignacio, Miguel and Lalo, followed them. Before they reached the bridge, they saw two caballeros burst, galloping, out of the gates of the fortress. The riders descended the hill and cut east along the river road.

"They're goin' fer help from the other haciendas, maybe even from the army," Ulysses said. "If this parley don't work, we've gotta hit 'em fast, finish it an' ride north—hard."

The Norteños crossed the bridge, rode up the hill through the hacienda's gates and into the courtyard. Diego and his vaqueros stopped before they got to the gates, twenty-five yards back. Several armed caballeros stood about the gates; Ulysses had ordered Diego to shoot them down if they tried to close the gates after he and the McCullochs entered.

Ulysses, the McCullochs and the two outlaws walked their horses slowly forward across the courtyard. The Kid was fascinated by the sights, sounds and smells of the hacienda. Men and women were all about, attending to their duties. To the right of the massive stone house at the back of the courtyard, before the stables, smithy and dairy, Indian women in cotton smocks and woven colored, cotton dresses tended a fire and grill. They sat on blankets all around and they had been gossiping and grinding corn on metates, cooking tortillas, carnitas on long skewers, and "cositas" corn, beans and other vegetables. But now all sat, silently, staring at the heavily armed intruders.

The Kid's sense of wonder evaporated and his instinct to kill and survive boiled up as he saw the two Pawnees—Dream Walker and Long Soldier— seated cross-legged on blankets amidst the women. Clearly, the Pawnees had been smoking and eating there. Their pipe lay between them. But now they held their rifles on their laps, cocked and ready, and they glared into the Kid's eyes as he rode forward. The Kid instantly judged that he could draw, fire and kill them both with his six guns before they could bring their rifles into play, but the Kid felt a hand on his forearm and he glanced at Ulysses riding beside him.

Ulysses shook his head and whispered, "Not now, boy. We'll get 'em later with no risk. Don't do it yet."

There were armed caballeros all about and the Kid choked down his urge to kill. The Kid yielded to his growing trust of Ulysses, but he never took his eyes off the Pawnees even as the riders reined up before the main house where three hombres stepped forward to meet them.

"Bienvenidos," the foreman said. "Welcome." He introduced himself as Marcelo, and he invited the men to enter the great stone house. Marcelo's men took the Norteños' reins as they dismounted.

Two stone staircases curved at either side of the main house up to the top of the first story and opened onto a carved-stone balustered patio before the high heavy mesquite doors of the Trujillos' great hall. The Norteños ascended the stairs, and followed Marcelo through the doors. Several armed caballeros stood just within the entrance, and a white-haired gentleman faced them. He wore an immaculate grey traje corto with silver lace, buttons and conchos running down each leg.

"I am Carlos de Trujillo," the man said in perfect but heavily accented English. "Welcome to my home. Please, pass."

Behind the man, the Kid could see the great hall, and at its far side a great stone hearth. Several people were standing and seated around the fire place.

"Don Carlos," Ulysses said, bowing slightly, "I am Ulysses O'Laerte. This man is Robert McCulloch."

Ulysses went on to introduce Angus McCulloch, Billy and Montoya.

Don Carlos looked into Robert's eyes. "Of course," he said. "I have expected and awaited your arrival for some time. Que pasan, por favor."

Don Carlos led the McCullochs' party to the hearth and, indicating a woman about his own age seated there, said, "This is my wife, Doña Elviria."

Doña Elviria sat on a high, intricately carved pine chair just to the left of

the hearth. She sat perfectly erect, dressed in black; a black silver-embroidered shawl covered her head and shoulders. She looked directly into the eyes of each visitor. Ulysses thought he detected a subtle flinch of shame behind her proud stare.

Don Carlos then introduced his sons, Paco, Antonio, Pedro, Placido and Hectór. Placido stood behind Doña Elviria's chair, his hand on its back. Antonio and Paco stood to Doña Elviria's right. At her left, Hectór sat on the elevated hearthstone shelf before the fireplace.

Hectór attracted the Kid's attention because he seemed so relaxed. He savored a long, sweet alfalfa sprout that extended from between his white teeth and dark red lips. Although he was seated, the Kid could see that Hectór was a tall man. He had dense, jet-black hair, combed straight back. He was clean-shaven and his jaw and chin were powerful. His skin was dark, his eyes darker still, and they were crowned by delicate eyebrows that conveyed an acute sensitivity and intelligence. Hectór's shoulders were broad, his chest deep. His legs were strong but lean and elegant.

Hectór leaned his back against the chimney, one foot on the hearth-stone banco, the other on the floor. He wore no jacket. The billowing sleeves of his white linen shirt exaggerated the considerable thickness of his powerful arms. He wore finely tanned leather breaches with conchos over soft yellow deer-skin boots. A Colt's .44 occupied an embossed leather holster on his right thigh and his right hand was near the gun, but Hectór conveyed no sense of belligerence as he sat back, and confidently contemplated the introductions, awaiting the negotiations that would follow.

Don Carlos looked into Robert's eyes and said, "Of course, you know Placido and Paco. Please sit down."

Hide-covered bancos surrounded a low table before the hearth and Angus, Ulysses, Billy and Patricio all sat down. Robert ignored Don Carlos's invitation. He stood, arms folded, staring balefully at Placido. Placido stared back with equal malice in his eyes.

The Kid continued to watch Hectór, whose eyes moved from Robert to Placido and back. Hectór looked interested, but calm and unconcerned—even slightly amused.

Don Carlos sat in a finely carved chair next to Doña Elviria.

"Elena," he called, "traiga refrescos, por favor. Please bring refreshments."

An Indian girl came forward bearing a silver tray with cups of cold, frothy chocolate. She set the tray on the table. The Kid looked behind Elena and saw finely dressed young women and children standing, watching, in the hallway from which Elena had come.

"These are the McCulloch brothers," Don Carlos said in Spanish to his wife. "And this is Señor O'Laerte, Señor Montoya and a famous pistolero del norte, Señor Bonney."

The Kid looked into Doña Elviria's eyes. He felt ashamed that he was being introduced as a threat to the fine lady and her family. The Kid did want to kill the Pawnees in the courtyard, but he felt no enmity toward the Trujillos. They seemed like fine and interesting people. The Kid hoped the whole problem could be worked out and he nodded and ventured a shy smile, showing his buck teeth, at Doña Elviria. The lady nodded toward the Kid, bent forward, raised and offered him a cup of chocolate.

The Kid took the drink and glanced to his right at Hectór, still watching all, his hand by his .44.

"Muchas gracias," the Kid said, sincerely. Then he drank.

"Por nada," Doña Elviria replied, smiling kindly at the young man.

When Billy tasted the delicious cold, frothy cinnamon and chocolate he smiled again, wider, raised the cup slightly and nodded at Doña Elviria and Hectór. Doña Elviria nodded back, slowly, and looked with maternal satisfaction on Billy's pleasure. Her gaze was entirely charitable, free of any prejudgment against the young man who had come with her enemies, armed, into her home. The Kid felt grateful for the lady's noble hospitality. He liked her. He liked her so much that he felt no blame as Hectór slowly and deliberately returned his nod and the Kid realized that Hectór saw him as a threat to his mother. The Kid knew Hectór intended to shoot him first if a fight broke out.

"Don Carlos," Ulysses began, speaking slowly, thoughtfully choosing his words with great care and exaggerated dignity as if he had entered the tipi of some war chieftain on the plains. "I thank you and my heart is filled with hope because you have welcomed us here to parley...to talk. We have come here in search of Señor Robert's wife, Helen."

The Kid saw that when Ulysses spoke Helen's name, Doña Elviria lowered her eyes at the floor, her jaw clenched; almost palpable shame at the uncomfortable situation seemed to emanate from her entire being. The Kid felt another rush of admiration and even compassion for the dignified lady.

Don Carlos raised his hand, palm outward, to stop Ulysses from saying any more. "Please Señor O'Laerte," he said. "Of course we know why you are here. I am informed that the McCullochs are noble and honorable men, entitled to the greatest respect. Please allow me to speak directly to the…punto de honor…to the very point.

"I have lain awake for many nights, as has my wife, knowing that Don Roberto McCulloch, man that he is, must come. I have thought a great deal of what is to be said.

"Helen and Placido informed us of what occurred. Of the…" Don Carlos hesitated, frowned, then almost spat the word: "…disgraceful…way," he looked with deep anger at Placido, "…my son and Helen behaved."

"I know that Don Robert was, unjustly, left with insufficient information. Since he was not accorded the courtesy of an honest, courageous explanation, he was forced to consider, as any honorable man would, the possibility that Helen did not come here of her own free will.

"Señor McCulloch, you are entitled to an answer to this question and I give it to you now. Helen chose to come here with my son. They fell in love.

"I must also say to you that Placido and Helen were married before God by a priest in El Paso del Norte before they came to my house, where Helen was then introduced and has been received as my daughter. I am informed that my they disclosed to the priest that Helen was previously married to you, Don Robert, in a civil ceremony carried out by a government official in the Territory of New Mexico. They informed the priest that the union was arranged by your brother and Helen's mother, and that the Holy Catholic sacrament of marriage was not celebrated or consecrated before God. Based on these facts, the priest rendered the opinion that Helen was not party to a true marriage and that in view of their…extant and ongoing physical union…it was imperative that the couple enter into the honorable state of true marriage. The priest then performed the ceremony and blessed their union.

"Now you are here. You have done no wrong and your honor has been offended.

"The next question is what is to be done. You have come, perhaps, for the woman. And you have, certainly, come to redeem your honor. Many people follow you. And my people must also deal with this grave matter." Don Carlos looked at Angus and Ulysses.

"As leaders of our people, we know that the problem threatens to harm the lives of many—not just Robert, Helen and Placido. It is our duty to find a solution which is civilized, yet honorable and just. My wife and I have carefully considered and discussed this matter. I now wish to propose a solution. But first, I wish to hear your views and," Don Carlos looked back at Robert, "to answer all questions which you must have."

"I want to see the girl," Robert said. "If she's here of her own will, let me hear it from her." Then he roared out, "Now!"

He leaned forward, his hand by his holstered .44. All, except Hectór, stirred. The vaqueros by the entrance stepped forward alertly. Placido stepped to his right, away from his mother, with his hand over his holstered revolver, glaring at Robert. Robert, shaking with rage, locked his eyes on Placido's.

The Kid looked at Hectór. Hectór remained calm and apparently relaxed, watching all, but especially the Kid. The Kid raised his hands and held them, palms outward, looking at Doña Elviria and Hectór, assuring them that he harbored no hostile intention. Doña Elviria glanced briefly away from Robert and Placido at the Kid, and she gave the Kid a satisfied and grateful nod. Hectór remained alert and watchful, not about to trust the Kid's peaceful gesture.

Ulysses rose, faced Robert and put his hands on Robert's forearms. "Be still, friend. Hear the man out."

Robert nodded and relaxed a little. Ulysses turned back and faced the Trujillos. "The man's request is reasonable enough. Bring Helen out here. Let 'im talk to 'er."

"Yes, Señor O'Laerte, the request is reasonable…but I cannot grant it," Don Carlos replied.

"Two Pawnees, rogues, really, implored our hospitality the day before yesterday. Their report led me to believe that you were near. Helen was informed

of this fact. Then, this morning, we were all informed that your arrival was imminent.

"Helen expressed her fears for Placido's safety and for the safety of our family. She begged my son, her husband, and she begged me to allow her to surrender herself to you. I questioned her carefully out of Placido's presence. I determined that she does not wish to return to Don Robert's home, she only wishes to protect her husband, our house and our family from danger. Of course, under those circumstances, Placido could not agree to such a course. Nor can I.

"Helen has accepted our judgment and guidance on this point. But, having accepted our position that no Trujillo will yield to force or intimidation, she is still understandably, ashamed. It is now, therefore, my duty to inform you that she does not wish to be seen by you, nor to speak with you.

"I am a man of honor. I must now ask you to acknowledge this fact. I respectfully request that you accept my word that the woman is free to leave here. But only of her own choice. I give you my word that, if you were to speak with her, she would say that she loves Placido. She would say that she is his wife. She would tell you exactly what I have told you. It is true that she has wronged you. But I now implore you, nonetheless, to show her kindness. Accept that she is full of shame and pain, respect her desire and her decision not to be seen by you or your men."

"The hell I will!" Robert's arms, hands, and face trembled with rage.

"Now hold on a minute," Ulysses said. "We come a long way. We come to git her back. You say you have a solution to the problem but I don't see it in what you say."

"I offer this solution," Don Carlos replied. "First, accept my word of honor that the girl came and remains here freely. Second, to vindicate your honor, we acknowledge that you, Don Robert, have been wronged. So that all may know your honor has been redeemed, and our family shamed by this acknowledgment and apology, I offer reparations...Paco! Traigame las mascaras y la espada. Bring me the masks and the sword."

Paco moved behind Don Carlos, and brought objects wrapped in fine leather to the patriarch. Don Carlos drew the leather back, revealing two masks, each twice the size of a human face, made of pure gold and finely wrought, and a broadsword made of blue, Toledo steel with a gilded handle.

"I offer you my family's greatest treasures to justify and redeem your honor. These masks were taken by my ancestor, Rodrigo de Castille, from the temple of Tezcatlipoca, in Mexico, when Cortez, trapped in the city, fought the Meschica and burned the idols of the demons which held sway in that land. The masks were won by strength of arm, courage, and only with great suffering and much loss of Christian blood.

"This is the sword Rodrigo wielded that day. Inscribed below the hilt are the words FOR MY GOD AND MY HONOR, and on the other side, the name of the sword—which, Rodrigo believed, has its own soul: 'Santiago.'

"Moreover, I offer you thirty of our finest horses as well as the two that Helen and Placido took from you when they left your hacienda. You may return to your land with these palpable and visible signs, as proof to all, that the wrong you justly complain of has been acknowledged. All may see these signs and proofs and know that your honor has been redeemed. All may see and know that we Trujillos suffer by displaying these proofs of our shame and dishonor. Because, if your cause were not just, we would fight to the death before giving you anything which could even suggest wrongdoing by any member of our family."

The Kid watched all as Don Carlos spoke these words. He saw Doña Elviria stare at the floor, her neck and cheeks flushed with verguenza—shame—as Don Carlos offered the reparations. He saw Placido's demeanor change from defiance to a look of remorse and soft hope that his wrongdoing and all the disastrous consequences which now threatened his people might be averted by his father's eloquent and logical plea. The Kid saw that even Robert had calmed some. He looked a little confused. Maybe he didn't really want the girl back after all, the Kid thought. He saw that Hectór remained calm and dangerous, ready, yet entirely placid.

The Kid felt hopeful that Don Carlos's argument might prevail. He imagined a dawn of hope and redemption. War might be avoided. The Kid's goodwill toward Doña Elviria and the Trujillos might live. The McCullochs might ride out satisfied with their spoils. Placido and Helen might live on, in love. The Kid might ride south, deeper into Mexico, with Tzoeh, to find his benevolent and happy alternate destiny.

Ulysses could see that Angus and Robert could not answer Don Carlos's logic, but that they were not about to accept his terms. He wondered how they would answer.

Angus knew his hot-headed brother would never accept Don Carlos's proposal, but Angus didn't want to reject it outright while they were all so vulnerable, surrounded in the heart of the Trujillos' stronghold. Angus decided to complicate the negotiations in order to buy time.

He said, "Yer ideas are just fine…for you. But we lost a man comin' here. The man that killed 'im is sittin' outside yer door. Even if we agree…and I ain't talked to my brother or Ulysses about it yet…y'er gonna hav' ta give the Pawnees over. We'll hang 'em here so ya can see they won't be tortured. They'll be hanged quick 'n fair."

Don Carlos looked at his wife, and at each of his sons.

"Those men have come here seeking hospitality which is an honorable custom, more ancient even than law. They warned us of your approach and they say you attacked them. They say you killed many of their company. Now you ask me to commit a cowardly act. You ask me to protect my own interests by allowing these men to be summarily seized and killed in my own house. I do not approve of their obvious occupation, but it is lawful here. We have always warred with the Apache. Your dispute with the Pawnees must be settled by submission to Mexican law and trial."

"Ya know we can't do that," Angus said.

"Yes. Your own presence here, and your purpose, is unlawful. It will subject you to sanction should you choose to await the arrival of our army. And, as you probably know, I have already dispatched riders to bring help. So I believe you are now fully informed of all facts necessary to make your decision. What is now to be done?"

Ulysses saw that Angus and Robert were both seething with anger. They were frustrated that they were powerless to answer Don Carlos's arguments or to act. The vaqueros in the entrance hall were all ready. Hectór, Paco, Placido, Pedro and Antonio were ready. Many more armed caballeros were outside. Robert wanted to draw and kill Placido but such action would be suicidal. Even with the Kid's quick hands and two guns all would die before they could make the gates outside. And Ulysses saw that the Kid didn't want this fight.

The Kid still sat with his hands extended far to either side, away from his guns. His eyes were wide and he felt uneasy. His hope that the McCullochs would accept Don Carlos's offer were now dashed. Robert looked ready to throw down. The Kid didn't want to die, but he didn't want to start shooting the Trujillo men before Doña Elviria's very eyes. The Kid had already figured how he could take Hectór. He could kick the banco back, draw and fire as he fell backward with it. If he did this, Hectór's first shot would probably miss. But the Kid was reluctant to do that. He hated the McCullochs and he felt paralyzed by Doña Elviria's grace, dignity and moral presence.

All were silent for a few moments. The room was filled with tension, like a bomb with a burning fuse. Ulysses knew he had to get his people out before the McCullochs did something stupid.

He spoke, "Don Carlos, thank you for bringin' us with such gentility inta yer home. The things you've said, the answers you give...Robert's gonna have ta think some about what it all means. So we're goin' now, ta think an' talk. I'll prob'bly bring ya Robert's answer myself."

"Of course you will," Don Carlos replied, knowing that the answer would probably be fired from the big Hawkin slung on Ulysses's back. "But I see no reason for dishonesty. We owe each other more respect than that. If you do not bring the answer at dawn tomorrow, I will know that my offer is unacceptable and I will act accordingly and expect you to do the same. Whatever the answer may be, I am satisfied that I have done all that I can, consistent with honor, to prevent tragedy."

Placido glared a question at Don Carlos. The Kid could see that if Placido had his way, he would order them all shot down in the courtyard where they would be surrounded by many guns.

Don Carlos fixed his eyes on Placido's, but spoke to the gringos. "You may go," he said. "Vayan con Dios. Go with God." Don Carlos' eyes on Placido's, were stern, his gaze withering. Placido lowered his eyes.

The gringos walked out, mounted up, and rode across the courtyard, through the gates and away, as all watched in silence.

Bonney, Montoya, the McCullochs and Ulysses rode down the hill, and the church bell rang warning for the second time that day as they crossed the river bridge. Apache warriors were visible on the mesa above.

27

DEVIL'S BARGAIN

**He took her again and again as the stars and moon spun
toward dawn on the dark, night sky dome.**

Women had brought hot food, and Angus arranged to quarter his men in and about the cantina. The cantina adjoined a store where tools and other goods were offered and Angus took a room on the far side of the store area.

Ulysses sat on the portál before the plaza as the sun set. He watched as five charros rode from the hacienda into the enormous attached corral. They skillfully rounded, then drove the entire herd of Arabians out of the corral, through the high gates of the hacienda's sally port and into the shelter of the fort's great courtyard for the night. The Trujillos would not leave their fine horses outside their walls with so many enemies all around.

The western horizon rolled up and covered the sun, and Ulysses watched as a band of sixteen armed riders came pacing up the river road through the gloaming. There was just enough light for Ulysses to see that one of the envoys who had raced from the fort earlier was among the company of reinforcements. Help from another hacienda, Ulysses thought.

Ulysses was right. Don Vicente Cabrera, the father of Hectór's wife Antonia, led the reinforcements. Advised of the Trujillos' danger, they had ridden hard from Don Vicente's hacienda thirty miles away. Don Vicente had come to protect his daughter and his grandson, Astayanio. The riders entered the courtyard, where Don Carlos received them graciously. As Don Vicente dismounted, Antonia ran to her father and embraced him.

Don Vicente's men were quartered and their horses stabled. Don Vicente and his headmen ascended the curved, stone stairway and passed into the great hall where they entered into a council of war with Don Carlos, Hectór, his brothers and their foremen.

After the Norteños had eaten and their men had settled for the night, Ulysses, Robert and Angus met in Angus's room.

"Did ya see them new men ride in?" Angus asked Ulysses.

"Yeah. There's sixteen of 'em. And I counted close to twenty more in the fort, not countin' them two Pawnees and the Trujillo boys. There's prob'ly more of 'em we didn't see.

"So they got about as many men as we do and they're forted up and ready. And one of their riders ain't come back yet. He'll be bringin' more. Hell. Maybe even the Mexican army."

"So what're ya sayin'?" Robert asked suspiciously, fearing Ulysses intended to urge withdrawal and retreat.

"I'm just sayin' we gotta act fast, before them Trujillos git more help. We prob'bly only got a couple 'a days, maybe three."

"How do we take 'em?" Angus asked.

"I may know a way. A good way. I'm still thinkin' it over. But we can't do nothin' 'till we parley with that war party up there. We got no time to waste. We gotta ride up there right now. Take 'em their women and their peoples' scalps we captured back. Talk to 'em. Hell. They followed them Pawnees here. Once they know who we are and what we're doin' they might even help us. We're gonna have ta give 'em a share of them Trujillos' horses, though."

Robert raised an eyebrow and felt greatly reassured. He now understood that Ulysses was determined. Ulysses was no longer just fulfilling his obligation to their alliance. He now had his own motive to destroy the Trujillos: he coveted the Mexicans' wondrous horses. And Robert was confident his cunning ally would come up with a way to get what he wanted.

Angus had never doubted Ulysses's commitment. He had also, immediately upon seeing the Trujillos' great caballada, noted with satisfaction the immense potential rewards likely to come from the success of their mission to take Helen and give Robert his revenge. Angus hadn't specifically thought about it, he just knew intuitively that Ulysses's loyalty and willingness to brave considerable risks were greatly fortified by knowledge of the great prize to be won by decisive victory.

When Angus, Ulysses, Diego and Robert walked out of Angus's room into the store and cantina, Billy and Tzoeh were lying against Billy's saddle,

talking. Evans, Croft and Montoya stood at the bar, drinking. Evanglina leaned against Montoya, her arm draped over his shoulders. Two of Angus's men stood there drinking too.

"Get the hell away from there!" Angus ordered his men. "There's likely ta be a fight tomorrow and drinkin' now 'll only make you slow and stupid."

Angus' men slunk away to their bedrolls on the floor. Evans, Croft and Montoya regarded Angus without interest, and kept drinking.

"You girls get yer things," Ulysses said. "Them 'er yer people up on the rim and we're takin' you back to 'em."

The Mescaleras had only their blankets, the pistols they had taken from Cain's people and the saddle wallets with their people's scalps. They embraced Billy and Patricio, and Billy watched with dismay as they walked out the door.

Diego and two cowboys followed Ulysses, the McCullochs and the sisters up the mesa.

Tzoeh took the lead as they topped the rim and rode by two young Apache sentries into the camp. The Indians' women and children had arrived only hours after the warriors. A dozen wickiups had been assembled and the people congregated around six fires in the little, ephemeral village.

Tzoeh led the whites through the encampment to the fire where her father, Don Tenorio, sat with prominent warriors and headmen. Everyone gathered about and Tzoeh and Evanglina were received with joyous embraces and songs. The young women were led away, and Angus, Robert, Ulysses and Diego were directed to places of honor at the chieftains' fire. Angus's two cowhands stood by, holding the horses.

Ulysses scanned the faces of the men at the fire as Don Tenorio prepared a pipe—and the hairs on Ulysses's neck stood up as he recognized Cuerno Verde. Cuerno Verde no longer wore his distinctive headdress. He was older and thicker about the middle. His long, black hair was streaked with grey and he was now dressed like the Apaches in a cotton blouse, vest, breaches and loin cloth with knee-high moccasins. But it was Cuerno Verde, all right. Ulysses looked around and realized that several of the other warriors standing and seated about the fire were Comanche also.

Cuerno Verde looked balefully at Ulysses and Diego, and grinned mirthlessly and with great malice. Ulysses rested his hand on his thigh near his six-gun and looked at the edge of the mesa, only a few steps away. He figured if he had to start shooting he might make for the edge, dive over, and maybe get away on foot in the darkness. Ulysses saw Diego looking at the precipice too, and Ulysses knew Diego would take the same chance. Ulysses could figure no way to warn the McCullochs.

"I'm Angus McCulloch and this is my brother, Robert."

"Gracias," Don Tenorio said. "I give you thanks for bring me Tzoeh and Evanglina."

Angus looked at Ulysses, perplexed at his counselor's uncharacteristic silence.

"We've come here because the Mexicans stole my brother's wife," Angus said. "Just like them killers stole your daughters. When I saw it, I knew I had ta help 'em. Right is right." Angus didn't intend to lie. He had convinced himself it had been his idea to fight Cain.

Don Tenorio handed Angus a feathered smoking pipe.

"I'm sorry for what them killers did ta your people, though," Angus said.

Angus paused and looked at Ulysses, expecting Ulysses to speak and begin the serious negotiations. But Ulysses still said nothing, so Angus continued, "Two of them scalphunters, Pawnees, are in that fort with the Mexicans. The Trujillos. They're holdin' Robert's wife there, too. We plan to attack 'em tomorrow night. We've got a good plan. We're gonna whip 'em and take their horses. I'm asking ya ta help us. We'll help you get the rest of your people's scalps back. You can bury 'em so your kin can walk whole on the other side. And we'll give you a fair share of the horses."

Don Tenorio spoke in Apache to the warriors in attendance. Several senior men spoke. It was obvious that Cuerno Verde was against Angus's proposal. Don Tenorio argued fervently for the alliance. Cuerno Verde looked smug and satisfied and Don Tenorio was clearly frustrated and concerned when he announced the decision.

"I help you. My son and brother follow me. The others…no." He tilted his head at Cuerno Verde. "This man say you not be trust." Don Tenorio nodded at Ulysses and Diego. "He say this man lie. That man have no name. He fight us. No give horses."

Now Angus understood Ulysses's silence and the meaning of his concentrated focus on Cuerno Verde and the Comanches. Ulysses and Diego were clearly old enemies of the Comanche chieftain. Angus now understood that only he could conduct the parley. "Tell 'em they can trust me. My word is true. I alone say what we do. This man's name is Ulysses O'Laerte."

Ulysses flinched when Angus told his true name.

"He does what I say," Angus continued. "You came on our trail so you've seen the bodies. And you've seen the grave of the man we lost in the fight. You can trust us ta fight your enemies."

The warriors continued their council and debate. Ulysses felt a shock and cold chill when Cuerno Verde ended his speech by pointing his finger at Ulysses and saying with great sarcasm, in English, "Nobody enemy. Nobody lie."

Don Tenorio ignored Cuerno Verde and calmly asked Angus, "You have wife?"

"No."

Don Tenorio's lips moved in a sly smile and he rejoined the Athapascan debate. When Angus had said Ulysses's true name, Don Tenorio knew Ulysses as one of Carson's army scouts from long ago. Don Tenorio was pretty sure Ulysses understood the natives' conversation. So when a consensus was reached, and even Cuerno Verde looked satisfied, Don Tenorio asked Ulysses, "Comprende?"

"Yes, I understand."

"Say to Angus McCulloch."

Ulysses then spoke carefully and humbly as he translated to Angus the war council's consensus:

"Don Tenorio and some of the others know you from the old days at Bosque Redondo. They know you still bring cattle to feed their people on the Mescalero reservation. Don Tenorio told 'em you are a strong leader. You have a strong voice among the whites in our home country. Don Tenorio told 'em that if you are kin, they can trust you in this fight and you can help 'em if we get back home. If you want their help in this fight you've gotta marry Don Tenorio's oldest daughter. They need horses for this fight. Theirs are rode down. So, you marry Tzoeh. Tonight. You give Don Tenorio six horses for Tzoeh. They lost a lotta men chasin' Cain. They got sixteen fighters left, includin' the Comanches. They'll follow yer orders accordin' to our plan. When we take the Trujillos, each warrior gits two horses. Thirty-two horses. Even if some of their people git killed, it's still thirty-two horses."

Ulysses looked at Don Tenorio and Don Tenorio nodded his agreement that Ulysses had accurately translated the offer. Angus and Ulysses stood and stepped away to talk alone at the edge of the mesa cliff.

Angus was thinking of the implications. What would Bonney and his amigos do? He thought of Tzoeh's incredible beauty. But if they got home, would he really keep her as a wife? What were the long-range effects of relations with the Mescaleros if he did not? How would his own people act if he did? But they had to get home alive, first. And Don Tenorio and his fifteen fighters looked real tough and good right now.

Angus and Ulysses looked at each other and thought. Ulysses considered that Don Tenorio and Cuerno Verde might not even let them ride out alive, tonight, if they didn't take the deal.

"It's real complicated," Ulysses said.

"Yes. It's the Devil's own bargain. It looks real good but there's a hundred ways it can go wrong."

Ulysses furrowed his brow, raised one eyebrow and frowned. He knew Angus and his weakness and he already knew what Angus would do. But he warned Angus, anyway.

"It looks good all right. And that pretty girl makes it look maybe too good. But there's no way to figure it all sure in the time we got now. Be careful."

Angus and Ulysses stepped back and stood before the chieftains at the fire.

"I agree," Angus said.

Don Tenorio was greatly relieved. He had felt bound by honor to help Angus in return for his daughters' rescue. And he had lost a young niece and nephew in Cain's initial attack on the hunting camp on the llano. Don Tenorio had also lost a cousin and a close friend in the running five-day battle that followed. He wanted revenge on the surviving scalphunters. The fact that the only survivors were Pawnee, traditional enemies, increased his burning desire for vengeance. So Don Tenorio had reluctantly agreed to follow Angus with only his brother and son. But Don Tenorio had felt great apprehension at the prospect of joining the gringos without the support of his people. Now Don Tenorio was very pleased that he had found a solution: they would all fight together. Don Tenorio thirsted for the Pawnees' blood and for the blood of the Mexicans who paid for Apache scalps.

Don Tenorio understood Cuerno Verde's hatred for Ulysses. Had not Ulysses scouted for the army against the Mescalero? But for now Don Tenorio would settle for the blood of the Pawnees and Mexicans, and for horses. Cuerno Verde could settle with Ulysses and Diego later. Don Tenorio was even inclined to help the Comanche kill Ulysses when the time was right. Cuerno Verde knew this. It did not need to be said.

Angus's two drovers left the horses Tzoeh and Evanglina had ridden into the camp. They rode down the mesa and returned with four more good mustangs from Angus's remuda.

The Apaches piled wood on the central fire and maidens and matriarchs brought Tzoeh forward. All gathered and sang there. Tzoeh was now adorned in a simple, white, beaded faun-skin slip. Her hair had been combed to sleekest blackness.

Angus arose and Don Tenorio placed Angus's hand on Tzoeh's. He wrapped a leather thong around their wrists.

"Angus McCulloch. You give word you defend this wife and her people with your sabido and blood?"

"I give it."

"Tzoeh. You give word be good wife for strong and defend your people?"

"Yes."

Her voice trembled and a tear descended her cheek.

When Ulysses, Diego, Tzoeh and the McCullochs re-entered the cantina, William Bonney rose to his feet expectantly and stepped up, but Tzoeh didn't even look at Billy. She looked at the floor and followed Angus into his room at the far end of the tienda. The door closed behind them. Ulysses and Diego stepped between William and Tzoeh as she walked away. Ulysses explained the alliance to the outlaws, Gates, and the cowboys who camped in the cantina.

"It was Don Tenorio's idea," Ulysses said to the Kid. "It's the only way they'll trust us and we need 'em ta get into that fort."

"Yeah, an' Angus didn't tell 'em she'd rather be with me and he gave the horses so he'd have her. I don't figure he complained too much."

"She's married ta Angus now, boy," Ulysses said. "I'm sorry. She done give her word ta her father and ta all of us."

Diego glared at Billy and Billy felt utter contempt. He could draw and kill Diego and Ulysses both in an instant if he chose to. He let it go. The Kid brooded, drank a little and slept very little that night.

Angus McCulloch was a strong leader and he considered himself an honorable, responsible man. But he had always had a weakness for good-looking women. Now, he was thrilled and astounded at the unexpected stroke of luck that had brought the exquisite Apache maiden to his bed and he took her again and again as the stars and moon spun toward dawn on the dark, night-sky dome.

Normally, Angus would have arisen to assume his duties two hours before dawn, but on this morning he remained with Tzoeh, savoring the full panoply of his newly acquired pleasures and privileges as husband to the young, perfect, dutiful, totally compliant yet absolutely uninterested Apache beauty.

Angus McCulloch was a good leader. But on this day, men would pay with their lives and descend, bloody, into black oblivion for his one weakness and resulting negligence.

The Kid got up at dawn, ate, then got his tack together and moved toward the door. Robert, Gates and Ulysses were there, and about ten hands were in the cantina too, eating, as Angus remained behind the closed door of his room with Tzoeh.

"Where ya figure you're goin?" Robert demanded, and stepped forward.

Bonney set his saddle and rifle down and turned to face Robert squarely. Bonney's arms and hands were at his sides, extended a little over the handles of his Thunderers. He was ready to draw. "I'm ridin' south. You got somethin' to say?"

"Ya promised ta help against the Mexicans." Robert's thick Irish accent

was always more pronounced when he was angry, and now his voice was loud, trembling with anger and hatred of the Kid. Robert was ready to draw and his men rose all around, focused on the confrontation, and stepped forward. They were all ready, too.

"Yeah, I promised—and you helped me get the girl. Now you took her. You took her. But you expect me to help you get your woman back. You think I'm a fool? I don't figure I owe you nothin'."

Evans, Croft and Montoya all stepped up to the Kid's side. The Kid looked around the room at the faces of the cowboys who backed Robert.

A slight, satisfied smile grew on his lips. He could see fear in the eyes of the cowhands. They had been ready to shoot him down when he stood alone against Robert, but he could see on their faces that their ardor was considerably cooled at the prospect of an all-out gunfight with the four professional pistoleros. They'd get the worst of it, by far, and everyone knew it. Ulysses sat, leaning back on a chair against the wall. "Let 'im go," he said.

Bonney scanned the room again.

"That's what I figured," he said.

He picked up his saddle and walked out. Evans, Montoya and Croft moved and gathered their gear.

"You ridin' out with 'im?" Ulysses asked Evans.

"Yep."

"That's fine. Git 'im out a' here, safe. But you boys talk it over. Where will ya go? If ya come back by sundown ya kin help us and our offer still stands. We'll get ya amnesty with the gov'ner. You kin still go home."

At the top of the mesa the outlaws said nothing to the young Apache sentries who waited there. They just rode by, defiantly. They rode a few hundred yards along the crest, dismounted, and stood looking down on San Apolonio, the valley, and the fortress beyond.

"Gracias, amigos," Bonney said. "Those skunks would'a shot me down alone, sure. Still, I figure you better get back to 'em. You all got reasons to go home and the governor's amnesty ain't gonna come twice. We all knew from the start, I can't go back. But you can. Go on. Live free an' happy. I got a chance for a new life here, a fresh start. That greedy bastard Angus McCulloch gave it to me, and I'm sure as hell gonna take it. So this is adios, amigos. I hope you won't hold it against me. I can't help you fight them Trujillos. Last thing I need is to turn into an outlaw down here. And, truth is, I don't want to fight them people. But if we're square, then this is a happy goodbye."

Evans swallowed hard. Croft looked at the ground. They had fought a few battles together and they had danced and laughed. Montoya had a tear in his eye and he embraced the Kid.

"Forgive me, hermanito. It is in my heart to return and live in peace with my wife and children. You know I would never leave you in danger."

"No hay de que, mi hermano," the Kid replied. "Don't worry about it, brother." He stood back, looking into Montoya's eyes, a hand on each of Montoya's arms.

"The word 'goodbye' is an English word," Montoya continued. "It means 'God be with ye.' It is almost the same as the Spanish, 'Adiós'—'to God.'"

Montoya, bent, pinched a bit of dirt between his thumb and forefinger, rose, and tossed the dust into the slight breeze which had arisen.

"Adiós."

28

FATES OF WAR

Adiós, amigo. Adiós para siempre. Goodbye, friend. Goodbye forever.

Just then, Hectór attacked. A sudden fusillade of gunfire grabbed the attention of the four outlaws and they looked down on the pueblo far below. They saw that the cowboys who guarded the corrales were suddenly enveloped in a flash flood of bullets from the buildings across the street. Two fell immediately, mortally wounded. Others, several less severely wounded, shot back as they retreated up the street toward the cantina, or through the corrales and up the alley which led to the rear of the cantina. Dirt, splinters and plaster kicked up from the ground, corral beams and surrounding buildings as the cowboys fled through the rain of fire.

The outlaws watched as caballeros burst out of the hacienda gates, galloped down the hill and across the bridge. The men charged up the main street firing wildly at the gringos around the wagons before the cantina portál. Other caballeros, who had been concealed among the houses south of the plaza, raced through the streets, dismounted and took positions behind the low wall before the cathedral. They sent bullets flying across the plaza into the walls, windows and door of the cantina.

From their vantage high above the pueblo, the outlaws saw that some of the Mexican horsemen, supported by campesinos running on foot behind them, rode past the plaza to the south end of town and invaded ruined buildings at the very bottom of the mesa where the camino entered the pueblo. The campesinos wore white cotton trousers and blouses and colored serapes. Some carried old muskets, others scythes and axes. But the horsemen who led them were armed with pistolas and rifles. They covered the camino, foreclosing any possibility that Don Tenorio's warriors could enter the pueblo to support the gringos.

On the black-cliffed rim above, Don Tenorio raged. He had not come so far and fought so hard to now lose Tzoeh to the Mexicans whom he had always held in contempt. And he wanted the Pawnees' scalps. Don Tenorio ordered his men to fire slowly but steadily down on those who covered the entrada and to keep their heads down. Maybe the McCullochs and Ulysses would find a way out of the trap.

The vaqueros who had charged up the street dismounted at the corrales and took cover behind the black, stone corral wall and at the corner of the adjoining buildings. From these positions they fired down the portál, enfilading the position of the cowboys who had attempted to fight back from behind the wagons in front of the cantina. All but three of the gringos were driven into the cantina and store.

Gates and two of Robert's young hands, Cooper and Smith, were in the plaza near the fountain when the attack began. They took cover behind the stone cistern which surrounded the fountain. They fired at the caballeros who rode up, dismounted and entered the walled patio before the cathedral. Gates calmly aimed his Henry rifle and shot a man as he dismounted at the corner of the cathedral. The bullet knocked the man into his horse and he fell under its legs and the animal kicked, bucked and skittered away. Another caballero rode forward and Gates shot at him, but his torso was partly covered by his horse's neck and head. The bullet cut through the animal's neck and clipped its spine; it screamed and collapsed. The rider leapt free and landed on one knee, and Gates pumped another round into the chamber and fired, hitting the man squarely in his chest as he rose to his feet. The man was knocked backwards and he lay, arms and legs sprawled wide, eyes staring unseeing at the sky. Gates fired rapidly at the men behind the church wall and he told Cooper and Smith to run for the cantina. The gringos in the cantina fired from the windows, covering the retreat.

Hectór and Paco galloped into the plaza. Paco reined up, aiming and firing his rifle at the cantina windows. Hectór charged at Gates. Gates, caught in the open, threw his empty rifle aside and pulled his revolver as Hectór rode him down. Hectór's stallion leapt into the air as Hectór rode over Gates. The animal's forelegs and chest struck a terrible blow and Gates was hurled, dazed, to the ground.

Hectór wheeled his mount as Gates rose to his knees, looking

desperately for his Colt's. Héctor held his reins in one hand, his rifle in the other, and he shot Gates in the belly. Gates collapsed onto his side and doubled into a fetal position, clutching his abdomen with both hands. He extended a bloody, trembling hand toward his Colt's on the ground beside him. Héctor leveled another round and shot Gates in the chest. Then he wheeled his horse again, lifted rifle to shoulder, aimed carefully, and shot Smith between the shoulder blades.

Cooper was sprinting hard for the cover of the wagons before the cantina. Héctor cocked his rifle and fired, quickly, hitting Cooper in the calf. Cooper's leg gave way under him, and he seemed to dive forward onto his face. Cooper kept moving, crawling toward the wagons, only a few yards away. Héctor aimed again.

Kneeling by a cantina window, Ulysses braved the suppressing fire hurled forth by Paco and the vaqueros before the church. Ulysses raised his Hawkin, aimed as carefully as he could as bullets splattered the adobe and wood frame around him, and squeezed the trigger. The fifty-caliber round hit Héctor's horse in its shoulder, tore through the bone and ripped through the grullo's lungs. The stallion collapsed onto its knees as Héctor fired at Cooper. Hector's shot tore through the top of Cooper's shoulder as he crawled between the wagons. Emboldened by Ulysses's daring, other gringos stepped up their fire from the windows.

Héctor leapt free from his mount as the animal rolled onto its side, spitting blood. Paco was there. Héctor vaulted onto Paco's horse and the brothers raced back to the corner of the plaza through winds of fire exchanged by the gringos and the vaqueros at the church wall.

Paco cut his steed around the corner into cover. Héctor sprang to the ground. "¡Vaya para los corrales! Sin caballos estan atrampados. ¡Nos los dejan recojer los caballos! Get to the corrales! Without horses they're trapped. Don't let them get the horses back!" Paco raced down the street and cut right toward the corrales to take charge of the men there. Héctor caught a dead man's horse, mounted and directed arriving vaqueros into the churchyard.

The outlaws watched the action from the mesa above. The Kid grinned at the ranchers' predicament.

"It don't look like them damn McCullochs 'er gonna get you no amnesty now. The Trujillos got their horses. On the other hand, this could be your chance to earn your part a' the deal. Chase the vaqueros away from the corrales long enough for them fools to get mounted an' they'll know they owe you."

"He's right," Evans said. "This is our ticket home. If we kin git down this pile of rocks, right here, we kin come in shootin' from this side. We draw their fire off the streets. If the boys are smart enough and got the huevos to hit 'em quick at the same time, they might just git their horses back and git out. Hell, old man Trujillo knows who we are. That means they all do. Most of 'em 'er probably scared of us. 'Specially you, Billy. We might jist chase 'em clean outta them corrales."

"You might. I ain't goin'. Sorry boys. I can't help them dirty rich bastards. You boys'll be all right. Just don't get too close. Let 'em see you comin' then fire from cover from a distance. Them vaqueros ain't fighters. They'll scare easy. Shoot at the Trujillo boys. They're the leaders. That old Indian fighter, Ulysses, is smart. He'll see what you're doin' and he'll take the chance if you give it to him."

"Guillermo Bonito," Montoya said to Billy, "I can ride and shoot but not so well yet. But what Jesse says is true. They fear you. Let me take your horse, your jacket and your sombrero. They'll think it's you. They're sure to run." Billy laughed and tossed Montoya his hat.

As the outlaws led their horses on foot down the steep, boulder-strewn mesa face, Ulysses was trying hard to figure a way out of the cantina. The street in front was controlled by the riflemen across the plaza and, Ulysses judged, there were two or three others firing up the street from the buildings opposite the corrales. The men behind the stone wall at the corrales covered the street behind the cantina. Anyone who exited either side of the building would be shot down immediately.

"Diego," Ulysses said, "shoot down that back alley at them corrales. Don't show yerself. Jest reach around the door and shoot, ev'ry little bit, to keep 'em watchin', thinking we might be comin'. Angus, tell yer men ta slow down their shootin' from the windows. They're not hittin' nothin'. Have 'em shoot steady but slow. Save ammunition. But make the Mexicans think the fight is still right here."

Ulysses led several cowboys into the store, seized shovels, picks and axes, then directed them to place chairs on the cantina bar and climb up. He set the cowhands to work carving an exit through the ceiling. The men chopped easily through the cedar rejas and between the long pine vigas, and the dirt roof caved in.

"When ya hear us start shootin'," Ulysses told Angus, "come, hard, out the back an' down the alley. But only shoot at men who look over the wall. Shoot careful. Don't gun down the horses. Leave the wounded men and the woman, and leave five men shooting' out the front windows. Keep all them vaqueros where they are, across the plaza. We'll ride back up the alley and pick them men up on our way out."

Ulysses was first through the hole onto the roof. Ignacio and ten cowboys followed. There was a low azotea, only about a foot high, so the men squirmed, concealed, on their bellies across the contiguous adjoining roofs until they reached the edge of the row of buildings, just above the corrales. Ulysses ordered four men into place on the side of the roof overlooking the main street. He ordered them to shoot on his command at the people in the windows opposite the corrales. Ulysses, Ignacio and five cowboys lined the roof over the north side of the corrales, ready to open up on the vaqueros below who guarded the horses. Ulysses, lying sideways, parallel to the parapet, removed his hat and raised his head so that only his temple and left eye rose above the cover. Ulysses saw Paco and his men behind the stone wall. And Ulysses saw something that exceeded all his hopes and expectations. Ulysses saw Evans, Croft and Montoya, who he thought was the Kid, wearing the Kid's sombrero and chaleco, and standing by the unmistakable black stallion, Bala. They were at the edge of the cottonwood bosque, 300 yards to the east, dismounted and firing their Winchesters at the corrales. They were too far away to be effective but they were drawing the attention of Paco and his men. Paco moved about half his men, seven in all, to the east wall to oppose this flanking threat. Paco stood behind them, their backs totally exposed to Ulysses and the men on the rooftop.

From his position by the church, Hectór heard gunfire from the east. He ordered Placido and four other men to mount up and they headed around the block and up the street to the corrales. When they reached the main street, they saw the outlaws.

"¡Vamonos!" Hectór charged forward past the corrales and across the open fields toward the outlaws. Placido hesitated a moment then followed his brother. The other four vaqueros hesitated even longer, then moved forward at a cautious trot, apprehensive at the sudden prospect of facing the notorious pistoleros in a gunfight on open ground. When Montoya saw Hectór galloping toward him, he leapt onto Bala and moved to meet him.

"Git back here, loco!" Croft yelled. "Stay down an' we'll hold 'em back!"

Montoya galloped full speed into the open, right at Hectór. Hectór thought he was facing the Kid, and his heart was filled with passion for the fight. He thought if he killed the Kid the gringos spirits and will to fight would surely be broken. He would then let the others escape, killing a few more, hopefully including Ulysses, and they would keep going, running north, never to return.

A hundred yards from Hectór, Montoya pulled back hard on Bala's reins, bringing the stallion to a sudden, sliding halt. Montoya leveled his Winchester at Hectór and fired. The .44 slug hit Hectór's horse in the chest. The animal collapsed, its body hurling forward into the dust. Hectór leapt free and tried to run onto the ground but he was flying forward too fast and he ran out of legs and tumbled, head first, over the earth. Hectór held onto his rifle. He came up on one knee and leveled his weapon at Montoya. Bala was kicking and circling after Montoya's rough handling and the sudden explosion of his shot at Hectór. As Montoya came around, Hector shot the outlaw through the right side, just below his ribcage. Montoya's torso swayed drunkenly in the saddle, then he slipped forward, still holding his reins, and dropped over the stallion's shoulder onto the ground. Bala skipped aside and Montoya lost the reins. Hectór fired rapidly at Evans and Croft in the trees.

Placido and the others rode up. Placido ordered his men to dismount. He held their horses as they knelt and began a hot barrage at Evans and Croft.

"That's all we kin do," Evans said. "Let's git."

The Mexicans' bullets splattered bark on the cottonwoods all around as the ladrones fell back to their horses, mounted up and high-tailed it back into the bosque.

Hectór rose and walked calmly over to Montoya. Lying on his side, Montoya tried to draw his revolver as Hectór walked up, but he lost all strength and his hand fell to the ground.

"¿Porque veniste aquí, a pelear por los gringos y morir?" Hectór asked mildly. "Why did you come here to fight for the gringos and to die?"

"Vino a pelear por me libertad y la libertad de mis amigos. I came to fight for my freedom and for my friends' freedom." Then dark death descended over Montoya's eyes and his spirit flew away…away, for all time.

Paco and his men were still fully exposed, watching Hectór's men and the fleeing outlaws, when Ulysses rose up, aimed his Winchester and shot Paco between the shoulder blades. All Ulysses's men began firing, putting the others to urgent, scrambling flight and suppressing the gunmen in the buildings across the street.

Angus and his men flooded down the alley over the wall, into the corrales, some bridling horses while others fired at any Mexican they saw, driving all to cover. Four cowboys, swinging picks, smashed an opening in the stone wall and the men and horses poured through, back up the alley.

Ulysses and his men slid over the parapet and dropped to safety in the cover of the alley. All mounted up. They paused, briefly, behind the cantina, picked up their saddles. The rear guard, Tzoeh, and the wounded, then thundered up the back street and cut across to the high bridge, firing at the guards who covered the escape route. The Mexicans adjacent to the bridge were already pinned down by the Apache's fire from above, and the gringos burst full speed across the bridge and up the switchbacks toward the top of the mesa.

Hectór's brother, Antonio Trujillo, was in charge of the men in the adobe ruins covering the road at the high bridge. He was filled with desperate anger, furious that he and his people were pinned down by the Apaches' fire, unable to kill the fleeing enemies of his clan. Antonio's boiling emotion burst the bonds of caution and he suddenly sprang up from his cover behind a low ruined wall, snapped his rifle into position over the barricade, and fired.

Ben Highsmith was riding double with and supporting the wounded man, Cooper. They were the last of the fleeing gringos to reach the bridge. Highsmith saw Antonio aiming right at him but both his arms were around the nearly limp, fainting body of his wounded friend, as he held the man in the saddle and tried to control their horse's reins at the same time. Highsmith reached for his revolver with one hand and Cooper tipped to the side and fell off their bolting, swerving mare as Antonio's bullet hit Highsmith just below his right clavicle, knocking him backward, over the rump of his panicky, sprinting horse. Highsmith's upper back and shoulders hit the ground first, bending and almost breaking his neck. His legs flew over him and the momentum snapped him up into a sitting position, legs extended, facing Antonio's position.

Antonio dropped back behind the cover of the wall in almost the same instant that he squeezed his trigger, but several of the Apaches above had already fired. Bullets ripped by as Antonio ducked and one severed Antonio's ring finger from his left hand and shattered his rifle barrel as he pulled his weapon down after him. Highsmith sat, dazed, in the street and Cooper lay behind him, weakly trying to push himself up with one arm.

Ten caballeros had advanced from the church, across the plaza onto the main camino, following the gringos' retreat. They were a hundred yards from Highsmith and Cooper but well out of range of the covering Apaches. The Mexicans opened fire and Highsmith's and Cooper's sagging bodies jerked and jumped as they were riddled with bullets and sprayed with their own blood.

Fleeing and cutting up a switchback halfway up the mesa, Angus looked down, shook his fist and bellowed, "I'll kill ye all ye God-damned bloody bastards! I swear before God my witness!"

Ulysses kept low in the saddle and whipped his horse, striving to get well out of range and looking back only to assure himself that his people, Diego, Ignacio and their vaqueros, were following.

When Ulysses had opened fire on the corrales, Hectór had moved, quick as a cat, seized Bala's reins, and lightly sprung onto the dangerous stallion's back. The masterful horseman instantly bent the elemental equine to his will. The animal exploded to a full gallop under Hectór's sharp, merciless, silver espulinas.

"¡Siga me! Follow me!" Hectór ordered Placido and their men, and they all followed immediately, dominated no less than the half-wild stallion, by Hectór's passion, courage and certainty.

Hectór had no fear of the gringos who were firing from the corrales as they mounted up and began their retreat. But he knew he couldn't stop them all alone. So he raced to the buildings at the bottom of the main camino, just above

the bridge on the Rio Scamandario where his men, driven by Ulysses's attack from the corrales, were regrouping.

The gringos were already fleeing up the alley as Hectór gathered his caballeros together and ordered those who had attacked on foot to follow. Hectór quickly organized and instructed his men. They would charge up the main camino and take cover around the bridge at the base of the mesa. Half would fire on the Apaches and the others would shoot gringos as they ascended the switchbacks.

There was already shooting at the upper bridge and Hectór was about to lead his men in pursuit when he saw his brother Pedro and Don Vicente's foreman, Escobar, riding toward him at a walk, somberly, calmly, backs perfectly erect in their saddles. They led Paco's horse, a fine grey, and Paco's dead body lay over his saddle.

Hectór stopped speaking. He dismounted and walked slowly forward with great dignity and profound sadness, leading the black captured stallion to meet his brothers: one alive and weeping, the other still and mute. Hectór and Pedro stopped and looked into each others eyes. Then Hectór walked past Pedro. He caressed Paco's grey, behind the ears. Then he ran his fingers through Paco's chestnut colored, curly locks. Paco had always been so full of mirth. There was an entry wound on Paco's back and drying streaks of blood ran from the exit wound on his chest down his neck and clotted in trembling droplets at his chin. Hectór looked up the camino and watched as the gringos fled up the mesa and the shooting died down. He saw Angus pause and shake his fist. He saw Ulysses riding hard, low and dangerous.

O'Laerte, you fox, Hectór thought. I know of you. It was your cunning that accomplished this foul murder. Perhaps even your own hand.

But all desire for black war and vengeance were banished from Hectór's heart by the inescapable knowledge that he must now take his brother to Doña Elviria.

The condemned outlaw William Bonney, "Guillermo Bonito," sat on the mesa's rim, five hundred yards to the south. He smoked and watched Evans and Croft slowly making their way up the steep slope. He contemplated Patricio Montoya's body lying in the dirt under the sun where Hectór had left him. He'd been the Kid's best friend...hell: his only real friend. Like a brother. The man to whom he owed his very life. Now, the Kid knew he must kill Hectór, or be killed trying. If he killed Hectór, he could have no life in Mexico. Nowhere to go. Except to death. Nothing for him and Tzoeh. Perhaps not even honor, since he must again serve the tyrannical McCullochs who had forced Tzoeh to betray him. Billy kept looking at Patricio far below. Patricio seemed so small now. His being was already shrinking toward nothingness in space as well as in the face of the vastness of never-ending time. William flicked his still smoldering cigarette butt out, into the wind over the escarpment and it was carried away.

"Adiós, amigo. Adiós, para siempre. Goodbye forever."

At sundown, Ulysses sat on the mesa at the Apache camp. He watched the pueblo below and calculated. He saw how the Trujillos again drove their horses into the fortress and he figured how to use the Trujillos' prudence against them. Ulysses looked at the outlaws' campfire on the escarpment half a mile away. Bonney's there, Ulysses thought, and Ulysses was thinking how to use Bonney. Ulysses looked over his shoulder at the Apaches' fires and he figured he could tell what they were capable of, what they wanted and what they were likely to do.

All the parts of it are complicated, Ulysses thought. And there's things I don't know. Like, when's the Mexican army comin'? We gotta finish it tomorrow and I've thought it through every way I can. But if it all works like I figure, I just might get all my people home safe. And with some horses and gold, too.

29

LOVERS DESPERADOS

They held each other all night and they tasted salty tears.

Ulysses, Angus and Robert sat at their campfire with Evans and Croft.

"You lads did us a good turn today," Angus said. "Ya made the right decision. We won't forget it. We get back to New Mexico, we'll make sure Chisum and all the ranchers support ya in favor of gettin' the governor's amnesty. We'll see ya get another chance to start clean, stay clear of the law. Hell, Robert an' me 've lost seven men killed already. When we get back, we can use tough hombres like you who've proven their loyalty. I'm sorry about your friend, Patricio, though. They say I'm cold hearted, but I liked the boy. That's the truth. He was real brave to fight Hectór like that, shot up like he was."

"Thank you, McCulloch," Evans said. "Patricio was really more the Kid's friend than ours, though. We only fell in with them two after our luck went as far south as theirs. We rode with the Kid a while back. He's always been too wild to read. First he rode with us. Then, he was with Tunstall, Brewer and McSween. They all got killed. Then he was with us again. Today he was gonna ride on alone, even without Patricio, an' him an' Patricio were muy amigos. You just can't tell what the Kid 'll do next."

"I can tell," Ulysses said.

"You figure we'll ride out tomorrow?" Croft asked Angus.

Robert's face boiled red with rage.

Before he could speak, Ulysses raised his hand, palm upturned—asking him to hold back—and said, "We came for the girl and we'll have 'er. Tomorrow."

"I don't see how yer gonna do that," Evans said. "We got shot up real good today and they've got about as many men as we do. They've got a strong fort. If we fight 'em in the town again, it'll be a blood bath. I sure as hell don't mind none, but I don't figure yer cowboys got much stomach left fer gun fightin' after what they seen today."

"We can do it." Ulysses said. "And there won't be no blood bath, except for the Mexicans. But we need yer guns and most of all, we need the Kid."

"Well, today we were too busy ta talk," Angus said, "but if we're gonna try again tomorrow, I guess we better know your plan now."

Ulysses replied, "This is how I figure it. We've gotta get into the hacienda ta git the girl. We've gotta surprise 'em and beat 'em bad, prob'ly kill most of 'em ta' git the horses. Evans is right. If Hectór brings the fight out to us again tomorrow, the fight will be even and we'll lose as many as they will. Just like today. If that happens, we lose. We got no back-up comin'. They prob'ly do. Most of our boys are green. We can't keep fightin' and losin' men here on the Trujillos' home ground.

"If Hectór attacks us, we can't surprise 'em and we can't get inta the fort. And anybody who saw Hectór fight today kin understand his nature. He will attack tomorrow. He's plannin' it now. Now, livin' on the border, I've heard of Hectór before. The caballeros follow 'im 'cause he's got the biggest cojones, and he's never been beat even though he's led 'em fightin' against Apaches and ladrones, and fer Diaz against mestizos, who figured old Spanish families like the Trujillos shouldn't be able to hold onto their big haciendas. Hectór hasn't been beat 'cause he can ride better than anybody I've ever seen and he thinks quick in a fight. He's real fast and good with his guns, and his people believe in 'im and follow 'im up. He's their leader."

"Well if he intends to attack, how do we keep him from it?" Robert asked.

"We kill 'im. That's the only way. We kill Hectór and the Mexicans lose their leader. They can't attack fer a day or so. They hole up in that fort. I've figured how ta' git in at sundown, surprise 'em, cut 'em down and burn the place. With surprise, there's little risk fer us. If it don't work we just back off, nice and safe, but if it works, they'll all die or run. We've got a few fighters among us and them Apaches and Comanches, too. We lead the cowhands in, git the Mexicans on the run and them boys 'll do jist fine, slingin' lead after them Trujillos who scared hell out of 'em today and killed their compañeros."

The ranchers and pistoleros all looked in silence for a while at Ulysses,

realizing that his logic was solid. But it led, inexorably, to the pivotal question.

Angus asked it. "Who's gonna kill Hectór? You? And how 're you gonna do it?"

"Me?" Ulysses scoffed. "No. There's only one man that kin git him out alone and only one man that kin kill 'im… maybe: Bonney. If he's as fast and accurate as they say. An' he may be. Judgin' by what he done ta them scalp hunters, I think he is."

Ulysses looked around the fire but perceived no understanding in the eyes of any of his listeners. "Look. Hectór don't know Bonney ain't with us. He figures Bonney's important to us, just like Hectór is with his own people. Hectór knows we'll have ta run if we git hurt bad again tomorrow like we did today. Look how Hectór fought today. He rode out front and killed Gates and that other boy where we could all shoot at 'im. Then he charged you boys across open fields. He was too far ahead of them that followed 'im ta be safe. He thought he was fightin' the Kid. He took a bad risk because he figured killin' the Kid would hurt us bad an' give his people the advantage they need to whip us fer good. He'll do it again. His heart only knows one way to lead. I've heard it and now I've seen it. I'm sure of it.

"Before dawn, we take cover along the river. Hectór and his people will know we're there but we'll build fires to make sure they know. Hectór won't be able to attack right off. He'll have to figure a way to hit our new position without losin' a lot of people. But at sun up, before he kin do anything, the Kid rides across the bridge and up the hill to where he's out of range of our rifles. He'll have to stop there and he'll be out of range of their rifles too. He jest has ta wait there in the open where they kin all see 'im. They'll know what he wants an' Hectór 'll come out, sure. He'll figure his people kin beat us all if he puts heart in 'em and takes ours away by killin' the Kid."

"That sounds real good," Jesse replied. "Except for one thing. How're you gonna git the Kid ta do what you want? Like I said, he's got his own mind."

"True. But we all know the Kid wants to pay Hectór back for Patricio. And he wants his horse back. Now, the Kid kin fight Hectór how and when he wants, so we've gotta git 'im on our side again. We gotta give the girl back over to 'im. That'll satisfy 'im."

The outlaws and the McCullochs all sat quietly, thinking about Ulysses' plan. Then, Robert said angrily, "How do ya figure my brother's gonna give his wife over ta that low gunfighter?"

Evans and Croft flinched at Robert's revelation of his opinion of the Kid and, by association, of them as well. Ulysses raised an eyebrow and looked at Angus. Angus looked back at Ulysses. Angus's face betrayed embarrassment at his brother's lack of understanding.

"It's all right, Robert," Angus said gently. "I never intended ta take that Apache girl back home as a wife. She's handsome enough, sure, but when this is over, and the time's right, I'll leave her behind. Fer the Kid or the Apaches, I don't care."

"It's settled then," Ulysses said. "I'll talk ta Bonney. Tell the girl ta git ready ta go with me."

William Bonney sat alone at his little fire on the rim of the mesa. He looked down on the lights of San Apolonio and the Trujillo's stronghold. He could see the fires of the McCullochs and their Indian allies, nearly a mile to his left. The Kid knew he must now kill Hectór to avenge Patricio, or die trying.

The Kid considered that he could be killed at any moment. Did the McCullochs want him dead? Would they send a couple of Apaches forward through the night? Would Ulysses come with his far-striking, death dealing Hawkin? Maybe Angus would send Evans and Croft, posing as friends, to kill him. Would the Trujillos send the Pawnees? Would the Pawnees come of their own accord, for revenge? Would Mexican ladrones or rebellious compensinos, revolutionaries, be drawn to the fire-light?

Perhaps raiding Chiricahua, the last "wild," free, untamed aboriginal Americans would see and be drawn to the dying coals of the Kid's fire. The Chiricahua war parties, led by Chato, Geromino, Chihuahua and Juh, were doomed just as the Kid was. They were hunted by the American and Mexican armies, by vengeful militias and by mercenary scalphunters. Yet they remained defiant and free. Dedicated to war of blood and fire, they plunged on relentlessly toward their inevitable destruction, both destined and chosen.

At least them Chiricahua got each other, Billy thought, feeling bitter and alone.

The Kid knew he was now doomed, even if he could somehow prevail

over Hectór—Hectór, who now sat in his stone fortress surrounded by his family and supported by many brave and loyal caballeros and servants.

Billy spoke to the wounded, lame horse Patricio had left him. "It looks like its you an' me, Relampago." The Kid chuckled at the irony, 'relampago' being Spanish for 'lightning.' "Any bastards come after us, we'll outrun 'em or run circles around 'em an' out-shoot 'em in a fight."

The Kid then spoke again, with melancholy and without bravado, to the big-eyed animal who looked back at him as if understanding. "You always gave all you had to my brother Patricio, and it looks like you're gonna give your last to me."

The Kid rose, took his saddle and kit, and walked away from the dying fire toward the Norteños camp. He sat under a broad-branched juniper, leaned back on his saddle, Winchester across his thighs, and smoked.

Billy saw four riders come down the trail from the McCullochs' camp, walking their horses quietly. They were leading a coiled prancing stallion.

The riders stopped a good twenty yards beyond the light of the Kid's fire and whispered to each other.

"Billy!" Croft called out.

The Kid stepped onto the trail behind the riders and levered a round into the chamber of his rifle. Ka-chink!

Ulysses wasn't surprised. He had expected just such a maneuver and was pleased at this proof of the Kid's cunning. Maybe the boy really is smart enough to take Hectór, Ulysses thought.

Ulysses raised his empty hands, looked at Croft and Evans, then called out to the Kid. "Easy, boy!" he said. "You wouldn't want ta shoot Tzoeh, or this fine horse Angus sent ya.'"

The Kid and Tzoeh lay together and knew each other and the earth, sky and stars. Billy explained what Tzoeh already knew. Once he killed Hectór, he would be an exile, north and south, an exile with no direction or hope of shelter, his death imminent and inescapable. The lovers could have no life.

Tzoeh explained what the Kid already knew. Her duty was to defend and support her people against their enemies, the Pawnees, and against the irresistible, powerful oppression of the Americans and Mexicans. If the Kid

248

killed Hectór, Tzoeh's people might take their vengeance on the Pawnees, even as the gringos destroyed the Trujillos.

The Kid and Tzoeh were alike desperado—"without hope"—and committed to vengeance, and they held each other blameless.

After they coupled, the lovers sank together into deepest love. They held each other all night and they tasted salty tears.

30

DAWN

She sleeps by a dark, haughty warrior who has killed many men.

A few hours after midnight, four Mescaleros slipped down the face of the mesa, spread out, and moved stealthily through the streets of San Apolonio looking everywhere for signs of ambush. But Hectór's people were all in their fortress and the citizens of San Apolonio stayed quietly in their homes, watching from behind their windows as the gringos then rode down through the town in the cold and dark just before dawn.

The gringos spread out and took cover among the trees along the riverbank. Tzoeh and Billy said goodbye atop the cliff at the edge of her people's war camp in the ashen grayness that exists, like this world, in the middle place between light and darkness. Tzoeh clung to Billy and they kissed many times.

"Stay by me, only little more, Beh-leh. Look on lighting."

"Lighting? Dawn. It's called dawn."

"Dah-hen."

"When I was a little boy a man sang a song…a story. He said Dawn is a beautiful girl with gold hair and skin, and she sleeps by a dark, haughty warrior who has killed many men."

"Haw-tee?"

"Yeah, you know, proud. Like a war chief. And she sleeps on a bed of roses and when she wakes up she rises up and she reaches out and she touches us with her fingers. Her fingers are gold, too. And her fingers make us warm. So we can live. She gives us life. Like fire. She touches away cold, dark, fear, and death. Just touches 'em away. And I used to like the story. But now, sometimes I think the light just makes us see the mean things people do to each other."

Tzoeh leaned against William, under his arm, and they watched the lighting.

The sun rose and light flooded the valley between the mesa and the mountains as the Kid rode alone across the bridge and up the hill toward the hacienda. Halfway between the river and the fortress, Bonney stopped, dismounted and smoked a cigarette.

Many caballeros, campesinos, ladies and peasant women joined the sentries on the front wall. The crowd watched the Kid, and the people spoke quietly among themselves. Behind them, at the far side of the courtyard, an Indian servant held Bala's reins at the base of the stairs before the Trujillos' great house. Don Carlos, Don Vicente, Antonio, Placido, Helen and others, stood on the high balcón and argued, imploring Hectór not to ride out. But Hectór thought of his people's safety and of his lost, beautiful brother, Paco. Hectór embraced Antonia, kissed their infant son at her breast, and descended the stairs. Hectór checked his weapons and made sure his cinta was securely fastened. He mounted Bala and walked the animal across the courtyard to the gates.

The Kid saw the gates open. Hectór rode forth, holding Bala to a walk. As Hectór slowly descended the hill, the gates closed. He scanned the gringos' position along the river below. He came on, satisfied the gringos were too far away to support the Kid.

The Kid swung up onto his horse, turned the animal a little to the right, and sat there, waiting. Hectór held his Winchester cocked in one hand, barrel resting across his saddle. The Kid's rifle remained in its sheath and the Kid sat still with both hands resting on his saddle horn. Hectór stopped only thirty yards from the Kid. The long rise was almost flat here and the riders regarded each other calmly.

"Señor Bonney," Hectór called.

"Que quieres? No hay nada que decir. What do you want? There's nothing to say."

"Hagamos un acuerdo. Si le mato, dejare a su gente que lleven su cuerpo para enterarlo con la ceremonia y el honor debida y les concedo el tiempo para hacerlo. Y le ruego que me conceda el mismo derecho y cortesia. Let us make an agreement. If I kill you I will allow your people to take your body for burial with all due ceremony and I will allow the time for it. And I respectfully request that you give me the same right and courtesy."

"No son mi gente. Ellos son, como usted, rancheros gordos y ellos me

ven solamente como un lobo hambriento. Pero solo quiero comer como ellos. Y como usted. Por lo tanto, no puede haber, nunca, tratos entre los hombres y los lobos. They're not my people. They're like you—fat ranchers who see me only as a hungry wolf. But I only want to eat like them. And like you. And so it is. There can never be agreements between men and wolves."

Hectór reflected for a moment on this answer. He shrugged. There was nothing more to say. He snapped rifle to shoulder and fired.

As Hectór raised his weapon, Bonney roweled his stallion and yanked his torso down hard behind the animal's shoulder. As the stallion leapt away, Bonney pulled his left leg over its back and dropped down off his saddle. Holding onto fender and pommel, he pushed off the ground twice with both legs, hopping along beside the horse, then dived to his right, rolled head over heels, and came up on one knee.

Bala broke in two, then kicked for the sky. Hectór knew he had missed. He reined Bala in, levered another bullet to chamber and swung the rifle to his left, seeking the Kid. The Kid's horse vaulted past him, and as Hectór looked down his barrel, bringing the Kid into sight, he saw two flashes of light. The bullets knocked Hectór backward, out of his saddle and over Bala's flanks. Bala panicked, reared and bolted. Hectór's right boot was caught for a moment in the stirrup and he was dragged a few yards before he came free on the ground. The release vector caused Hectór's body to roll onto his chest and face and the Kid, walking forward, firing Thunderers in turn, shot Hectór four more times and Hectór bit the dust and died.

Bonney heard a high keening of the women and bellowed objections and denials of men on the ramparts as he strode quickly past Hectór, toward Bala. As he reloaded his Thunderers, he glanced apprehensively at the gates, expecting vengeful caballeros to break and charge at any moment. But none came.

Bala stood off, ready to bolt, front legs spread, ears back, tail twitching. Bonney spoke softly as he approached then caught the stallion's reins. The Kid led the horse back to Hectór's body.

The Kid had forced himself to remain calm and clear for the fight. Now that the killing was done, his anger boiled up. Anger that Angus took Tzoeh. Anger that Hectór killed Patricio. Anger that the McCullochs used him and

Patricio. Anger that he was now a hunted exile, desperado, in Mexico as well as in the north. Anger at the loss of his dreams and fleeting hopes. The Kid choked with wrath and irrational passion for vengeance. He put his hand on his knife and he considered, for a moment, cutting Hectór's scalp, digging the blade into the skull and ripping the hair away from Hectór's head. Bonney had never scalped a man. He looked at the wailing people on the walls and knew he could not do the barbaric thing. Tears welled up in his blue eyes. Bonney removed the lariat from Hectór's saddle, tied Hectór's ankles, mounted, and dallied the rope around his saddle horn so he could drag the body away.

Billy heard Ulysses' voice, distantly, shouting a warning. He looked up and saw Don Carlos and an Indian servant riding down from the gates. The Kid waited. The Indian veered off and retrieved the horse Angus had given the Kid.

Don Carlos rode up and dismounted at Hectór's feet. Don Carlos dropped to one knee and placed his hand on the Kid's rope. He looked at the Kid. "Te ruego. Dame mi hijo. No lo llevas. I implore you. Give me my son. Don't take him."

"Mató a mi amigo. He killed my friend."

"Yes, but their deaths show us that this war is madness. And now, all is equal. I implore you. Think of your father." The Kid thought of his father. He was unmoved.

"Think of your mother."

The Kid thought of Catherine, and he thought of Doña Elviria. The Kid dropped the rope from his saddle horn. The servant brought the stallion and handed Billy the lead.

Billy rode down to the river, crossed the bridge and rode past Angus, Robert and Ulysses. They looked satisfied and expectant. Billy rejected his urge to draw and shoot Angus. He rode on through the town.

Atop the mesa, Billy gave Angus' stallion to two Mescaleras. One was old, one was pregnant. He told the women the horse was for Tzoeh. He did not see Tzoeh. He rode on, north. He did not look back.

31

WAR OF BLOOD AND FIRE

I cannot ask God's forgiveness.

By mid afternoon, Hectór's body was washed and dressed in a clean, swallow-grey traje corto with silver conchos on the jacket and trousers. Hectór and Paco lay side by side in fresh-cut and fragrant pine coffins on tables in the entry of the Trujillos' great house.

On the wall above them was a blue Cristo. Many candles burned on the tables around the dead brothers. Doña Elviria lay in her quarters on her bed, shrouded in black, curled in fetal position, weeping and occasionally attempting to vomit into a silver bowl held by an Indian servant girl who attended her.

Don Carlos, his surviving sons Pedro and Antonio, Hector's widow Antonia, and all the women and children of the household kept vigil before the hearth in the great hall. Antonio lay on a wooden banco clutching his bandaged, shattered hand to his breast and taking deep draughts of tequila, offered by his wife, against the pain. Don Carlos sat in his throne-like carved chair and hung his head. Tears ran down his cheeks, his shoulders slumped and he seemed, now, as never before, very small and devoid of power or wisdom.

Placido stood with Dream Walker and Long Soldier by a cook fire in the courtyard. Placido handed Dream Walker a bag of gold. "Muerte. Dead. If you bring me El Pistolero's head as proof, I will give you two more bags of gold, and any horses you want."

"We hunt him and kill him, for what he done to Hectór and for the fight he done before. We take him, we kill slow. We bring head. We go tonight. We need good horses now. He can ride far and fast on the stallion he take from Hectór. We know horse's track."

"Marcelo."

And the foreman stepped up.

"Give them the best horses we have—those you judge to be equal in speed and endurance and well broken. Give them four, so they can change often and take the ladrón."

Secluded in shame in her room, Helen stood before a little table and mirror. She carefully folded her note and laid it on the little stand:

Amada Doña Elviria, I do not ask your forgiveness. I cannot ask God's forgiveness. I give my life instead. I know God will burn me in hell forever for what I do now. Accept this as my apology. Give my body to Robert. Then there can be no reason for war. I am sorry. Con todo remordimiento, Helen

Helen lifted a sharp Spanish dagger with a gleaming blade, gripped the hilt with both hands, placed the point touching her breast over her heart and looked at her reflection in the mirror. She raised the blade and prepared to plunge it down. She looked again at her reflection. Her hands trembled and she could not do it. She fell, weeping, to her knees. Then she found the strength. She reached up, took hold of the little table and pulled herself, shaking, back to her feet. She knew she had to do it fast. She threw her forearm down onto the mirror-stand and raised the dagger over her wrist. She looked at her face in the mirror one last time.

She saw Placido there. She slammed the blade down but Placido stepped up behind her, caught both her wrists, pulled them apart, wrestled the blade from her hand and threw it aside. Helen's knees gave way but Placido caught her, turned her to face him and pulled her up against his chest.

"Por favor, mi amor. Let me die. If I die, you can give me to Robert and this war's gonna end."

"No!"

"Por favor. I caused many men to die."

"No. Our people are born to war and we do not ask Death his reason. Hectór and Paco fought many battles and they fought in the ways which they believed were most honorable. War is man's way and we accept it. Once a man is dead there is no use in saying it might have been otherwise.

"You must not leave me. We are safe here. In three hundred years of warfare, this fortaleza has never fallen. Our soldiers must arrive here at any

moment. Then we will destroy the gringos, and we will live on in peace. I must lead our family now and I need you."

Helen's cheeks were wet and raw and the rough leather of Placido's chaleco scratched and burned her face as she pressed against him. Helen had once imagined that she and Placido would live in peace and happiness in this family and place but she now knew those things could never be. With the deaths of Paco and Hectór, the fleeting wisps of her dreams were taken by the wind.

Don Vicente entered the hall with five caballeros, carrying their rifles ready. Don Vicente gestured subtly, and two of his men took his daughter Antonia by her arms, raised her from her seat and ushered her with her baby Astayanio toward the door.

"¡No, pápi, por favor! ¡Tengo que enterer a mi esposo! No daddy, please! I must bury my husband!"

"Es mas importante vivir para sus hijo. It is more important that you live for your son and Hectór's," Don Vicente replied.

As Antonia was pushed and carried out, Don Vicente's riflemen covered the hall and the guards at the doors.

Like Don Carlos, Don Vicente had been educated in Spain and England. Now, in order to avoid shaming Don Carlos before those who might not understand, he chose to speak English.

"I have always despised your presumptuous pride and false pretense of honor. Now your hypocrisy has caused the death of two sons and all because you cherished the beauty of that slut, Helen, and supported Placido's dissolute and immoral crimes. I could do nothing when my daughter chose Hectór as husband. He was, truly, honorable and brave. But, now that he is gone, the tie between our families is broken and I refuse to support you further in your folly. There is a black curse on this house. I am taking my daughter and my grandson home to safety. May God be with you."

Don Carlos never even looked at Don Vicente. He remained shriveled and bent in his place. His sons, Antonio and Pedro, looked confused. They had the strength and will to act, but absent guidance and direction from Hectór or Don Carlos, they knew not what to do and they remained frozen in doubt.

Don Vicente and his men walked out. The rest of Don Vicente's people were mounted and ready in the courtyard below. Antonia and Astayanio were forced into a spring wagon next to two shrouded, dead men. The contingent rode out of the fortaleza and took the road east and south out of the valley and around the base of the Sierra Madre.

Ulysses sat in council with Don Tenorio and Cuerno Verde in shade by the river. They passed and smoked herb from a long feathered trade pipe with a tomahawk blade on one side and a fire bowl on the other. Ulysses rose to his feet, stamped, slapped his thigh, and grinned at the chieftains when he saw Don Vicente's powerful contingent of reinforcements ride out and away. Don Tenorio and Cuerno Verde smiled, nodded and grunted in satisfaction. Ulysses's stratagem was working better than they had dared hope.

But Cuerno Verde was not surprised. Reflecting on his first meeting with Ulysses, when he had barely escaped with his life, Cuerno Verde knew, now more clearly than ever, that Ulysses was a liar, a thief and a trickster. A coyote. A perfect ally. Cuerno Verde intended to wait until the Trujillos were destroyed. Then he would kill Ulysses for what Ulysses had done to White Wolf and his Comanche brothers so long ago.

The McCulloch's men worked through the afternoon gathering wood along the river. The gunfighters, Evans and Croft, disdained the hard labor and they sat in the shade, cleaned their guns and watched as the cowboys prepared a huge pyre just west of the bridge on the river Scamandario. The cowboys doused the wood-pile with coal oil. Sentries watched apprehensively from the front wall of the hacienda as the gringos marshaled and saddled their horses just before sundown.

At dusk, five vaqueros rode out of the gates into the vast corral and pasture next to the fortress and began gathering the Trujillos' fine horses, preparing to drive them inside the protection of the walls for the night. The vaqueros herded the horses into the far corner by a cistern against the front of the corral. Ulysses, Diego and Ignacio, wearing colored serapes similar to the vaqueros', lay concealed in the tall grass just outside the corral. Once the horses were gathered together there, the raiders crawled under the lowest rung of the fence and moved, crouching, below the equines' backs. They slipped through the crowded herd toward the vaqueros working on the far side.

Angus watched through a spyglass and signaled his men. They torched the bonfire and it flared through the deepening darkness. The Trujillos' men on the walls and at the gates were distracted by the sudden diversion and they saw nothing as ten Apaches rose, suddenly, from behind the cistern and loosed arrows which flew like wind and impaled the herders. The Indians immediately loosed a second volley and Ulysses, Ignacio and Diego rose from among the horses and pulled the dying men from their mounts as they gasped, swooned and clawed at the many feathered shafts which seemed to have suddenly sprung from their torsos.

Diego's man tried to pull his pistola as Diego yanked him down, hard, onto the ground. Diego held the dying man's wrist and slashed his throat with a Bowie knife.

In an instant, Ulysses, Ignacio, then Diego were mounted and wearing the murdered men's sombreros. They whistled, shouted and lashed the animals, hazing them into a hard run toward the open gates of the corral and hacienda just beyond. The man at the gate of the corral, and two in charge of the gates of the Fortaleza, tore their attention from the gringos who came charging up the hill at a full gallop. The Mexicans waved their arms and whistled, turning the streaming herd into the hacienda as it burst out of the corral. The horses raced under the parapet above the gates and thundered into the cobblestone courtyard.

The gatemen moved toward the shelter of the fortress and prepared to pull the big gates closed, but Ulysses and his men, following at the back of the wild remuda, shot the guards down with six guns and rode into the fort.

Just inside the arched, stone passage through the front wall, Ulysses and his men leapt from their saddles, knelt against the sides of the opening and began firing their Winchesters at anyone they could see inside and on the high walls around the confused, panicked, milling horses. The McCullochs and all thirty of their men whooped, yelled and fired wildly with rifles and pistols, at the six caballeros on the front wall as they galloped full-on into range.

The caballeros saw the open gates, their dead compañeros on the ground below and the irresistible speed of the overwhelming force as bullets zipped through the air and splattered the wall before and all around them. The caballeros fired only a few despairing shots at the attackers and they ducked, ran along the parapet to the east wall and fled away along that rampart. This brought them into Ulysses's field of fire and they followed other sentries and men, women and children of the rancho who were climbing over the wall, dropping into the corral below and fleeing across the pasture toward the rising, forested heights beyond.

The few guards who had been posted on the rear battlement behind the Trujillos' great hall turned and rushed forward along the balcónes and fired across the courtyard, over the crowded horses and running people, at Ulysses's group crouching at the opening of the sally-port.

As the guards turned and moved away from the back wall, Don Tenorio, Cuerno Verde and all their warriors arose out of concealment and came swiftly forward, like ghosts, through the darkness. They tossed lassos over the merlons on the crenellated parapet. Within moments, warriors scaled the wall and slipped through the crenels onto the rampart behind the defenders. They fired Sharp's rifles and muskets and loosed bows at the sentries' backs as the gringos rode into the courtyard and through the chaos of the swirling mass of horses, hurling forth an overwhelming barrage of lead in every direction. The sentries jerked, twisted and crumpled in the crossfire.

Placido, Antonio, Pedro and four caballeros charged out of the great doors, onto the balcón, firing. Five were cut to pieces in an overwhelming fusillade from the cowboys below. Marcelo and Dominico fell back, both badly wounded. At the rear of the house, warriors ignited torches of hemp and cotton soaked in pitch. They fired the roof and hurled faggots onto the roofs of the smithy and stables and into the hay below.

The Pawnees climbed a ladder onto the west wall and as Dream Walker jumped over the parapet, Long Soldier turned and looked through rising flames on the back rampart. Cuerno Verde locked eyes with Long Soldier and bared his teeth in a malignant grin. Long Soldier raised his rifle and was hit by bullets and arrows fired from the warriors around Cuerno Verde, and he was slammed backward as he squeezed his trigger. His shot flew high into the dark sky and the darkness filled Long Soldier's eyes and heart.

Cuerno Verde made his way along the rampart toward Long Soldier.

He looked over the wall at Dream Walker, dodging and loping away into the darkness beyond, headed toward the river and the bosque. Cuerno Verde knelt and took Long Soldier's narrow, high, magnificent scalp lock.

The Trujillos' most loyal Indian servant, Ramón, stood at the base of the curved stone stairway that rose to the balcón before the great house. Ramón had served Don Carlos loyally for nearly fifty years, since he was sixteen years old. Ramón calmly raised an old "Brown Bess" muzzle-loader and aimed carefully at one of the young cowboys, Andrew O'Connor, as the boy galloped forward across the courtyard. Ramón's ball blew O'Connor backward, out of his saddle. A fountain of bright blood erupted and spewed up out of the boy's chest, then his shattered heart pumped no more.

"That nigger killed Andy!" Young Bayless called to their friend McGee, and the two young hands rode up, jerked their horses to a skidding halt and lassoed Ramón as Ramón tried to reload his musket. Bayless snapped his rope tight around Ramón's neck and McGee's noose snagged an ankle as the old man was jerked off his feet. Clay Wright shot Ramón in the side as the cowhands dragged him across the courtyard to a ramada by the front gate. They threw their ropes over the wooden scaffold, and pulled their mounts back, hoisting Ramón into the air. They tied the rigs to supporting pillares and the old man hung there by one ankle and by his neck. Ramón gripped the garrote at his throat and kicked with his free leg as he choked and black blood dripped from the gash between his ribs and puddled on the ground.

Cuerno Verde rose to his feet, held Long Soldier's scalp high and shrieked a hoarse, triumphal Comanche war cry: "Kaa-kaw! Ka-ka-kaw!"

At the same time, Jenkins kicked in the door of the servants' quarters against the wall below Cuerno Verde. Rob Duralt and Hays followed him inside, rifles ready. Clara Mendoza cowered against the far wall. The old mestiza held her fifteen-year-old granddaughter, Patricia, tightly against her.

"Haw!" Jenkins bellowed, and strode forward. Clara released Patricia and stepped to meet him, open palms raised before her. Jenkins bashed the side of Clara's temple with his rifle butt and Patricia bent to embrace Clara as she fell, unconscious. Jenkins grabbed the girl's hair, jerked her back and threw her onto the hard dirt floor. She clawed and kicked as Jenkins straddled her and ripped off her clothes. Then Jenkins slammed his fist into her mouth, forced her legs apart and raped her.

When Evans and Croft had ridden a little behind the leaders into the courtyard, they cut right, pulled up, scanned the dangerous environment carefully, then sat their horses and fired slowly and with deadly accuracy at men on the west wall. They killed several and wounded others. The surviving vaqueros jumped over the wall and fled. The outlaws reloaded their rifles and watched calmly as Cuerno Verde scalped Long Soldier. They looked across the courtyard: most of the wild horses had bunched into the northeast corner, and there were bodies on the ground. The McCullochs' wild, inexperienced young cowboys had killed mostly unarmed peasants, women and a couple of children.

Croft and Evans had seen the Trujillo boys shot down, and they saw that a couple of caballeros who followed the Trujillos out initially had fallen back into the hall. The men had gotten off a couple of ineffectual shots and now the McCullochs' people maintained a steady fire at the huge, thick, mesquite doors of the great house. The back of the house was afire and the stables and forge were, too. Mexicans could be seen crouching behind cover about the courtyard and some, probably women and children, were in the quarters which lined the walls.

The pistoleros looked at each other morosely. They had raised hell in New Mexico Territory, riding hard, robbing and rustling. But they never killed innocents and they had fired off missives to the newspapers in which they mocked and challenged powerful authority. They had pride and they had only fought worthy opponents. Never peasants or women.

Now, in the space of five minutes, each had shot and killed more men than they ever had in all their lives before.

"Looks like the Kid was right," Evans said.

"Yeah. But I'll still take the amnesty." Croft replied.

"May's well. Now, after all."

"But I'll never ride with these bastards or work for 'em, after we get back."

"No. But till then, we better end this bloody dung 'fore it gits worse."

"Let's go."

The outlaws rode their horses forward, slowly, toward the right staircase

leading to the Trujillos' hall where Marcelo and Dominico had fled.

Marcelo and Dominico had charged forth, just behind Placido and the others, but they had immediately retreated back into the household as they saw their patrónes and amigos sliced to pieces in the impassible wall of fire from the gringos coming across the courtyard below.

Marcelo and Dominico had each been shot several times and Marcelo collapsed onto one knee, but the caballeros managed to close the big mesquite doors and drop a heavy bar across iron braces. But even before they could prepare further defense, they were shot down from behind by Apaches who had broken into the back of the house, butchered male servants in the cocina, and were coming through a passage into the great hall. Warriors pushed, dragged and hazed Helen and the Trujillos' other wives, as well as female servants and the children of the household, toward the front doors.

Don Carlos stepped out from his quarters and opposed the warriors, holding only a long, fine-steel, swept-hilt rapier. The old ranchero had choked down his pain and recovered his composure when the sounds of the attack boiled up around him. Now he stood, proud and ramrod straight, and he raised and pointed his rapier at the advancing Apaches.

"Que vengan," he said, "Come on."

Several warriors raised their rifles but a lithe young warrior, Kahthili, raised a hand to stop them. Kahthili tossed his rifle to Daklugie and took a spear from Nayiitch. Kahthili grinned in anticipation of the sport and stepped forward, spear in one hand, a dagger in the other. He thrust the spear at Don Carlos. Don Carlos parried and thrust back. They fenced and Don Carlos, aged and no longer quick, was forced back in the face of the lightning fast thrusts and supple strength of the young Apache. Doña Elviria rushed through the door toward Don Carlos, holding before her in both hands a loaded blue-steel Colt's .45.

"Carlito!" She called out the name she had used for her sweetheart, decades before. As Don Carlos glanced at her and reached for the gun, Kahthili thrust his spear past a weak parry into the old man's stomach and another warrior shot Don Carlos. Doña Elviria cried out and Kahthili kicked the revolver from her hands and caught it in the air.

As smoke from the fire at the rear of the house roiled forth below the ceilings throughout, the Apaches and Comanches drove the women and children toward the front doors. They pulled the doors open. Daklugie called to the gringos and they ceased fire. The captives were pushed out onto the portico, past the bodies of Placido, Pedro, Antonio and their men. They shoved and hazed their prisoners down the stairs into the courtyard.

Doña Elviria had to be dragged off Don Carlos and past her dead sons. Two warriors threw her down onto the stone escalera. Doña Elviria's hip was broken and Helen rushed to help her. But Robert McCulloch saw Helen, shouted a curse, rode up, lassoed her and yanked her down off the stairs. Helen hit the cobblestones, five feet below, hard. Robert cut his cayuse and dragged Helen across the courtyard and under the legs of the panicking, blooded tarpans in the far corner. The frightened animals kicked, skittered and danced away from the tumbling, screaming woman. Robert cut back, pulled a bullwhip from his saddlebag and lashed Helen, opening a ragged gash on her left cheek. Robert pulled the whip back but Angus rode up and grabbed his arm.

"No man! It's enough for now. We'll take an' deal with 'er later!"

Angus ordered two of his drovers to get Helen on a horse.

Meanwhile, the other captives had been herded into a group by the cook fires at the west side. Doña Elviria had been dragged and dumped there too.

As Jenkins raped Patricia, Duralt and Hays shifted nervously in the doorway.

"Let's go man!"

"Leave 'er be, we got no time fer this!"

Jenkins got off Patricia. She curled into a ball. Jenkins stepped over to the fireplace and tossed burning faggots onto the bedding against the wall. He raised a burning brand and ignited the dry, cedar latillas between the pine vigas, which supported the roof.

The men left and Patricia, naked, mouth and thighs streaked with blood, dragged her grandmother out the doorway. Indian women among the group of captives who huddled there helped the girl get Clara clear of the burning structure.

Many of the McCullochs' cowboys and the Apaches and Comanches,

most mounted, some on foot, were arrayed in a wide arc before and on either side of the prisoners, and they regarded the wretched survivors there. The victors hesitated but many leaned forward in anticipation, with murder and rapine in their eyes.

Doña Elviria lay at the front of the group of captives. She forced back her pain and pushed herself up on one arm. She glared at the enemies, raised her chin with bitter pride and prepared to die with the last of her family and people.

Tzoeh galloped into the courtyard and reined up, hard, before the captives. She slipped from her saddle, tossed a blanket to Patricia then stepped between Doña Elviria and the victorious raiders. She scanned the faces of the cowboys, Apaches and Comanches, defiantly. A Colt's .44 was visible in her waistband.

Croft and Evans had intended to shoot their way into the house, retrieve Helen and end the slaughter, but before they could get there, warriors had emerged with the survivors. Now the outlaws walked their horses over and watched the standoff.

Tzoeh saw the pistoleros. She had considered them friends when she rode with them, Patricio and Billy. Now she looked at them and cocked her head, questioningly, to one side.

"You boys best settle down, now," Croft said to the excited drovers, fidgeting on their saddles. Croft glared at the warriors too. His Winchester rested, cocked, across his saddle. Jenkins stood across the arced line from Croft. He gripped his rifle, knuckles white.

"You got no say here!"

"Shut up!" Evans said, cold death in his voice. Jenkins seemed to shrivel before Evans' deadly gaze. Jenkins looked at the cowboys all around. Clearly, nobody wanted it.

Angus, Robert, and Don Tenorio rode up.

Angus scanned the scene. He looked at Tzoeh, and nodded several times. He spoke to Don Tenorio. "Let's leave 'em."

Don Tenorio nodded. The leaders gave orders and their men, white and red, moved away and got to work rounding up the horses and driving them out of the gates, past Ramón's hanging corpse.

Angus tilted his head at Tzoeh and said to her father, "Y'd best take 'er, friend. Truth is, she won't have me." And, Angus thought, If I ever bedded her again, she'd prob'ly slit my throat in my sleep. "Ya can keep the horses, I gave. And take this." Angus handed Don Tenorio Dream Walker's saddle bags, full of the scalps of Don Tenorio's kinsmen.

"And I give this." Don Tenorio pulled Don Carlos's elegant rapier from his quiver and passed it to Angus. The two leaders of their people grasped each other's wrists in sincere gesture of friendship.

Don Tenorio gave orders and two of his men pulled Doña Elviria's ten-year-old grandson from his pleading mother's arms and put the boy on a horse.

Doña Elviria had collapsed back onto the ground. A servant girl held her head in her lap. Doña Elviria's eyes were brimming with tears but she refused to weep or moan in pain before her enemies.

Don Tenorio spoke to the matriarch, saying, "I take this boy as son. He grow to be blood bond between our people. Because he live, your people live. Never again be war between our clans."

Atop the mesa, the allies divided the horses. The Apaches and Comanches broke camp, quickly and headed northeast. The white men rode straight north.

In the waning moments of the fight, Cuerno Verde had looked for Ulysses, hoping for an opportunity to shoot him in the chaos of battle so no one would know. He had seen Ulysses entering the burning house, probably seeking loot, but Ulysses was watching Cuerno Verde too, and Ulysses was ready. No other chance had presented itself.

And so, before they parted atop the mesa, Cuerno Verde spoke to Ulysses.

"Good fight."

"Yes. A very good fight," Ulysses replied.

"We meet again," Cuerno Verde said with respect, and both men knew the assertion was no "farewell," but rather an honest affirmation of malice that demanded revenge.

"Maybe so," Ulysses said, with respect also.

The gringos drove their share of the prize horses at a good pace out across the vast, high llano. Bayless led O'Connor's horse and the boy's body was tied to his saddle. They would bury him at first rest.

Robert gripped a braided rawhide lead, drawing Helen's mount along behind him. Helen's hands were tied to the saddle horn and she hung her head and her shoulders shook as she sobbed. Her clothes were torn and her golden hair was now dark and matted with dirt, ash, sweat, blood and tears, and it hung down concealing her face. Her tears fell onto her hands and mixed there with her blood, which dripped from the ragged whip gash that ran from her temple to her chin and would remain always, a scar and sign of her shame, until the day of her death.

After all had gone, Ulysses sat his horse, alone, on the mesa. He watched the valley below. He regarded the burning hacienda, saw survivors, some supporting or carrying the wounded, straggling down to the river where they were being received by the people of the pueblo. Ulysses looked down the valley to where the camino curved out of sight around the base of the Sierra Madre.

Ulysses felt no emotion of pity or remorse. He was merely calculating the distance from which the flames could be seen, calculating the nearest point from which any pursuit might come. He was just trying to figure how best to get his people home safely.

Ulysses turned his mustang and rode north. The quillon, hilt and pommel of the sword of Rodrigo de Castille protruded from Ulysses' feathered quiver beside the stock of his big Hawkin, and in his saddle bags Ulysses carried the golden masks Rodrigo had seized, long ago, by strength of arm, great courage, and with much loss of Christian blood, from the high temple on the great pyramid of Tezcatlipoca.

32

JUH

**The Apaches did not understand and would never know
the meaning of his name.**

Dream Walker ran hard. He reached the shelter of the bosque along the Rio Scamandario and he moved upstream in the cover of cottonwoods, carrizo, and dense oak brush. He slowed to a long, walking stride and he slipped carefully from shadow to shadow, looking back for signs of pursuit. He saw the glow of the burning stronghold through the trees.

When he was satisfied no one followed, he trotted down a narrow footpath. As he passed a dense oak thicket, a burl war club, thrown from the bosket, struck the back of his skull. Dream Walker's knees buckled and he twisted his body and tried to bring his rifle around as he hit the ground, but men were suddenly on him. He fought desperately, knowing he must escape or die. But his assailants were many and within a few, brief moments he found himself on his feet against a tree. His arms were stretched behind the trunk and his wrists were tied there with strips of rawhide.

Leather thongs encircled his neck, chest, hips, thighs and ankles. All the ligatures were knotted tightly behind the trunk. Now he knew he could do nothing. He ceased to struggle, recovered his breath and studied his captors. They were Apaches, but not Mescaleros.

The men were Chiricahua, free, wild, defiant and ruthless, sworn to unending war against all—Indian, Mexican and white alike—and this was the ancient and unrelenting virtue of their people. Dream Walker knew the Chiricahua would not give nor ever request mercy.

A man, stocky, yet lean and wiry, and among the shortest of the Chiricahua, stepped forward. He carried himself with an air of great authority and the others moved aside in deference. The chieftain wore a calico shirt, a leather vest, cotton pants, a loin cloth and hide moccasins which reached to

his knees, secured by leather thongs circling and crossing around his forelegs. A scarf, wrapped like a turban, covered his head. His long, jet-black hair hung half way down his back. He wore turquoise and silver on his wrists and about his neck. The chieftain casually cradled a Sharps rifle in his arms, and bullet-filled bandoleros crossed his chest.

The chieftain raised his eyes, scanning Dream Walker from his feet to his head. The Chiricahua warrior nodded and projected a soft, almost musical, grunt of satisfaction and respect as he considered the high scalp lock, which Dream Walker wore in deference and as a challenge and gift of honor to any enemy who might be bold and lucky enough to take it.

"Yo soy Juh," the chieftain said. Juh spoke the words mildly, with a lilting, almost kind, inflection.

"I am Dream Walker," the prisoner replied in Pawnee, knowing the Apaches did not understand and would never know the meaning of his name.

The reply was given simply and matter of factly and with calm courage, barely invoking the melancholy knowledge that by dawn Dream Walker's bloody scalp would hang among the silver conchos on the Chiricahua chieftain's belt.

Dream Walker felt strength and confidence that he could endure his torture and die without crying out.

33

BILLY THE KID

Maybe they'll sing songs and tell stories.

Guillermo Bonito, "William Bonney," traveled north under the stars. He had covered many miles after killing Hectór, at dawn, that day. Billy had rested during the hottest hours of the afternoon. Now, he rode Bala at an easy canter that the stallion could maintain for hours. The Kid had decided to return to Fort Sumner, to see Paulina and the few friends who still bore him good will.

It's true, nobody can win, the Kid thought. All I can do is fight against dyin'. Maybe they'll sing songs and tell stories, like Luz said, about that.

William Bonney was sure in his knowledge of the great country. He was confident that the many young warriors who rode by command of powerful chieftans—the president, the governor, high shire-reeves and wealthy ranchers—fast, hard and unrelenting over sun-scorched deserts, through snow-blanketed forests and icy arroyos with his blood only in their hearts— would never catch him on the open road. And Billy knew, when they finally cornered him, there could be no purchase in surrender. He would simply have to take dark death, brutal and terrible. And he would do it, with an Irish laugh and a little Spanish flair, he hoped.

Billy the Kid was twenty-one and he figured he'd probably die, as Luz foretold, before another year would pass. He rode alone into the night in sweet knowledge that defiance and freedom only must endure in his being eternal or bounded and temporal under the wide compass of infinite, black, star-sparkling western sky.

34

UNEMPLOYMENT

I bring a last gift for you.

Percy awoke late the morning after the dance. Bright New Mexico sunlight flooded his room. His writing was done. It was time to move on. He packed his things, carried his suitcase down the pine-board portál and passed through the door into the Salazárs' kitchen.

Doña Flora was stirring a pot of chile on the wood-stove. "Buenos días, Señor Percy. ¿Ya te vas? Good morning. You're leaving now?"

"Sí."

Doña Flora placed coffee and a plate of eggs, bacon, corn tortillas and red chile before Percy, and he ate the food with relish.

"Señor Percy, you came here looking for the Kid. Did you catch him? Many have tried. But he has been before you all this time."

"I think I did." Percy answered.

Doña Flora smiled. "Sí," she said. "Tu sábes, ¿No? You know, don't you?"

"Sí, but how did it happen?"

" When Bee-lee returned to Fort Sumner, he stopped to see me one last time in Santa Cecilia."

Percy sat and listened as Doña Flora told him the story of the Kid's last run, just as Billy himself had told it to her forty years earlier, only a few days before he met his fate at Fort Sumner. She concluded, "We lay together under the stars of the desert. Rosario is his grand-daughter."

"Yes, I think I understood that. Where is Rosario?"

Doña Flora hesitated. She did not wish to hurt her guest, but there was nothing else to do.

"She rides with Matéo."

Percy winced and looked down at the table for a moment. He had known in his heart that the phantasms of his budding romantic love for Rosario could have no true substance. He smiled ruefully at Doña Flora.

"Of course."

"Claro," she said gently, smiling back. "Rosario is a bit like Bee-lee, no? No one can catch her for long," she said wryly.

They both laughed at that, then sat together in silence, sipping coffee for a time. Percy arose and lifted his travel bag.

"Wait un momento, Señor. I bring a last gift for you."

Doña Flora left the room and quickly returned with an old straw Mexican sombrero. "This was Bee-lee's."

"Doña Flora! This was the Kid's sombrero?"

"Pues. There are many old sombreros in this house. But I think this one could have been Bee-lee's."

Percy put the sombrero on his head with great pride. Doña Flora embraced him.

"Goodbye, Doña Flora. Thank you."

"Goodbye, Señor Percy."

He walked out and put his things in the Hupmobile. As he drove out of town he saw Matéo sitting his horse atop a far rise. Rosario sat behind him, her dress pushed up over her strong, brown thighs as she straddled the animal. Her upper lip curved into a most graceful arc over her prominent front teeth and sparkling white smile. Rosario and Matéo both raised their hands high above their heads and waved briskly.

"Adiós," Percy thought he heard them call.

"Adiós." He waved back, pulled his sombrero snugly down to the top of his goggles, tightened the stampede strap under his chin, and tooled north at a fair speed toward Santa Fe.

It had only been three days since his return, but everyone in the New York Daily Herald's offices had noticed a change in Mr. Percival Baron Chesterfield. It wasn't just the ratty, filthy-looking straw Mexican sombrero that had taken the place of his fedora, nor the cowboy boots he now sported. There was something different in his whole demeanor. He had taken to bellowing, "¡Buenos días!" as he entered each day, and a slight swagger carried him through the lobby.

The reporters all knew Percy was the only bachelor on the staff, and they understood that this was why Mr. Magruder had chosen him and spared the family men from the lengthy absence required by a trip to New Mexico. They were all glad for that. But Percy's new, cocky attitude caused the married men to feel a kind of envy.

Mr. Magruder had not yet pronounced judgment on the articles Percy had written in New Mexico, and most of the reporters secretly hoped he would take Percy down a peg or two when the work was edited. They feigned lack of interest, but watched askance when word spread that Miss Pritchard had summoned Percy to Mr. Magruder's office to discuss the New Mexico project.

Everyone was shocked when Percy donned his sombrero, and at a rakish angle, as he sauntered casually toward Mr. Magruder's door—without even a hint of the urgency he would have formerly displayed. But none of them would ever know what happened in that office.

"Take that goddamn stupid thing off your head, Percy."

It was true. Percy had been feeling pretty cocky. But now, facing Mr. Magruder and his profane command; a lightning bolt of the old fear struck Percy's heart. He began to raise a hand toward his sombrero, but something stayed it. In later years, he often supposed it was the spirit of Billy the Kid.

Percy was so scared that his asthma flowed over him and he could not breathe, and he wondered if he could even speak; but he straightened and managed to say, "I don't think I care to."

Blood pumped visibly into Mr. Magruder's face. He rose to his feet and tossed Percy's articles across the desk.

"'I don't think I care to?' Well, do you care that these articles have next to nothing to do with Pat Garrett? Do you care that they read like they were written by some damn anarchist? 'Billy the Kid! Billy the Kid!' I want answers and I want them now!"

"No, I guess I don't."

"You don't what?"

Percy was now facing the fact that he would be seeking other employment. And with that realization, he suddenly acknowledged that he would survive. At least they wouldn't murder him like they murdered William. It might even be a good thing.

"I guess I don't care, Mr. Magruder, sir."

Mr. Magruder took a deep and evidently calming breath. He reached down, opened a drawer and took out two cigars.

"Want one?"

"No, thank you, sir."

Mr. Magruder sat down, leaned his chair back on two legs, put his feet on his desk, lit his cigar, and chuckled. "I'm sorry to let you go, amigo."

"¿Amigo?"

"Yeah, that's right, Mr. Chesterfield. You see, I've been to New Mexico, too. You were once my most promising reporter. But you lost your passion, so I sent you there. I hope you found it again. I think you may have. Write with passion, son."

"Will you publish the articles?"

"No, you can take 'em."

"Thank you, Mr. Magruder. Adiós, sir." Percy took up the manuscript, turned, and walked out.

Percy felt stunned and confused when he stepped out of Mr. Magruder's office, pulling the door closed behind him. But, upon seeing Miss Pritchard standing there, he found that all confusion had fled his soul. She stood off to the side and turned her head to look at Percy. He met her eyes, then lowered his, and considered her immense bosom, all buttoned up beneath her high lace collar, and the opulent curve of her rump, which caused the hem of her gabardine dress to end at a point much higher in the back than in front. Percy wondered how these attributes could have escaped his attention so thoroughly and for so long.

"Is everything all right, Mr. Chesterfield?" Miss Pritchard asked, clasping her hands tightly before her and looking truly concerned. As Percy scanned the newsroom, everyone looked back at their typewriters. He stepped over, removed his sombrero, placed it over his heart, and took Miss Pritchard's hand.

"May I ask you a personal question, Miss Pritchard?"

Miss Pritchard looked around, and again, everyone in the room turned their eyes back to their work. She blushed, but managed, "Of course you may, Mr. Chesterfield."

"Do you like ice cream?"

"Absolutely, Mr. Chesterfield."

"Would you be so kind as to accompany me?"

"Absolutely, Mr. Chesterfield. Please call me Juliana."

"Please call me Percy."

The Monthly Book Club

November 21, 1924

Mr. Percival Baron Chesterfield
324 Mulberry Lane
Manhattan, New York, New York

Dear Mr. Chesterfield,

I am pleased to inform you that, based on the glowing reviews it has received, we have selected your novel, Billy the Kid's Last Ride, as the first choice of the Monthly Book Club which will launch in January, 1925, offering mail-order sales across the nation. We are confident that this debut will be a successful one and look forward to a long (and mutually profitable) literary association.

On a personal note I wish to apologize to you and your beautiful bride, Juliana, for having been unable to attend your wedding last year. Time flies, and I was surprised to hear last week of the birth of your first child. Congratulations and warmest regards:

Max Scherman
President, the Monthly Book Club

ACKNOWLEDGEMENTS

I wish to thank my editor, the incomparable Mary W. Walters. Thanks also to Bob Boze Bell whose book The Illustrated Life and Times of Billy the Kid inspired me, and whose kind counsel pointed me to the best contemporary sources of Billy history. I also want to thank my friends Jeff Fielder, Gary Gardey, Elizabeth Kales and Richard Lienau who were kind enough to read this work and provide useful feedback. Tom Ketcheson, David Campbell and my primo James Maurice provided moral support and tequila throughout the writing process. June Armijo, my administrative assistant, was strong enough to type endless illegible hand-written drafts. And last, thanks to Jim and Carl at Sunstone Press for publishing this book, and bringing it to the attention of its intended readers.

www.ingramcontent.com/pod-product-compliance
Lightning Source LLC
Chambersburg PA
CBHW031938010726
47493CB00007B/1987